All characters, places, and events in this story are fictitious. Any and all similarities are coincidental.

This novel is based on the life experiences of

Laurel Forte.

This Novel is written for:

Every Parent and Child.

Anyone, who has ever been bullied,

Fallen in love

or been heartbroken.

Anyone that ever wished to be famous

And last, but *always first*,

My son.

Part I

There has never been,
nor will there ever be,
anything quite so special as the love
between a mother and a son.

-Author Unknown

Chapter 1

Lightning

I walked down the trail and glanced up at the sky through the balcony of swaying trees. In the distance the sky was a grayish purple canvas of angry, growling clouds as a thunderstorm approached. My dog, Nimbus, a black and grey brindle pit bull, quickly followed my lead as we ran across the moss-covered rocks and the fallen tree trunks. A loud crack of thunder bellowed from the sky in the distance.

He whipped around and darted next to my legs shaking in fear. I studied the swirling clouds above. "We should pick up the pace so we don't get caught in the storm," I said aloud. The fearful look on his face gave me a sense that he was thinking the same thing.

I began jogging but the path was too uneven to run. Nimbus stayed close beside me, petrified of the thunder. As we made our way back towards the edge of the woods, a flash of lightning brightened the sky. Nimbus whimpered with fear.

"It's alright boy. We aren't too far from the cabin," I assured him, though I began to question if we were going to be alright. The sky was getting darker by the minute and the storm was getting louder and much closer.

As we came to a clearing in the woods I paused and looked up at the sky. I could see the translucent black sheets of rain moving down the mountain like a tsunami overtaking the forest.

I took a few deep quick breaths. "Fuck," I thought as I started running full speed through the field. "We have to beat the rain across the river or we're screwed. Why I didn't check the weather forecast before we went hiking?"

Thunder clapped around us as we dashed into the woods on the other side of the clearing. I scaled the branches of a fallen tree trunk across the path. As I straddled the trunk, Nimbus pushed his way through the broken tree limbs beneath me. I carefully crawled down the branches, gracefully hopped to the ground, and sprinted full speed down the path.

The hair on my neck stood on end as a deafening thunderclap bellowed around us. Nimbus and I looked at each other as fear poured from his big brown eyes and his body shook in terror. I reached down to nuzzle his neck and noticed the goose bumps covering my arms, each with a blonde hair standing at attention. "It's okay, boy, we're almost home. Five minutes. We can make it." I patted his hind end. "Let's go."

I propelled myself over broken branches, pushed through brush, and dodged trees as we hustled through the woods towards creek. I gasped as we abruptly came to a halt at the edge of the embankment. *Holy shit.* The water was aggravated and quickly rising.

I'd been hiking through these woods for about 19 years and had never seen the creek like this. The water level crested the embankment and the current was fiercely trying to move everything in its path. To add to it all, the rain clouds were now hovering above us. As I searched the clouds for answers, huge spheres of rain stung my skin. Looking for a sympathetic partner in this mess, I said, "Here comes the rain, Nimbus." He looked up at me as if to say, "I noticed."

We approached the metal bridge at the creek's edge. I thought, "Figures. Two ways to get home and both could kill me. Do I risk drowning in the creek or getting struck by lightning on the old rickety metal bridge?" The best choice I could see was to risk crossing in the current.

I looked at Nimbus. "You ready Nimbus? We've got to cross in the creek. No problem, right?"

He fearfully looked at me and I read his eyes, *Don't make me do this, I'm already scared.*

"I don't trust the bridge, so we've got no choice," I told him. "Let's go."

As I stepped into the water. a chill shot through me like ice. The farther I stepped into the rushing water, the stronger the current got. My sneakers tried and failed to grip the algae covered rocks. The water wrapped around my knees as I, step by step, pushed my way through the infuriated water.

The clouds exploded and the rain stung my skin as we got thrashed in the vigorous winds. Nimbus paced back and forth on the embankment, displaying a not-so-acute desire to not be in this situation anymore. I called out to him, "C'mon, boy."

I was half way across the creek as the freezing water was now as high as my thighs. It pushed me farther downstream with each step. Just as I was reaching the other side, I lost my footing and

4

plummeted under the surface of the creek. The shock of the cold water shot through my submerged body as I was swept under by the agitated current and barrel-rolled across the rocks. I sat up, stunned as my breath escaped me and I gasped for air. My body was throbbing from being pulverized against the rocks. I reached out and tried to grab for a vine or root or rock to stop myself from being swept away by the rushing water. Eventually I found a tree limb and grasped onto it with all I had. The water pushed me backwards, slamming me into the exposed tree roots on the embankment. I braced my battered body against the creek's bank of entwined mud, roots, and rocks as my teeth chattered. I struggled to regain my balance as I gasped for air and yelled, "Nimbus come!" Nimbus stopped pacing as he realized I'd reached the other side safely and that a rescue mission wouldn't be necessary, after all. He climbed down the bank and jumped in the river. He doggie-paddled faster and faster as the current quickly pushed him further downstream.

I grabbed a tree branch that stretched across the surface of the water and hoisted myself up the bank. Nimbus greeted me with whimpering kisses. I struggled to my feet, exhausted from resisting the current and trembling from the iciness of the water. My teeth chattered and goose bumps covered my body as we took off running to the cabin. "Home free," I thought. "Almost there."

5

As we approached the cabin, I lunged and jumped onto the porch. Thunder slammed above while a bolt of lightning struck where the creek wrapped around the cabin. I was horrified as I thought "Whoa, that struck barely 30 feet away." I noticed that my hands were raw and bleeding. Nimbus yelped and ran for cover under the porch swing.

I plopped down on the swing, gasping for air and enjoying the shelter of the porch. I watched as the rain blurred the forest. *Mother Nature, in all her glory.* I untied my right sneaker and loosened the laces, struggling to pull the shoe off over the drenched sock. After succeeding in this task, I turned my sneaker over and poured out what seemed like a gallon of water. I took off my sock and wrung it out onto the chipped paint of the wooden porch and then shoved the sock inside my sneaker and tossed the whole drenched mess towards the screen door.

The thud of the sneaker startled Nimbus and he bolted out from under the chair. He whimpered as if to say, "Really mom? You had to add insult to injury? I'm terrified here, and you're throwing shoes."

I giggled, "I'm sorry, I didn't mean to scare you anymore than you already are." I grabbed him around his sopping wet neck and kissed his head. "Mommy loves you, I'm sorry buddy." He whimpered as if he were forgiving me and kissed my face. "The thunder booms are loud aren't they? We're safe and sound now. Don't be scared." He started to relax as I comforted him. He stared out at the woods that surrounded the cabin with ears perked, listening to the torrential downpour. I rubbed his back and chest as he continued to watch the rain intently.

I began to chant as I rose to my feet, "HI-ya-hi-ya!" I performed my version of a rain dance as Nimbus barked and joined in by spinning in circles along with me. "HI-ya-hi-ya-HI-ya-hi-ya!" We danced together for another minute, diluting the tension of the situation. I sat down on the swing and giggled as he plopped down at my feet.

As I untied my other shoe the thunder grumbled above us and I froze. I could feel anger in the thunder; something I'd never felt before. I paused for a second longer and waited for the thunder to cease.

Nimbus darted from my feet and pawed at the screen door as he shook in fear. I shuffled over and opened the door. He dashed inside frantically searching for a place to hide.

I balanced myself on the swing trying to remove my other sneaker. I fumbled with the laces just as a bolt of lightning cracked and struck the swing.

I felt an explosion of electricity surge through me. I was suddenly airborne and the rest of my body followed my head as I collided with the porch rails. I gasped for breath as my body convulsed and my head writhed in agony. My vision ricocheted as everything glowed white. I gasped for breath again as a low mellow buzz rang in my ears.

I just got struck by lightning.

I stared at the roof and gulped for air as my heart hammered in my chest and everything went fuzzy.

A feeling of horror overtook me as the fuzziness began to settle. I took long, slow, deep breaths, blinking my eyes and trying to focus. My muscles contracted around my bones and I began twitching uncontrollably. My hands trembled. The left one was dripping and scattering blood spots on the porch.

I wanted to jump up and run but my body wouldn't respond to my thoughts. I laid there convulsing involuntarily for what seemed like hours. My stomach quivered in unison with my muscles as they twitched. I felt a wave of nausea pass through me as if I was in a small boat and the swell of a wave rolled out from underneath me. "Nimbus," I whispered as my breath escaped me.

He cowered inside the door.

"Nimbus, come," I managed to vocalize slightly louder. Nimbus pushed his way outside and walked over to me with his head lowered in fear of the storm and whined as he licked my face.

In need of comfort, I reached out to him while my arms were still buzzing and grazed my bloody hand across his drenched coat. I wrapped my arms around him as sharp pains shot through my arms and chest and a burst of tears poured from my eyes.

He whimpered as he licked my quivering hand and cleaned off the blood.

My heart was racing as soft tears drenched my cheeks. I tried to roll over but my head was numb with confusion. However, I knew enough to realize that the storm was not finished. Thunder slammed above us like an explosion of fireworks. The downpour of raindrops illuminated the sky and fizzled by the time they hit the ground. I stared up at the sky. *Lightning never strikes the same place twice.* I repeated the words in my head. *Lightning never strikes the same place twice.*

I tried to bring myself to focus and control my thoughts. "Focus, Laurel," I whispered and blinked my eyes. I wasn't sure if I wanted to get up, I wasn't sure if I wanted to lay down, I wasn't even sure if I could stand. More than that, I wasn't sure I was going to be alive to know the difference. I closed my eyes and pushed all those thoughts away as I rubbed my hands along my thighs in an attempt to get the blood to circulate through areas where I wasn't sure there was blood anymore.

The world around me began to come back into focus and my disturbed breathing finally began to mellow. I mustered every ounce of strength I could find and rolled over onto my hands and knees. Fighting to urge to puke, I forced myself to crawl towards the door. My arms didn't want to support me, my legs didn't want to follow me. I was terrified and confused as more questions funneled through my brain like a tornado. *What if I die? What if I can't ever walk again? What if I can't ever get pregnant? What if I can't do gymnastics anymore?* Tears poured from my eyes as all of these thoughts horrified me.

Nimbus stared at me whimpering; sad that he couldn't lift and carry me to get help.

I found a water bottle on the table next to the door and sipped it slowly. The water quenched my ravenous thirst as the shock of lightning had dehydrated me instantly. The water absorbed in my throat and a feeling of relief began to settle. I gulped more of the water feeling my body become quenched further into my stomach.

I closed my eyes and lowered my head into my hands and cried ceaselessly, releasing the panic and fear. *I need more water…and a hospital. Get inside. Get your phone. Move nice and slow. But move. Now,*

Laurel. My legs groaned as I commenced crawling towards the door. My head spun as another wave of nausea ripped through me. I froze and then slowly lifted my head to try to keep the contents of my stomach where they currently sat. I took long slow breathes, forcing the nausea to retract. I opened my eyes and tried to focus on the trees around me that seemed to be glazed with a white radiance. I felt my body weaken. *I need a hospital right now.* I chugged the rest of my water, feeling my body absorb every drop like a dried out sponge.

I moved as slow as I could. The floorboards dug into my knees while I braced my hands into the ground, everything throbbing with pain. Trying not to move my head too quickly, I crawled to the door. I reached over for the door, swung it open quickly, and propped it open with my barefoot. I wrenched my body through the doorway, agonizing with every movement. At a snail's pace I crawled across the braided carpet towards the coffee table where my cell phone was.

I grabbed my phone and kept moving towards the kitchen. After slumping into the refrigerator I called my parents. *They shouldn't be too far away. If I call 911, the ambulance could get lost trying to find the cabin because it's so secluded.*

I heard my mom's voice. "Hey Hun."

"I'm okay. How far…from cabin…are you?" I said, trying to catch my breath.

11

"About 5 minutes. What happened?"

"Swing, jus' got struck…by lightning. I…got zapped," I panted.

"Oh my God, are you okay?!" she shrieked.

"I'm okay, jus' *need you here*…an' a hospital…I think."

"We'll be there in a minute. I'm going to call the ambulance and direct them there."

"H-hurry u-up…I'm *freakin' out*." I hung up the phone and reached out for more water. I struggled to open the bottle because my body was weak and trembling. My bloody hand held the bottle while my other hand shook uncontrollably. Both hands were numb and tingling but I was finally able to get the cap off. I drank it so quickly I almost choked. Coughing, I leaned back against the refrigerator with my legs straight out in front of me. I still had only one sneaker on. I stared at it. It was melted, singed, and reeked of burnt rubber.

I heard a car pull up in the driveway. Nimbus barked and ran to meet the drivers. By the time he had pushed through the door, my parents came running through the other way and the rickety screen door did a full rotation on the hinges. They both ran over to me as I was finishing the bottle of water.

I reached for a new bottle but my mom held me back and grabbed one for me. I drank more.

"Tell me what happened," she whispered. Her blonde curls were drenched by the rain and her blue eyes were filled with fear.

"Swing…go'struck…You call ambulance?"

"Yes, they'll be here soon. They said you shouldn't move around too much."

"How'd you get in here?" my dad asked as he perched on the island. His salt and pepper hair had rain drops dangling from the tips.

"Crawled. Had…t'get phone…an' water." I gulped down another swig of water as the plastic bottle crackled. My chest seemed to be settling as my breath evened out and my words became easier to dictate.

I looked at my father absently. "Don't feel good. Body hurts. Really tired."

My dad moaned and shook his head. "Ya' just got struck by lightning, Laurel. You're not gonna feel good."

My mom glared at him over her shoulder.

"Makes sense, huh?" I joked with him trying to lighten the mood but it seemed to upset him more. He'd always taken good care of us and set us as his top priority. He definitely had a lot to deal with when it came to me. As a gymnast and a tomboy, I was always looking to master the next challenge. Whether it was building something with my dad, traveling, or sports, he'd always challenge

13

me. He always had an answer. But this time, there was nothing he could do.

My dad dropped his head into his hands, frustrated with the situation. He stared at me knowing that he himself was helpless in my near death encounter. He was unable to help his little girl as he had so many times in the past. I could sense the fear and pain in his frustration.

My eyes started to feel very heavy and I closed them, wanting nothing more than to fall asleep. My mom grabbed a washcloth, wet it with cold water, and dabbed my forehead saying, "No, Laurel. Don't go to sleep; the ambulance is on its way. They told me not to let you sleep. It's like a concussion."

"Can't sleep? Not gonna work...I'm *tired*...and eyes...heavy." I sipped my water as it drizzled down my face.

Nimbus came over and laid his head on my leg, whimpering as he stared at me. I struggled to raise my hand and pet him. "We did have...good walk...didn't we...buddy? Didn't know...was gonna storm...like that. Did you?"

He whined as if to say, "Of course I did! Weren't you paying attention? It was raining cats and Nimbuses out there!"

Dad glanced out the window, "The ambulance is here." He darted across the kitchen and out the door.

My mom continued dabbing my head with the cloth and nervously whispered, "I'm glad you're okay." But I could tell she didn't completely believe that I was okay.

My mouth didn't want to move. "Thanks mom. Love you." My eyes lowered and my head bobbed.

"I love you too," she replied.

My dad led the paramedics into the kitchen. They checked everything they could with the tools they had. They put a neck brace on me, which relieved a lot of strain, though it made me want to sleep even more than before. They laid me onto a board, strapped me down and asked as many questions as they could on the short trip into the ambulance. I answered their questions as best I could considering my brain had just got struck by lightning.

I faded out of consciousness as they placed an oxygen mask over my mouth. "It's so bright in here," I thought.

Chapter 2

Already?

My eyes fluttered open. A halo glistened around everything in the room but nothing was in focus. I blinked a few times trying to get my eyes to focus on the ceiling tiles above.

"Where am I? What happened?" I thought. I felt something on my face. I tried to push it away but my arms were so heavy that I couldn't move them. I saw machines with blinking lights when I tilted my head to the right; I winced in pain as I rolled my head to the left. I caught sight of my mom's curly blonde hair when the room stopped spinning.

I tried to speak but instead I gurgled.

My mom stirred and jolted out of her light sleep. "Laurel?" She jumped to her feet. "Laurel, can you hear me?" I felt her hand on my forearm. "Laurel?"

Another sound bellowed from my throat. My mind scrambled to make sense of where I was, how I got there, and what was happening in this strange room. Just then my mom called out for the doctor.

"Doctor?" I whispered as I realized I had an oxygen mask strapped to my face. "What happened?"

"Laurel, you were struck by lightning. Do you remember anything?" Her eyes filled with fear as she frantically pushed the call button.

I was utterly confused as to what she was saying. I vaguely remembered the trek through the woods, but everything after that was a blur at best. As I tried to lift the clouds from my memory, I screamed out in pain as my mom touched my right leg.

She jumped back saying, "What? What hurts? Your arm?"

"No, my leg! What's on my leg?" I screamed.

"Just the sheet, hun. Hold on, the doctor's on his way in."

"*Where am I?*" My throat felt scratchy as I questioned my surroundings.

"You're at the hospital in the mountains."

"Why? How'd I get here?" A whisper was all I could muster as I cleared my throat.

"The ambulance picked you up at the cabin. Don't you remember anything?"

I shook my head, "It's all so fuzzy. What happened?" I looked at my hands. The left one was bandaged and throbbing and the right one had an intravenous needle plugged into a vein. I twitched ever so slightly while my legs and back strained in the dull pain that bellowed through my body.

My mom sighed as she explained what had happened. "Just before Dad and I got there you were struck by lightning. Thank God you're awake."

"Where's Nimbus? He okay?"

"He's fine. He's at the cabin with everyone. He's been sitting by the door waiting for you. We've all been very worried."

Just then the doctor walked into the room. "Well, Miss Forte, it's about time you decided to wake up. I'm Dr. McKinley," he said as he stretched out his hand, though mine was unable to meet his.

"How long I been here?" I asked.

"Well, you've been unconscious since you were brought in. It's been about seventy four hours now."

"Three days?" I struggled to understand.

19

He removed my mask and said, "You're math is good. It's been three days, two hours, and twenty five minutes to be exact. We've kept a close eye on you. Your vitals have been fine and your brain function has been productive, so we knew not to worry too much." Despite the positive reinforcement of his prior diagnosis, I could see he was relieved that I was not only conscious, but cognizant as well.

"You watched my brain activity? Is everything okay?" I shielded my eyes from the lights as my arm throbbed in agony.

"We've had you monitored for days now. We could tell your brain was functioning at a normal level. Your heart rate fluctuated a little here and there, but we knew your body needed a lot of rest. You had a large amount of electricity pass through your body."

"It hurts." I looked at my mom. "I hurt."

She forced a smile and dabbed the tears in her eyes.

Dr. McKinley interjected, "I can only imagine that you do. Now that you're awake I can give you something for the pain if you'd like. But I do have some questions to ask before I administer any type of medicine."

"Okay, but I don't really remember anything. It's all so fuzzy right now." My arm felt like it weighed a ton as I lifted it to put my hand over my eyes. "Why's it so bright in here?"

"I'll give you a small dose, just to take the edge off and then we'll get you some food. After you eat we'll discuss a few things. Sound good?"

"Uh-huh." I tried to adjust myself in the bed and cringed in anguish. The doctor helped me sit up and used an extra pillow for support.

"Can I have some water, please? I'm so thirsty."

Mom jumped up and poured me a cup from the plastic pitcher at the foot of my bed. "I'm going to call Dad and let him know you're awake." She paused, "We've all been so worried even though the doctor told us not to be." She tried to leave the room but kept looking back with excitement that I was, at the very least, conscious. She eventually disappeared into the hallway.

I began to take in my surroundings; my head spun with confusion. "What's your name?" I asked the doctor.

"Dr. McKinley."

"Can you turn off the lights, Dr. McKinley? They're so bright."

He stared at me. I couldn't figure out if he was diagnosing me, or if he just thought I was an idiot. Maybe he thought I was crazy. I was too confused to care.

"I've been asleep for three days?" I asked the room, hoping it would provide a better answer than the staring moron who was in charge of my survival.

A nurse came through the door. "Hello, Doctor," she said. He nodded and quickly retreated from the room. "Hi Laurel, good to finally meet you. I'm Kelsey, your nurse. I've got some pudding for you."

"Thank God, I'm starving. Oh, and yeah! Nice to meet you too." I mumbled, "Can you turn the lights off, please? It's so bright it's stinging my eyes. I feel like I'm getting a headache."

She stared vacantly at me. The look was oddly similar to the doctor's confused face. She hesitantly walked over to the light switch and turned off the light.

"Thank you, that's *so* much better. I'm really sore. Is that normal?" I shoved spoonfuls of butterscotch pudding into mouth, sending my taste buds into hyperactive mode. "So good."

The empty look that she had on her face since our initial meeting persisted as she explained, "Lightning strikes aren't very common."

"Maybe not in your world," I thought and pushed her rambling into the distance.

"You took one hell of a hit," she said and went on to explain the severity of the thunderstorm and the local flash flooding that had apparently wiped out a few roadways and trees while I slept off the pain. "That's bound to make anyone tired and sore. Or any two, in your case."

She grasped my attention at that last comment. "Two? Two what?"

She fumbled the tray and turned to rush out of the room.

"These people are weird," I thought to myself, "Mountain folk are kooky." After that little exchange and the newly added confusion, I rubbed my hands down my legs and my right leg hurt much more than the left one. The pressure of my hands felt good but made my stomach cringe. My left hand was bandaged tightly and throbbed as I pressed it to my thigh.

I took a deep breath and searched the room for something familiar, but nothing jumped out at me.

The doctor returned with a syringe full of clear liquid. He injected the fluid into my intravenous line and then dropped the needle into a large red container marked "Contaminated." Dr. McKinley pulled the clipboard from under his arm, sat down on the stool, and spun towards me. "Alright, Laurel. Do you remember anything that happened?"

I struggled with the question for a few seconds as I stumbled over my words. "I know…um…I was on a hike…with my dog. We, ah…got caught in a storm, but, um…we made it back to the cabin." I paused, unsure of what had happened next. I winced in pain as I lowered my head in my hands.

"Do you remember where you were when you got struck by the lightning bolt?"

I paused in shock as the reality of my situation hit me all at once. I got struck by lightning. *Lightning*.

I shuttered and hesitated, trying to jog my memory. "At the cabin, I think, on the porch. Not really sure." The pain medicine really took effect in that instant. It made my head spin and everything in my insides wanted to be on my outside.

"Was anyone with you?" he continued.

"No…um…Nimbus was there, but I think he was inside. I don't really know." I paused, looking around as I tried to jog my memory. "I was in the river, I think."

"When you got struck?"

"Um…no…I don't think so…but I remember being soaking wet. I think I was…ah…swept under…?"

"So you were in the creek before you got hit?"

"I think so. I'm sorry, nothing makes sense. It's all so fuzzy." My mouth was dry and chalky. "My legs really hurt, especially this one." I slowly grazed my right leg.

"From what we've gathered, you came in with one sneaker on your left foot, which would explain why your right leg hurts more. The sole of the sneaker on your left foot insulated you and probably saved your life. We think the bolt of lightning hit the arm of the chair directly where your left hand was," he pointed to my bandaged hand, "propelling the surge through the rest of your body." He waved his hands across the length of my body, insinuating that all of me should've been fried and that I was lucky I was here to have him tell me about it.

I looked at him with a blank expression. "My sneaker saved my life?"

"Absolutely it did. Now the question is this: did it affect your baby?"

"My baby? What baby?"

"Miss Forte, you're three and a half months pregnant. Weren't you aware of that?"

A rush of heat overtook my already aching body, "Pregnant? Already?" I thought. "I'm pregnant?" I whispered as a smile kissed the sides of my lips.

"Yes, Laurel, you are. And from the looks of the test results, your sneaker didn't just save you, it saved your baby as well. Your baby seems to be doing just fine."

My head began to spin and my heart pounded in my head. *Pregnant? How'd I get pregnant so quickly?* I tried to recall. *Did I know I was pregnant before I got struck? Or am I finding out for the first time that I'm pregnant?* I looked at the doctor. "Did you tell my parents that I'm pregnant?"

"We did discuss it and they seemed quite surprised." He paused, studying my reaction. "However, *you* don't seem to be that surprised."

"I can't say that I'm *surprised*. I don't think I knew definitely." I felt somewhat stripped of my doctor-patient confidentiality because I was 19 and he told my parents without my consent. But I figured what's been done is done and it was probably best to have the cat out of the bag before I woke up anyway.

"Even though you're not a minor, due to the extreme circumstances I needed to discuss each aspect of the situation with your parents. I'm sorry that may seem unfair to you but if it's any consolation to you, they didn't seem to be upset," he assured.

"Did you just read my mind?" I thought as I nodded and lied. "I understand."

"At this point, Miss Forte, they're so thankful that you're alive. To know that you're pregnant means that sneaker saved two lives, not just one. Instead of looking at this negatively, we're all looking at it very positively. You're giving them a grandchild. Their first, from what I understand."

"Yeah, it's a first for me too." A surreal feeling brushed across my aching body. "I'm going to be a mother," I thought as a joyful tear rolled down my cheek.

"Are you okay, Laurel?" Dr. McKinley asked.

I stared at the blanket covering my body. My vision blurred and I felt very faint.

"Why don't you finish your pudding and lay back. You've had one exciting vacation."

"Can I ask you a question, doctor?"

He turned and nodded. "Sure."

"Is it normal for someone to be struck by lightning?" I paused as I realized what a stupid question that was, but I couldn't take the words back. The events of which I had been made aware in the past hour had dumbed me down to the point where I could ask if breathing was optional without thinking it was an awkward question.

He looked at me quizzically. "No. It's not normal. But this has been one of the better outcomes anyone could ask for. You're alive and your baby's doing well. You should be grateful. I'll be back in a bit but in the meantime, relax. Your baby needs to rest too."

"Yeah, but..." I stopped, staring at him as I adjusted myself slowly in my bed and cringed in agony.

He turned back towards me. The look on my face must've made it clear that I was overwhelmed with confusion. "I'm sorry. I didn't answer your question completely?"

Trying to figure out how to word it properly, I organized my question. "Well...um...if it's not a common thing for someone to be struck by lightning and survive, how strange is it that this is the third time that I've been struck by lightning, or at least been in the vicinity of lightning striking, and have still survived? *And* that my baby is okay?" I couldn't stop my rambling at this point. "This is the most severe and direct hit. But still, this is the *third* time. Shouldn't I be dead?" I forced myself to stop as I saw the expression change on his face—it had gone quickly from *I pity her* to *She's crazy*.

He said, "I suppose it's just not your time to go yet," and he turned and briskly walked out of the room.

My stomach sank in sheer disappointment. I laid back and stared at the ceiling. The tiles were yellowed with age yet had a radiance about them that glowed with life. "It's not my time to go yet," I repeated. I studied the ceiling and pondered. *Why does this keep happening to me?*

The doctor returned and gave me another dose of medication. "Is this healthy for the baby?" I asked.

He generalized, "Anything I'm giving you is safe for the baby, but you must realize that you're our first concern." He smiled. "We need a healthy mommy to raise her healthy baby."

"A healthy mommy," I mumbled to myself. "How weird is that? I'm a mommy."

"With everything you've informed me about, I'd say it's the least 'weird' event of your life.

Teenage pregnancies are definitely more common than someone being struck by lightning multiple times," the doctor replied.

I winced as I adjusted myself in my bed. "When can I go home?"

"We're going to release you in the morning. I'd like to observe you for one more night. You'll need the rest of your vacation to relax."

I chimed in, "And figure out what my life is going to become."

"Something tells me you're going to be okay, Laurel. You've got a great family that loves you, and soon you'll have one more person to love." He grabbed the TV remote and held it out for me. "Now relax and watch some television. You deserve to unwind."

My mom came back into the room. "Why's it so dark in here? I can barely see you."

I stared at her. "Are you kidding me? It's so bright in here! Everything is glowing."

Her face went blank. She handed me a bottle of water. "I opened the cap for you."

"Thank you, I'm so weak and the lights are hurting my eyes," I replied.

"Still? The lights are still hurting your eyes?"

"Yes, everything's glowing. It's so bright I can't focus." I shielded my eyes. "Can you close the blinds?"

Softly she stated, "Laurel, the blinds are closed. It's almost pitch black in here."

Chapter 3

Discharged.

The nurse pushed my wheelchair through the wide hallways of the hospital towards the information desk. The medicinal stench in the air made my stomach queasy. I kept my eyes closed; the sunlight blinded me as I sat slouched in the wheelchair waiting to be discharged. "Mom, do you have sunglasses? My eyes are watering from the brightness."

She rummaged through her purse, pulled out her case, and handed the sunglasses to me.

31

I put them on and opened my eyes. "Much better," I said as I looked around the waiting room, watching each person and wondering what brought them there.

I listened in the distance to the conversation between my parents, the doctor, and nurses. My head was heavy and my eyes were very tired. I leaned my head on my hand with my eyes fixed on the people in the waiting room.

I wondered about each of their lives. *Why are they here? What did they do? Do they have kids?*

I stopped questioning their lives.

I started questioning mine.

When we arrived back at the cabin, Nimbus was the first off the porch, quickly followed by my brother, Lance, and my sisters, Sarah and Hillary. My dad rushed around the side of the cabin to join us in the stone driveway.

Lance helped me out of the car saying, "I've been so worried about you," and he hugged me.

I cringed as he squeezed me but accepted it openly. Considering everyone had expected me to die, I could handle the pain of a hug. Obnoxiously, I muttered, "I'm sorry to make you worry. I certainly didn't mean to."

My parents escorted me across the porch. As we approached the swing I paused and stared at it. A chill shot through me and everything went silent as flashbacks filled my head. I stared at the rail, then out towards the river. I released a deep breath as my head spun. "I need to sit down." I stepped inside the door and resisted support from my parents as I sat down on the couch, exhausted from the walk.

I was starving. I tried to stand up and instead fell forward, then jerked myself backwards onto the couch. My head spun and I groaned.

My mom quickly came to my side. "What do you need?"

"I'm hungry. I need real food. No more pudding."

"You're not supposed to eat solid foods."

I cut her off. "Mom. Just a half a sandwich. I'm starving."

My younger sister, Hillary, chimed in, "She's got to be hungry. She hasn't eaten real food in days."

My mom checked my dad's face and saw that he seemed to agree. She got up and went into the kitchen. "What do you want?"

Hillary brought me a bottle of water. I flopped back onto the couch and gave my mom a grateful smile. "What lunch meat do we have?"

"I have ham and cheese."

"Yes please." I said.

Hillary asked, "What'd it feel like?"

I winced as I muttered, "It felt like I got electrocuted by a high voltage shock. Everything was glowing white. My whole body was buzzing and convulsing."

Lance asked, "What happens from here? Do you have to go back to the doctor's to see how you're doing?"

My head buzzed with uncertainty as I tried to answer his question. "I've got to rest a lot and as soon as we get home I need to get more testing done to make sure the baby is fine."

"Baby, what baby?!" Lance exclaimed.

I looked at my mom. "You didn't tell them?"

She shook her head. "We figured you wouldn't want us to, so we decided to wait until you came home."

I huffed, "Oh." I turned to my stun-faced siblings. "I'm having a baby. I'm a little more than three months pregnant."

Sarah and Lance exchanged glances as Hillary screeched, "I'm going to be an aunt?!"

Lance, dumbfounded, said, "Congratulations, sis." He kissed me on the top of my head, "Have you told Greg yet?"

"I've been unconscious in the hospital for days and just found out myself. How could I have told him?"

"Dumb question, sorry."

"Wasn't I the one who just got her brain fried by lightning? Maybe you should get checked out," I teased.

He laughed and I giggled as best I could, wincing through the pain.

He said, "Well, I see you haven't lost your twisted sense of humor, Elektra."

We giggled so hard, "Ow! It hurts! Stop making me laugh."

He kept laughing, "Spark."

I looked at him. "Spark? What's spark?"

He laughed relentlessly as he said, "That's your baby's nickname: Spark."

I roared with laughter as I cringed in pain. "Ow-ow-ooow! It hurts."

He tried to contain his laughter. "Sorry. I couldn't help it."

I looked at him, "I think I'm going to take a couple more days to figure it out."

As I drank half of the bottle of water, Sarah brought the sandwich over and set it on the table in front of me. I still felt very dehydrated even though I apparently had more than a dozen bags of saline drip over the past few days.

I inhaled the sandwich. I was full for the first time in days and very thankful; I knew I'd made it through one hell of an experience.

I tried to get to my feet. Lance wrapped his arm around my waist and I winced as he helped me up. I shuffled into the kitchen with my dish in hand and set it in the sink, turned around, and bent down to get another bottle of water.

I yawned, "I'm going to lie down. I'm exhausted."

Everyone agreed with my decision. "You've had quite a vacation, I think you deserve a nap," Sarah chimed in.

"C'mon, Nimbus. Let's go." I shuffled back to my room with Nimbus trotting at my heels. I crawled into bed and fell asleep without hesitation.

Chapter 4

Eventful...

The next few days flew by as I tried to wrap my mind around the concept that in the past week I not only got struck by lightning again, but found out that I was pregnant, too.

We headed home on Sunday. My brother rode with me to keep me company. "You want me to drive?" he suggested. "You did just get struck by lightning."

"Nah, I'm okay," I replied. "At least for now. I'll let you know if that changes."

"Whatever you want."

Our conversation was minimal throughout the duration of the trip. Nimbus passed out on the back seat with his head on my duffle bag, snoring like a human. I asked my brother, "What's your opinion on Greg and the pregnancy?"

"You've gotta tell him," he said.

"Obviously." I paused. "We kinda planned this," I admitted.

He glared over his shoulder. "You planned the pregnancy?" he repeated.

I slowly nodded as I exhaled. "*Something* told us to have a baby. That's the best way I can explain it."

He huffed. "*Something* told you to get pregnant? At 19? That's the stupidest thing I've ever heard." We sat in silence. "Well, that changes the dynamics of the situation. At least you know he won't run from it."

"I know he won't. He's a good guy."

"Do you think you two will last? Just because you two wanted a kid doesn't mean that your relationship's going to work. You *know* Mom and Dad are gonna make you two get married."

"I know. I already warned him about that. I don't think either one of us expected it to be so easy."

"Easy? C'mon, Laurel. You know we're fertile people. You knew exactly what you were doing," he rebutted.

"I know. What's done is done."

"It is…what it is." He took a deep breath, releasing a groan as he exhaled. "You're both young but you'll be just fine. I'm not worried."

"19. He'll be 21 in a month."

I looked out the windshield in silence as I watched the world pass me by. The trip went by so fast as I wondered how difficult my life was about to become. My head was spinning with confusion, fear, and a million questions. I answered each question as best I could and placed them according to their level of importance. I had many concerns about being a mother, not to mention having been struck by lightning in my first trimester. I was worried that the baby would suffer. *What if the baby was affected mentally or physically because of this? I know the doctor said the baby's fine, but it still makes me worry. After all, how many pregnant women get struck by lightning and survive without death or serious injury for either of them? How am I going to coach gymnastics with a huge belly? Am I a good influence for the kids I'm coaching? What are their parents going to think?*

I awoke the next morning with my stomach rumbling. I quickly got ready for work and ate a bowl of cereal. Grabbing my purse, I headed out the door. I called my doctor on my way and scheduled an appointment for the following day. After my classes that night, I needed to go tell Greg.

I called Greg in between work and my classes, "Can I stop by tonight?"

"Uh…yeah. I'll be here," he replied.

"Okay, I'll call you on my way. See you then," I said.

"Sounds good. Talk to you later."

I hung up and wondered if he had an inkling as to what I was going to tell him. I didn't believe he would be shocked, though this may be slightly unexpected. We'd only had sex once unprotected with the intention of having a baby. I decided not to worry about it; I knew he'd be there for me no matter what.

I drove to his house after my class as my stomach danced. I took a few deep breaths as I drove down his street.

He opened the front door as I pulled up. "Hey, how was your vacation?" he asked as I closed the door behind me.

"Eventful I must say."

"How's the middle of no-mans-land eventful?"

I took a long, deep breath and began my story. "Well, on the way back from my hike with Nimbus there was a severe thunderstorm. We ran back to the cabin through the woods, got swept under in the river, and finally made it back. Then I leaned against the porch swing…and it got struck by lightning." I held up my bandaged hand.

He turned towards me, his face empty with shock. "What? You got struck by lightning?" He stared at my hand.

"Well, yes." I studied his face and added, "And so did our baby."

His face went through an array of emotions: horror, then a quick smile, then back to horror. "I was unconscious for about three days in the hospital before I woke up. The doctor told me I was pregnant." I studied his face. He seemed fearful about the health of the baby, so I continued. "They did tons of tests on both the baby and me. The doctors believe that we're both healthy."

Stuttering, he asked, "Y-y-you, got s-struck by lightning and you're p-pregnant?"

"Yes."

Silence spread through the room as he absorbed the information. I held my breath as I waited for him to process it.

"So you're pregnant. And you both got struck by lightning," he repeated, trying to absorb the reality of his words.

"Yes," I repeated. "Are you okay?"

He nodded, still in shock, "Uh, yeah." He reached across the counter, grabbed a bag of chips and started shoveling them in his mouth.

"The doctors think you're both okay?" he asked as little bits of chips flew out of his mouth.

"Yes. They've done every kind of test on both of us: brain functions and blood samples. You name it, they did it," I assured him. "I made an appointment for tomorrow at the hospital here, just to confirm everything, but the doctors up there are confident in their test results."

He nodded. "What time tomorrow?" he asked.

"9:30."

"I'll be there," he assured me.

"Um, I've got to remind you of this," I hesitantly continued, "I know it was mentioned before but, um, my family is, ah…"

"…going to want us to get married," he said, finishing my sentence.

I nodded.

He didn't seem surprised. He nodded, "Okay, I just need some time to absorb all of this."

"I know. It's overwhelming for me too," I assured him.

"Yeah. Overwhelming is a good word for this," he mumbled.

"Call me if you want to talk. I'm going home to rest and absorb this more, myself."

"Okay." He followed me to the door.

"Laurel?" "Yeah?"

"I'm glad you're okay. And the baby, too," he said.

"Thank you." I walked out the door and climbed in my Jeep. As I started it, I looked up. He was standing there, staring at me with an absent look of shock on his face.

I smiled, waved, and drove off. I felt somewhat relieved. He'd handled it all very well. I guess he really had no choice.

I pulled into my apartment complex, admiring the stars as I pulled into my parking space. I turned off the Jeep and stood outside staring up at the sky. A shooting star darted across the grayish black sky speckled with thousands of dancing lights. I smiled as I wished upon that star, "I wish that my baby is healthy." As the words left my mouth, chills shot through my body and I choked up. Tears streamed down my face as my throat knotted and quickly dried out. I wiped away the tears, ran inside, and chugged a bottle of water. Flashes of the kitchen at the cabin sparked in my brain. I started dripping sweat and felt very weak and dehydrated. I grabbed another bottle of water and went into the bathroom to shower. As I stripped out of my gym clothes, I warmed the shower water and brushed my teeth. I stepped into the shower and felt relieved as the water hit my skin. It absorbed the drops like a dried out sponge. It seemed as if my skin itself was dehydrated. I plugged the drain and sat down in the

43

tub. The water fell on me like warm, refreshing rain. I pushed down the nozzle and let the spigot fill the tub almost full with hot water as I soaked in its warmth. As the water wrapped around my body, I felt relaxed and refreshed. I laid there with my eyes closed and drifted off to sleep.

Chapter 5

Exam

     I jumped to attention as I heard my alarm going off in my room. The freezing bath water shocked my pruned and shivering body as I realized that I'd slept the entire night in the bathtub. I laughed at myself and drained the water from the tub and warmed the water for a shower. I covered myself with a towel and ran to turn off my alarm. My teeth chattered as I shivered and retreated to the bathroom to shower again. The warm water thawed my skin as I quickly soaped and rinsed and dried myself off.

I called my work and left a message for my boss, "I wanted to remind you that I've got a doctor's appointment at 9:30. I'll be in as soon as it is done."

I hung up and quickly dressed. I flew out the front door and headed towards the hospital for more poking and prodding.

As I signed in, Greg appeared in the waiting room. "Thanks for being here," I said.

"No problem. It's my baby too. I want to make sure he...she...it's okay," he smiled.

"Well, we appreciate you being here," I giggled. "Ya know, I got pregnant the first time we had sex after I stopped the pill."

"We must be fertile people," he replied.

"And it must be meant to be."

"It must be." He grabbed my hand and kissed it. "We can do this."

"I agree." I kissed his lips.

A nurse came through the door. "Laurel Forte?"

"That's me." I motioned for Greg to follow me.

He stood up and followed as the nurse led us to the observation room. "Remove your clothing and put on the gown with the opening in the front."

I nodded.

She closed the door and I rolled my eyes at Greg. I removed my shirt and bra and tossed them on the stool in the corner of the room. I slid my arms into the light blue paper towel gown and removed my pants, which I also tossed on the stool in the corner.

I sat myself on the table to wait for the gynecologist to come in. We waited in silence as I crossed my ankles, swung them back and forth, and hummed a tune.

The doctor knocked on the door and entered, pushing in an ultrasound machine. She introduced herself to Greg, "Hello, I'm Dr. Gold."

"Hi, I'm Greg Boyce."

"Nice to meet you, Greg." She took a deep breath and spun on one heel towards me. "Hello, Laurel, I understand we've got an outlandish situation. Can you explain to me what happened?"

"The swing I was leaning on got struck by lightning." I held out my bandaged hand. "Then I found out I was a little over three months pregnant."

"Uh, huh." She paged through my file. "Dr. McKinley sent me your test results. I've looked over everything. From what I can see, you and your baby are just fine."

I nodded as I looked at Greg's face from across the room. He appeared to still be slightly confused. He said, "Doctor, how can someone that's pregnant get struck by lightning and everything be okay? I'm baffled."

"It's quite a miracle." She paused and looked at me. "Well, I'm going to assume, you were insulated by something?" She looked over her rectangular glasses with wide yet squinty eyes.

"I had a sneaker on."

She repeated, "*A* sneaker? As in one?"

I nodded.

"Well, that'll do it." She looked at Greg, "Is that a good enough answer for you?"

He rationalized, "I guess. If you say so, Doc."

She turned back to me. "How are you feeling, Laurel? Is your energy level good? Are you feeling fatigued? Any morning sickness?"

I shook my head as she asked each question. "Just really thirsty."

"Well, I normally wouldn't require an ultra sound or blood tests again so quickly but under these circumstances I think it's acceptable. I'm also going to pull some amniotic fluid out of the uterus, just to confirm."

"I figured you'd want to re-run all of the same tests, and then some. Just to confirm." I said.

"Well, lay on back and we'll get started. I figure it's best to get the internal done first."

I laid back on the table and crossed my arm over my eyes. As she performed the exam I felt a wave of embarrassment cascade through my body. I shifted my body, as I was extremely cold and uncomfortable. I sucked in a quick, deep breath and held it, imagining I was on a white sandy beach overlooking the crystal blue water. I imagined inhaling the saltwater smell deep into my lungs. I envisioned the seagulls as they soared above me, cawing for food.

"Uh-huh, uh-huh, uh-huh." She confirmed, "Well, everything feels great in there."

I took my first breath in what seemed to be minutes. "Well that's good so far."

"That's one of the most important exams in this particular case; we need to know your uterus is happy and healthy so you can carry this baby full term."

I nodded. "So what's next?"

"A quick breast exam and then the ultrasound." She jumped off her stool, slid out the table's leg extension and pushed my paper towel dress to the side of each of my breasts. I lowered my legs covering myself, still embarrassed.

She pressed on my right breast in a circular motion and then the left. "Well, they look good," she said as she covered me back up.

Silence conquered the room. I could feel my embarrassment prickling across my skin. I glanced at Greg. He seemed to be sheltering his face from a direct view of my exam. I was relieved, forcing myself to believe that he didn't see anything.

Dr. Gold broke the discomfort in the room as she blanketed my lower half with a paper towel sheet and said, "Time for the ultrasound." She wheeled the cart over to the side of the table, grabbed the jelly, and squeezed it out in a circle around my belly button. The screen popped on and she began moving the transducer around my stomach.

She moved it back and forth and then settled in one spot. "There's your baby." She pointed to the black and white speckled body floating around. "There's the heartbeat." She pointed to the white speckle that pulsed in conjunction with the heartbeat pulse we could hear through the monitor speakers.

A tear trickled out of the corner of my eye as I saw the baby growing inside me. Hearing the heartbeat reassured me that the baby was fine. Relief, excitement, and love washed the worry away immediately. Our baby was like a miracle. The baby was just fine.

Greg jumped up. "I need a better view." He pushed between the doctor and the countertop and grabbed my hand as he positioned himself in front of the monitor.

I squeezed his hand tight as we watched and listened to the heartbeat jolting across the screen. The baby moved its arm and then its legs. "It's a boy. I know it." Another tear rolled down my face.

Dr. Gold said, "It's about two weeks too early to determine the baby's sex, but here's to wishful thinking."

Greg said, eyes welling up with tears, "That's our baby. Oh, my God, that's our baby."

I knew he was as happy as I was.

Dr. Gold said, "The heartbeat looks great. The little one is moving around in there pretty good, too. I'm rather pleased so far. Now, for the hard part: the amniocentesis. We've got to go to a different room for that so I'm going to ask you to get dressed so we can change rooms, and then you will get undressed again."

I giggled as she wiped my stomach clean and tossed the towel away. "I'll be back in one minute, go ahead and get dressed." She closed the door behind her.

I got up and wiped more of the lubricant off as best I could and got dressed.

"That's amazing," Greg said.

I was somewhere in the back of my head thanking Jesus as he spoke. I snapped back into focus as I turned towards him. "What? What's amazing?"

"We just saw our baby. We're going to be parents. I'm so freakin' excited!"

I smiled as my hair brushed across my chin. "I am too. Even more now that I know you're excited about it. I wasn't sure how you were going to react at first."

"Well…I am." He gave me a bear hug, picked me up and spun me around. "I love you, Mommy."

"I love you, Daddy."

He threw his hands up in the air and exclaimed, "I'm gonna be a daddy! Whoooo-hooooo!"

The doctor burst through the door as Greg quickly regained his composure. "Good to know you're happy," she said. "Now let's go."

We followed Dr. Gold down the hall. Her assistant joined us as we walked into what seemed like more of an operating room than an exam room. As the door shut behind us I got queasy. I knew one of these procedures was already performed on me, but I was unconscious at the time. My palms started sweating. "Can I have some water?"

She pointed to a cup already filled with ice water. I quickly drank it. "Can I have more, please?"

She looked over her rectangle rimmed glasses, her mousy brown hair highlighted with gray, "Thirsty?"

"Yes, very."

She looked at Greg, "Do you want to stay during this procedure?"

"Should I?" he asked.

"I don't recommend it unless you're in the medical field. The last thing I need is you passing out. But if you stay near her head and hold her hand, it shouldn't be a problem."

I squeezed his hand. "Stay. Please don't leave me.   Just don't look."

He reluctantly nodded.

She walked over to the wall and pushed an 'N'- shaped bar on wheels about four feet wide halfway up my chest. She took a paper towel sheet and three clips and created a makeshift barrier between us and her.

"*That's* your barrier?" Greg asked sarcastically.

From behind the sheet she said, "Can you see me?"

"Uh, no. No I can't," he replied.

"Then it works," she justified.

The nurse wheeled another ultrasound machine next to my stomach. She applied a topical numbing agent and moved the transducer back and forth.

"There," said Dr. Gold. "Hold it right there."

I felt pressure as the needle pierced my belly button. I took a deep breath through my nose as I squeezed Greg's hand, bit down on the inside of my lip and closed my eyes. I was imagining I was back on the beach again, lying out in the sun. The seconds felt like minutes passing though before I knew it, the procedure was over.

"You may feel a little crampy or nauseous for a few days. It's very normal," she said as she cleaned up. The nurse wiped my stomach clean and covered me.

"I don't want you to worry. Your previous test results look good, and I'm confident that these will read the same," she reassured.

I nodded. "Okay, how soon will we have the test results?"

"In about a week or so. I'll call you when I get them. Go ahead and get dressed. I'll meet you at the front desk."

Greg wiped his brow. "This is all so intense."

I quickly got dressed. "All you've had to do is sit there. Imagine being me."

"No thanks. I'm glad I'm a guy and don't have to deal with any of this."

"It's really not fun, I must say."

"Is it wrong of me to say that I hope it's a boy?"

"Not at all; I know it's a boy. I can just feel it. Not to mention, I don't know if I'd be a good mother for a girl unless she was a tomboy like me. I don't think the world needs another 'me.' I know I'll be a great mom for our son."

"I never thought of that, but I see what you're saying. I don't know if this earth could handle a 'Mini You.'"

I laughed. "One is enough."

He opened the exam room door and we headed down the hallway towards the front desk. Dr.

Gold was waiting for us behind the counter. "Everything looks great Laurel; I'll get back to you in a few days with the results of your amniotic fluids. Until then, no worries." She reached out and handed me an envelope. "Open that after you leave. Have a great day and we'll see you soon."

I cracked a small smile, wondering, "What's this?" I signed the papers the receptionist put in front of me. She tore off my copies, saying, "Have a great day, Laurel."

"Thanks, you too." I turned around and followed Greg into the hallway. I stopped after three steps and flipped over the envelope and slowly pulled out its secret prize. In my hands were the first pictures of the baby, in utero. I looked at Greg and said, "It's our baby."

He wrapped his arms around me and squeezed me tight.

"There's a copy for you, too," I said.

"I can't wait to show everybody. Whoooo! I'm a daddy!"

When we got in the elevator, Greg spun me around and kissed me. "I love you. I'm so happy we're having a baby."

"I love you, too."

We both got into our cars, each with the first picture of our child, and went to work.

As I drove, reality quickly set in. *I'm going to be a mother.* I laughed so excitedly, honked the horn, and screamed out the window, "I'm gonna be a mommy!"

I floated through the rest of my day.

My parents knew I was pregnant before I did, so the hardest part, spilling the big news to the folks, never really existed for me. And Greg's parents were thrilled at the news when he told them.

We decided to get married to respect my parents wishes. After all, we both were so excited to be parents and loved each other dearly. Since we had very little money, we decided to have a judge marry us in my parents' well-groomed back yard. The most expensive part was having it catered.

I found a gorgeous spaghetti-strap gown that had white satin with embroidered flowers and pearls strategically placed around each flower. The train of the gown was long and flowing. Everyone's biggest concern was about the growth of my pregnant stomach over the next two months before my wedding. My mom, an extremely skilled seamstress, was able to settle everyone's concerns. The gown itself was a size too big. She knew she'd be able to alter the gown a week or so before the wedding so I wouldn't have to stress or go back and forth to the seamstress at the gown shop. She also made the veil: a tiara with tulle, pearls, and lace.

My dad immediately started working on a project in the basement and none of us were allowed down there anymore.

Chapter 6

Nineteen

As the wedding day grew closer, I began to realize that I was no longer a child. I was going to be a wife at the age of nineteen. My twentieth birthday was three days after the wedding, and then I'd become a mother a few months after that. I often got a chuckle out of referring to myself as "the girl whose life took a major detour in development." I hadn't gone to college and I wasn't even of legal age to drink alcohol, yet I was bringing a life into this world. I never regretted the fact that I was pregnant, especially with both of us surviving the trauma that occurred at the beginning of the second trimester. I couldn't imagine regretting our choice to have a baby.

I definitely had a lot of stress about the thought getting married, though. I began to have second thoughts about this huge step we were about to take.

I was awakened by my mom on the morning of our wedding. "Rise and shine, Laurel. You're about to become a wife!" she said with drastic enthusiasm.

I rolled over in bed, choosing to ignore her wake up call.

"Everyone's starting to set up the back yard and you need to get up and get ready."

"I'd rather just sleep this day away," I groaned as I sat up. "You know how excited I am for this."

"Laurel, we talked about this. You and Greg need to do the right thing and give this baby a proper home."

"Ugh. Mom, it's almost a new millennium. People have kids out of wedlock all the time."

"Well, Laurel, our *religious* family is upset enough about the situation. You had to make a choice between single motherhood or married life."

I slumped over onto the bed. "I know, Mom. It's better in the long run to be married and play the part. I get it."

"You're making the right decision, Hun. You know you are."

"Yep." I grabbed my white button down shirt and my blue and white linen striped pants as I walked out of my bedroom to shower.

I stood under the steaming hot water with my hair pulled up in a bun. I felt my stomach cramp and swell. I looked down, rubbed my baby bump, and smiled. "I'm doing this for you." I jiggled my rock hard stomach. The baby responded with a rather strong and solid push, its way of saying "Thank you, Mommy."

I groaned in pain because the kicks felt like an alien pushing out of my stomach. I rubbed my stomach as the baby finally released from its stretch. I took a deep breath of relief and relaxed.

After my shower, I took my time getting ready, mostly staring in the mirror at myself. After stalling for about twenty minutes, I went downstairs for breakfast.

"Here's your eggs and bacon. The toast and sausage will be ready in a few seconds," my mom said.

"Thanks. It'll all be coming back up anyway," I replied, referring to my morning sickness.

"No one said pregnancy was easy," she said.

"No one said I was going to have morning, noon, and night sickness either."

"Just brush your teeth again before you kiss your husband."

I picked at my breakfast and looked at the clock. *Two hours till I am to be wed.*

I watched the hustle and bustle of the caterers setting up as my family and friends started to arrive. I disappeared upstairs.

I went into the bathroom and threw up. I didn't understand how this baby was going to be healthy due to the constant vomiting, though I'd had more than the normal amount of gynecological appointments for the average pregnant woman. Dr. Gold said everything was fine. She told me that morning sickness was normal. I chose to continue to believe that she knew what she was talking about.

I plugged in my curling iron, brushed my teeth, and rinsed my face with cold water. I began preparing myself for my day. My *wedding* day. I curled my hair and pinned it up in a bun with a few ringlets dangling down, and then applied my makeup. I sprayed my perfume on my chest and wrists.

I walked down the hallway to my parents' bedroom and stared at my dress. The white silk sparkled in the sun. The scattered flowers and pearls on the train of the dress individually reflected the sunlight.

I had hoped that seeing myself in the gown would make me feel differently about becoming a wife. Maybe I'd be happy. I doubted it, but decided to try and see if the effect worked anyway. I pulled the dress off its hanger and stepped into it. I pulled on the spaghetti straps up and zippered as much as I could. I rubbed my stomach, the gown slightly stretched across my belly. *Well, at least your stomach didn't pop and you fit into your dress.* I giggled. My heart began to thump in my head. I could feel the baby move with the beating. I knew the baby could sense my emotions: I was so excited to be a mom, though I never thought I'd have a child. Especially so young.

Nothing made me more proud and excited than to have this baby. I wanted to make this baby proud of his parents. I turned back and forth admiring my dress. Suddenly I realized that I was actually looking forward to getting married and embarking on our journey together as a family.

My mom entered the room. "Laurel, you look so beautiful."

"Thanks, Mom."

"You look like an angel." She tasseled the train of the gown.

I smiled with embarrassment and said, "I…um…actually am excited to get married now. I know it's all been so sudden and crazy but I do love Greg and I want our baby to have a proper home. Sorry I've been so crabby about it."

A tear touched the corner of her eye and a smile overtook her face. "It's okay. You've had an exciting few months. It's been more than anyone else could've ever handled but you're strong. after all, that's what our last name means. "Forte" means "strength." God gave you that gift so you could be strong for your husband and your child."

I nodded. I'd heard her say that my entire life. *Forte means strength.* I stared at myself in the mirror as I swayed back and forth. I thought, "Somehow my name makes complete sense. 'Laurel' means 'flower' and 'Forte' means 'strength.' I'm a strong flower."

I snapped back into the moment as my mom interrupted my thoughts. "It's time. I love you and I'm proud of you." She spun me and zipped my gown the rest of the way.

"I love you, too, Mom."

She helped me slip on my white satin shoes with short thick heels, intentionally picked so they wouldn't pierce the ground as I walk across the backyard and down the aisle. She pulled my train out, flapped it and rustled the gown. "It's perfect," she whispered as she stood up behind me in the mirror. "Let's go downstairs. Everyone's waiting on you."

We walked down the hallway as my mom guided the train behind me. As I descended down the stairs, my heart began beating fast and my stomach turned as a knot formed in my throat.

I stood at the back door of the house waiting for the crowd to silence. I took one long, deep, final breath in preparation for taking the first step out of childhood and directly into adulthood.

As I exhaled the baby kicked hard, sending a shooting pain through my stomach and side. I grabbed my stomach and tapped where its foot was, trying to tell the baby that he was hurting me. The baby pushed back each time I tapped, like Morse Code. I giggled as I tapped against its foot twice. I stood waiting to feel a response.

I wondered if the baby knew that I was communicating with him. As seconds ticked by, I held my breath. I placed my hand on my stomach and waited.

Thump. Thump. The baby responded. Tears of joy doused my cheeks as my entire being was overwhelmed with love.

My dad walked through the kitchen and met me at the back door. "What happened? Are you all right?"

I dabbed my tears. "He's talking to me. Like Morse Code," I quivered. "Come feel."

I tapped twice again, grabbed my dad's hand, and put it on my stomach. "Shhhh, just wait."

The seconds ticked by. And then…Thump. Thump.

"Wow, that's neat!" His face lit up with excitement. "It's been a long time since I felt a baby in your mom's stomach. And now I get to feel my grandchild in my baby's stomach."

I smiled as tears welled up in my eyes. "I love you, Dad."

"I love you too, Laurel." He put his hands on my shoulders and kissed my forehead. "You ready?"

"Yes. Are you?"

He nodded.

We were ready. The baby was ready, too. I picked up my bouquet of beautiful red roses, which were handpicked from our garden, and opened the door before my father escorted me across the porch. When we reached the stairs, the crowd stood up with their attention directed at us. My nerves sparked as we walked down the steps through the garden that my parents had cultured for years. The aroma of the roses and hyacinths calmed me as I inhaled the sweet smell of the gardens.

I heard cameras snapping and saw flashes out of the corner of my eyes as we approached Greg. My cheeks twanged as my nerves twitched. I watched Greg as we walked towards him; he looked as nervous as I was. He stood under a white awning, draped in vines; the secret project my dad built for the wedding. My father shook Greg's hand and then kissed my cheek, "I love you, Laurel," he said.

"I love you, Dad."

He turned and proudly took his seat next to my mom.

The judge spoke, "Dearly beloved, we are gathered here today to join Laurel and Greg in Matrimony."

We stared at each other and shared a moment of bliss. As the judge went through his lines, my thoughts drifted into the back of my head:

We made a commitment to have a baby. We are making a commitment to each other. We are choosing a path that makes sense to us. I know without a doubt, at this moment, that this is the right decision. I know this in the depths of my soul. I know by the love swirling in my heart. I know from the serenity that inhabits my mind, this is what life is about. This is where I want my life to go.

Chapter 7

Twenty

I finally forced myself to lie down on the floor. I'd been cleaning all day. The baby was on its way in five days. I knew I'd need a few days to recover after the baby was born and I was trying to get as much done as possible before that time.

Because stomach was so big, I could only lay on my back or side. I was so uncomfortable and my ribs felt like they were going to push through my chest. I stretched my back and rolled from side to side. My back cracked all the way up the spine.

"Ahh. That felt so damn good," I said to Greg who sat in his recliner watching the news.

"You're about ready to pop. Do you need anything?" he asked.

"No, I'm okay. Just ready for this to be over."

He looked at me. "Are you ready to be a parent?"

"Definitely. How 'bout you?"

He nodded. "Yeah, I am. Not that we have much choice now. It's almost time."

I giggled. "Five days. Unless I go late, which doesn't really seem that desirable to me. I can't remember the last time I ate a meal that I didn't throw up."

He chuckled, "That's got to be rough. Six months of morning sickness."

I stretched my arms out across the floor, "Or what I like to call 'morning, noon, and night sickness,'" I said accompanying finger quotations. "I just hope he isn't malnourished."

"The doctors have done enough testing and kept a hell of a close eye on you and the baby since you got fried. I'm sure everything is fine."

"I know. I've been pricked and prodded enough, too. Add the puking and it's literally been one hell of a pregnancy. I'm kinda worried about the delivery."

"Don't worry; everything's gonna be fine. I'm going to get a drink, you want anything?" He said as he slammed down the recliner's foot rest and wrestled to get out of his chair.

I laughed, "You gonna be able to handle being a dad, ol' man?"

He chuckled, "Right? I'm not even that old yet." He started imitating me by stretching, "Maybe I should workout as much as you do, then I'll feel better."

"You'll at least get rid of that gut that I see starting to form. Are you pregnant too?" I teased.

"I had womb envy." He jiggled his belly. "I wanted to be fat too." He chuckled at himself, "Do you want something to drink?"

"I'll have a Coke. I need some carbonation to make me burp. I'm rather gassy."

He walked into the kitchen as I arched my back against the floor trying to relieve the tension in my back and rib cage. I relaxed back on the floor and pulled my knees up around my stomach, then stretched my legs back out. I relaxed as I lay perfectly still.

Greg handed me a glass of Coke when he returned. I rolled up into a sitting position being careful not to spill any soda. As I leaned forward on the ottoman and took a sip, I started feeling a burning sensation in my lower back. I set my drink on the ground and stretched my back from side to side. My head spun as a sharp pain shot through my back, "Ahhh!" I groaned.

"What's wrong? You okay?"

I took a long, slow, deep breath as I nodded and massaged my lower back. I took a sip of my soda; the carbonation seemed to help suppress the nausea that had begun to rise. "Can you rub my back a little? I must've twisted the wrong way while I was cleaning." I knelt in front of the ottoman and laid face down across it as far as my belly would let me.

He sat down next to me and rubbed circles up and down my back. When my back seemed to relax, I hobbled over to the bathroom. I sat down on the toilet and as I relieved myself, a sharp pain shot through my sides and I screamed again, "Uuuhhhhh!"

Greg came running in. "You okay?"

"Get my mom on the phone."

He darted away and quickly returned with my cell phone already calling my mom.

My mom's voice answered on the other end, "Hello?"

"Does labor start with sharp shooting pains in your back and sides?"

Excitedly she said, "Yeeeaaaah!"

"In the last few minutes, I've had two of them. I'm coming over."

"See you soon," she said.

I flipped the phone shut as my eyes met Greg's. "Get my hospital bag. I'm in labor. We're going to my parents right now."

"Oh shit. You're in labor?" His eyes widened as reality hit him and he sat frozen.

"Go grab everything I need."

He stumbled up the steps and fumbled around as he reminded himself aloud what to grab for the hospital. "Bag of clothes. Car seat. Baby bag full of goodies."

I slowly pulled myself together and put on my coat and boots. I put Nimbus on his leash and met Greg at the car. "Can you please grab my soda? I'm really gonna need that."

Without question, he ran back inside.

Nimbus danced in the back seat of Greg's Mountaineer, always happy to go for a car ride. "Nimbus, sit down," I ordered. "I can't deal with this right now." I rubbed my stomach in circles. Nimbus sat immediately, his tail wagging as he watched Greg lock up the house and return to the car. We then headed over to my parents house.

I felt my stomach tighten and release a few times along the way. I braced myself for what I believed to be a contraction.

As we pulled down my parents' driveway I screamed in agony. Another sharp pain shot up from my lower back into my shoulders. This one lasted about thirty seconds, "Ahh-AHHHH-AAAAHHH-FUUUUUCK!"

Greg, trying not to laugh, quickly put the car in park. "You okay?"

"Uh-huh," I said, rubbing my back and stomach simultaneously. My parents met us in the driveway as I was unbuckling my seat belt. My dad opened the door and helped me out of the car. Lance and Hillary were standing at the edge of the carport, both smiling and excited. I slowly walked into the house with my dad escorting me. I waddled my way into the living room as Greg informed everyone about the details.

"What'd you do today?" my mom asked me.

"Cleaned."

"Yep, you're in labor alright. You were nesting today, preparing for your baby to arrive."

"He's not due for another five days," I objected.

She shook her head. "It doesn't matter. Your body knew the baby was coming today and you couldn't sit still." She then turned to Greg saying, "How far apart are the contractions?"

"About every fifteen to twenty minutes," he answered.

"When was the last one?"

"Right when we pulled down the driveway," he said nervously.

She looked at the clock on the stove, "About two minutes ago." She grabbed a piece of paper and titled it "Labor Pains - November 5th, 1995." On the line under it she wrote, "3rd contraction 10:46 PM."

The contractions continued to get closer together and around 3:30 AM we headed over to the hospital. As we drove I rested my head back, sweating profusely and extremely exhausted. We pulled up to the emergency entrance and I slowly sat myself into a wheelchair that Greg had found. When we entered the hospital, another contraction surged through my body. "Oh, Jeeees-uuuuus! Ahhhh-ahhhhhh-uhhhhh-huh!"

The nurses ran over towards me and asked Greg, "How far apart are her contractions?"

"About seven minutes."

"She's about ready to go." The nurse in the pink swirled scrubs pushed my wheel chair down the long hallway towards the birthing rooms.

As I continued to breathe heavily and rub my stomach, I began to feel more nauseous than I ever did during my entire pregnancy. I lowered my head as the rapid movement, the smell of the hospital, and my nausea combined. A hot and cold chill crawled across my body. I leaned to the right and vomited onto the floor.

The nurse stopped immediately. "Are you okay?"

"Yeah. Sorry, it came out of nowhere." I hung my head down, trying to make the hallway stop spinning. "Soda isn't so good coming back up."

The nurse in dark blue scrubs rolled her eyes and huffed as she ran to the nurse's counter we'd just passed. She called for a janitor and grabbed towels from the cabinet. They wiped down the chair and the wheel. I hung my head and held my breath as the smell made me want to throw up again.

They quickly cleaned off the chair and continued towards the room. They wheeled me into the waiting area and another wave of nausea over took me. I motioned to the nurse to grab the trash can. Just as she handed it to me I leaned over and puked. With each heave I could feel my muscles tightening. My entire body was dripping with sweat. My hands were quivering and my heart was jumping out of my chest.

They pushed me into a room and helped me get onto a bed that was layered in sheets and towels. The nurse in the dark blue scrubs pulled my shirt off and dressed me in a paper towel gown. They laid me back and removed my sweat pants. I rolled to the side, searching for the trash can as I began dry heaving. The nurse quickly moved the trash can underneath my face. I hurled up the soda that was left in my stomach. "Oh, God" I moaned. I felt a contraction coming on and I screamed in agony as I held my stomach. My back was on fire; I felt like I was inside an industrial-sized furnace engulfed in flames. I tried to breathe through the heat but instead I kept dry heaving.

The nurses rushed to my assistance. "Here you go, Laurel." The one in pink handed me ice chips as she toweled the sweat off my forehead. "You need to keep yourself hydrated."

"Thanks," I huffed. "Does everybody puke during contractions?" I tried to avoid the stench of my cotton mouth wafting through the air as I spoke.

Both nurses shook their heads. "Not really, but everyone's different."

The one in blue said, "Lay back and relax. You need to conserve your strength. I'm going to give you a dose of Demerol for the pain before your epidural. I'll be right back."

I laid back and closed my eyes. I had a heat flash, and my head was still spinning. I leaned over to throw up again and then passed out.

I jolted awake as a contraction surged across my stomach and I screamed in agony. My hands clutched around my stomach and I puked again. I looked at my left hand and noticed that they had inserted an intravenous needle in the vein.

The nurse rubbed my back. "We administered the Demerol, that's why you were able to rest. The anesthesiologist is on his way to administer the epidural. You'll feel much better after that."

"Uh-huh." My eyes rolled back in my head as got another waft of my rotten breath. At this point, I really didn't care. I slumped back into the bed and closed my eyes again.

I screamed out as another contraction shot through my back. My toes curled up and began to twinge. Sweat dripped profusely from my pores as my legs suddenly began to spasm. I tried to massage them but instead my head spun and I threw up again. This time, I didn't make it to the trash can, but I really wasn't concerned.

I shoved an ice chip in my mouth. The chill felt so refreshing. I thought of the day I got struck by lightning and was right back there again. I shoved more ice chips into my mouth. I closed my eyes and savored the relief.

A doctor entered the room. "Did you do an internal yet?"

One of the nurses said, "I was just getting ready to."

She said, "Let me know where she is."

The door opened again as the doctor and anesthesiologist left the room. The pink nurse helped me adjust into position for the internal, as the blue nurse put on her vinyl gloves and said, "I'm going to do an internal. Do you need me to explain it or are you used to the routine by now?"

"I got it. Just do it and get this fuckin' kid outta me."

She chuckled and began to perform the exam. "How old are you?"

As my tired eyes batted I quietly said, "Twenty."

She nodded her head as she felt around for a few seconds. "You're about halfway there. The baby is facing the right direction, so we'll administer the epidural now."

"Thank God. I'm exhausted." I shoved another ice chip in my dried crusty mouth.

"I bet you are," the pink nurse said as she left the room.

I laid back and closed my eyes, wishing I had a soda.

The pink nurse returned with the anesthesiologist. Both nurses came to the left side of the bed and helped me sit up.

"Swing your legs off the side of the bed, towards us," the one nurse said. "We need you to hunch over and curve your back. Just hold still."

The anesthesiologist said, "You're going to feel some pressure as I insert it the needle. Make sure to hold completely still."

I closed my eyes and followed their directions. I leaned into the shoulder of the pink nurse. The next thing I knew, I was comfortably lying in bed. "Feel great," I said to the blue nurse as my eyes rolled back into my head.

"Everyone loves that epidural. Makes a world of difference," I heard her say as I drifted off to sleep.

I heard movement in the room as I slowly came to. "Did I have the baby yet?" I asked the nurse groggily.

"No sweetheart, but you've slept through about six contractions." She lifted the paper streaming out of a machine down to the floor. "We're going to do an internal to see if you're ready."

She positioned my feet into the stirrups and pulled on her gloves. "You know the routine?"

"Yes," I said.

I barely felt anything as she checked the dilation of my cervix. "You're ready to go. We need to break your water."

"How do we do that?"

She reached to the bottom shelf of her cart and lifted a long rod with a sharp hook at the end. "We're going to pop it. With this."

I shook a few ice chips into my mouth as I looked at the hook. "Great. Will it hurt?"

"You're numbed from the waist down. You'll only feel pressure. Now lay back and relax."

The pink nurse dabbed my forehead with a wet cloth. "You're doing great, Laurel."

I felt pressure as the nurse in blue inserted the hook inside me and positioned it. I heard a popping sound come from inside me followed by a gush of warm water. As the disposable sheets absorbed the water flowing out of me, it hit me: *I'm ready to have this baby. It's time.* "Can Greg come in yet?"

The pink nurse opened the door. "Greg, do you want to come join Laurel?"

He popped his head in the door. "Hey, how you doing?"

"Exhausted and nervous, I guess. They just broke my water, so...it's time."

"I can't wait." He kissed my forehead. "You're sweating."

I pointed to the cup. "Ice chips."

He handed the cup to me and shook the ice chips into my mouth. "I've thrown up so freakin' much. I'm exhausted."

"I heard them talking about it at the desk. You'll be fine."

"How long we been here?" I asked.

Greg looked at the clock, "It's 8:50 in the morning, so about 5 hours."

The pink nurse came over. "We're going to lighten the dosage of the epidural so you'll begin to feel the contractions again. We need you to be able to push."

I nodded and looked at Greg. "Here we go."

"You'll do great. No worries."

I instantly began to feel the pain again as she lowered the dosage. "Where's the doctor?" I asked.

"She'll be here in a few minutes."

I felt a contraction coming on as I grabbed my stomach and screamed.

"That'll do it. You should be completely dilated. You're ready to push. The baby is ready too."

I rolled to Greg and motioned for the trash can. As he lifted it, I puked. Almost nothing was left in my stomach. As I cramped and contracted again, the blue nurse said, "Push."

I bore down, pushed hard, and moaned, "Huuu-uuuh!"

The blue nurse looked at the pink nurse and said, "Call Dr. Gold."

The pink nurse hustled out the door and returned within seconds. "She's on her way."

Greg whispered, "You're doing great. Squeeze my hand."

"Push," the blue nurse said. "The baby hasn't moved yet."

I bore down again, squeezing Greg's hand. "Huuuuuuuhhh, Huuuuuuuuuuuuh!"

She inserted her fingers inside. "You've got to push like you're going number two. You haven't moved the baby at all. Push down."

I pushed down harder and harder.

The blue said, "That's better. Now do it again."

I pushed again. I groaned and pushed until I had nothing left and then flopped back in the bed as I rolled towards Greg and started dry heaving. He put the trash can under my face and rubbed my back as I ejected more of my stomachs content.

The pink nurse dabbed my forehead with a wet towel as the blue nurse said, "I need to check where the baby is." As she checked she huffed and rolled her eyes, saying, "You still haven't moved this baby. You need to push." She shook her head and mumbled under her breath, "Too young to have a baby."

"Where's the *doctor*?" I asked. "Shouldn't she be in charge by now?"

The door flew open as the doctor came in. She immediately put on her coat and gloves. "How are we doing, Laurel?'

"In agony."

The blue nurse updated her. "She has pushed a few times but the baby hasn't moved."

"Well, let me see what's going on in there." She gloved her hand and did an internal. She turned to the blue nurse. "The baby's head is turned the wrong way, its chin is caught in her hip. We need to physically spin the baby. You didn't realize that?"

"Sorry, Doctor. I thought I was feeling the crown."

"You weren't. You were feeling the chin. You'll need to push on the outside of her stomach while I spin from the inside."

She nodded, "Yes, ma'am."

I sensed the urgency in her voice. "Is everything okay with the baby?"

She pulled up her gloves saying, "Everything's going to be fine, Laurel. We need to spin this baby immediately." Without further hesitation, she inserted both of her hands inside me.

I screamed in pure agony.

"On three, you push that way." She jerked her head to the right. "One, two, three," she said as she and the blue nurse worked to spin the baby.

I bellowed in pain as I felt my uterus shift, and the placenta tear from my interior walls. My hands clutched the arms of the bed I release a blood curdling scream as my entire body cringed in anguish.

"Okay. Now the baby's facing the right direction," Dr. Gold said.

I leaned over and threw up again; down Greg's leg; it was fluorescent yellow. My stomach was starting to reject its lining.

He jumped back in an attempt to avoid getting puked on again. He grabbed the trash can and shoved it under my face. I ejected everything left

84

in my stomach. With each heave I felt like my insides were ripping apart.

"I'm going to let you rest for fifteen minutes. Then we need to get this baby out." The doctor pulled the blue nurse out of the room with her.

I lay there, wishing I could hear the doctor reprimand the blue nurse, though I didn't feel I had the mental capacity to wrap my brain around the situation. I couldn't even muster the strength to keep my eyes open.

I felt the baby move. My stomach turned and I puked again. This time Greg was quick to get the trash can back under me.

My eyes rolled closed and I blacked out for a moment.

The doctor and the blue nurse came back into the room. The doctor sat down and said, "You ready, Laurel?"

Barely conscience and dripping with sweat, I mumbled, "Uh-huh."

"I need you to push."

I forced myself awake. I shifted in my bed, took a deep breath, and bore down with every ounce of energy I had. I felt the baby's head pushing out of me as I screeched in pain.

"Good job! We need another good push."

I bore down again as I felt my insides tearing away from parts of my body that I never knew existed. "Ahhhhhhh! God damn. Holy shit, I can't do it."

"Yes you can, Laurel. You're almost there. Give me two more good pushes and you'll be done."

I bore down. It felt like I was giving birth to a spiked bowling ball as I screamed in terror.

"One more, Laurel, and you're done."

As I bore down, I felt the blood vessels in my face popping. Then I felt a pop and a gush of warm liquid pour out of me. And then I heard a cry.

"The head is out, Laurel. Great job," Dr. Gold said. "Give me just a slight push, to help get the rest out and then we're done."

I pushed again. I felt the shoulders and arms, and, finally, the legs come out. Before I knew it, I had given birth.

"It's a beautiful baby boy," the doctor reported. "9:31 in the morning, November 6th, 1995. Congratulations. What are you going to name him?"

I knew it. I knew I was having a boy. "Hunter Elliott Boyce," I said. I gasped for air and wiped the sweat off my brow as I collapsed back. I realized it was over and smiled; our son had arrived. My weak arms reached for him.

Greg jumped for joy and kissed my forehead. "It's a boy!"

The doctor said to Greg, "Do you want to cut the umbilical cord?"

"Yes I do." Greg followed the directions from the doctor. While he cut the cord, I saw that Hunter was purple from crying so hard.

The blue nurse cleaned him off and wrapped him in a blanket. "He's got a good set of lungs."

"He gets that from his mother," Greg joked.

She set him in my arms and he stopped crying immediately. We looked at each other as I held him close and tears filled my eyes. "Hey there, Hunter. It's so good to finally meet you, my precious baby boy."

He made tiny cooing noises as he shifted in his blanket.

Greg came over and kissed his forehead and then mine. "We have a son," he said, eyes filled with tears of joy. "You did so good. I'm so proud of you."

"I'm exhausted." I smiled and stared at Hunter with my heart so full of love.

The doctor and nurses cleaned up the delivery room and then opened the door and called our families to come into the room.

My mom was the first through the door, tears in her eyes. She was followed closely by my dad and Greg's parents.

Greg proudly announced, "It's a Boy. Hunter Elliot."

They all gathered around the bed, ecstatic to meet Hunter. Everyone cooed over him for a few minutes, snapped pictures, and congratulated us.

The doctor interrupted, "We need to move them down to a room and make sure both mother and son are doing well. You'll be able to visit them shortly."

Everyone slowly started leaving the room and poured back out into the hallway.

I enjoyed the silence while I held my son.

Chapter 8

Yellow

The nurse helped position me in the bed in my recovery room. I moved incredibly slowly as I tried to get comfortable. She pulled my gown aside exposing my breast, and lifted Hunter out of his wheeled cart. She laid him in my arms and shoved my breast in his face. He opened his mouth as he lifted his head, searching for my nipple. He found it and latched on as we began our first breast feeding.

The pink nurse said, "Did he just lift his head?"

I nodded.

"Strong son you have there. Most babies don't understand how to nurse for a few hours. He's smart, too."

I smiled. "Does he seem healthy? In *every* way?"

"He seems fine: ten fingers, ten toes, and a healthy cry."

I grinned as I watched him nurse. "You okay buddy? We went through a lot already, didn't we?" I closed my eyes, exhausted and sore.

As we finished nursing, Greg and our families came in. I adjusted in bed as they all swooned around Hunter. They each took turns holding him and introduced themselves to him.

I closed my eyes and fell asleep.

When I awoke, Greg was the only one still there. He was holding Hunter. "Good morning, Mommy."

"How's he doing?"

"He's perfect."

"Yes he is." I whispered, "Thank God."

"What a relief it's over."

"You're tellin' me." I stared at Hunter. "I knew you were going to be fine. I had faith."

He stood up and laid Hunter in my arms so I could cuddle him. He opened his eyes and stared at me before closing them again.

Dr. Gold came in. "How's everyone doing?"

"We're good," I said.

"Excellent, we did a thorough exam on him before we brought him in here and everything looks great. Under the circumstances, I'm thrilled." She paused, "the only thing we want to watch is his bilirubin levels. Jaundice may occur from the stress of the delivery. Nothing to worry about now, but we'll keep an eye on it. If he starts to look yellow call us right away."

"Jaundice?" Greg asked. "What's that?"

"It often happens in newborns from the stress of the delivery. The liver isn't completely developed so it's not filtering the blood sufficiently yet. His delivery was slightly traumatic, so we'll keep an eye on it."

"Okay," I said. "And everything looks fine from the lightning incident?"

"Laurel, you have a miracle child. Everything is fine." She shook my foot. "Get some good rest tonight; you deserve it."

"Believe me, I will."

She looked at Greg, "Visiting hours are over in five minutes. They both need their rest."

Greg nodded. "I'm leaving soon."

She picked up Hunter from my arms and set him in his cart. "He'll see you in a few hours." She turned and left the room with Hunter.

"Okay," I called behind her.

Greg grabbed my hand. "I'm going to head home and make sure everything is ready for you two to come home tomorrow."

"I'm so excited to bring him home," I said.

"Me too."

"You've got the next few days off from work, right?"

"I have a week off to spend with my family."

"Good, I'm gonna need to catch up on sleep and heal. I'm in agony."

"I bet. I wish I could've made it easier on you, but you did great."

"I'm glad it's over."

"Me too," he said. "Sweet dreams."

"Good night." I laid back and enjoyed the silence, drifting quickly off to sleep.

Despite being woken up every three hours to nurse, I slept well throughout the night. As soon as we were finished nursing I fell into a deep sleep again. The nurse woke me up at 6:15 in the morning. "Laurel? It's time to nurse."

My eyes fluttered open and I sat up in bed. My eyes focused quickly as she laid him in my arms. I focused on his face and smiled. As my eyes adjusted, I noticed his skin had a yellow tinge.

"Nurse, he's yellow. The doctor said to tell her if he starts to look yellow."

"All babies have a slight yellow coloring right after birth. If it gets worse, then we'll worry," she said with a smile.

I wasn't confident in her knowledge of jaundice and I was quite sure she was unaware that we'd been struck by lightning. "Please call the doctor. His skin is yellow and so are his eyes."

She huffed, "I will, but she's going to tell you the same thing."

"If she does, then she does. But I want to see her."

She shuffled out of my room and I began to feed the baby. My breasts were swollen, rock hard, and sore. My nipples were incredibly tender and sensitive.

The doctor entered the room. "Good Morning, Laurel. I hear you want me to look at Hunter. Is he slightly yellow?"

"Yes, he is." I said.

"Can I hold him so I can look at him?"

I broke the suction between his mouth and my breast and began to pump. He started to wail.

The doctor opened the hospital blanket wrapped around his fragile body. "We're going to have to put him under the lights."

"Put him under the lights?" I repeated swallowing the knot in my throat. "What does that mean?"

"In order to control the jaundice we'll put him under ultraviolet lights in an incubator. That'll slow down the yellowing and then reverse it."

"So he has jaundice?"

"Yes, he does. But don't worry, he'll be fine."

"You should tell your nurse to stop offering her diagnosis. She told me that all babies are yellow and he's not yellow enough to worry about."

"Well, then, it's a good thing that you had her call me anyway."

"The nurse…in the delivery room," I paused, "She didn't know what she was doing either. She didn't know that his chin was caught in my hip bone and at one point mumbled, 'too young to be having a baby.' I'm quite uncertain about the maternity ward at this hospital."

"You have very legitimate concerns and both nurses will be reprimanded properly. Can I get you anything else?"

I shook my head. "Maybe a new nurse."

She pursed her lips, "Her shift is over in less than a half an hour."

"I'm not trying to complain, but you know the details of my pregnancy and I've had enough to worry about already. If the jaundice gets worse I'm not going to politely handle being belittled by professional nurses just because I'm young."

She handed Hunter back to me. "I wouldn't want you to have to deal with that. I'll make sure the head nurse is aware of the situation. You and your son will get the best of care."

"Thank you."

"You're welcome. I'll see you in a bit."

As she left the room, I began to nurse again, this time with the pump on my other breast. As I 'double-breasted' the nurse came back in.

"We need to take him back to the nursery," she said.

"Okay. Dr. Gold wants him under the lights."

She nodded with defeat, "She informed me. We'll have him there in the next fifteen minutes."

"Thank you," I snapped bitterly.

"You're welcome." She laid him in his wheeled cart and pushed him out of my room.

I stared at the ceiling and prayed, "Dear God, I pray that it please be your will to keep him healthy and safe. Lord, I ask that you protect him. In Jesus' name, Amen." I drifted back to sleep.

I awoke to my mom shaking me. "Laurel, wake up."

I rubbed my eyes as I sat up. "What time is it?"

"About ten. Where's my grandson?" she excitedly asked.

I searched the side of the bed for the call button that hung next to my bed dangling near my pillow.

"I'll get a nurse. He should be ready to eat again."

A different nurse entered my room. "What can I do for you?"

"Can you bring Hunter in?"

Reluctantly she shook her head. "I can take you to him. Are you able to walk?"

I shook my head, remembering that he was under the lights. My mom, confused, said, "Where is he?"

"He's in the NIC unit," I reported.

Her eyes filled with horror and tears. "What? Why?"

"He has jaundice. They've got him under the lights," I said slowly. "He's going to be okay."

The nurse backed in a wheelchair. "Here you go. I'll take you down in five minutes."

My mom said, "I'm so sorry. You've gone through so much from day one of this pregnancy. Are you okay?"

"Yeah. Dr. Gold said not to worry. It's more of a precaution than an emergency." I pulled sweatpants out of my bag and my mom helped me put them on. I tied my hospital gown around my waist and hobbled over to the wheelchair. "My boobs are huge and painful. Can you grab my pump?"

She grabbed the bag and then wheeled me into the hallway while we waited for the nurse. The nurse came within seconds and started pushing me towards the elevator. As the doors opened, she wheeled me in and pushed "2." The doors slid closed and we descended to the second floor. They opened again, this time to an empty hallway. We turned right towards an oversized wooden door. The nurse swiped her identification badge in the slot and the oversized door swung outward towards us. We continued around a corner and stopped outside a door. As my mom helped me get to my feet I saw tears in her eyes. "Mom, what's wrong?"

She shook her head and wiped her eyes.

I turned towards the glass and looked into the room where my son was. I stared through the window as my fears suddenly skyrocketed. The room was huge, divided in half by a thick glass wall. The right side of the room was radiant white with about thirty enclosed carts, each containing a baby. Each of the carts had glowing blue lights shining on a naked newborn. Some had breathing apparatuses and intravenous lines taped to their arms. The front side of the room had scattered rocking chairs and a few tables. It looked like one of the most solemn nurseries ever.

The sight of it all brought me horror and anxiety. I instantly teared up and covered my mouth with my hands as I gasped for air. I met eyes with my mom and she quickly hugged me. "He'll be okay," she consoled. "This too shall pass."

"Call Greg. Get him here," I said.

She nodded and walked towards the nurse's station.

I turned towards the nurse. The fear in my eyes must have explained it all. "Laurel, he's got the best care," she assured. "The doctors in here are the best in the hospital. Let's go see him." She pointed to a rocking chair for me to sit in. I forced my feet to take the eight steps over towards the chair. Those eight steps felt like steps taken on a plank to my demise.

I watched as the nurse pushed through the glass door into a sterilizing room. She scrubbed her hands and covered her mouth with a mask as she pushed through another door into the back room.

I lowered my head in my hands and prayed: "Dear God, please keep him safe and healthy. Please let him be okay." I lifted my eyes to meet my mom's as she peered through the glass barrier that separated us. Worry and fear swept her face. I leaned back in my rocking chair and closed my eyes.

The nurse approached me with Hunter in her arms. "He's a fighter. I can already tell." She laid him in my arms. My breast milk began to flow again and

I started leaking in my gown. He was ready to eat. I pulled one breast out and he quickly found it and began to feed. The nurse grabbed my pump out of the bag and handed it to me saying, "Breast milk is the healthiest thing for him. You need to pump so we have plenty of milk. You should be prepared to spend a lot of time in here over the next few days."

The end of the statement caught my attention. "The next few days?" I shifted uncomfortably as the words left my tongue and sent my mind into massive confusion.

"His bilirubin levels have jumped quickly and the doctor has required him to be admitted into the neonatal intensive care unit, officially."

My eyes instantly overflowed with tears as my stomach churned. "What does that mean? What can happen to him if his levels keep climbing?"

"Well, the higher his levels climb, the more yellow his skin will get and his brain will swell." She paused, "If his brain doesn't stop swelling, he could possibly have brain damage."

I began whimpering as I absorbed her warning. Unable to free either of my hands, she grabbed a tissue and dabbed my face. Through my machine gun whimpers I asked, "Wh-wha-at is hi-is le-ev-vel?"

"When we first brought him in today he was at 6.3, which is slightly high for a newborn. He's now at 13.9. If he reaches a 16, brain damage could possibly set in."

My chest searched for air as my brain tried to escape the hurricane winds blowing in my head. My heart stopped beating as my blood pumped angrily through my veins. My stomach crashed into my toes and my body went limp. I stared down at my yellow son, my precious, precious baby. My vision blurred, "Why? How?"

"You had a traumatic delivery. That's normally the reason."

I lifted my head. It felt as heavy as an anvil. I met my mother's tearing eyes and I felt everything empty out of me. I felt numb, vacant, powerless.

"Can she come in?" I whispered.

"Unfortunately, only the mother and father can come in here, and only for feedings."

I slowly turned my head up and my fearful, worried eyes met hers. "Only for feedings?"

"We've got to keep germs away from these babies as much as possible. I know this sounds harsh but there are other babies in here that are in a much graver situation and are holding desperately on to their lives."

I stared down at my son, my vision blurred with tears. "Please get better. I love you so much. I promise I'll never let anyone or anything hurt you. With every ounce of my soul I *will* protect you." I looked up and saw my mom in the hallway, hugging

Greg as he cried. He turned and as our eyes met we both wiped our tears away. "Can he come in?"

The nurse turned and opened the door and Greg slowly entered the room. He dried his tears away again as he approached us. "Your mom told me what's going on. Are you okay?"

I reluctantly nodded and sobbed, "I'm s-so-oh worried about him. I ne-heed him to be okay. I know this is my fault, and..."

Greg cut me off, "This isn't your fault, Laurel. He's a fighter, just like you. You're the strongest person I've ever met and I know he'll be okay."

"I'm s-so sorry."

"Don't be sorry. He'll be fine. How long does he need to stay here?"

"A fa-few days. That's a-a-ll she said."

He hung his head in his hands. "What about you?"

I shook my head. "I don't know. I don't care about me right now."

"Shhh, Laurel, it's going to be okay."

The nurse overheard our conversation and she came to my side. "You'll be getting discharged today. You can come here during the days and we'll need you to pump so we can feed him during the nights."

I sat there as a surreal feeling over took me. "I have to go home without my baby?" Tears drenched my face as my head spun and I sunk back into the rocking chair. "You're telling me that I can't stay here?"

She shook her head. "Only during visiting hours."

I began to whimper as my stomach churned. "How many days will he have to stay here without us?"

"Realistically, count on four more days."

I wiped my tears away as the reality hit me: *Four more days.* Greg and I sat in silence, dumbfounded.

"We need to get him back under the lights," the nurse said. When she removed Hunter from my arms I felt a wave of weakness pass through me. I became very faint as my eyes fluttered. I searched for breath as I rubbed my hand across my aching chest. I sat there helpless, empty, and stunned.

Every third hour one of the nurses brought Hunter in so I could feed him. The joy I felt while our precious baby nursed eased my soul. My mind settled; his fragile little body felt so perfect in my arms and so in tuned with my presence. But when they took him away again only fifteen minutes later, any joy or relief I'd felt with him in my arms got sucked back into the tornado of absence.

I was miserable all day. I hated the nurses. I resented their faces and hated their presence.

When visiting hours were over we had to leave. I despised the nurses even more because they got to stay with our son.

As I was discharged from the hospital, Greg quickly pushed my wheelchair out to the parking lot. He helped me into the car. I felt empty. I never imagined that I would leave the hospital without my baby. I didn't feel good. I was sick to my stomach. As soon as we got home I threw up. I wasn't pregnant anymore but I was still puking. Only now I was puking for a different reason: my son's life was on the line and there was nothing I could do about it.

I barely ate that night. I didn't answer the phone. I couldn't focus on anything. I didn't speak to Greg. I didn't think. I merely existed. I was simply absent and fell asleep on the couch curled up with Nimbus.

I woke in the morning with rock hard throbbing breasts, sore from head to toe. I looked down and grabbed my deflated stomach. I knew I had given birth, but where was my baby? Confusion spun in my head as I slowly recollected the events of the past 24 hours. *He's still in the hospital.*

My chest tightened. "Greg?"

I heard him come downstairs. "Good morning. How are you feeling?"

"I wanna go see Hunter."

"Me too. Get showered and we'll go."

I walked into the bathroom and sat down on the toilet to pump my breasts. They were so sore I felt like they were going to pop. After I showered we left for the hospital.

As the hours drug, by the nurses kept us informed with the details. "His level has been at 14.7 since last night. It seems to be slowing down. After it levels out it'll drop as quickly as it jumped."

"He's close to the dangerous level. What else can we do?" I asked.

"Besides keeping him under the lights, you need to keep pumping; breast milk is the best thing for him now."

I nodded. "I brought you a few bottles, they're all labeled." I handed her my bag. "That should get you through tonight."

She disappeared with the bag of bottles and went back to the incubator. We were escorted out of the nursery and down the hallway.

I found it harder to leave the hospital the second day and even harder on the third day. Uncertain whether or not our baby was going to have brain damage, I feared the worst but hoped for the best. I walked like a zombie through the days.

104

The only times I felt even slightly human were during the fifteen minute intervals I got to nurse Hunter. His level kept rising and my strength kept falling. His bilirubin level rose to 15.8 by the end of the third day, just under the danger zone. Our nerves were wearing as his level kept climbing and the hours passed us by. Our fears peaked as the bad news kept coming.

Sitting there helpless, waiting and praying, I felt that my spirit had plummeted. My energy level was at zero and my brain function: nil.

Greg found a wheelchair to help me get out of the hospital. I wouldn't have made it out any other way. Like lifting a sack of potatoes, he managed to get me into the car. I slept all the way home and hardly remembered getting home or how I got into bed.

When the alarm went off in the morning I was still exhausted. I slid out of bed and shuffled over to the closet. I removed my pajamas and stared at the naked person in the mirror. I knew I was looking at myself but I didn't recognize the person staring back at me. She looked exhausted, sad, and in some ways pathetic. I blinked a few times trying to focus on her face. Her empty green eyes met mine as I studied her face: dark circles under her eyes, puffy and swollen cheeks, broken blood vessels broke out across her nose, cheeks, and chin. Her long blonde hair was wiry and greasy. I watched as she ran her

105

fingers across her face and through her hair and felt
the same motions on my body. I knew that we were
one in the same, yet I felt nonexistent. I slowly
followed her hands as they traveled to her stomach.
The deflated stomach reminded me that the past few
days were all real while the rock hard breasts
screamed for relief from our absent son. I stared at
my naked body in the mirror and was disgusted with
what I saw. Tears drizzled down my cheeks. I was a
skeleton wrapped in skin, that's what was left of me.
I slowly turned and walked into the bathroom,
craving a long hot shower.

As I showered, I cried. I hated not being
pregnant anymore while feeling unable to be a
mother. My stomach, my hands, and my mind were
empty.

We drove to the hospital and I stared at the
landscape that passed us by. "Day four," I thought,
"God, please let us have some good news today." As
we approached the NIC unit the nurse saw us
through the glass waiting in the hall. "Good
Morning. We've got some great news. His levels
have dropped down to 11.5 this morning."

My chest quivered as I flopped into a chair
and a rush of relief cascaded through my body.
"Thank you, Jesus. Where is he?"

She quickly turned to retrieve Hunter.

"Thank God," Greg said as he rubbed my
back. "We can start to relax now."

I nodded and wiped away my tears. "My nerves are shot. I'm so weak. I feel like I just took my first breath in days."

"Me too. I'm going to call our parents and let them know. I'll be right back."

The nurse returned with Hunter in her arms. I squeezed him as I kissed his forehead and his hands saying, "I'm glad you're feeling better, my precious baby boy."

He lifted his head as he rooted for my breast. I began feeding him and prayed, "Dear God, thank you so much for keeping our baby safe. Thank you for this great news today. In Jesus' name, I pray, Amen."

Greg returned and quickly kissed his forehead. "I'm glad you feel better, my son. You've had us all so scared."

"I wonder how much longer he'll have to stay; I just want to take him home," I said.

The nurse overheard me. "Most likely tomorrow. As long as his levels keep dropping, you'd be able to take him home tomorrow."

I would have preferred to take him home that day, but I was just so thankful that his health was finally on the rise.

Greg said, "Everyone was thrilled to hear the great news and they all send their love. Your mom in particular is waiting for her grandson to come visit."

"I'm sure he can't wait to get away from those blinding lights. It's got to be annoying."

"I'm sure he doesn't know any different," he countered.

As our day ended, I prayed that this would be the last time that we'd have to leave the hospital without him. We drove home in silence. When we pulled into the parking lot I said, "I'm so tired. I'm going lay in bed, watch TV, and pass out."

"You should eat first. Your appetite hasn't been good at all," said Greg.

"I'm not hungry. I'm sure after he comes home, I'll get it back. I have no desire to eat right now."

We walked inside and I went right into the bedroom and laid down with my hopes high that we would be bringing him home tomorrow.

I woke early the next morning extremely rested with extremely swollen boobs. I was so sore that my shirt lying across my chest was too much pressure against my breasts. I excitedly got moving, praying that today would be the day our baby finally came home.

When we arrived at the NIC unit they informed us, "His levels have normalized and you can take him home today."

My heart jumped for joy as the nurse handed him to me. "We're ready to discharge him. I have everything ready for you to sign."

"Oh, thank God. I'm so happy!" I squealed.

Greg wrapped his arms around us, "You're comin' home today, Hunter. You get to see your home and meet your dog."

I kissed Greg on the lips, "I love you."

He smiled, "I love you, too." He nuzzled Hunter, "And I love you."

"Follow me. We'll get you all set to head home," said the nurse.

As the relief began to spread through my mind and body, I looked at Hunter and I promised him, "I'll never let *anyone* or *anything* ever hurt you. I'll protect you with every *ounce of my body*."

When we settled back at home, I refused to lay Hunter down. I had been craving to hold him for almost five days. To finally have him in my arms felt magical. I finally had the chance to embrace him for more than fifteen minutes and I didn't have to put him down him down. Greg would hold him for a few minutes but then I'd take him back; I had to get my fill.

Nimbus loved his scent. He followed him everywhere he went. He'd nestle his nose into Hunter's blanket to sniff him and then whine as he licked his face. He was instantly in love with Hunter.

My soul was finally settling, my spirit was rising, and my smile began to shine again. I was finally able to be a mother. I was finally happy and I finally felt complete.

Chapter 9

Twenty One

Over the next few months Hunter grew so quickly. His strength was amazing to me: from the day he was born he held his head up by himself, by six months old, he was crawling, and by nine months he was walking. His first words in his twelfth month were "ball," "dada," and "mama." I was astounded by his brilliance. He was forming complete sentences by the time he was a fourteen months and the doctors were completely amazed.

Despite our mutual love for Hunter, somehow Greg and I drifted in opposite directions.

As I stayed home with Hunter while Greg was on the road all day, our relationship began to dwindle. I stayed confined within four walls all day. As easy as that sounds, it was a very wearing and lonely situation. I had no one to talk to and began to feel isolated from the rest of the world. I did what I could to get out of the house: we went for walks around the block, went to my parents' house, and visited my neighbors.

We had very little money and many bills. We applied for and received assistance through the state, which helped but didn't solve any problems. Sadly, I began to look forward to going to the grocery store. I was mostly excited just to get out in public.

Greg's job required him to be on the road by 6:00 in the morning, so he was gone before I woke up. He drove all day, answered calls, and by the time he got home, he was exhausted. We'd eat dinner in silence and shortly thereafter he'd go to bed. Our conversation dwindled down to next to nothing and I realized that our love had slipped away.

I was, once again, alone.

I loved being able to spend my days with Hunter but I knew my life needed to be different. I've been on the go since the day I was born and this solitude was depressing me.

Hunter was just over a year old when I began coaching gymnastics again at the local gym on Saturdays. Because I was able to get out of the house on a regular basis, I felt like I had purpose in life again. My days began looking up as my spirits lifted. Though I had little faith in our marriage actually lasting, I prayed every day that things would change.

Tired of pretending nothing was wrong, I finally brought it up to Greg one day while we were lying in bed watching TV. "Are you happy?"

"Huh?" He didn't move his eyes from the television.

"Are you happy? With me? With being married? Are you happy?"

"Yeah."

"Well, things are very different. Slowly but surely we have drifted apart," I said.

"Well, it's not my fault," he huffed. "You should be happy; you get to stay home all day."

"I'm happy that I get to raise our child as opposed to taking him to daycare but if you aren't happy being with me, then I want to know."

"You want a divorce?" he asked.

"Well, I don't want to live in misery. I feel like I don't matter to you anymore. We never talk, let alone have sex. I was hoping for more of a change in our marriage instead of a divorce."

"I work all day. We have no money, and by the time I get home, I don't wanna talk anymore. And you wanna talk all night."

"Well, since there's no one around to talk to all day, yeah, I wanna have an adult conversation by the time you come home. It's hard not having anyone to talk to all day other than a one year old, so yeah, I wanna talk."

"I wish I got to stay home all day. Maybe you should work more. Saturdays aren't enough." He paused, "But if you're not really happy and I'm not really happy, then what's the point in staying married, right?"

"So, you aren't happy and you want a divorce?" I asked.

He shrugged. "It's crossed my mind. I mean we did this to try to make things right. Things aren't right, so let's get divorced. At least we gave it a shot."

"Yep, at least we gave it a shot." My heart sank as we sat in silence. He watched TV as I stared at the ceiling. *I'm now twenty one, and getting divorced. I'll be a single mother and on my own.* A cold feeling of worry traveled through my body.

I began working full time as a receptionist at a restaurant equipment sales company. Within two months Greg had moved out. Our divorce took 90 days; about as quick as our shotgun wedding. We had no assets to divide let alone fight over. Greg kept his car and I kept mine and the apartment. He moved in with one of his friends. We knew we weren't going to fight over custody of Hunter; we wanted to keep it out of the courts, so we came up with our own civil way of sharing custody.

My mom was able to watch Hunter while I worked, so I didn't have to take him to daycare. She worked out of the house reupholstering furniture. I often left work and had dinner at my parent's house so I could spend time with them.

I strived to develop a good life for us.

Chapter 10

Is There A Future?

Shortly after our divorce, Greg arrived to pick Hunter up for the weekend. He seemed really nervous about something as he came inside.

"Are you okay?" I asked.

He shrugged his shoulders. "I, um, kinda wanted to talk to you about something."

"Is everything alright?"

He nodded and said nothing.

"Are you gonna tell me or make me guess?" The frustration made me want to jump in my skin.

He took a deep breath. "I sorta met someone."

I hesitated. I was confused, "Why he was so worried about telling me and should I be worried about Hunter?" I thought. "Congrats," I finally said. "Does she know about Hunter?"

"She has a daughter too. She's three and a half."

"Well, I'm happy for you."

I heard him sigh with relief. "Well, she, uh. They're going to meet Hunter this weekend and I didn't want you to be bothered by it."

I froze for a few seconds and chose my words carefully. "I guess my main concern is, well...Is she a random chick or is there a future?"

"There's a future. Otherwise I wouldn't be introducing them." He paused, "I just wanted to be respectful of you."

I nodded. "Well, thank you. I'm sure there's going to come a time when he gets introduced to someone I am dating. I hope you'll be respectful of that."

"Absolutely. I just don't want anyone to feel awkward, I guess," he said.

"Well, I'm sure it may be a little awkward when she and I meet, but I don't have any plans of causing problems if that's what you're worried about. We decided to get divorced. I accept that and so do you. Our main concern is Hunter's happiness and safety. As long as she treats him well I won't have a problem."

"Thanks, I appreciate that."

"I will say, and maybe this is jumping the gun, but I don't want Hunter calling anyone else 'Mom.' That's my right and my right only."

"That's definitely jumping the gun, but I understand what you mean," he said as we walked out onto the front porch.

"Thank you." I picked Hunter up, "Have fun at Daddy's house. I love you." I wiped his slobbery face with my sleeve and kissed him goodbye.

"Wuv you, Mommy," he waved as Greg carried him to the car.

"I love you. Bye." I went inside as my thoughts danced around our conversation. Part of me wanted to be jealous but I knew he and I weren't meant to be together. Another part of me wanted to cry because I wanted to be with someone, too. But there was no sign of that happening in my life any time soon. Most of all, I was worried about Hunter and whether or not this new woman was good enough for him.

I went for a jog to clear my mind. I knew Greg wasn't going to put Hunter in an unsafe situation; I knew better. I also wondered how long it would take for me to actually meet her. It was a little nerve racking not knowing who she was, but I had to trust his judgment. I had no control over what

Greg did and that included who he chose to date. I wanted the same respect when it was my turn to date someone.

As my weekend progressed, I accepted the possibility that this could be the woman that stuck around. I had to admit, I didn't think it would've happened so quickly considering it had only been a few months since Greg and I finalized the divorced. At the same time, it gave me hope that it could happen for me too.

On Sunday morning, Greg called me saying, "Hey Laurel, how are you?"

"Good. How was the introduction? Did it go well?"

"Yeah. It went great, actually."

"Glad to hear it. What time are you dropping him off?"

"Well that's what I wanted to talk to you about." He paused, "We were invited to go to Tony's, Gina's brother's, for a barbecue. I wanted to make sure you'd be fine with that. We won't be home until seven or eight tonight."

"Wow, so it went really well then, huh?" I took a deep breath and ran my fingers through my hair.

"Yeah. She's great. You'll really like her. And for the record, she adores Hunter."

"Well, what's not to love?" I chuckled, as I tossed my hair over my shoulder with pride. "Have you met anyone in her family, or is this a first for you too?"

"No, I'll be meeting everyone for the first time today. I'm kind of nervous."

"You'll do fine. I'm sure Hunter will take the focus off of you. He's good at that."

"Yeah, no kidding! I'll call you on our way back so you'll know when we'll be there."

"Sounds good. Do you need any clothes for him or are you all set?"

"Nope, I'm good."

"Talk to you later and good luck."

"Thanks."

I hung up. My heart fluttered as my jealousy level increased a little. I took a deep breath and grabbed Nimbus's leash. *Today needs to be a Laurel day.*

We jumped in my Jeep and headed to my parents' house. I was grateful to find that no one was there when I arrived; I wasn't in the mood to talk to anyone. We walked across the trail to the river.

The fresh fall air lifted my spirits, yet my concerns grew as I thought about Greg and Hunter being at a family barbecue with some strange woman. I was jealous, not because Greg was with someone else, but because I wanted to find someone for myself. I had accepted, a long time ago, that things with Greg and I wouldn't have worked. I was thankful that we had the respectful relationship that we did, but it troubling me that he'd already met someone, and her family, and I still hadn't even had a date. *This fuckin' blows.*

I took a deep breath and prayed, "God, if there's a guy out there for me, can you please put him in front of me?"

I stared out across the river as I played fetch with Nimbus. After a few hours, Nimbus was finally worn out and we walked back across the trail to my parents' house.

My mom was home. I walked inside and Nimbus plopped down in the sun on the back porch.

"Hi! How was the walk?" she asked.

"Good," I said with little enthusiasm.

"Why are you moping?"

"Greg met someone."

She studied my face. "And that bothers you, why?"

I shrugged. "I'm mainly concerned about Hunter, I guess."

"You guess? What else is there?"

"I guess I just wish I had someone." I paused. "I get lonely."

"I'm sure you do. It's hard being a parent, not to mention, a single parent. It's a very trying situation; you don't have the freedoms most people your age have. You've got more responsibilities."

"Yes, I do. I'm happy to have them but it's definitely lonely and stressful." I inhaled a deep breath. "I guess I'm jealous it's happened so quickly for him, and I haven't even had a date."

"Well, you don't want to just date anyone, that's for sure. But your time will come. Don't worry." She rubbed my back. "Did she meet Hunter yet?"

"Yep. They're at a barbecue at her brother's house today, so they're meeting the entire family."

"Wow. That was fast."

"Yep," I agreed.

"Well, don't worry. Your time will come."

"Yeah, my time will come." I paused. "I'm gonna go home and take a nice hot shower."

"Ok, I'll talk to you later." She hugged me goodbye.

I quickly left; I felt like I just wanted to get away. I opened the door for Nimbus and he jumped in and lay across the back seat. We pulled out of the driveway and headed towards my house.

A few hours later, Greg arrived with Hunter. Nervously I asked, "How'd it go today?"

"Really well. Everyone loved Hunter. He was really good."

"Well, that's good to hear." I bounced Hunter on my hip and asked him, "Did you have fun today?"

He nodded, "Yeah, it was lots of fun. How come you didn't come?"

"You had a daddy day today. Sometimes I have to share you." He slid down to the ground and ran inside as Greg and I followed.

"Um, she's here if you'd like to meet her," Greg ventured.

I stood still for a second, dumbfounded and unprepared, "Yeah, of course. If you guys are going to start spending a lot of time together and she's going to be around Hunter a lot, I'd definitely like to meet her."

I slowly followed him outside as he motioned for her to come up to the door. I watched as she got out of her car. She had long blonde hair pulled back in a pony tail. She was tall and skinny, and very pretty. Her daughter impatiently climbed out of the car and followed her. We shook hands as Greg introduced us, "Laurel, this is Gina."

"Nice to meet you," I said, as part of me settled.

"You too! Hunter is great. This is my daughter, Gianna."

Gianna waved, "This is where Hunter lives?"

"He sure does." I paused as I admired her long dark curls.

"Is he going to come over and play again?" Her big brown eyes widened.

I nodded, "I believe he is, but we'll leave that up to your mommy and Greg."

Gina said to her daughter, "He lives here with his mommy, and we'll hopefully see him on the weekends."

I looked at Gina, "She's really cute."

"Most of the time, but you know how it is: sweet one minute and sour the next."

"Yeah, they do seem to know it all, no matter what the age," I replied.

"Right? I guess I thought I knew everything at that age too. Didn't realize everything I *didn't* know."

"Yeah, I hear that. We just have to take it day by day."

"Episode by episode," she added.

"Well, let's get going. I'm exhausted," Greg said as he walked towards the car.

Gina said, "Thanks for letting Hunter come today. We had a blast. We'll see you soon." She waved as she helped Gianna back into the car. "Nice to meet you."

"Nice to meet you, too," I smiled as I retreated back into the house. Hunter was already naked, waiting to take a bath. "You want a bubble bath?" I asked him.

He danced in front of the bathtub. "Baa-bbles."

As I ran the bubble bath I realized that I felt relieved; Gina seemed to be a good person and a good mother. She understood parenting. I had to admit, I liked her, which took a load of worry off my back.

I believed things were taking a turn for the best; Greg met someone and hopefully someday soon, I'd find a boyfriend that was not only excepting of Hunter but worthy of being around him. Until then, I'd keep focusing on Hunter.

Part II

Be careful what you wish for…

Chapter 11

The Set Up

A gust of wind rustled my hair as I stood in Hunter's bedroom. I packed a bag full of clothes for a trip to his father's he was taking over the four day weekend. There were very few Saturday's when I didn't have to coach gymnastics, so I was thrilled to have off for Memorial Day weekend. The weather forecast for the weekend called for sunshine with temperatures in the 80's. Since Hunter was going away with Greg and Gina for the weekend, I'd made plans to meet up with my friends Kelly, Stacy, and Chelsea that night to go to a local club where bands played every weekend. Our favorite band, "The White Walls" were playing that night.

I had fixed pancakes for Hunter that morning. "Did you like your breakfast?" I asked him.

"It was delicious, Mommy. Can we have pancakes tomorrow morning, too?"

"Well, Daddy's picking you up around lunchtime today and you're going to stay at his house for the weekend. Maybe he or Gina can make them for you tomorrow or Sunday."

"Mmhmmm. How come I have to go to Daddy's all the time?"

"Well, you have to spend time with your daddy and his family too. They miss you when you're not there. Your lucky your daddy wants to spend time with you."

I could see him processing something in his brain before he said, "Mommy?"

"Yeah, hun?"

"Why can't we all live in the same house?"

"Uh," I knew this question would come up sooner or later.

He pleaded his case, "If we all lived in the same house, we'd all see each other *all* of the time." He paused, "And both of Kenny's parents live in the same house, so he never has to go visit his daddy on the weekends."

I took a deep breath and carefully chose my words. "Well, first of all, Kenny's mommy and daddy are still married, right?"

"Right."

"Daddy and I aren't married anymore. Daddy's going to marry Gina soon, so they live together because they love each other."

"You don't love Daddy anymore?"

"I do love your daddy but not the same way Gina does. I love your daddy as a friend." I tapped the tip of his nose. "You're the best thing that ever happened to me, and I love Daddy for giving me you. We decided to go our separate ways and that means we don't live together anymore."

"Do you love Gina?"

"I love Gina as a friend, too. She's the best step mommy I could've ever asked for for you. But, again, she loves Daddy in a different way than I do; she's *in love* with Daddy."

"So you and Daddy aren't in love anymore but you still love him as a friend," he confirmed.

"That's right. Daddy and Gina are in love, so Daddy takes care of Gina, Gianna and you. And because of that, your family's different than Kenny's. It's much bigger and in two different homes."

His eyes were full of life and questions. "Well, Mommy, since Daddy takes care of Gina now, who takes care of you?"

I choked on my thoughts. I smiled and brushed my fingers through his hair saying, "You do, Sweetheart."

He smiled, "I do take care of you, don't I?"

A tear crept into the corner of my eye and my chest tightened. "You're the only man I need in my life."

"I love you, Mommy. You're the best." He wrapped his arms around me and kissed my cheek. "I'm gonna go play outside."

"Be careful and stay close."

He darted out the back door. "C'mon, Nimbus."

I stood at the kitchen window watching as he played with Nimbus.

He giggled as Nimbus barked impatiently, waiting for him to throw the ball. I slumped into the counter as his words rang through my head. *Who takes care of you?* My chest tightened more as I wondered, "Is there anyone out there for me?" and, more importantly, "Is there anyone out there good enough for Hunter?"

Nimbus darted after the ball as it soared across the back yard. *Can most three year olds throw a ball like that?*

Nimbus jumped in the air, soaring with grace as he caught it in mid-air, about fifty feet from where Hunter stood. *I don't even know if I could throw it that far...*

Slobber dangled from the side of his mouth as he sprinted back towards Hunter with the ball. I watched as he darted back and forth past Hunter.

"Nimbus, bring me the ball." He turned to chase Nimbus, giggling intently.

Nimbus instantly turned and headed back towards Hunter. He zig-zagged back and forth, teasing Hunter, as Hunter zigged and zagged chasing him. "Nimbus, come!" he commanded. Nimbus turned and darted right into Hunter and he fell face first over Nimbus onto the ground. Instantly, an ear piercing shrill cut through the air and Nimbus immediately started yelping in fear.

I flew out the back door and dropped to my knees next to Hunter, who was still lying where he fell. "Where are you hurt?" I demanded as I saw blood dripping from his lower lip.

"M-m-my fa-fa-faaaa-ce h-h-hu-rts!" he said, gasping for breath.

"Spit for me, Buddy. I think your lip is cut."

Hunter let out a long low bellowing moan as he spit the blood out and tears raced down his bright red cheeks.

Knowing he was okay, I couldn't help but giggle at the "Woe is me" drama that produced his exaggerated bellowing.

I gently pulled down his lower lip and saw a small cut from his tooth. "I'm gonna roll you over. Tell me if it hurts anywhere else." I started to roll him as his body quivered in my hands and he pushed his way to his feet.

"I'm not hurt anywhere else, Mommy, but

133

my face hurts." He touched his pointer finger to his lower lip and saw the blood dripping down his finger. His eyes instantly filled with tears and he began to cry so hard and loud. "I hurt my face, Mommy! My beautiful face!"

With absolute agony I pursed my lips and held back laughing at his remark. "I know you did, but it's only a little cut on your lip. You'll be just fine." Still trying to repress laughing hysterically in his face, I added, "...and as handsome as ever. Let's go inside and get a popsicle so it doesn't swell anymore."

With tears welling to the brink of overflowing, he took a few quick breaths and replaced his pouty bloody frown, with a grin. "Yeah, cause it's swollen and bloody, and the popsicle will make it stop!"

"That's right."

Nimbus came over and kissed Hunter all over his face, apologizing for the collision.

"You knocked me down, Nimbus. You made me fall and hurt my face," Hunter said.

Whining as if to say, "I'm so sorry I hurt you. I only wanted to play," Nimbus laid down at Hunter's feet and laid his head out across his paws.

"He didn't mean it, Hunter. He just got so excited that he got to play with you, he couldn't contain himself," I said. I then turned to Hunter, saying, "Let's go get you fixed up." I squatted down and turned my back to him so I could give him a piggy back ride. He wrapped his arms around my neck and stepped his feet into my hands. I stood up and walked him inside to the kitchen, bouncing with each step. I turned my back towards the counter next to the sink, and made reverse back up noises like I was a trash truck backing up, and sat him down on the countertop. "Beep-beep-beep!"

He giggled and said, "Pah-schuuu!" imitating the sound of the release valve on the garbage truck. We both giggled.

"I'm sorry 'bout your lip, Babe, but it's not as bad as it could've been. You should be glad your teeth didn't go all the way through your lip." I raised my eyebrows and continued, "...then we'd have had to go to the hospital and get stitches."

"Stitches? What're stitches?" he asked as I dabbed the blood from his miniscule cut.

"Well, if anyone cuts themselves really badly, they go to the hospital. The doctors have a special needle and thread that they sew your skin back together with so you don't scar."

"Woah. Have *you* ever had stitches?" His curious eyes studied me, waiting intently for an answer.

"As a matter of fact, I've had thirteen sets of stitches."

His eyes exploded with shock. "Thirteen times? You got hurt a lot."

"I'm a tomboy, so I was always getting hurt when I was little."

"What's a tomboy?"

"That means I'm a girl, but I didn't want to play with Barbie dolls or make up. I wanted to play in the dirt with my trucks and I played a lot of sports. I was a rather aggressive little girl, so I was always bruised and battered from climbing trees, riding bikes, and playing football." I studied his face as he seemed to understand. "Grandmom said that because I always had cuts and bruises on my face she used to get stared at because people would always assume that I was getting beaten and abused by her and Danpop. Even the doctor's brought it up to her a few times."

He cackled, "Grandmom and Danpop would never hit anybody."

"Well, we know that. But sadly, there are many children that get beaten by their parents and need help from people like us." I watched his face. "So there's something you can be grateful for: you may have two separate families in different homes but you don't get beaten. You get loved."

"Yeah, I do."

I walked over to the freezer and pulled out a popsicle. "Cherry flavored?" I asked over my shoulder.

"Yep. I like cherry. Are you gonna have one, too?"

"I sure am. I'm going to have orange."

I unwrapped the popsicles and handed

Hunter his as I lowered him to the floor. "Wanna go sit outback with me?"

He turned and darted to the sliding glass door, pulled it open with his free hand and hustled outside. I followed as I slid the door closed.

He grabbed the ball and threw it for Nimbus. Nimbus barreled after the tennis ball, snatched it out of the air after it bounced, and trotted back to Hunter.

I smiled. I knew that my dog understood that he hurt Hunter and was aware of himself enough, in his doggie brain, not to hurt him again.

As Hunter's popsicle melted it dripped down his hand and Nimbus licked the juices clean. I jumped up and threw the ball for Nimbus and then grabbed Hunter, tossed him in the air, and then flew him like an airplane towards the house. We approached the sliding glass door, saying, "Open sesame!"

Hunter reached out and slid the door open. I flew him into the kitchen, as he came to a landing lying on the counter next to the sink. We were washing the popsicle juice off our hands when the doorbell rang. I yelled out, "Come in, Greg."

Greg cracked the door. "Did I hear you say come in?"

"Yeah, we're washing our hands."

He walked into the kitchen and said to Hunter, "Hey, Buddy. What's up?"

"I hurt my face, Daddy. I fell over Nimbus."

"What? Where?" He squatted down to see him close up.

Hunter pushed his lower lip down and forcefully pointed at the cut. "Wite heel."

Greg looked at it. "Boy, that's nothing. When I was your age, I put my two front teeth through my upper lip. I went the hospital and got six stitches."

Hunter's eyes got big as he processed his newly acquired knowledge of stitches. "How many times did you get stitches?"

Greg thought for a second. "Um, I wanna say five or six times."

"Really, Daddy? Mommy beat you. She had *thirteen* sets of stitches."

"I know your mommy was crazy when she was little."

We all giggled at my expense.

"Not crazy," I defended myself. "More like adventurous."

"Adventurous, my ass! You were crazy. And way too strong," he teased.

"Thanks to gymnastics. Thirteen years of training would make anyone strong," I added.

"Laurel, you're way too strong. Physically *and* mentally."

I shrugged my shoulders. "I'm going to take that as a compliment." I grabbed Hunter, saying, "You have fun at Daddy's this weekend. I love you."

"I love you too, Mommy." He kissed my cheek and jerked back quickly as he remembered his cut. His eyebrows scrunched and he touched his lip softly. "I need another popsicle for my lip."

Greg said, "You can have one when we get to the house. You'll be fine until then."

Hunter gave me a quirky smile. "Bye, Mommy."

"Bye, Sweets."

I took a deep breath of fresh air as Nimbus laid at my feet with his favorite rubber tractor tire toy.

As they drove out of sight, I grabbed the tire and Nimbus jumped to attention and barked at me. I tossed the tire across the front yard and he bolted after it. I sauntered towards the front door of my apartment, excited for my holiday weekend to begin.

I stepped inside with Nimbus carrying his tire at my heels. He pushed through my legs to beat me inside. I opened the sliding glass door, letting Nimbus outback so he could run. I inhaled a deep breath of fresh air; the birds outside were chirping and the flowers were blooming. Spring was finally here.

I went outside and sat down on my lounge chair. Nimbus dropped his tire next to my chair and barked for attention. I threw it again and he darted after it, grabbing a hold of it and shaking it into a black blur.

I shook my head with a smirk; I knew I had finally found a toy he could not rip apart, which made it the only toy that didn't end up in pieces on my floor. After about an hour of watching Nimbus whip around his tire, I went inside and started getting ready for the evening.

My phone rang. "Hello?"

"You're definitely coming tonight right?" Kelly seemed overly excited about us meeting up tonight.

"I'll be there around 9:00. I'll call you when I get there," I assured her.

"Okay. Talk to you then." The line went dead.

I hung up the phone shaking my head. I rarely went out; I had little very little time or interest for going to the bars. My friends would usually come over to visit me because they knew that my schedule didn't allow me the freedoms that theirs did. Kelly especially would come over and hang out. Hunter was one of her most favorite people. She has been enthralled by him since the first day she met him and often took care of bragging about him for me. I usually sat back, listened, and smiled as she did.

"Her son is such a little man and he's only three. He's so intelligent and funny, and he's going to be a lady killer when he gets older. They'll all be wrapped around his little finger," she'd say.

"I'm pretty sure he's already got *you* wrapped around his finger. You're his puppet!" I'd caution.

"I'll be his puppet as long as I can. He's fantastic."

I knew from the day he was born that there was something very special and different about him. After all, I was struck by lightning while I was barely out of my first trimester, and then he was in the NIC unit for days. That must be a sign of strength and power. His demeanor and his intelligence have always been out of this world. It was inexplicable and somehow genius.

His physical skills never ceased to amaze me. They were naturally undefined yet controlled and deliberate. I knew he would be a great impression on this world everywhere he went.

I walked into the bar and looked around for the girls. I pushed through the crowd and said hello to a few people I knew. I called Kelly. "Yo, I'm here. Where are you?"

"We're upstairs near the bar. Hurry up, I've got someone for you to meet," she said excitedly.

"What do you mean you have someone for me to meet?"

"Get off your high horse and get up here, Bitch." Click.

I rolled my eyes, took a deep breath, and pushed my way up the stairs. Kelly was there with her new boyfriend, Phil. I hadn't yet decided whether I liked him or not; he was so quiet, it was creepy. And Kelly, Stacy and I were loud, happy, and obnoxious.

Stacy saw me and came running up and gave me a hug, practically tackling me.

Chelsea, a good friend of Stacy's, was just behind her holding a beer for me. It was looking to be a perfect night. We all said cheers and took drinks.

Kelly grabbed my arm and pulled me into the bathroom. "You *have* to meet this guy Bryan."

"Oh, Kel. You know I'm in no mood to get into another torturous relationship that's going nowhere. Especially with some guy that doesn't know shit about life and hangs out in bars looking for his next victim."

"Yeah, but Bryan's awesome and so funny. He's perfect for you."

"I don't want to be a victim again. I want something real."

"That's exactly why you're not with Vince anymore, Thank God." she said. "I'm telling you, *Bryan's* your *one*. Just get over yourself. He came here tonight just to meet *you*."

"You mean to tell me that you told him about *me*? What the hell's *wrong* with you? You know I don't believe in that set-up, blind date horseshit, Kelly."

"Would I hook you up with someone that I didn't think was fabulous? He's hysterical and so cute."

"What about that guy, the one that managed the coffee shop? He turned out to be a stalker and you thought he was perfect for me. What does that say about how you think of me?"

"Oh, come on. He was so enthralled by you; he didn't want to leave your side! Did you give it to him good?" she pursued.

"Screw you! You know I didn't give it to him at all, especially after I saw the tattoo of his ex-girlfriend's name across his stomach. Apparently he obsessed over many a bitch."

"Come on, let's go. I can't wait for you to meet him so you can tell me I'm right. 'Cause I love it when you do."

"I'm making no promises, Kel. If anything, I promise to kick your ass when this turns out badly." I stretched my hand out. "Deal?"

"Deal." She shook my hand, winked at me and brushed past me out towards the bar.

When we left the bathroom I saw a few friends from high school and stopped to say hello.

Kelly rudely interrupted, "Excuse me, I need her right now. Can she come back in a few?" Without hesitation, she grabbed my arm and pulled me through the crowd towards our friends.

"Kelly, you've got to stop pulling me around the bar. I think you pulled my arm out of the socket. That hurt."

"Yeah, like I can hurt *you*, She-Ra. Quit you're complaining." She turned to Phil. "Where's Bryan?"

"He ran to pick up a friend. He'll be right back," Phil said.

I looked at her as if to say, "I'm already right."
She glared back.

"I'm going to dance," I said as I spun around and Stacy and I went to our favorite place on earth: the dance floor. We usually became the center of attention before too long; we both can dance, yet somehow we make complete fools of ourselves and everyone around us laughs and cheers.

"I need water and a fresh beer," I said after a few songs.

Stacy nodded and pounded the rest of her beer. We walked over to the bar and I leaned in and ordered our drinks. We giggled, laughing at ourselves and at the fun we'd been having and unaware of much else. When the drinks came, we clanked our bottles, saying, "Cheers to the dance floor!"

Just as I tilted back to take a sip, Kelly showed up and grabbed my arm that was holding the beer, making it spill all down my face. I swallowed what was left in my mouth. "What the hell?" I wiped my mouth clean. "What's wrong with you? Why can't you stop grabbing me? It's really starting to piss me off." I quickly froze, realizing that she was trying to introduce me to someone.

"Laurel, this is Bryan Cease. Bryan, this is Laurel Forte," she interjected.

He smiled the cutest crooked, pleased, little smile. His blonde hair tasseled and his blue eyes sparkled. He reached out and grabbed my hand to shake it. When he touched me I jumped from the surge I felt through my body; it felt like a warm sensation shooting up my arm. Speechless, I cracked a half-assed, bewildered smile.

"You're a great dancer," he said.

I smiled, a real smile this time. "Thank you. We tend to get a little goofy."

"That's the best part. I'm Bryan."

"Of course you are, and I'm wrong," I admitted, eyeing Kelly as she stood at his side, tucked slightly behind him.

"What?" he asked.

"Oh, nothing. I'm probably going to have to swallow my pride and tell Kelly that she's right, but that can wait. I'm Laurel. It's nice to meet you."

"Likewise, Laurel. I've heard a lot of great things about you."

"Oh, have you?" My eyes caught Kelly's peaking around his shoulder. "And how long have you been hearing about me?"

"Um, how long have Kelly and Phil been seeing each other?"

"About a month and a half." My eyes narrowed.

"Then, I guess about a month and a half."

"Oh, really?" I glared at Kelly. "Why was I never informed of you until tonight, *after* I got here?"

Bryan replied, "Well, if you knew I was interested in meeting you, you never would've shown up tonight because you hate being set up."

I stared at him, astonished, while Kelly had a huge smile on her face.

"What *else* do you know about me?"

"I know that you coach gymnastics, you're an office manager, and that you have a son, Hunter, who's three. And apparently he's a ladies' man already."

I was speechless.

I turned to Kelly, "You've been busy."

She smirked, "You're welcome."

"I didn't say 'thank you.'"

"Not yet, but I'm waiting for it." She blew me a kiss, waved good bye, and disappeared into the crowd.

I turned back to Bryan puzzled. "So how do you know Phil?"

"We've been friends for years; my cousins grew up next door to his family and we all hung out. I stayed with Phil when I lived here before."

We started walking off of the dance floor since the music was so loud that we could barely hear each other.

"So where are you from?" I asked.

"Ohio. I moved back to Milltown about eight months ago."

"Ohio?" We sat down at the far end of the bar, where it was quieter.

"I'm a hick at heart; I grew up there with my family until I was about nineteen. I moved here for a year, lived with Phil, and then moved back to Ohio. I missed it here so much, I came back after six months."

"Interesting. So what do you do?"

"I install audio visual equipment. It pays the bills," he said.

"I know that feeling. Its hard making ends meet."

"Well I won't be struggling for too much longer. My friends and I are hoping to get signed soon."

Baffled, I asked, "Signed for what?"

"We videotape movies and stunts. Can I get you a drink?"

"No thank you. I'm still full. I seem to have forgotten I have a beer in my hand."

"Now that's a compliment if I ever heard one."

"What kind of movies do you film?" I asked.

"Stupid humor skits. When we get together we act like idiots and film it."

"Sounds cool. I hope it works out for you."

"It will. I know it." He hesitated, "So what're your plans for tomorrow night?"

I shrugged my shoulders. "I don't have any, really. I don't go out that much."

"Any chance you'd like to accompany me to our premiere tomorrow night? It's at the skate park right in town."

I blushed and lowered my head, hiding my embarrassment behind my tasseled blonde hair. Then I turned my eyes up towards him and said, "That'd be great." My lips pulled up into a smile and I felt my face turn bright red.

"I was hoping you would."

"What do I wear? Is it dressy or casual?"

"Casual, all the way." He added in a funny voice, "No black tie required."

I giggled. "Okay, what time should I be ready? Where should I meet you?"

"How about I pick you up around eight?"

"Perfect."

I couldn't help but know that Kelly was right. We spent the night talking and learning about each other. We connected with each other immediately and we didn't realize how late it was when we were finally ready to go home.

"Can I walk you to your car?"

I batted my eyes, saying, "I'd love that."

He grazed his hand down my arm, grasped my hand, and led me out of the bar. We walked towards my car, planning for the next night. We wanted to make sure he had my phone number written down correctly, so he dialed me immediately. We waited to hear my phone ring. I reached for my phone as it buzzed in my purse, and quickly answered it. "Hello?"

A smile overtook his face as he looked into my eyes. "Hi Laurel, this is Bryan. I met you at the bar tonight. Do you remember me?"

I giggled and stared back into his eyes. "I'm sorry, who is this? I don't usually give my phone number out when I'm in a bar. How did we meet?"

We laughed uncontrollably.

He closed his phone as he reached over, placing his hand on the back of my neck and pulling me towards him. My heart pounded as he kissed my left cheek, then kissed my right one and whispered, "I'll call you tomorrow. Be safe getting home."

He opened my Jeep door for me and I climbed into the driver's seat. I turned the key and the engine roared to life. "It was great to meet you. I'm actually glad I got set up tonight," I admitted.

He threw his hands in the air and chuckled. "Kelly was right about us! Who knew?"

He walked back towards the bar and I drove home. I was extremely tired but incredibly giddy.

Suddenly, I heard my phone ringing. I hoped it was Bryan.

I answered and Kelly chirped in my ear. "Are you ready to thank me yet?"

"He seems great. Thank you, Kelly."

"Great? He's absolutely perfect for you, my dear. Are you going to see him soon?"

"As a matter of fact I am. He asked me to be his date tomorrow night for some movie premiere."

"That's my girl!" she exclaimed.

"Any chance you're going?"

"We've all been planning on going. We hoped you'd be joining us." Her giggle was ornery this time.

"Glad to know you have my entire life planned out on this one night, Kel," I said obnoxiously.

"Oh! He's back. Gotta go pick his brain. Love you." Click.

My stomach turned as I closed my phone. "Uh-oh," I huffed and said aloud to myself. "Well, Laurel, she's been right so far. Let this take its course. She's not going to do any damage now."

When I got home and crawled into bed, I heard my phone alert me with a text message: *I'm so glad I finally met you and I can't wait for tomorrow night. Sweet Dreams, Beautiful.*

I smiled and quickly responded: *I'm happy to admit I had a great blind 'set-up' and I'm ecstatic about tomorrow night. Nighty Night.*

I closed my phone, curled up in bed, and fell asleep with a smile on my face.

Chapter 12

The Premiere

I awoke the next morning still smiling and giddy with excitement. I stretched as I stood up out of bed, and went straight into the shower. Nimbus was sitting by the sliding glass door waiting to go outside when I got out. I slid it open and he darted into the back yard. I stepped out on to my porch and sat down in my lounge chair. I had plenty of things to do that day but my head was filled with excitement for tonight. This would be my first official date since Greg and I divorced. It had been years.

Nimbus trotted over to me, dropping his slobbery tennis ball in my lap. I grabbed it quickly and threw it across the back yard. *I'll be picking up the pieces of you off my floor very soon, fuzzy yellow tennis ball.*

I filled his bowls with water and food. He inhaled his food quickly and slurped down the water. "Why don't we go swimming today?" I suggested to him.

He began running in circles. I often knew he could understand what I was saying.

I quickly put the dishes in the dishwasher, threw in a load of laundry, and tidied up a bit. I changed into old shorts and a tank top, expecting to get filthy.

I grabbed his leash, his bag of toys, and his harness. He started jumping and ran towards the front door. I pulled it open and he darted right for the passenger side door of my Jeep. I opened the door for him and he jumped up into his seat. As I buckled him in his feet danced on the front seat. I got into the driver's seat and headed over to my parents' house.

After about three hours of swimming, Nimbus was exhausted. We walked back across the trail to my parents' house; both of us soaked and covered in sand and dirt. I kept a bag with extra clothes and towels in my Jeep to dry off and change. I slipped into my dry clothes and circled around to put the towel down for Nimbus. I buckled him in and headed home.

I checked my phone: I had four missed calls. One each from Hunter and Bryan and two from Kelly. I called Hunter back immediately.

He answered, "Hi Mom. Guess what!"

"Hi, Sweets. What's goin' on?"

"We are going to Uncle Tony's house."

"Cool. Uncle Tony's the best," I said.

"I know. It's his birthday, so we're getting ready to leave now."

"Tell him I said 'happy birthday.' Did you bring you're bathing suit with you?"

"Yes, I did. I'll call you later."

"I love you," I said.

"I love you too, Mommy."

"Bye." I hung up.

I called Kelly next but she didn't answer, so I hung up, took a deep breath, and called Bryan. He answered on the first ring. "Hello, Beautiful."

"Hi, how are you?"

I could hear him smile through the phone. "I thought you were blowing me off for a minute."

"Why'd you think that?"

"I called about three hours ago, and about two minutes after that I started worrying."

"I took my dog to go swimming. You must've just missed me."

"It's a good thing. After having met you, I don't know if I'd ever be able to find anyone like you ever again," he said.

"You're too cute."

"What kind of dog do you have?"

"He's a brindle pit bull. His name is Nimbus."

"Nimbus, like the clouds?"

"Exactly. I'm impressed that you knew that. Most people don't know where I got the name from."

"I'm guessing you're into astrology and weather?"

"Yeah. I love thunderstorms, astrology, and outer space. I have a red beta fish named Jupiter."

"Why didn't you name him Mars? That's the 'Red Planet.'"

"I thought about it, but I figured most people would relate it to the candy company. And I don't eat too many sweets, so Jupiter made more sense. Everyone knows exactly what Jupiter is."

"I see your point, and I'm rather impressed, myself."

"Well, thank you. That's nice to hear. How has your day been so far?"

"Well, my stomach is in knots; I can't wait for the premiere tonight."

"Do you always get nervous for the premieres? How many have you had?"

"Well, this is our fourth premiere, but I don't get nervous for them." He inhaled a deep breath and chuckled. "Tonight's the first time I'm bringing an incredible and gorgeous woman as my date. You're gonna piss off a lot of my fans, you know."

"You're nervous because of me? *Little 'ol me*?"

"I have to admit, I've been nervous since yesterday when I found out that you were definitely coming last night."

"What? Why?"

"No, I'm wrong about that. You see, when Kelly first started telling me about you, I reacted the same way that you did: 'Yeah right. Whatever. You're full of it.' You get the picture." He paused, "Then one day, we were at Phil's and Kelly had you on speaker phone, and I heard your conversation, and *that's* when I became very intrigued."

"I was on speaker phone?" I asked, surprised.

"Yep. And after you got off the phone, I asked to see a picture of you. She showed me one and from that point on I've been nervous."

"How long ago was that?"

"About a month ago."

"A month ago?" I repeated. "What was our conversation about? I don't remember conversations that I had yesterday, let alone a month ago."

"You were telling Kelly about going for a motorcycle ride with someone named 'Diablo.'"

I choked as I recalled the conversation perfectly. "No." I turned bright red and smacked my hand against my forehead. "Dear Lord, I'm so embarrassed."

"Why are you embarrassed?"

"I just am. Had I known you or Phil were listening," I rubbed my hand along my face and through my hair, "I wouldn't have been so vulgar."

He burst into laughter.

I cringed. "I'm so sorry you heard that."

"Heard what? That you got so turned on by the vibrations, or the crazy sex you had afterwards?"

I glanced in the mirror. I brightened to a shade of lobster red and inhaled a deep settling breath. "I'm so glad that you can't see how red I am right now."

"Don't be embarrassed. Like I said, hearing your conversation made me want to meet you."

"Why'd that make you want to meet me? You wanted some crazy sex of your own?"

"No, no, no. When you were talking about the bike itself, you knew the type of bike you were on and how fast you were going. You knew about wheelies, leaning, and how to ride in general. I have to say, to hear a woman speak like you did about a motorcycle is a huge turn on. For me, at least."

"Uh-huh." I shook my head and mumbled, "I'm mortified."

"Don't be. If it makes you feel better, I'm not a virgin, nor do I speak like one."

"Well, that's not the 'first impression' I thought you had of me. But thanks for the insight."

"I have to admit, hearing you talk about sex was a turn on, too. But I'd rather be with a girl that I can hold a real conversation with. A conversation about anything, not just motorcycles. When you were finally able to be at the same place at the same time I was, I canceled my plans to be there. I'm not interested in just sex. I can get sex from almost any girl. I want something more meaningful."

"Uh-huh," I replied.

"I came to realize last night that you're very intelligent. We talked about music, bands, kids, life, and family. And I can't wait to find out more about you and your son."

"Well, we'll see about that. For now, I'm going to pretend we never had this conversation. That way, I won't back out on tonight."

"Don't be like that. If I only wanted one thing from you, I wouldn't have spent the entire night last night picking your brain. Did sex come up once last night?"

"Not at all," I admitted.

"There you go. Enough said."

There were a few seconds of silence until he broke it. "Can I ask you one question, though?"

I squirmed, "I guess so."

159

"Who is Diablo?"

"His real name is Vince. He's my ex-boyfriend. I nicknamed him Diablo because of his eyes. They're orange."

"Is there anything still going on between you two?"

"I haven't seen him since that day, nor have I talked to him. We've always had a touch and go relationship, if you know what I mean."

"I do. I just didn't want to get my hopes up for having you all to myself someday if you were already taken."

"I'm definitely not taken but I'm not ready to jump into anything either. But I am thoroughly intrigued by you. I've never been the girl that meets a guy and goes home with him that night. I take my time."

"I respect you even more now," he said.

"I have more responsibilities than most people my age, and those have to come first in my life," I informed him. "Don't get me wrong; when I get an itch, I scratch it. Obviously you know, from overhearing that conversation, I do have a high sex drive. But I control it; it doesn't control me."

"Well, that makes me feel much better," he said.

"Do I dare ask if *you're* seeing anyone?"

Without hesitation, he answered, "Not in the least."

"Good. Now I need to take a nap because some guy had me at the bar all night and I have a hot date with him tonight. I need to get my beauty sleep."

"You don't need to be any more beautiful than you already are. But if you start to slack on your sleep, you'll get dark purple circles under your eyes and start to look like a zombie...and probably start to smell like one, too."

"Or like a beaten down homeless woman wearing that perfume, *Eu de Unflushed Toilet*," I cackled.

"Yeah. Or an ungroomed street dancer that smells like dead fish in a swamp," he snorted.

We laughed wildly as I walked into my apartment.

He said, "I'll let you nap. See you around 8:00?"

"I'll be ready and waiting."

"Sweet dreams."

"Thank you." I hung up the phone, smiled, and laid down immediately, drifting off into a deep sleep.

I jumped up at 7:30, startled by my phone buzzing. It was Kelly. Confused with sleep, I answered, "Yeah?"

"Please tell me you're not just waking up. Bryan's going to be there in a half an hour! You should be ready and waiting by now."

"Oh, shit! I have to shower. I'll call you back." I hung up the phone and ran towards the bathroom, removing my shirt as I rounded the corner. I turned on the shower, pulled my hair up and stripped down. The water was barely warm enough when I got in. I rushed through shaving, hoping I'd covered everything. As I showered, I sifted through my closet in my head, picking out the outfit I was going to wear to the premiere.

I stepped out of the shower and quickly brushed my teeth as I plugged in my curling iron. Then I ran into my closet, pulled out the jeans I wanted to wear, and rummaged through my drawers for my favorite green shirt, and suddenly remembered it was still hanging drying in the laundry closet. I pulled my jeans on as I hopped down the hallway and grabbed my shirt. I pulled it over my head. *Almost ready.* I know most girls cannot pull off getting ready as quickly as I can; it's a quality that I truly appreciated about myself. I have a very natural beauty so I wear very little make up, if any at all. My hair is long and a golden natural blonde. I wash it once a week and all I have to do is brush through it.

I straightened up my shirt, applied deodorant and perfume, brushed through my sun kissed blonde hair and bumped the ends with the curling iron. I applied an orange-gold eyeliner and mascara to brighten my hazel eyes.

I took a deep breath; I was ready. I looked at my clock in the hallway: 7:56. Four minutes to spare. I switched my laundry into the dryer, changed my purse to a smaller one, and then called Kelly back, though she didn't answer. I pulled on my black sandals and I opened the back door to let Nimbus outside. We stepped out the door onto the porch and I heard a knock on the front door. Nimbus started barking and my stomach plummeted as I slid the door closed, leaving Nimbus outside, and went to answer the door.

I smiled as soon as I saw him standing there; he looked like a model. He had on a black t-shirt and jeans with a fitted black suit jacket that lay perfectly across his broad chest. I opened the door the rest of the way, allowing him to see all of me and I invited him in.

He stepped inside and pulled me into him. He kissed me on my cheeks. "You look stunning." Then he pecked my lips.

"Thank you, sir. You look handsome yourself."   His cologne smelled so delightful.

He looked at the back door as Nimbus kept barking and swatting at the door to come inside to say hello.

"This is Nimbus," I said as we walked over to the back door. "He'll kiss you to death, so let me

163

grab a hold of him before he goes too berserk. I don't want him to jump up."

"I'm used to it; I've been around dogs my whole life."

I opened the door and grabbed his collar. "Sit, Nimbus." He sat immediately and Bryan started petting him. "I've heard a lot about you, boy. You're handsome." Nimbus snuck in a kiss or two, then flopped on his side, forcing Bryan to rub his belly.

"Good boy," he said.

"He's a lover all right. Everywhere we go, he makes friends. I guess we should get going; I don't want to hold up your show."

"Sounds like a plan. I need to stop and get gas before we go. I meant to stop before I picked you up but I was so excited, I drove straight here."

"That's sweet." I grabbed my purse before we walked out the door and locked up.

He escorted me over to his Lexus and opened the door for me. I sat down and buckled up. He walked around to the driver's side, as I made myself comfortable.

"A lot of my friends are gonna be there tonight, along with a talent agent," he said.

I looked out the window. *Are you preparing me so you can ignore me all night, or because you want to introduce me to everyone? Time will tell, I guess.*

"That's cool. Are you nervous?"

He shook his head. "I told you, I'm really only nervous because of you. I want to make a good impression on you."

"Well you already have, so no worries," I assured him.

He grabbed my hand. "So which park do you go to with Nimbus?"

"It's called Strubble Trail. It's more of a bike path that follows the Milltown River. There's a dam there where people bring their dogs to swim." I hesitated, unsure if he was listening to me ramble.

"I know the place. There's a huge house across the trail on the other side. It's gorgeous over there. Lots of kids, too."

I nodded as I bit my tongue. I didn't want to tell him that the big house across the trail was my parents' house, so I quickly changed the subject. "How many people usually go to your premieres?"

He shrugged his shoulders, "I guess about five hundred or so. It really depends on how many people we comp in."

"Five hundred? That's a good amount. How long have you guys been doing this?"

"Well, I've only been doing it for about three or four years on and off. But it's a lot of fun. I get along great with the guys. They've been doing it since they were twelve years old."

"Twelve? Wow, that's impressive," I said.

"Yeah it is. I hope you enjoy the craziness you're about to witness me doing."

"I learned not to judge a long time ago. It's hard being a single mom that gets judged simply because she's a single mom, and young."

"I think it's great. I was raised by a single mom. I give her all the respect in the world and I'll give the same to you. No worries," he assured.

I smiled as my stomach settled. This was my first official date in years; my nerves were trying to take over but I refused to let them. After we gassed up, we turned into Skate Freight. Bryan put the car in park, quickly removed the key, got out of the car, and walked over to open my door for me. I was taken aback. He held his hand out for me to hold as I got out of the car. Grabbing my hand, he escorted me inside. We walked to the counter and put on florescent orange wrist bands. "I feel special," I said.

"No, *I* feel special." He wrapped his arm around my waist. "Because you're here with me." My heart fluttered as he escorted me in.

"I need to find Spam," he said.

"Your friends name is *Spam*?"

"Yeah, it's his nickname."

"Ah," I said. "I guess he's fat and eats a lot of spam?"

"Yep, *that's* it," he snickered. "Nah, his name is Gus Spamanti."

"Ah, I see."

He saw Spam out of the corner of his eye and pulled me behind him as we pushed through the crowd.

"Damn, there are a lot of people here," I commented.

"Well, a lot of them are Spam's fans. He's a professional skateboarder."

"Really? That's cool."

"That's really how this got started. He had someone film while he practiced so he could study himself. He realized that people that watched it reacted to his crashes. So it spread from there."

"Sounds brilliant," I said as we met up with Spam.

"Spam. What's up?" he said.

They slapped hands as Spam stared at me. "Who's this?" He cocked his head towards me.

"This is Laurel."

I smiled, "Nice to meet you."

Spam looked at Bryan. "I didn't know you were bringing a date."

"I didn't know either until last night." He shot a wink at me.

"Where'd you find her?"

I shifted uncomfortably, realizing he was talking as if I wasn't even there.

"Kelly introduced us. I told you about her."

Spam nodded, slowly. "Uh-huh."

Spam looked at me as his right eye twitched, "You gonna be one of those groupie whore bitches?"

Caught slightly off guard, I said, "No. I don't see the point in throwing yourself at someone who doesn't want to be with you. They only wanna use you. Not to mention, I have other responsibilities that keep me busy the majority of the time."

Spam said, "Oh right. You're the one with the kid."

"Yes, I am."

A tall lanky guy with shaggy blonde hair who was listening intently to the conversation chimed in, "How old is it?"

"He's 3," I said.

"How old are you?" the tall lanky guy asked.

"23," I said, starting to feel as if I was on the firing range.

"23? So you're older than Bryan," Spam confirmed.

"I am. How old are you again? 21?" I said, turning to Bryan.

"Yep, just turned it, too." He winked at me and smiled.

"What's your son's name?" the tall lanky guy asked.

"Hunter."

"Well, at least we know you won't be one of those whores who stalks us," the tall lanky guy added. "You're preoccupied with life." They shared a giggle at my expense.

I stared into Spam's eyes. "I'm not here because I'm a groupie. I have no idea who you are or what you do."

Spam glared at me with his jaw clenched. I could feel his hate and anger burning into me.

I ignored his glare. I turned to Bryan and said, "I'm going to use the bathroom. I'll be right back."

"Can I get you a drink?" Bryan said.

"I'll have a beer, please." I turned away and walked towards the bathroom. As I walked, I felt all of their eyes on me, burning a hole in my back.

I closed the door behind me and looked in the mirror. I didn't have to go, I just needed to regroup. I felt very uneasy about the comment about groupie whores. It made me feel unsure of who I was getting involved with and what I was getting myself into.

I stared at myself in the mirror. "That guy's *horrible.*" I washed my hands and checked my makeup and hair, completely stalling. I didn't really want to rush back out there. I was secretly hoping that I would be gone long enough to change the topic of conversation.

I walked out of the bathroom and looked for Bryan. He saw me and started walking towards me. Handing me a beer he said, "All of your drinks are on me."

"Thanks. I don't plan on drinking too much, it's not my style."

He looked deep into my eyes and said, "Whatever you want, I'm just glad that you're here with me."

A smile touched the corner of my mouth.

He grabbed my hand and pulled me into a nearby office and quickly closed the door behind us. He spun around and wrapped his arms around me, pulling me into his chest and kissing me. His soft lips slowly teased my lips and my head spun as his tongue touched mine. I grabbed the back of his neck and felt his muscles flex as he kissed me. I felt myself lift from the ground and I wrapped my legs around his waist.

He carried me over to the black leather couch and sat us down. I felt his heart beat faster as we began to make out more and more aggressively. His hands caressed my back and then traveled down to my thighs.

The door flew open. Startled, we turned our heads to see Spam and three guys standing in the doorway laughing and cheering.

One of them said, "Maybe she *will* be a groupie-whore after all."

I turned a shade of red, recoiled from Bryan and stood up. My heart was beating in my throat.

Bryan jumped up and stood in front of me. "Thanks guys, way to ruin the moment."

"We wanted to share it with you, that's all," the tall lanky guy teased. "We're happy for you."

I ran my fingers through my hair and adjusted my clothes. Bryan looked at me and saw how embarrassed I was.

He grabbed my hand and led me out of the room. I watched the floor, letting my hair cover the embarrassment on my lobster red face.

I heard one of the guys say, "Can I take her for a ride on my motorcycle?"

They all burst into laughter as I felt another lightning crash of embarrassment strike through me. Speechless and mortified, I turned and headed straight for the front door. Fuming with anger, I stomped out onto the sidewalk.

Bryan was right behind me. "Laurel, wait."

I stomped down towards the corner, paused and said over my shoulder. "I need to be left alone right now. I'm so pissed."

"I'm so sorry. I didn't think they'd be ignorant enough to say anything."

I spun instantly and glared at him. "I didn't think you were ignorant enough to tell them."

He dropped his head, "Phil, Kelly, and I were talking about you and it came up. They were wondering why all of a sudden I was so excited to meet you and wanted to know what changed my mind. I didn't think it'd be used as ammunition when they met you."

Tears welled in my eyes. "So it *was* because of the sexual comments I made and not because of my 'brain.' I feel like an idiot and I'm mortified all over again."

"Please don't be; it's my fault. I should've never said anything. I promise I'll fix this."

He reached to grab my hand but I pulled away. "I'm going to go for a walk by myself. I'll be back eventually." I turned and marched away from him.

"Laurel, please come back."

I huffed and kept walking.

Hearing footsteps behind me, I spun on one heel and stopped him dead in his tracks. "I told you, I need to be alone right now. I'm going for a walk *by myself*. I'll be back, but for now I need to be alone."

"I'm so sorry Ace said anything about taking you for a ride and I know I shouldn't have told them that story, but..."

I cut him off, "Which one is Ace? The tall lanky one with the blonde hair?"

"Yes."

"Well, the damage is done. I feel like the asshole and you look like the man." The knot in my throat tightened. "This bullshit is why I don't go out and exactly why I don't date. I hate knowing women are pieces of meat to guys. It makes me crazy." My hands were clenched into fists, I felt my heart jump into race mode, my face and shoulders got very hot, and I began breathing heavily.

He stared at me. "I didn't know that would upset you so much, I just repeated what you said, and…"

My eyes glued to his chest, I wanted to beat my fists into it. "The beauty of that is, I didn't say that to *you*, I said it to *Kelly*, a friend of mine, someone who knows me. I had no idea that you even existed, *let alone* that you were listening in on my conversation."

"Yeah, but…"

I continued without hesitation. "Then I come to find out, not only were you listening in on the conversation, but you told everyone about it. Now I feel like the asshole. I never set myself up for this situation, you and Kelly did. So I'll make sure to thank her, too."

I spun and stomped away. "Don't follow me, I'm a big girl." My ears were burning with anger and my head was fuming with confusion.

I walked about five blocks towards town, never looking over my shoulder once. As I approached people on the sidewalk they moved around me, stepping aside to let me blow past them. I felt like I had smoke coming out of my ears.

I turned onto Market Street, the main strip in Milltown, and walked into Chestnut Street Pizza shop. I walked up to the counter and ordered a slice and a soda. I wasn't really hungry, but I was angry. I always ate when I was angry; it calmed me down.

As I sat and scarfed down the slice of pizza, my phone rang. It was Kelly. "Yeah?"

"I just got to Skate Freight. Bryan told me what happened. I'm so sorry Laurel."

"Well, thanks Kelly. I hope you know that I feel like such an asshole. I am so freakin' embarrassed."

"I know. I'm so sorry," she repeated.

"I didn't know Bryan and Phil were listening in on that conversation, nor do I appreciate that you two told those other guys about it."

"I know. He's so upset, and we're both so sorry."

"He is? Why's *he* upset?" I hissed. "He looks like the fucking man with the groupie-whore that gets off on riding motorcycles."

"Laurel, no one judges you for saying that; we all get off on it. Stop making this about you and come have fun with us."

"Why would you let him listen to the conversation?"

"I just wanted him to hear you talk; you have a way with your words. I didn't know where the conversation was headed. It was as innocent on my part as it was his."

"Well, I'm so embarrassed. You have no idea."

"Laurel, you have this way about you that you don't even realize that you possess. People hear you speak and they listen, not just about motorcycles or sex, about anything. It's a wisdom that you carry about yourself. I can't explain it thoroughly, but you have a power."

"Uh-huh."

She paused, "You make people want to be around you. Hell, every girl wants to *be* you and every guy wants to be *with* you."

"I don't believe that for a moment. Not in the least."

"Well, you should. You're gorgeous on the outside and your personality is captivating. He didn't want to meet you because of your sex jokes. He wanted to meet you because you grabbed his attention from the first sentence he heard you say. You just happened to lead into a story about a motorcycle ride and sex; none of us coerced you to go there." She continued, "It wasn't what you said but how you said it. How you present yourself, the confidence, the security, the happiness, your personality…it's enchanting."

"So why has the motorcycle conversation bit me in the ass twice today?"

"Please stop focusing on the motorcycle conversation because that's not what made him to want to meet you. It's the way you carried yourself on the phone during the whole conversation, the knowledge, the jokes, and the smiles. You don't have to be present in the room for people to know that the voice that they are listening to has a smile attached to it. And that smile is infectious."

I listened to her and processed what she said, breathing deeply.

"Please come back. It starts in twenty minutes and he's so upset."

"When I calm down, I'll be back. Not sure when that'll be, but eventually I'll be back." I hung up the phone, still irate.

I picked at my pizza crust. I debated whether to go back now or wait a while. *I'm on a date, even though it hasn't started out great, I'm on a date none the less. Those guys mean nothing to me, why should I care about what they think of me? Bryan's the one I'm here with, and even though he's the reason they know the story, I do get a really good feeling from him. Maybe I need to let this go. If I drag this out, I'll lose him before I ever really have him to begin with. Can I forgive and forget? Or will this come back and haunt me again? Time will tell. I don't want to walk away from a potentially good relationship because I can be overly sensitive.*

I stretched in my seat, cracked my knuckles, and ran my fingers through my hair. I stood up, threw out my plate, and I slurped my soda. I walked outside and headed back towards the skate park.

I strolled along, feeling no need to rush back. I was definitely feeling much more relaxed about everything.

As I sauntered past a popular bar along the strip, I heard someone call my name. "Laurel?"

I turned around, almost sure that I recognized the voice. I looked through the crowd and saw Diablo heading towards me.

"*Shit,*" I thought as I forced a smile. "Hey. How are you doing?"

"I can't believe that you're out tonight. What's the special occasion?"

"Its Memorial Day weekend and I'm out with some friends. I needed something to eat; it's going to be a late night."

"So were you hungry or angry? I know how you are," he said.

"Hungry," I lied through my teeth.

"Who'd you come with? Kelly?"

"No, but she just got there." I spoke too quickly. "I should get back."

"Why are you in such a rush? Who are you with?"

"I'm with Bryan," I said without thinking. I knew Vince wasn't going to like hearing it. *Too much information, Laurel.*

"You're on a date?"

A chill passed through me as I stared at him, "I'm on a date," I confirmed.

"So then, where is he? Shouldn't he have bought you dinner?"

I arranged my thoughts quickly. "I took a nap earlier and didn't have time for dinner, so I ran out to grab a slice." I had left out the major points of the evening, but I knew he could sense the frustration in my voice. "I've got to get back to the skate park." My stomach dropped as I realized I'd said too much again. I cursed myself in my head. *Bitch, you have diarrhea of the mouth.*

"The skate park? I heard about that. It's a movie premiere right? A few of my friends are going. I'm supposed to meet up with them later," he said.

"Cool, well, I have to get back. I'll see you later."

"Well then, I won't hold you up. Maybe if it doesn't work out, you can give me a call. I've missed you."

"The phones work both ways, Vince. Don't try to make our failure my fault again. I know how you like to place blame."

He smiled at me. It was the smile that always melted my insides. "Maybe I should call you anyway. We can go for a ride."

My heart shot into my head. *Don't react to that; he has no idea.* I smiled and said, "I'd like that." I turned and started walking away.

"Maybe I'll see you later."

I peered over my shoulder, smiled and waved my hand. *I hope you don't show up. Fuck, I always say too much.*

I called Kelly when I got to the skate park. She answered immediately, saying, "Where are you?"

"I'm at the corner of the parking lot. Can you come out here?"

"I'm on my way," she quickly responded.

"Can you bring me a cigarette?"

"No problem." She hung up.

I sat down on the curb and waited for her. She was there in seconds and threw her arms around me. "Please don't be mad. We never thought they'd say that. I take full responsibility." She handed me a cigarette and lighter.

I lit it and choked on the smoke. "No, no, no. I'm thoroughly embarrassed; you know how I am. I don't like people knowing personal shit about me. I don't care if my friends know because that's why they're my friends. But people that don't know me don't need to know details." Motioning towards the door, I said, "But since they don't know me, why should I care?" I inhaled my cigarette.

"I'm so glad to hear you say that. Bryan is so upset and people know it."

Bryan suddenly showed up right next to Kelly. "You're back! I've been so worried. I'm so sorry, Laurel. Please forgive me?"

"I forgive you. I'm sorry too. I shouldn't care what they say about me or what they think. I'm here with you, not them." I took another puff of my cigarette.

He glanced at the cigarette. "I didn't know you smoked." Suddenly he grabbed me, picked me up while constricting my arms, and squeezed me. He kissed my neck and spun me around and then set me back down saying, "I'm so sorry. I never want to hurt you again."

"I only smoke when I'm upset. Its okay. I'm sorry for leaving. Did I miss anything?"

"We had some technical difficulties, so it's just starting now."

"I'm sorry, but I could use a drink right now. I think I've earned it." I smiled and tossed the remainder of my cigarette on the ground.

"Anything you want, I just want to see that smile on your face." He grabbed my hand and led me inside. I looked back at Kelly and saw in her face that she was relieved.

We approached the makeshift bar and he ordered drinks as I looked around at my surroundings. I found Ace on the other side of the room and stared at him. His eyes finally met mine and his face became stone cold as his jaw tightened.

I stared at him and an evil smirk turned my lips upwards. "Thought you got rid of me that easily, huh?" I thought. "You're not that lucky."

He broke away from my stare and whispered something to the other guy from earlier who was wearing the floppy hat and had hair like Slash. He glanced over towards me making sure not to make eye contact with me.

I repeated in my head, "You're not that lucky, jealous bastards."

Bryan handed me a beer and a shot. "I know you don't drink liquor, but I need a shot. This one's for you."

He handed me a test tube shot. "Might as well. I could use a shot to take the edge off. One won't hurt." I swallowed it down and chased it with a sip of beer.

Ace and Slash suddenly showed up next to Bryan. My heart plummeted into my toes.

I squirmed as Ace said, "We didn't mean to upset you, Laurel. We were just playing around. I'm sorry."

My heart started climbing its way back up my legs.

Slash said, "I'm sorry too. I didn't mean to upset you or Bryan."

I stood there, amazed. "It's okay. I'm sorry, too. I just found out today that he even knew about that conversation and I was already embarrassed as hell about it. When you said something, I just didn't know how to react. But the damage is done. You

181

already knew about it, so what can I do about it now?"

They smiled at me as relief overtook their faces.

I sipped my beer and eyed up Ace. "What kind of bike do you have?"

Confusion flashed across his face. "I have an R1."

"Yamaha, nice." I locked my eyes onto his. "Maybe I'll take *you* for a ride on her one day. Show you what she can really do."

Bryan giggled under his breath.

Hesitantly, Ace asked, "Do you have a bike?"

"No, I have a child," I grinned. "I will one day. I used to ride often."

"Whose bike did you ride?"

"I used to ride with my ex-boyfriend, Vince. He has a few bikes."

Slash stared at me. "You'd ride on the back with him, right?"

"Sometimes, but not usually. It depended on his mood."

"What'd you ride?" Slash asked.

"I usually rode his R1 or the Hayabusa. Again, it depended on his mood. Personally, I preferred the R1. He lowered it so I could touch the ground better."

"Bullshit," Ace said.

I stared at him, smiled, and shrugged my shoulders.

Bryan asked, "Why would she make that up?"

"I don't need to make it up." I looked at Bryan. "But boys have a hard time when a girl can handle a bike. Especially someone like me." I grinned as I flipped my long golden blonde hair.

"Time to start the movie. Let's go guys," Bryan said. He kissed me on the cheek. "Stay here; I'll be back after they introduce us." I watched them make their way through the crowd.

Kelly came up and whispered in my ear, "Guess who just showed up?"

I knew instantly. "Diablo?"

"Yep. Did he know you were here?"

"I ran into him on my walk back here tonight. I had diarrhea of the mouth and told him I was here on a date."

"I suppose he wants to make sure that he ruins it? Haven't you had enough drama already?" She looked over her shoulder. "Here he comes."

I was glad Bryan had to be up front for the introductions so I had some time to diffuse Diablo.

I felt him grab my waist. He spun me towards him as I acted surprised to see him. "Hey, you made it."

"Of course I did." He looked at Kelly. "How are you doing?"

"Good," she said. "How's racing?"

"Good. I just got 2 new bikes from Yamaha."

"Exciting. Anything else new?"

Shaking his head he said, "Same old shit, different day."

He turned towards me. "So which guy is your date?"

Kelly pointed to the stage. "The blonde, the really hot one."

I chuckled, "His name's Bryan."

Vince glared over his shoulder. "Okay, I'm going to get a drink. Do you need anything?"

"We're fine, thank you," I said. As he walked away, I grabbed Kelly's hand and pulled her towards the back wall. We found a spot for us to stand as they began introducing people.

"Why do I feel trouble on the horizon?" I asked her.

"I don't know, maybe because the *Devil* is stalking you?" she said sarcastically.

"It's just a nickname; it's not to be taken literally," I said.

"There's a reason you gave him that nickname. Maybe you should read between your own lines."

I nodded, choosing to end the conversation there.

As the movie began, the crowd was instantly laughing hysterically. The guys were jumping off of buildings into trees, smacking each other into oblivion, and bounding off of trampolines into pools. The crowd roared with laughter.

I leaned towards Kelly. "Damn, this is hysterical."

"Yep, they're going to be huge one day."

"I can see why. I've never seen anything like this," I said. "I need a beer. Do you?"

"Yeah, grab me one."

I fought my way through the crowd towards the bar as I got knocked back and forth between bodies. "Can I have two please?"

"So, you're what the fuss is all about, huh?" the bartender said.

"Fuss? What fuss?"

"Apparently Bryan ripped into the guys. He was really pissed at whatever they said to you."

"Oh," I said. "No wonder they were so nice when I came back."

"No worries; you're a beautiful girl. They're just jealous that you're not here with them."

I nodded my head. "I guess that makes sense." A false smile spread across my face. "Thanks for the beer."

As I walked back to Kelly, I felt like a midget pushing my way through the crowd. Everyone stood between four to six inches taller than me. I loved being a gymnast, but damn, at times like this, I wished I was just a few inches taller so I wouldn't get ricocheted through crowds.

185

I noticed that Bryan had returned from the stage as I said, "I feel like I just made it through a mosh pit."

"Well, She-Ra, if you weren't so damn short you wouldn't get pushed around," said Kelly.

I nodded. Suddenly Bryan whispered in my ear, "Can you come with me?"

I nodded my head as I looked at Kelly. "I'll be right back."

"Take your time."

Hesitantly, I followed him into the office. I reminded myself that what had happened was over and done with.

Bryan pulled me into the room and shut the door. I saw that the entire crew was in the room.

I quietly sat down in the corner, trying not to bring anymore unwanted attention to myself. I was thankful to have my beer to sip on as I tried not to listen to their conversation. I was somewhere in the back of my head when I heard my name. "What? I'm sorry, I wasn't listening."

Ace said, "Don't you think that we should be selling more DVDs during the premiere? No one's buying them."

"Do you have someone trying to sell them? Or did you just announce that you have them available?"

"We announced that we have 'em, but only a few people have bought 'em," Slash said.

"Why don't you have someone walking through the crowd to sell them while it's showing?" I paused. "Just because you announced that they're for sale doesn't mean people are listening. Put it in front of their face and then they'll buy it."

They all stared at me.

My eyes skipped from one of them to the next. "That's common sense." I felt flushed for a second. "And whoever's selling them should also tell them that they can get it autographed at the end. You guys have to be ready and willing to do that."

Bryan said, "I agree."

I looked over at him as he smiled from ear to ear. He turned to Slash and said, "Why don't you ask your friend to sell them?"

Slash said, "Dustin? Hell no, he'd pocket the money in a heartbeat. I'd never trust him."

They conversed back and forth about who they could ask to do it as I listened intently. Before I spoke, I cleared my throat. "I'll do it."

They all stopped talking.

"Are you serious?" the guy in the pink sport jacket, with rather bad acne, asked.

"Sure, why not?" I answered.

They each looked over their shoulders at one another, at Bryan, and then back at me.

"Am I not good enough to sell your DVDs?" I sent a quick grin to Bryan.

"That'd be kick-ass," the Pink Panther said.

"Start me off with ten DVDs and when I need more, I'll let you know. How much are they?"

"Ten dollars each," Bryan said.

"Okay, where are they?"

Slash dug into a box, pulled out the DVDs and handed them to me.

I took them and then immediately walked out of the office and made my way through the crowd selling the DVDs.

Vince approached me from behind. "He's got you hustling for him already."

"Nah, I offered to help out. Do you want to buy one?"

"Sure, why not? It's fuckin' hilarious." He handed me a ten. "I can get your man to autograph this, right?"

I studied his face. "After the movie's over, the crew will be signing DVDs."

He smirked, winked at me, and disappeared into the crowd.

"That's not good," I thought.

As the movie ended I went back into the office with Bryan. When Slash returned I handed him three hundred and twenty dollars. I smiled at him and said, "You better get your markers ready; they want your autographs."

Shock filled Slash's face. "How'd you sell so many?"

"I have a way about me."

Just then, there was a knock on the door. Bryan opened it.

A voice echoed into the room. "Is Laurel in there?"

My shoulder's tightened. It was Vince. *Oh shit!*

Bryan, dumbfounded, replied, "Ah, yeah." He turned to me, "Laurel? There's someone here to see you."

I slowly turned towards the door. My stomach was ricocheting all over the place. *If any one of them figures out who's standing at that door, it's all over for me.*

My eyes met Vince's as he peeked into the room. "I wanted to say good bye." He stepped into the room and stared Bryan down. Vince's black t-shirt wrapped around his arms and showed off his broad physique. His forearms were covered in tattoos that danced as he moved.

I nonchalantly walked over towards the door as Bryan stood watching, confused about what was happening.

I hugged Vince good bye. "It was nice to see you."

He whispered in my ear, "Call me tomorrow."

"Have a great night and be careful getting home," I said.

Vince eyed up Bryan again. "Bye guys. Good movie; very funny stuff."

I stepped back into the room as Bryan closed the door and said, "How does that happen?"

"How does what happen?" I asked as worry danced across my face.

"Your fans are banging on the door and ours aren't?"

"Like I said: I have a way about me."

"Who was that?" Bryan asked.

"An old friend."

"An old friend?" he repeated as he reluctantly nodded. "An old friend."

There was another knock on the door, making my stomach drop as my chest jumped. I turned slowly to open it, praying that it wasn't Vince again. I slowly cracked the door as Kelly pushed through. "Did Diablo just come in here?"

My lips tightened and my eyes bulged as the words escaped her lips. I felt every ounce of personal integrity escape me as her words owned the room. There was a gasp among the crew members. I turned to Bryan and held my breath before I admitted, "That's Vince."

"*Diablo* Vince?"

I nodded, hesitantly.

Knowing she just spilled the beans, Kelly quietly backed out of the room and silently shut the door, leaving me to deal with the mess.

"That's the guy you said you ride with?" Ace asked.

I nodded, hesitantly. I knew exactly where this was headed. I've been in this conversation too many times before. Guys have a difficult time accepting female riders. They always need proof, and my proof just waltzed right into my night, which added more confusion to the already bewildering situation.

I slowly nodded. Slash got up from his seat and bolted through the door.

I saw Bryan shift uncomfortably. My eyes strained as Slash returned with Vince. *Great. Here we go.* I rolled my eyes and plopped down on the couch.

Vince introduced himself to everyone.

Ace asked the first question. "So, I understand that you ride?"

Vince nodded his head, eyeing me from where he stood and not yet understanding where this was going.

"What kind of bike do you ride?" Ace asked.

"I have a few," he answered, crossing his tattooed arms in front of his broad, muscular chest.

"Like two or three bikes?" Slash asked.

Vince huffed, "Something like that." He peeked between Ace and Slash. "Laurel?"

I knew the question on his mind. Without making eye contact, I answered, "I didn't say anything."

"Uh-huh." He looked around at each of them. "What'd she tell you, then?" His eyes met Bryan's taunting him with a smirk.

I stood up and turned towards Vince. "I didn't say anything. They didn't even know you were here until Kelly opened her mouth."

All eyes were on me. I didn't look towards any of them. I started fumbling with my purse.

"Laurel said that you let her ride your bike," Ace said.

Vince chuckled, "Did she?"

I felt Bryan's eyes burning through me. I glanced up, catching his eyes, and then glared at Vince.

"Laurel and I used to ride together a lot," he said. "It's been a while, though."

"Yea, but did she ride her own bike or on the back of yours?" Slash asked.

"Both." He glanced at me.

I quickly jumped up and attempted to push Vince's chest towards the door, saying, "Thank you for clarifying that, Vince. It was good to see you."

Vince didn't budge. He stood in the doorway, eyes locked on Bryan's with a smirk of satisfaction across his face.

Bryan watched as I grabbed Vince's arm and tried to pull him out the door. He still didn't move.

"What else did Laurel tell you? I'm very curious now."

Bryan quickly responded, "Not much. She just talked about riding with you. I gather there wasn't much more to say."

Vince grinned. "Well, it was nice to meet you, Bryan." Vince turned to me and said, "I'm glad we had time to catch up tonight, Laurel."

Bryan glanced at Vince and then me. "You've been hanging out with him all night?"

Vince shrugged, "For the most part. We ran into each other while she was in town."

Bryan shifted his glare at me. "Were you going to tell me that you brought your ex-boyfriend to our date? And after we argued about him?"

Vince laughed, "You fought about me, already? I thought you didn't tell them about me."

I turned to Bryan. "We didn't fight about him. We fought about a conversation *I* had that *involved* him; a conversation that you told everyone about." I felt a rush of horror cascade down my body. *Hat trick! This is now, the third time in one day that this conversation has bitten me in the ass. And this time, it's my own damn fault.*

I spun back towards Vince. "I didn't tell him you were here because I didn't think I was going to have to make an issue of it. But you just *had* to make sure that *they* knew that you were here by the end of the night."

"Can I talk to you in the hallway?" Vince grabbed my hand and suddenly I was outside of the door. "What's all this about? Why do they know about *me*?"

"It's a long story."

"Well, I'm interested in hearing about it," he pried.

"Some other time," I snapped at him shifting my weight into my left hip and crossing my arms in front of me.

He stood there watching my eyes and waiting for me to explain.

"We got into a conversation about motorcycles and they were impressed with what I knew and, of course, that's how your name was brought up."

"I'm not sure if that's the whole story, but it'll do for now. I'll call you tomorrow and you can fill in the rest of the details for me." He winked at me and smacked my ass.

"I don't know what to tell you. I haven't talked to you in a while. I met him and we started hanging out. You know that I don't make snap decisions about a guy I just met two days ago," I said.

"Two days?" he inquired.

"Yes, two days," I repeated, realizing I had just said too much again. *Fuckin' dumb bitch.* I spun around and walked back into the room, slamming the door shut behind me.

I stopped dead in my tracks, realizing that all sets of eyes in the room eyed me where I stood.

"What was that about?" the Pink Panther asked.

"That's my ex-boyfriend, Vince, a.k.a. 'Diablo.'" I hoped to end it there but I knew all too well that this conversation was nowhere near over.

"Why does he look familiar?" Ace asked. "What's his last name?"

"Stockton. Vince Stockton," I said quietly, knowing I was shooting myself in the foot.

"Vince Stockton?" Ace repeated. I could see him making the connection in his mind. "The professional motorcyclist? The one that tours the world?"

I slowly nodded as my chest tightened. "Yes. He's a professional motorcyclist. He *is* Stockton Racing." It took a second for the information to sink in. I watched as the triggers went off in all of their heads.

Ace said, "That's cool."

Bryan shifted uncomfortably when he heard Ace's comment. "*Cool? Really?* I don't think any of this is *cool.*"

"Now you understand my knowledge of motorcycles and where it came from," I said. "Unfortunately for me, you've met my ex and he has met you."

"So, he's got a lot of bikes?" Slash said.

"He has at least sixteen street bikes and probably thirty dirt bikes in his garage, most of which I've worked on and ridden with him."

I looked at Bryan. "I ran into him on my walk tonight. I had a slip of the tongue and told him I was here on a date and, of course, he had to show up."

"So now I'll have to worry about this guy?" he asked.

"Unfortunately, he'll interfere. And he already has. As I told you before, though, I'm *not* a stupid girl."

"You were stupid enough to bring him here, weren't you?" Slash said.

"I didn't bring him here. He showed up on his own," I said, defending myself.

Spam chimed in, "I knew I had a bad feeling about you. For a good reason, too."

I glared at him and then shifted my eyes towards Bryan. "I didn't bring him here."

He said, "Tonight's been a very interesting night, hasn't it?"

I slowly nodded and bit the inside of my lips.

"I don't know what to think. It's one thing to have a misunderstanding about a conversation, a motorcycle, and a guy from your past. But it's another thing for you to invite him to *my* premiere, right in front of me, on our first date."

Spam glared at Bryan.

"I didn't invite him here. He showed up on his own and as for the argument, I wasn't the one who told everyone about a conversation that I was listening in on and use it to make myself look better in the eyes of my friends." A feeling of uneasiness traveled through my body. "I'm not going to sit here and feel like this is my fault. Should I get a ride home with Kelly?"

"I think that'd be best," he said. "I'm pretty confused and pissed right now."

"I know the feeling rather well." I grabbed my purse and headed out of the room, slamming the door behind me. I reached in my purse for my phone and called Kelly. She didn't answer. I tried again. Nothing.

I walked past the bartender. "Thank you, have a good night. It was nice meeting you," I said. Without waiting for a response I walked out the front door and retraced my steps towards town; I wasn't going to be left standing alone out in front of the skate park just waiting for more bullshit to occur.

My phone rang. Assuming it was Kelly, I answered. "Where are you?"

I heard Vince say, "I knew you wanted me and not him."

"I thought you were Kelly," I said.

"Kelly left about twenty minutes ago."

"Great." I threw my arms up in the air.

"Is something wrong?" he asked in a sly voice.

"I don't have a ride home."

"What happened with 'Golden Boy?'"

I shifted my weight. "I'll give you one guess, *Diablo*."

"What? He didn't like that I showed up?"

"Why would you do that to me?" I snapped.

"Where are you?"

"I'm walking towards town," I said.

"Would you like me to take you home? I haven't even pulled out of the parking lot yet."

"How convenient." I looked up to the sky. I knew this game of chess: Diablo saw an opportunity and he made a move. I tried to recover, but it was already too late. *Checkmate.* I knew he saw me leave the skate park by myself. He waited for it. And here I was, once again, forced into a corner by Vince. *A Damsel in distress. Who will save me? Who will take me home?* I threw my hands in the air, an act of surrender. "Come get me, please."

"Wait at the corner, I'll be right there." His phone went silent.

He knows exactly what corner I'm standing on. He watched me walk out of the skate park and up the street. I stood there, sheltering myself in the shadows of the trees and digging my heels into the sidewalk in disgust. I stared into the evening sky. Thousands of stars glistened across the grayish black canopy as I shook my head in disbelief. I inhaled the crisp spring air that somehow tasted bitter in my mouth. The weight of the evening bore down on my shoulders, though I simultaneously felt as if I was getting sucked right into the middle of a cyclone. I leaned against the tree trunk, trying to regain my composure. I knew my hands were tied.

Bryan was mad at me, Kelly was gone, and Diablo was on his way to "save the day." I closed my eyes and shook the thoughts out of my head.

He pulled up in his jet black Mercedes-Benz with tinted windows and I got in. I slammed the door, buckled my seat belt, and looked out the window in aggravation.

I wondered, "How the hell did I get here?" as my brain wrapped itself back around the anxiety of my night. I was baffled over how I had started the night with one feeling, and was finishing it with a completely different feeling.

"What's wrong?" Vince said as he put his hand on my knee.

I laughed as I brushed his hand away. "Trying to figure out the irony of my night."

"What's so ironic?"

I swallowed the knot in my throat, held back the tears forming in my eyes, and filled him in on every detail I could think of: the phone call that Bryan had listened to, the comment Bryan's friends made, why I had been walking into town, and the entire situation. "If it weren't for bad luck, I'd have no luck at all."

"So you *were* angry when you went for a slice. I knew it. I could sense it."

I hung my head and nodded. "Yep. I was angry, so I ate."

He touched my cheek. "I know you too well, Laurel. You didn't have me fooled for a second."

I wiped a tear off my cheek. "I think that's half our problem: we know each other too well. I knew you were going to show up at the skate park and make a scene. And honestly, I wasn't a damn bit surprised when you did."

"I'm sorry, but I don't want anyone else to have you. I love you too much."

I sniffed, still holding back tears. "Yeah, you don't want anyone to have me but you don't want to be with me either."

He grabbed a hold of my hand. "Our schedules don't allow us to be together. It's not because of my heart. You can't be on the road because of Hunter and I have to travel. It's not fair to either one of us."

"Then why would you prevent me from being with someone else? Why would you show up and ruin that for me?" I asked.

"Laurel, *who are you kidding?* You're *crazy* if you think that guy's going to stay with you after he makes it big. He's going to become famous and leave you high and dry. I never left you high and dry. We've been on the same page since we met." He paused, "If there's one person on this earth I could see myself with, it's you. It's always been you. I'm sorry, but it hurts to know that you want to date someone else."

"Vince, if you wanted us to work, it could work. We'd *make* it work. You use it as your excuse so you can stay single and bang chicks when you're on the road without a guilty conscience. It's not because of *me*; it's because of *you*."

He smiled and shook his head. "I haven't been with anyone since you. I know I won't find what we have with anyone else. We're perfect for each other. You're my beautiful tomboy."

I stared at him speechless and astonished. "Then *why* do you always disappear on me?"

He tilted his head and took a deep breath. "I don't think I'm good enough for you. I think you deserve better."

My tears started flowing. "How can you claim in one breath that you and I are *perfect* for each other, and in the next breath claim that you don't think you're good enough for me? And even worse, try to ruin things with anyone else I start to date because you don't want me with anyone else? You did all of this on purpose! You have to know that I've been in love with you from the second we met. And it makes life so hard to *know* that I was lucky enough to find the perfect guy for me, but I can't have him because he's worried that he's not good enough for me."

We sat in silence for what felt like hours, though only seconds had passed. "You're good enough for me. You're *perfect* for me. Why can't that be enough?" I sniffed.

"I'm leaving for tour in three weeks and then I'll be gone for eight months. If I'm not dating you, I won't worry about you. And if I don't worry about you I can focus on riding. When I'm not focused, I lose. My job is to win. That's why I make the big bucks."

"And that's why you'll be single for the rest of your life: so you don't have emotions that get in the way. But you'll have money and that's what matters."

"Laurel, this is who I am, not just what I do. Yes, I make a shit-ton of money. This is my life. It's not easy on me, either, but I can't live life like you do. Nine to five is not my style."

More tears flowed down my face. "And I have to live nine to five, because of Hunter. So, we'll never work." I shook my head. Under my tears, the irony made me smile: our lives were in opposite places.

My heart was bleeding with sadness and sorrow. This whole night was shot. I reminded myself in my head, "Laurel, this drama is why you don't go out."

He pulled into a spot in front of my apartment. I leaned over and kissed him on the cheek. "I have to go. Thanks for the ride."

I reached over and pulled the door handle, stepped out of the car, and slammed the door behind me. I drug my heels as I walked to the door. After fumbling through my keys till I found the right one, I let myself into the house. I quickly turned the lock behind me, pressed my back into the door, and slowly slid down to the floor as I began bawling my eyes out.

Nimbus greeted me with kisses as my pent up emotions for the entire evening released all at once. I cried in anger, in embarrassment, and because of the reality of the entire situation. *I hate dating.*

Nimbus began whining as he witnessed my release and nudged me with his nose. I grabbed him and held him tight as I bawled my eyes out. I reminded myself, "Laurel, this is why you choose to stay close to home. People are vicious out there."

I whispered to Nimbus, "I don't know why I even bothered going out tonight. I was a fool to think something good would've come out of it."

Then, there was a knock on my door.

I slowly pulled myself up by the door knob as I wiped my tears away. Nimbus barked as I unlocked the door. I cracked the door and saw Vince standing there.

"I'm here now. Can that be what's important? Not our problems. Not that guy. Can we please just be us?"

I smiled, my cheeks still wet with tears. I reached out and pulled him close. I laid my head on his chest, wrapped my arms around his waist, and I lost myself in him.

From our first touch, he sent chills up my spine. My body awakened as I heard his voice. I forgot about everything when I was with him.

I locked the door and kicked off my shoes. As my shoes hit the floor, he flung me over his shoulder with ease, spun us around, and marched into my bedroom.

He pitched me onto my bed. His shoulder muscles danced in the shadows as he towered over me and removed his shirt. He leaned forward and slid his hands from my waist toward my ribcage, sliding my shirt out of his way. I pulled my shirt off over my head as his tongue vigorously fondled my midsection. I jolted from the chills. I grabbed his head moaning as he aggressively kissed my stomach. I tried to push him back to myself half a second to regain my composure.

He grabbed my hands and pinned them next to my hips. I moaned louder, knowing he had me right where he wanted me. I struggled to free myself from his powerful hold, but the more I struggled the more control he gained over me.

He braced his knees outside of mine and I convulsed as his tongue ravenously traveled up my stomach and sucked my nipples. He paused and softly blew across my breasts. I shook in total and utter bliss.

He released my left hand and popped open the button on my jeans and quickly pulled them off. I gripped his arm tightly and pulled myself upright and enveloped my lips around his shoulder muscle. I felt him weaken as I slightly bit down. He growled with pleasure as I savored that split second of control. I then wriggled my other hand free and quickly unfastened his jeans.

He grabbed the hair on the back of my head, softly forcing me to lie back down. I resisted but he tightened his grip on my hair. I released a quiet whelp and inhaled a quick gasp of air.

"Do not resist me," he whispered as my body ached with desire.

I wanted nothing more than to obey his every command. I felt my guard go down as I became submissive to his demands. I wanted to feel him, *all* of him. My eyes rolled back in my head as I conformed to his control. My legs quivered and my body surged as he touched me. My head emptied. I wasn't concerned about anything or anyone as we entered into our alternate realm: pure, unadulterated, mind-blowing passion.

Chapter 13

Caught

The phone began to ring. My head jolted up from the pillow. "Hello?" my scratchy voice asked.

"What's going on?" Kelly demanded.

"Huh?" I said deliriously.

"I got a phone call from Bryan this morning. He asked if I got you home safe last night. He was rather surprised when I informed him that I didn't know what he was talking about."

I sat straight up in bed. *Oh, shit.* My hand covered my mouth as the recollection of my night ricocheted through my head. "Uh, can I call you right back? I just woke up and I gotta pee."

"Uh-huh. I've got all day," she said.

I hung up and looked at Vince lying naked next to me in bed. *I haven't even gotten out of bed yet and I'm already caught.*

Vince rolled over. "Who was that?"

Quickly, I thought up a lie. "Kelly. She's on her way over. You gotta go."

He chuckled, "Yeah, she would flip if she knew I was here."

He got dressed and kissed my head. "Call me when she leaves. We'll go for a ride."

"Sounds good. Talk to you then." As I heard the front door close behind Vince, I forced myself to call Kelly back.

"Yeah?" she said when she picked up her phone.

"Hey, sorry about that. I had to pee," I said. She was silent.

"What's going on?" I asked, after a moment.

"Uh, what happened after I left? How'd you get home?"

"Am I on speaker phone?"

"Nooooooo." She slowly spoke. "How...did you...get home...last night?"

I knew she already knew the answer, I just didn't want to say it. I clenched my teeth. "Vince."

"What the fuck, Laurel? How the hell did that happen?"

"It's a long story. I don't want..."

She interrupted me. "Give me the short version. How did *Vince* end up bringin' you home?"

I stared at the floor and ran my fingers through my hair. My wrists were sore. I noticed that I had slight bruising around my wrists from where he had restrained me. "Uh, Bryan told me to get a ride home with you. I called you twice but you'd already left. And, uh, Vince was my only option." I quickly re-capped in my head the stupidity of the evening. I dropped my head in my hands, knowing what the next question was going to be.

After a long period of silence, Kelly quietly asked, "Did you fuck him?"

I took a deep breath. "Uh. Yeah."

"How could you? I can't believe that you were so quick to throw Bryan away just to bang the guy that'll never be with you."

"I didn't throw Bryan away. He told me to get a ride with you, and..."

"Well, he didn't tell you to fuck your ex-boyfriend, but you did that. Was that just a bonus?"

I sat in silence.

"What were you thinking? Bryan is such a great guy and he likes you so much. How could you do that to him?"

I tried to defend myself. "I wasn't thinking, that's the problem. Last night was just one ridiculous situation after another. My thoughts were like a piece of paper in a windstorm."

"And you made it much worse by screwing the one guy who won't be with you. *Smart move.* Laurel, I have so much respect for you--raising Hunter on your own and everything--simply because you knew you'd never be happy with Greg. Most girls would cling onto the first guy that gave them attention and you know it. *Not you, Laurel.* You'll walk this road alone until you find someone who's fit for you. I put him right in front of you and *this* is what you do? You screwed it up before it ever really got going. I doubt Bryan will ever talk to you again. *I'm* questioning whether *I'll* ever talk to you again."

I wiped away the tear forming in my eye. "I'm sorry. I didn't mean for this to happen. You know how weak I am when it comes to Vince. I didn't mean to hurt anyone."

"You better not lie to Bryan. That'll only make things worse."

"I know." There was a knock on my door. "Someone's here. Let me call you later."

"Don't bother." Click.

I solemnly turned towards the door. "Who could this be?" I wondered as I slowly walked over to the door, dreading the answer. I held Nimbus back as I opened the door.

Bryan stood there. He looked at me for one second then spun around and took off.

The look on my face must have screamed "guilty!"

"Bryan, wait." I ran out behind him.

He stopped and looked at me. "Lemme guess: Diablo brought you home? And you fucked him, didn't you?"

"Please. Come inside. Let's talk," I begged as I ran towards him.

He stared at me. "I've got nothing to say. I'm so pissed right now. I don't want to hear you're pathetic excuses." He slammed his car door and drove away.

I stood on the front lawn as chills radiated from my spine and my body quivered with emptiness.

I just lost every one.
Kelly's pissed.
Bryan's pissed.
Diablo doesn't care enough to be pissed.
Once again…I'm alone.

Chapter 14

Ice Cream

Two weeks passed. I called Kelly and Bryan almost every day. Not once did they answer or return my calls.

I kept moving forward with my life as normal. My work schedule and Hunter kept me busy as usual, but it wasn't enough to distract me from the fact that I'd hurt two people in my life who meant a lot to me. The guilt hung over my head like a dark cloud.

I called Kelly and left her a final message. "Kelly, it's Laurel. I'm calling to say I'm sorry one last time. Please forgive me for the mistake I made. I know I fucked up, but I'm only human. I know I hurt both you and Bryan and I'm truly sorry. I'm not going to keep bothering you cause if you can't forgive me by now, I assume that you never will. We've been friends for years and I'll accept the loss of your friendship if I have to. I miss you. Just so you know, I miss Bryan, too. It's crazy but I didn't realize how much he meant to me. I don't even think I've got the right to miss him after all of this, but I do. Very much. I love you. Good bye." I hung up the phone.

I got ready for my Thursday night gymnastics class with Hunter and headed over to the gym. After class ended, I worked out on the trampoline for a bit. Hunter cheered from the crash mat at the base of the trampoline. I flew through the air flipping and twisting like a leaf being blown by the wind. I cleared my mind for the first time in weeks. I felt free: free from my troubles and free from my guilt.

I hopped off the trampoline and stretched for a minute. "Go put your shoes on, Spark; it's time to go home."

Hunter jumped up and ran over to the shoe bin. "Good job flipping tonight, Mommy."

"Thank you, Sweets. Did you enjoy class?"

He jumped in place. "It was so much fun! Did you see me roll?"

"Of course I did, Silly. You're the best roller around."

He jumped into my arms. "That's cause you taught me." He squeezed my neck and kissed my cheek.

I turned off the lights and locked up the gym. "Do you want to stop for ice cream on our way home?"

"Mmmmm. Ice cream."

I drove to the Dairy Queen in town. While we stood in line, Hunter danced around and sang, "*Ice cream. Ice cream.*"

I giggled as I watched him. The couple standing in line behind us laughed. "What a happy little guy you have. He's so full of energy."

I nodded. "He's a handful." I looked down at him, smiling and full of pride. I glanced over my shoulder.

Bryan stood there smiling and staring at Hunter and me.

My heart jumped out of my chest as our eyes met. I shot him a quick smile as I searched for Hunter's hand.

"Pick me up, Mommy." I reached down and hoisted him up as he quickly wrapped his legs around my waist. I could see from the corner of my eye that Bryan was still staring at us.

Hunter climbed from my hip up around my shoulders, giggling and making monkey noises. He held my hands and started bouncing on my shoulders. "Flip me down, Mommy, flip me down!"

I reached back and grabbed him by his waist and popped him up off my shoulders, flipping him forwards to the ground. He giggled, "Do it again!"

"Not right now, Sweetie. We'll get in trouble. We're next in line. What you want?"

"*Chocolate ice cream cone with jimmies,*" he sang.

"You're favorite, of course."

The girl behind the counter asked Hunter, "What can I get you?"

"Chocolate ice cream cone with jimmies!" He threw his arms in the air and spun around.

I laughed, "I'll have the same."

"Make that three, please."

Startled, I turned around. Bryan was standing right behind me and reached past me to put money on the counter.

I smiled. "Hi." My heart pitter-pattered in my chest.

He smiled back. "Hello, how are you?"

My throat was clogged as my heart had leapt into it. I nodded as I stared into his eyes and a tear formed in the corner of mine.

Hunter looked up at him. "Hi, I'm Hunter. Who're you?"

"I'm Bryan. I'm friends with your mom."

Hunter shook his hand. "Nice to meet you. Mommy didn't tell me about you. I know all of her friends." He looked up at me with his eyes glowing green. "Mommy, why didn't you tell me about your friend Bryan?"

"We only met a couple of days ago," I said, reaching for the ice cream cones and handing one to Hunter and the other to Bryan.

"Is he comin' over to play?" he asked shoving his cone into his mouth.

"Well, I don't..."

Bryan interjected, "I'd love to come over and play."

I swallowed my heart. "You would?"

Hunter started jumping up and down. "Yeah! Bryan's comin' over to play."

Bryan then looked at me and said, "I'm so sorry."

"*You're* sorry? For *what*?" I asked, bewildered.

"I shouldn't have told you to go home with Kelly. That was the worst mistake I've ever made. I should've driven you home myself instead of throwing you to the wolves."

I nodded. "I'm sorry. There's no excuse for what I did. You didn't deserve that and I'm so, *so* sorry."

"Its okay. Have you, um, talked to him?"

"Not at all and I don't want to."

"Thank God."

We walked outside, enjoying our ice cream cones. Hunter was dancing and singing in between bites.

"He's so full of energy. You've got your hands full," Bryan said.

"He's the best. The light of my life."

Bryan stared at me. "So, can I come over and play tonight, Mommy?"

"I'd love that." I leaned against the car. "I've really missed you."

"I missed you, too." He wrapped his arm around my shoulder. "I'd only known you for two days, but it felt like I lost my lifelong best friend." He pulled me into him and kissed my forehead.

"I know," I agreed. "Weird, huh?"

We watched Hunter finish his cone as chocolate dripped down his mouth onto his shirt.

"You're a mess; you've got chocolate all over your face," Bryan chuckled.

"Then it's time for chocolate kisses." He ran over to me and jumped into my arms. As he kissed me, he smeared ice cream and jimmies all over my face. "Mmmmmm, yummy. Chocolate kisses are my favorite," I giggled.

We all laughed as I set him back down and wiped both of our faces clean. "It's time to go home and get ready for bed."

"Yep," he said as he jumped up. "Bryan, are you comin' over?"

"Yes I am, Hunter."

Hunter climbed in the car and I buckled him in.

I looked at Bryan, "I'll see you there?"

He winked at me and walked around the side of the building and disappeared.

I drove home wondering if he was really going to show up.

We raced into the house as Nimbus greeted us at the door. Hunter ran down the hallway pulling his clothes off. "I wanna bubble bath."

I followed him down the hallway and started a bath for him. As the minutes passed by, I began to doubt that Bryan was coming over.

As Hunter bathed, we sang our bath time version of "the Backstreet Boys" song, *Everybody*.

"Everybody, yeah
Wash your body, yeah
Everybody, yeah
Wash your body right."

We giggled as I drained the tub and gave him one final rinse. I wrapped the towel around him and pulled the towel back and forth vigorously, drying his skin. I dropped it over his head and shimmied his head between my hands. I pulled the towel off and his hair spiked in all directions.

"Let me see my hair," he giggled. I lifted him up to the mirror. "My hair's big and pointy."

"It sure is. It's time for a haircut."

219

The doorbell rang. Hunter slid out of my arms and ran towards the door, naked as could be. "Who's there?" he asked.

"It's Bryan," a voice said from the other side of the door.

Hunter pulled the door open and stood butt naked and proud. "Hi, Bryan. I got a bubble bath."

"Well that'd explain why you're naked."

Hunter turned around and ran, bare-assed, back down the hallway past me.

Bryan smiled at me. "Hello, Mommy."

"Hi, come on in. Let me finish getting him ready for bed. I'll be right back." I walked back into the bathroom and helped him put on his Batman pajamas.

Hunter ran out into the living room with his arms stretched out, pretending to fly like Batman.

Bryan started pretending to be his sidekick Robin. Hunter jumped off the back of the couch into Bryan's hands and then they ran around the room as they fought the "bad guys."

I stood there watching. I couldn't help but love what I was seeing. It was like they'd been best friends for years. They did karate kicks in the air, dive rolls across the couch, and then tumbled down onto the ground. They were having the time of their lives.

About an hour later I said, "Spark, it's time for bed. Let's pick up the pillows and then say good night to Bryan."

Bryan looked at me out of the corner of his eye. "Spark?"

"It's my brother's nickname for Hunter."

"Why Spark?"

"It's a long story for another time."

He nodded as he helped Hunter pick up the pillows. Hunter placed the last pillow on the couch and hugged Bryan, saying, "Thanks for comin' over to play, Bryan. You comin' back soon?"

"I'd love to, Spark. I had lots of fun." Hunter high-fived Bryan.

"Goodnight," he said as he crawled up the stairs.

I looked at Bryan, "I'll be right back." I walked upstairs into Hunter's room.

He was already under the covers so I tucked him in nice and tight. We said our prayers and I kissed him goodnight. I closed the door behind me, took a deep breath, and walked down the steps into the living room.

Bryan was on the couch waiting for me. He got up from his seat, pulled me into his arms and kissed me.

Hunter called from his bed. "Mommy?"

"Yeah?"

"Can Bryan come tuck me in, too?" My heart skipped a beat, but before I could answer, Bryan took off up the stairs into Hunter's bedroom.

I stood there. Not knowing what to do. My hands were shaking as I climbed a few steps and tried to listen. "Good night, Spark. I'll see you soon."

"Good night, Bryan. Will you come play again soon?"

"I sure will. See you then." Bryan pulled the door closed behind him as I jumped up and quickly stood by the couch. He came downstairs. "What a great kid."

I smiled as he came towards me. "Thank you. He's a piece of work."

"Can we forget about everything and start over? My life hasn't been the same since we stopped talking."

"I'd love that," I said. "I haven't stopped thinking about you. But I didn't want to keep bothering you. I didn't think I had the right."

"I'm sorry. After Kelly reamed me out for not taking you home instead of putting you in that position, it took a lot for me to admit I was wrong. I've been trying to figure out for days how to call you and apologize. I didn't think you'd want me back."

"You didn't think *I'd* want *you* back? But I called you so many times, hoping..."

He cut me off. "When I saw you earlier, I knew it was fate. I'm so glad we ran into each other."

"So am I." I threw my arms around him. "Have you talked to Kelly recently?"

He shook his head. "She's pissed at both of us. I guess you haven't talked to her?"

I shook my head. "No, I called her as much as I called you, maybe more, but I never got a response."

"Maybe she'll forgive us when we tell her that she was right and that we're back together."

"I hope so. I miss her."

We stood holding each other in our arms in silence.

"So what'd you think of my little man?" I asked.

"He's fantastic. So full of life. He made me feel like a little kid again."

"Believe me, I know. But, um, it's not like me to introduce him to someone until I know if the relationship's going somewhere. I guess it's my way of protecting both of us."

"I can understand that." He paused. "When I saw you two walk in I got so nervous. I watched you for a few minutes before you saw me standing there. I completely understand why you are the way you are."

I cocked my head. "What do you mean?"

223

"Just why you're so set in your ways. Why you're not a party-er. You're just different. That's all I can say. You're just different in a good way. No, a great way. It's inspiring."

"Well, as long as you see it as a good thing, then, um, thank you. I'm definitely not like most girls my age; I'm an 'old soul,' if you will."

"Yes you are, and it's captivating. It makes me want to be around you as much as possible. I realized that when we stopped talking, and it hit me full force tonight when I saw you and Hunter together. I don't want to live another day without you in my life."

Chapter 15

Un-lie-able Introduction

As the weeks passed, Bryan and I mended our relationship very quickly. We spent every free minute together. Hunter and Bryan became the best of friends; it was hard to separate the two of them. We spent our week nights taking walks with Nimbus, shopping, or simply watching movies. On the weekends, while Hunter was at his dad's, we'd gallivant around town, usually we went to Johnny's where he was very well known.

Bryan and I went to the mall one Saturday afternoon to pick out an outfit for Bryan to wear to a meeting that Spam had set up with the producers of MusicVision about the crew having a TV show.

As we browsed the stores, Bryan's phone rang. "Hello?" His eyes widened. "Uh-huh." He glanced across the clothing rack at me. "Uh-huh." He stopped looking through the clothes.

I wondered, "Who's he talking to?"

"Yeah, we did." A smile crossed his face. "We're at the mall." He glanced at me again. "I will... Okay... Definitely... Thank you, bye." He looked at me and smiled.

Before I could even ask what was up my cell phone rang. It was Kelly. "Hello?" I said nervously.

"Hi, Laurel."

"Hi, how are you?" My heart swelled.

She started talking. "I'm ecstatic that you and Bryan were finally able to get past your egos and forgive each other."

"Me too."

"You're at the mall?"

I knew she had just called Bryan. "Yes, we're looking for an outfit for him."

"Good. I'm sorry it took me so long to get off my high horse. I just couldn't believe the absurdity of the situation and I somehow felt responsible. I miss you and I'm sorry for taking so long."

"It's okay," I said. "I'm sorry for my part in everything."

"Have you talked to that asshole?"

"Not at all."

"Good. Keep it that way."

I chuckled, "I will. No worries."

"Call me soon. We need to catch up."

"Okay, I will. Love you."

"Love you, too." Click.

We looked at each other from across the clothing rounder and smiled. Kelly's phone call seemed to have brightened both of our days.

"Finally, everything is how it should be. *Phew*," he said as he wiped his hand across his forehead.

"Thank God." My phone rang again. "Hello?"

"Hey Laurel, it's Dad."

"Hey Dad, what's up?"

"Can you stop by? I need your opinion on something."

"Sure, when?"

"As soon as possible, unless you're busy."

"I'm at the mall with Bryan. I'll see if he minds."

"Let me know if you can't. It'll only take a minute," he assured.

"Okay." I hung up the phone and nervously glanced over at Bryan.

"What's wrong?" he asked.

227

"That was my dad."

"I figured that when you called him dad."

"Okay, smartass."

"What'd he want?"

"He wants me to stop by so he can get my opinion on something."

"When?"

"Um, today. He said as soon as possible."

"So, you're telling me that we need to stop by your parents' house?"

"Well, *I* do. If you're uncomfortable meeting them, I…"

"No, that's cool. I'd like to meet them. They seem really cool from what I hear from you and Hunter."

I nodded slowly. I always had a thing about my boyfriends meeting my parents. With Hunter, I could play off the guy as just a friend because he didn't know any different. Now, *my parents*, on the other hand; that was a whole new level of *un-lie-able introduction*.

"What's he want your opinion on?" Bryan asked.

"Probably something he's building or re-modeling in the house. He's always got projects going."

"Why's he need your opinion?"

I shrugged. "I guess it's a tie."

"A tie? What's that mean?"

"A tie breaker. I'll be the deciding vote. They probably can't decide on what carpet or tile to use, or which curtains to use in what room. It's really a never ending issue at my parent's house."

"Ah, I see. Well, that's cool. I'm game for meeting them."

"Cool."

We finished picking out his outfit and then we stood in line at the checkout counter. I zoned into outer space. Before I knew it, he was pulling on my sleeve ready to go. We walked out of the mall and across the parking lot. As we approached the car, he opened the door for me. "Off we go to meet the family," he said.

I forced a smile as I sat down. The truth is I was nervous. Extremely nervous. After "the boyfriend" meets the parents, things tend to change. The relationship either sky rockets immediately, or drops off like the first step off a sandbar in the ocean. I couldn't decide whether I was more nervous for them to meet him, or for him to meet them. Both caused great anxiety. And afterwards, opinions would fly from all sides. I would've rather waited a little longer before this introduction. Although things had been great between us, we'd only been back together for a few weeks since the incident at the skate park.

I knew I could get out of it if I wanted to, but Bryan didn't seem bothered by it. *Why not? Maybe it's time.*

"Where to?" he asked, eagerly.

"Head down 30 and get off at the Parkland exit."

"Right near the Strubble Trail?"

"Mm-huh." I swallowed, trying to dislodge the knot in my throat.

As we drove, I watched the scenery go by. My stomach knotted tightly, about as tight as the knot in my throat. As we exited off the ramp I said, "Make a right and go around the bend. Then it's the third driveway on the left."

He came to a stop and repeated my directions, "Make a right. Wrap the bend." As we went around the corner he counted the driveways. "One, two, and three." He turned down the driveway lined with trees and shrubbery. We descended down the driveway and my parents' house came into view.

I heard him gasp. "Wait. This is your parents' house?"

"Uh-huh." I bit my lip as I caught the look on his face in my peripheral vision.

His mouth was wide open, similar to his eyes. "This house is huge."

"Um, thanks? My dad built it."

"You grew up here?"

"We moved here when I was fourteen."

"So this is where you come when you take Nimbus swimming? To your parents' house?"

"Well, yes, but we cross the trail and go down to the river."

"You conveniently left that part out." He parked and got out, spinning around to take in the view.

"No, I didn't. I'd just met you. I didn't disclose all the facts and neither did you." I slowly followed him and, once again, felt like I was walking the plank to my demise.

I lead him past the three car garage and through the carport.

"This house is gorgeous."

"Thank you." I opened the back door. He blew past me across the deck and looked out across the rose garden and manicured back yard. "Wow. Your dad did all of this, too?"

"My parents did, yes."

"Wow, I'm impressed. I love the pond up here and the river out there." He looked down towards the trail. "So this river meets down there with the Milltown River, right?"

"Yep, we're always in one or the other."

"I would be, too."

My dad opened the back door at the other end of the deck and said, "What's goin' on out here?"

Bryan jumped as he spun to see my dad. "Hi, I'm Bryan. Nice to meet you." He stretched his hand out.

"Nice to meet you," Dad said as he shook Bryan's hand and squeezed it very firmly. I could see Bryan's eyes ready to pop out of his head.

My dad had a 2nd Degree black belt in karate and was a rather intimidating man. He was not a huge man but he had a lean, muscular build and his presence in a room was simply intimidating.

"Hi, Laurel," my dad said, turning to me. "Thanks for stopping by."

"Hi, Dad." I kissed his cheek.

Bryan said, "This house is incredible. You built it?"

My dad nodded. "Yep, still working on it. That's why I needed Laurel to stop by."

I said, "I figured it had something to do with it. What're you working on?"

"Mom's reupholstering the couches in the Magic Room so we're going to repaint the walls. We can't decide. You're the tie breaker."

I chuckled as I shot Bryan a quick "told ya so" glance.

Bryan stood with his hands in his pockets, smiling at me. "Did you say, the 'Magic Room'?"

"I named it the 'Magic Room,'" I said.

"Why?"

"I always did my homework in there and

that's where we all practiced our instruments. Our music was like magic. Hence, the 'Magic Room'."

"What instrument did you play?"

"I played viola. Sarah played the flute."

"I didn't know that."

"Well, now you do." I winked at him. "Well, let me see the choices," I said as I motioned for my dad to go inside.

He walked back through the door he came out of and over his shoulder he demanded, "Take your shoes off before you come in my house."

I rolled my eyes as I followed him inside. Bryan began fumbling with his shoes. I put my hand on his shoulder. "He's kidding. It's his ridiculously obnoxious sense of humor."

Bryan stood there with one shoe in his hand. "Are you sure? He sounded serious."

"He's messing with you. He has his shoes on, too." I pointed to my dad's feet. "Put your shoe back on and come inside."

He shoved his foot back in his shoe and followed me inside. We all gathered around the kitchen table.

My mom came in. "Hello, everyone. It's nice to finally meet you, Bryan. How are you?"

"I'm great. Nice to meet you, too. This is a beautiful home."

"Ah, thank you. It's a never ending project."

I cut in. "Which ones do I choose from?" I pointed to the paint colors on the table.

"Well, this is the fabric for the couches and this is for the curtains." She laid the fabrics on the table. "We have narrowed it down to these two: Desert Camel and Sandy Beige."

I studied the colors next to the materials. "Considering the lighting isn't great in the room, I'd go with the lighter of the two: this one." I picked it up and read the name. "Sandy Beige."

Mom smiled, "Of course you'd go with that one. That's the one your dad wants."

"Sorry, Mom. He's right."

My dad, with his arms crossed, turned his head and stuck his tongue out at my mom.

Bryan burst into laughter.

I rolled my eyes and shook my head. "You two have serious issues."

Bryan asked, "Can I see this 'Magic Room'?"

My mom motioned for him to follow her and they walked out of the kitchen.

My dad whispered, "He seems nice."

"He is. He treats me wonderfully."

"Good. What's he do?"

"He installs audio visual equipment." I left out the part where he does stupid human tricks for entertainment; I wanted him to start out with a good impression.

"That's good. How's he with Hunter?"

"Really incredible. They're like best friends."

"That's the most important thing."

I nodded as I heard footsteps going upstairs. "Sounds like Mom is giving him the grand tour."

"The grand tour from the grand-poo-ba," he joked.

I giggled and snorted. "The grand-poo-ba."

"Well, I'm going down in the basement to finish my shelves. I'll see you later. Thanks for your help and thanks for making me right."

"No problem," I chuckled as I opened the refrigerator and poured myself a drink. I sat down at the island and waited for them to come back downstairs, staring out across the back yard watching the people pass by on the trail.

I heard them walking back down the stairs, only there were double the amount of footsteps stomping down the wooden steps. Lance and Hillary had joined them. They all rounded the corner into the kitchen. "Hey, Sis," Lance said. "Your boyfriend's funny."

"He's a quick one, he is," I confirmed.

"Hi, Laurel," Hillary said and then whispered in my ear, "He's cute too."

I smiled. "Yes, he is."

She tapped my shoulder with her fist. "Good job."

I chuckled.

Lance said, "Did my dad do the whole shoe thing with you when you came in? That's his favorite joke on newcomers."

Bryan nodded, "Dude, he sounded so serious. I was kinda scared."

Lance nodded and obnoxiously said, "He's only kidding. Don't worry; it's mainly a joke about Laurel."

"What does taking your shoes off at the door have to do with Laurel?"

Before I could react, he said, "Because of when she got struck by lightning at the cabin."

Bryan gasped as he stared at me, unsure of whether or not to believe Lance.

I pursed my lips. "Thanks for that, Lance."

"Oh, what? He didn't know?"

I shook my head. "He does *now*."

"You got struck by lightning?" Bryan asked.

"Twice," Lance said. "It's a running joke in our family. There's a one in 750,000 chance that someone gets struck by lightning and she got struck twice."

My mom chimed in. "Three times, Lance. Three times."

Everyone burst into laughter.

I sarcastically said, "I'm so glad to be the brunt of your jokes people. It's a miracle I'm still alive."

"What?" Bryan said. "You got struck by lightning three times?"

I nodded. "It's a story for another time and place."

"We call her 'Elektra,'" Lance said.

Bryan burst into uproarious laughter.

"And Hunter, we call 'Spark,'" he added.

They all burst into laughter again.

I sat there, smiling and shaking my head.

This introduction was a complete success. I was the brunt of the jokes, but I was used to it at this point in my life. Thankfully, he fit right in with the obnoxious, ball busting family that I was spawned from. Perfect.

"Okay, I'm going to quit while I'm still ahead. Are you ready to go? I have a lot to do at home," I said.

"No, no I'm not. I love it here!"

I rolled my eyes. "Well, I want to go home, so, get in the car." I stomped my foot and pointed to the door, trying to keep a straight face.

He shuffled his feet and lowered his head. "Alright, can we come back and play soon, Mom?"

"Yes, dear. We'll be back."

My whole family escorted us out to the driveway. "It was really great to meet you all," Bryan said. "I hope to see you again soon."

"Nice to meet you, too. Come for dinner anytime," my mom said.

237

We said our goodbyes, and before we made it to the top of the driveway he said, "Your family's awesome. No wonder you're so great."

"Thank you. We're a one of a kind family."

"I think it's great. Now you need to tell me about you getting struck by lightning *three* times. Who does that? How does that happen?"

I hesitated. "Well, twice I was just in the *vicinity* of lightning striking, but I felt the surge of it. The first time I was about seven and we lived in a 150 year old farmhouse. My dad and I were watching the Phillies play during a wicked thunderstorm. There was a rusty nail in the wood on the outside of the window that I was sitting in front of and the nail got struck right behind my head. The TV went blood red and I felt the surge."

"Uh-huh, keep going. This is good stuff."

"Not if you're me. It's kinda scary if you think about it."

"Tell me more."

"We had just gotten home from Florida, at this house."

"The house we just left?"

"Yes. We'd only lived there a few months and the tree where my dad has the dog runner got struck by lightning. The tree split in half from top to bottom and the surge of that strike blew holes under the tires of the cars and shorted out everything in the house: the alarm system, refrigerator, alarm clocks…pretty much everything that was plugged into the sockets. That one wasn't as bad because I was farther away from the strike, but I still felt the shock through my shoes."

"You're like a lightning rod; you attract it."

"The last time was the worst, though."

"Tell me," he pursued.

"I was at the cabin in the mountains."

"What mountains?"

"We have a cabin near Bloomsburg."

"Love Bloomsburg."

"I went for a hike with Nimbus and it started storming. We had to cross through the river, so needless to say, I was soaked from head to toe. I got to the porch and leaned on the porch swing. I started *taking my shoes off*, and the swing itself got struck by lightning. The surge shot through me and threw me into the porch railing. My sneaker insulated me."

"No shit."

"When it threw me I hit my head and I could barely move or breathe. My hand was burned." I showed him what was left of my scars. "I *really* felt that surge."

"Holy Shit. What happened after that? Did you go to the hospital?"

"I called my parents who were almost there and they called an ambulance. The next thing I knew I woke up in the hospital three days later."

We pulled into the parking lot of my apartment.

"That's crazy, Laurel. How'd you survive?"

"I asked the doctor the same thing; he said, 'I guess it's just not your time to go yet.'" I hesitated, "And then he told me I was pregnant."

He almost wrecked the car trying to park it in my spot. "What? You were pregnant with Hunter when that happened?"

"I was in the beginning of my second trimester."

"I don't know what that means."

"I was about three and a half months pregnant."

"No fuckin' way. Was he okay? I mean, he's okay now. But holy hell, Laurel. How'd you both survive?"

"I guess it wasn't our time to go yet."

"That's the most outlandish story I've ever heard. I can't believe it."

"It's crazy, but it's true. That's where we got the nicknames 'Eleckta' and 'Spark.' And that's why there's a running joke about shoes in my family. And that's why I'm so protective of Hunter. It's a miracle I'm alive, let alone Hunter."

"I've never in my life heard such a story."

I slid out of the Jeep; he met me in front of it and threw his arms around me. "I'm so glad you're alive. I never would've imagined that you'd gone through something like that. Pregnant, none the less."

"Someday I'll show you the sneakers," I said.

"You still have them?"

"Hells yes, I still have them. They saved our lives."

He bounced his head back and forth. "I guess I would've saved them too."

"Let's go inside. I'm exhausted. For some reason I get extremely dehydrated and tired when I think about it. Kinda like I relive it all over again."

We walked inside and I grabbed two bottles of water. I chugged one completely down and set the other on the floor next to the couch. I turned on the TV and relaxed.

Chapter 16

I Loved My Life

From that moment forward, Bryan became very close with my family. Lance and Bryan would often hang out together and my parents treated him like their own son. Hunter and Bryan would play together for hours on end and I often wondered if they remembered that I existed. I couldn't complain; it was nice having someone else to help me entertain Hunter. Bryan was a positive influence on him and was accepted by my entire family.

I truly appreciated that Bryan and I were able to give Hunter a decent sense of a family unit. Greg and Gina got married shortly after they met and I knew that Gina loved Hunter like her own son. That alone made my life much easier. I can't claim we were best friends, but we all kept our situation very civil. It was one less stress that we didn't need in our lives. We had our disagreements, but all in all we all got along respectfully. Hunter had begun pre-school at a daycare in Milltown and he quickly made many friends.

About a year after they got married, Greg and Gina had a beautiful baby girl who they named Angel. I was excited and happy for them but also a little jealous. I always wanted to have another baby, another son preferably, but either way I wanted another baby. My current situation was setting itself up perfectly for the opportunity. Bryan often made comments about getting married and having kids and it always made me glow. My dream was in the palm of my hands.

As our lives unfolded, it all seemed to mesh together. Everyone and everything was great; perfect, if you will.

I *loved* my life.

Almost ten months had soared by and Bryan was pretty much staying at our house all the time. When Hunter was at his dad's, Bryan missed him just as much as I did. During the weekdays, they both wined when it was Hunter's bedtime. Half of the time it was like I had two kids, but it was too cute to complain about.

It was a stormy Friday night when Bryan and I decided to go out to dinner. We went to our favorite Italian restaurant, Giovanni's.

Brianna, the owner's daughter and hostess greeted us. "Well hello, you two. Long time no see. How are you?" She flipped her board straight dark brown hair over her bony shoulder.

Bryan quickly answered. "Great. Had to get our Giovanni's fix. It's been too long."

She giggled, "Well here's your table. I'll send your server, Amanda, right over."

I smiled. "Thank you, Brianna."

Neither of us needed a menu; we knew exactly what we were ordering. Amanda quickly appeared at our table. "Hi, I'm Amanda." She paused and looked at Bryan, "Can I, um, get you something to drink? Maybe an appetizer to start?" She was slightly plump and had reddish brown ringlets. Her brown eyes studied Bryan.

"My girlfriend and I want two beers to start with. Laurel? What'd you want for dinner?"

She uncomfortably shifted her eyes to her notepad as she began to write down our order.

"She must recognize him from the videos," I thought, and then said, "Eggplant Parmigiana, please."

She wrote it down and quickly shifted her eyes back to Bryan. "And for you, darlin'?" She cocked her head, batted her eyes, and bit her bottom lip.

"I'd like the Chicken Parmigiana."

"Sounds good. I'll be right back with your beers." She winked at him as she turned away.

"That was rude," I noted.

Baffled, he looked at me. "What was?"

"She didn't even look at me when she took my order. That's just plain ignorant."

"She didn't?"

"Nope. She couldn't take her eyes off of you and she winked at you when she walked away."

He rolled his eyes. "Pfft, whatever." He quickly changed the subject. "What would you say if I asked you if we could move in together?"

I stared at him. My focus quickly shifted from Amanda's rudeness to Bryan's question. "Really?"

"Yes, really."

A smile crossed my face. "I'd love to live with you."

Amanda delivered our beers, listening intently to our conversation.

"What about Hunter?" he asked. "Do you think he'd like that?"

I chuckled. "I'm pretty sure he'd jump for joy. He adores you."

"That's what I was hoping to hear."

"We'll talk to him when he comes home. That way he'll feel like part of the decision. I know he'll be delighted. Where do you want to live?" I asked.

"Well, I figured it's not worth uprooting you and Hunter, and there's plenty of room at your place. So I was hoping to move in with you."

I smiled from ear to ear. "Perfect. When were you thinking?"

"My lease is up at the end of the month," he said. "I can rent month to month but what's the point? I'm already at your place the majority of the time."

"That sounds good to me. Maybe we can start going through my stuff this weekend and then start bringing your stuff over. That way it's not a huge project."

"Sounds like a plan to me."

I smiled. "I love you. I'm so happy."

Amanda approached our table with our meals. She abruptly set the plates in front of us, almost spitefully.

He grabbed my hand. "I want to spend every day of the rest of my life with you, Baby. The sooner I can start, the happier I'll be."

My heart fluttered in my chest. "I love you, Baby." I kissed his hand. "I can't wait."

"Anything else?" Amanda interrupted.

"Nope, we're all set. Thank you," Bryan said.

She retreated from the table. We ate our meals and began to plan the move.

Amanda brought our check, Bryan quickly left cash, we said our goodbyes to the staff, and we ran out to the car, shielding ourselves from the torrential downpour.

We decided to stop by Spam's house; most of the guys in the crew were there editing their film. My excitement level was high, but I never enjoyed spending time around Spam. He was a killjoy.

Bryan held my hand as we walked into the living room, shaking off the rain. He announced, "Guys, Laurel and I are moving in together."

Spam froze and glared at me.

"Really? Congratulations." Slash said with much surprise.

I smiled. "Thank you. I was surprised, too."

"I'm not," Spam mumbled. "I saw this fuckin' comin' a long time ago."

Bryan said, "Well, then I guess you were right." He leaned over and whispered to me. "I saw it coming a long time ago too."

I smiled. "I'd had my hopes, I'm not gonna lie."

Ace rolled his eyes and turned away.

"Jealous," I thought. "Typical."

Bryan leaned over Spam's shoulder as Spam showed him the video clips he was editing.

I stared at Bryan from across the room and I felt a peace settling inside me. My life was everything any one person could've wanted. I felt like my excitement was seeping out of my pores. I could do nothing but smile, from the inside out; I was glowing.

Every once in a while, Bryan would peer at me over Spam's shoulder, giving me goosebumps. Spam threw a glare my way every few minutes. I ignored him. I despised him.

After about an hour we headed home. "What's that guy's problem? He's such a dick," I said, referring to Spam.

"He definitely can be. I just think it's because his last girlfriend fucked him over. She cheated on him after a year. Now he, like, *despises* women."

"Well, I didn't cheat on you. We both know that. But he really fuckin' likes to make me feel unwanted. I'm just glad you're smart enough not to listen to him and his wounded ego."

He vigorously shook his head. "Spam hates all women and uses them for ass. Believe me when I tell you it's not just you."

"Well, if you guys become famous, he's gonna want you to be using and abusing all women, too. Mainly me."

"That's not gonna happen. I lost you once and I'm not gonna lose you again." He kissed my hand. "Famous or not."

"He's gotta be jealous, too. I mean, we get along amazingly." I chuckled, "If you ask me, that was a smart woman that cheated on his dumb ass. She did herself a favor."

He laughed. "You're hysterical."

"Well, I'm not trying to be funny. More like honest. He's *horrible*."

We pulled into the apartment parking lot and quickly ran inside to avoid the rain. We got out of our soppy wet clothes and put on our comfy clothes. "Movie?" he asked.

"Sure."

We sat down on the couch and the next thing I knew, he was sound asleep. I flipped through the channels and slowly drifted off as well.

As the weekend progressed, we went through my closets and belongings. We cleaned and organized almost everything, and before we knew it, Hunter came home on Sunday evening. Greg unbuckled him from his car seat and he went running straight to Bryan and jumped into his arms. He lurched from Bryan's arms into mine. We were so happy to see him. As Greg was getting back in the car, I ran over to him. "Hey, Greg."

"Hey."

"I wanted to let you know that Bryan's moving in."

Greg's eyes widened. "Okay. Is Hunter going to be happy about that?"

I smiled and looked over my shoulder at Bryan he tossed Hunter in the air. "Hunter'll be thrilled. I know Bryan's excited."

Greg nodded his head. "He does speak very highly of Bryan. Well, congratulations."

"Thank you. Tell Gina and the girls I said 'Hi.'"

As Greg pulled away I stepped inside the house. Bryan and Hunter were already playing with trucks. I smiled. I stood there and wondered, "How'd I get so lucky? I've got a beautiful child and an amazing boyfriend. I'm blessed."

"Mommy, come play with us," Hunter said.

Without hesitation I grabbed a dump truck out of the basket and joined in. My eyes met Bryan's; I winked at him and smiled. "Hunter, we wanted to talk to you about something."

"What's up, Mommy?" He pushed the truck across the carpet.

"What do you think about that Bryan moving in with us?"

Hunter's face lit up. "That's awesome!" He jumped up and threw his arms around Bryan's neck, tackling him to the floor. "Are you going to be my other daddy?"

We all giggled.

I said, "We'll see about that; we wanted to make sure you'd want Bryan to move in here."

Hunter beamed with happiness. "Yes, I do. What about Nimbus?"

"What do you mean?" I asked.

"Did you ask Nimbus if he wanted Bryan to move in?" Hunter asked.

"Well, I never thought about that," Bryan said and turned to Nimbus. "Nimbus, do you want me to move in?"

Nimbus nudged Bryan's jaw and licked his face. Hunter laughed hysterically as Bryan wiped his face off. "I think that's a 'yes' in doggie talk," Bryan said.

Hunter jumped up and danced around the room. "Bryan's moving in. He's gonna be my daddy. Bryan's moving in. He loves my mommy."

Bryan and I watched as Hunter celebrated. I rested my head on Bryan's shoulder and tasseled his hair. "I love you. I told you he'd be thrilled."

He kissed the top of my head. "I can't wait."

Nimbus joined in with Hunter's dancing around the room. He began barking and spinning in circles.

"Looks like Nimbus is just as excited," Bryan chuckled.

"Mommy, can Bryan stay in my room?"

"I think Bryan will be staying in my room, Spark."

Bryan crawled over and whispered in Hunter's ear. "We'll make forts in your room; it'll be our secret hide out. Mommy will never know."

"Let's go build one now," Hunter whispered.

Bryan jumped to his feet. "Mommy, we're going on a secret mission." He said pointing his finger in my face. "There are no mommy's allowed." He tapped the end of my nose with his finger.

Hunter grabbed Bryan's hand, pulling him towards the stairs. "Come on, Nimbus. Bye, Mommy."

"Have fun, boys," I giggled as they hustled upstairs.

Chapter 17

The Root of the Problem

Over the next few days, I rearranged my closet. I wondered whether or not I was making the right decision. I looked around at my three piles of clothes: one to keep, one for Goodwill, and one to throw out. *I'm well on my way.* As I finished my closet, I made what I hoped to be my last drop off at the Goodwill and then met Bryan at his apartment. We finished packing what was left and loaded up his rental truck as we emptied his apartment.

As we both pulled up out front, Nimbus

started barking. Bryan backed the truck up to the door as I jumped out of my Jeep and waited to meet him at the front door.

He threw his arms around me, picked me up, and spun us in circles. "Today's the big day. The first day of our life together."

"I'm so excited. I love you, Baby." I kissed him and pulled him in tight. I knew we were meant to be.

We propped open the screen door and started moving boxes inside. I grabbed his clothes on hangers and laid them across my bed.

He wrapped his arms around me. "That's about it, my love. We're now living together."

"Let's get you unpacked and settled. I cleaned out the closet for you. Let's start there." I moved a few more boxes aside on the shelf and gathered his clothes, then I walked them into the closet and handed them to him.

He winked at me as he hung them. Then he grabbed the only shoe box on the top shelf and pulled it down. "For a girl, I would've expected more shoe boxes. I'm surprised."

I turned and looked at the shoe box and froze. I reached out to take the box from him as a tear formed in my eye. "I'm not that kinda girl. You should know that by now." A smile formed as he caught the tear rolling down my cheek. "Most of my shoes are sneakers and boots, not heels."

"Are you okay? Why are you crying?" He put the box under his arm.

I pointed at the shoe box. "Open it."

"Is this a box full of stuff from your past boyfriends?"

"Open it." Another tear streamed down my cheek, which I quickly wiped away. "You'll understand it once you open it."

He grabbed the shoe box from under his arm and slowly lifted the lid. He gasped as he pulled the sneakers out, one in perfect order and the other with charred holes blown into the fabric. "Ho-ly shit." He slowly turned the sneakers over and stared at the soles in disbelief. Studying the burnt and melted rubber, he twisted the shoes slowly and looked up at me.

Another tear rolled down my cheek, followed by a stream of tears. I smiled. "Those are the sneakers that I was wearing when I got struck by lightning. They saved our lives."

"I don't know what to say. One is perfect, the other is fried."

I giggled. "So was I." I wiped away more tears. Every time I looked at them I couldn't figure out how Hunter and I survived. "It's a miracle."

"It *is* a miracle. I can't believe it. You told me what happened. But I just didn't realize it was that serious." He looked at me. "I'm sorry."

"It's okay; I don't talk about it too much.

People think I'm crazy when I tell them, no matter how much I try to downplay it. So instead, I usually don't mention it."

I looked at him, his eyes still admiring the soles. "I didn't realize," he said.

"Of course you didn't realize. I didn't go into detail about it so how could you understand?"

He studied my face. "Will you tell me the story, in detail? Inquiring minds want to know."

I laughed, "I'd rather not. You pretty much know what you need to know."

"Well, I want to know more. *Details:* where you were when it happened, how it felt, what the doctors said. Now, after seeing this, I want all of the details."

"I'm sure I don't know the details about the tragedies in your life."

He stared at me and held out the sneakers.

I huffed. "If I *have* to tell you, then I will. It's just hard, ya know, to talk about. I tend to relive it when I talk about it or even think about it." I wiped my face dry.

He held the sneakers up to my face. "*Details.*"

"Fine. I'll tell you but not right now. We've got enough going on right now."

He hugged me with a sneaker in each of his hands. "I love you, Laurel Forte. You're my hero."

I giggled. "Put those away. I can smell the burnt rubber and it's gross."

"Okay, but I can't wait to hear this story. Will you *please* tell me after we finish unpacking my crap?"

"No. We've got enough going on right now. Another time, so I can prepare for it." I turned and walked into the bathroom and splashed my face with cool water. I stared into the mirror, admiring how green my eyes became when I cried. *What is my purpose on this earth? How'd I survive? How'd we survive? Why did we survive?*

My eyes were very heavy. Whenever my brain remembered getting struck by lightning, my body tended to 'relive' it. The amount of emotions and fear that I felt that day and many days after still overtook me very quickly before I even had a chance to prevent it. It happened so suddenly. After I worked my way through it, I'd sleep for hours. I assumed it was my body's way of recovering again.

We settled Bryan in over the next week or so. My home was now *our* home. I felt so complete; I was perfectly content. As the weeks passed I was light on my toes. I danced through my days as graceful and happy as a princess.

Kelly and I met for a drink at Lucky's Pub. I walked in and sat on the barstool next to hers. "Hello, Lady. How are you?"

"I think Phil's breaking up with me," she huffed.

"What? Why?" I asked, though I wasn't too surprised.

"He's acting really weird the lately. I haven't talked to him in three days other than, 'Hi, can I call you back?'"

"Sorry to hear that. Did something happen?"

She shrugged her shoulders. "I think he met someone else last weekend."

"Well, I know he was with Bryan on Saturday night, but I don't know the details."

"Do you know where they went?" she asked. "I'd ask Phil but he's been playing games all week. It's really pissing me off."

"I think they went to Spam's house and then went to Johnny's, from what I gathered."

"That's what I figured but apparently I don't matter enough for him to talk to me anymore," she spit.

"Should I ask Bryan if he knows what's going on?"

"I don't know. I think I've got a right to know what's going on. And if Phil isn't going to answer his phone and talk to me, well I have other sources of information, right?"

"Right. You and Bryan are friends too, so I don't see why you can't ask him," I rationalized.

"But then there's that 'Bro's before Ho's' clause that throws a wrench in the gears for us ladies."

She dropped her head into her hands. "I just want to know what's going on with my boyfriend. That's not too much to ask, is it?"

"I don't think so. I'd want some answers. Bryan was going to stop in and say hi. So when he gets here, just ask. If you don't ask, you may never know."

We sat in silence for a few minutes. Finally, I ventured, "Can I, um, say something?"

She nodded.

"Would it make you feel any better if I told you that I didn't see you and Phil lasting from the beginning? I think you deserve much better."

She rolled her eyes. "I know. I just feel like I put in so much time and energy so that it'd work."

"Well, maybe that's the root of the problem."

She glared at me. "What do you mean?"

"Well, Bryan and I just mesh. We make sense together. It's effortless. That's why it's so good."

"You're welcome again, by the way."

"And Kelly, you were *right*. All signs pointed to 'go' and you were right. Maybe *I'm* right about this. Maybe you're wasting your time and energy forcing something to work that didn't even have any reason to start."

She dropped her head and nodded. "I know."

"What do you really have in common with him?"

She stared at her beer bottle and scraped the label with her nail. "I don't know."

"Is the sex even good?"

She giggled, "Not really."

"So why are you wasting your precious time on someone who you have nothing in common with and don't even enjoy sleeping with?"

She shrugged a shoulder.

"Just to say that you're in a relationship? Just to feel better about yourself?"

She slowly nodded. "I guess that has something to do with it."

"Well, that doesn't make any sense. You aren't happy in the relationship but you'll stay in it just to say that you're in one? That's absurd."

She let out a little giggle.

"Being single's better than being in a dead-end relationship with a 'dud' any given day of the week."

"Yeah, but look at *your* relationship. It's perfect," she said.

"Yeah, but think back to how long I was single. I didn't want to waste my time in a dead-end relationship. Think about all the guys I passed up because I knew they didn't understand my life. And think about all the great times I've had while I was single and not stressing over a man."

"You've got a child to keep you busy," she countered.

"And you don't. You're free to move about the country as much as you like, but I'm rooted here. I can't go out on a Tuesday night for wings with you. Not because I don't want to, simply because I can't; my schedule doesn't allow it. My responsibilities are to Hunter, and your responsibilities are to yourself. I don't know what that feels like."

She huffed and nodded.

"Think about all the nights I've spent alone," I said.

"You're never alone; you have Hunter."

"You're right. I have Hunter, but I didn't have a boyfriend to go to the movies with, or the mall, or to snuggle up in bed with at night. I'd been single and alone for what felt like a lifetime before Bryan," I paused and then added, "...other than Vince. And we both know that was a no-go from day one. Just because I have people around me, or a son, doesn't mean I never feel alone. I hadn't had the comfort of a man in years, let alone one who wanted to take care of me and Hunter. And sadly, I got used to being alone. And believe me, that sucks."

"I see what you're saying."

"Do you?" I asked.

"I have freedoms that you don't and I should take advantage of that instead of wasting my time on 'The Dud.'"

"Precisely. I think you should look at it like this: You're *way* too good for him. Your personality is happy and bubbly and he's a derelict."

She burst out in laughter.

"He's taking a weight off of your shoulders by being distant this week, if you ask me. He should go be someone else's problem. You deserve a man with some personality attached to him. And one that'll get you off in bed," I added.

We both burst out in laughter.

"You're right. Damn you, but you're right," she said.

"Glad you see it my way. I do what I can," I joked.

"It does suck that I've wasted so much time."

"You live and you learn, and then you grow. At least you've figured it out and can move forward."

Bryan popped his head in between us. "Hello, ladies."

He gave me a peck on the lips and wrapped his arms around me. "You look beautiful as always."

"Thanks, Babe. How was your day, Mr. Cease?"

"Fantastic. And now I'm with you, Mrs. Cease, so it's perfect."

"Are you headed out with the boys tonight?" I asked.

"I'm not sure. Phil wants to go to Johnny's, of course. And, ah, Spam's out of town."

When he mentioned Phil, Kelly breathed a quick deep breath and held it in.

Bryan stared at her. "Is something wrong?"

"I haven't heard from him in days and you know his itinerary. It's kinda upsetting."

"He hasn't called you?"

"Nope. I've called him but he hasn't called me back."

"I told her she deserves someone better for her anyway," I chimed in.

He pounded his hand on the bar. "I second that motion. I didn't think it was going to last this long to begin with."

She shifted on her seat. "You too, huh? It just would've been nice for him to tell me and not just disappear on me."

Bryan vigorously nodded. "I agree that's kinda lame. You deserve better; you two together were like oil and water."

She spun on her seat and hopped to her feet. "I know. I guess I'll just have to find a new man. Maybe Prince Charming will sweep me off my feet tonight."

"Maybe you should let me find you a man. I'll repay the favor," I shot Bryan a wink.

Bryan smiled. "I know someone you'd get along great with."

"So do I."

"Who?" she asked.

"Yeah, who?" Bryan asked, puzzled.

"James, from your work," I said.

Bryan grinned. "Amazing. That's who I was going to say."

"Then we must make it happen," I said and then looked at Kelly. "We both agree. You should meet James."

"Call him up! See if he wants to come out," she said.

"He's away until tomorrow but I'll make something happen. He's a good dude," Bryan said.

"And he's cute, too," I added.

Bryan looked at me. "Oh really?"

I smiled and brushed my hand across his back. "No worries, Babe. You've got my heart." I looked at Kelly. "But he is cute."

"Makes good money too," Bryan added.

Kelly said, "Well, make it happen damn it; you two owe me." We all giggled as Kelly disappeared into the crowd.

"So where'd Spam head off to this time? Hell, I hope?" I asked.

I could sense the hesitation in his voice. "He's in Florida. For the meeting."

"The meeting I've heard about with the executives of MusicVision? The one you were supposed to go to?"

"Yep. This meeting could change our future. I wish they hadn't moved the meeting to Florida; I really wanted to be there. Who knows what Spam'll agree to."

"It'll be a good meeting, I know it. You guys have something too original to be passed up. No worries."

"You're awesome." He brushed his hand through my hair.

"*You're* awesome." I tapped my finger on his chest. "You're the bestest."

"I'm going to go meet Phil. I'll see you in bed." He raised his eyebrows and winked at me. "Have fun."

"You too."

He vanished into the crowd.

"I'm so lucky," I thought.

Kelly sat back down. "Did Bryan leave?"

I nodded. "He went to go meet Phil."

"Figures." She pursed her lips.

"What're your plans for the rest of the evening?"

"Chelsea's coming to meet me. Wanna stay and hang out for a while?" she asked.

"No, I've got a lot to do tomorrow. I have to be good."

"Figures."

"Hey, girls," Chelsea sang.

In unison we both answered, "Hello."

"Any new news, ladies?" Chelsea asked.

"Guess what Bryan just told me," I said.

Kelly sat straight up. "What?"

"Spam's at a meeting with the executives of MusicVision. For the show."

Chelsea confirmed, "MusicVision? The TV station?"

I slowly nodded my head. "Yep."

"How cool would that be if you guys became famous?" Kelly gasped.

"'You guys'? No, no, no. This is his deal. I'm just dating him."

"Dating him, my ass. You guys are married without the paperwork. Give me a break." Kelly rolled her eyes.

I chuckled. "Yeah, but that's his stuff. I have no part of it."

"So then your husband would be famous. Can you handle that?" Kelly said. "And I hooked it up."

"Thank you, and thank you. That'd be weird," I admitted. "To actually see them on television would be cool."

"I know. Cause we're friends with the real them and not fans of the show," Chelsea said. "The question is: will they still be friends with us when they're famous?"

"What do you mean?" I asked.

Chelsea said, "Well, you know how people change after they become famous. Will they forget about us? Will they still need or want our friendship?"

A chill struck through my body as the words left her lips. That very thought had snuck across my mind a few times. *I know things will change, but how much will they change?*

Kelly said, "They're already known in this area, so it wouldn't be that different around here."

I nodded, hesitantly. I just didn't know if I believed that to be true.

"Time will tell," I said, trying not to think about it. "I'm going to head home." I jumped up from my stool.

"Did I say something wrong?" Chelsea asked.

"Not at all. But it does raise a question in my head."

Kelly said, "You and Bryan'll be fine. I have no worries."

I forced a fake smile on my face. "I hope so."

As I drove home I couldn't help but worry. *Will they forget us? Will Bryan forget me? And Hunter? What will happen if they do become famous? Time will tell.*

I threw in a load of laundry and straightened up the bedroom some more. I turned on the television to watch E News, listening to updates about the famous actors. *Is every bit of their privacy is gone? Is this how my life will someday be if they sign? Could this be my future?*

As I hung our laundry in the closet, I decided to focus on the present. We'd taken a big step together. I wanted to continue to be happy and not worry.

As midnight came, I curled up in bed and easily dozed off into a deep sleep.

Nimbus barked; I sat straight up in bed. I looked at the clock: 3:11 in the morning. I heard someone downstairs. Nimbus wined and pawed at the bedroom door to get out. I quietly got out of bed and cracked open the door. Nimbus flew down the steps barking and wagging his tail. I shuffled myself halfway down the steps and peered around the stair rail. "Bryan?"

No answer. Nimbus walked out of the kitchen and stared at me, his tail wagging. I knew if it was an intruder his demeanor would be different.

I stepped the rest of the way downstairs and shuffled towards the kitchen. I turned on the light in the hallway and peered around the corner; Bryan was laying in the fetal position on the floor in the corner of the kitchen, shaking, Cheerio's scattered across the floor surrounding him.

I quickly ran over to him. "Bryan, are you okay? What happened?" I wrapped my arms around him. He was convulsing. "Bryan, what's wrong?"

270

He sounded like he was hyperventilating.

"Should I call an ambulance? Are you hurt?"

"Nah, nah, nooooooo," he sputtered out. "Not h-hurt."

I smelled the alcohol on his breath.

"What's wrong? What happened tonight?" I searched for the answers.

His whimpers started getting louder and louder as he squeezed me. "I didn't re-mem-ber. I didn't tell."

"What didn't you remember?" I racked my brain to think if it was someone's birthday or anniversary, but nothing came to mind. I couldn't think of anything. "What, Bryan? What didn't you remember?"

In between his machine gun whimpers and chattering teeth he whispered, "Th-the g-g-guy."

"The guy? What guy?" I said rocking him in my arms.

"I d-d-d-didn't re-mem-ber him hurt me," he forced himself to say.

"Hurt you? Who hurt you?"

"M-m-my n-n-neigh-b-bor."

"Our neighbor hurt you?" I asked.

"N-n-no. When I w-was eh-eight. S-so s-sorry."

"How'd he hurt you?"

"H-he touched m-me a-and h-hurt me."

Shock cascaded through my body. *Did he just tell me what I think he told me?*

"Bryan," I whispered. "Bryan, what'd he do?"

"P-put his d-d-dick in m-me and h-hurt me." He began convulsing harder in my arms.

I sat there in the dark absorbing what he had just told me. Every breath I inhaled felt colder and colder. I pulled him closer to me and he slid his head down onto my lap. Tears trickled down my face and I whispered the only thing I could think to say. "Bryan, it wasn't your fault." My brain raced through possible scenario's of how it happened. With hate and disgust I asked myself, "Who would do such a thing? I swear if someone ever touched my son that way, I'd kill them."

My mind froze on that thought. *Hunter.*

Could I have opened my doors up to an occurrence like that with my own son? No. No. I don't believe Bryan would do such a thing. He is a different person than that. But who's this guy in my arms right now? How didn't I know this had happened to him? Did I just put my son in danger? No. No. I'm sure I didn't.

"Relax, Bryan. It wasn't your fault," I repeated as I rubbed his back and tears slowly streamed down my face. I pulled my fingers through his hair and rocked him back and forth in my arms.

His whimpers began to fade. Then I heard him mumble, "I'm s-sorry, Dad."

That was the first I'd ever heard him mention his dad. "Your dad?"

He nodded his head in my lap. "Th-that's why my dad left. C-cause the guy h-hurt m-me."

"No, Bryan, it wasn't your fault. There's no need to be sorry," I whispered in his ear. "You were a child; it's not your fault. It's his fault, not yours."

I felt his tears soaking into my cotton pajama pants. "I'm s-sorry," he whispered again, before drunken exhaustion overtook him and he passed out.

I sat in the kitchen leaning against the cabinet, my legs stretched out in a sea of Cheerio's. I stared across the darkness into the lit up hallway. My mind ricocheted around the many questions in my brain. I stared blankly into the darkness and asked myself again, "Who is this guy, in my arms? How did I not know that this happened to him?"

All at once, it hit me...

I knew who he was...

A scared little boy.

I awoke in the morning, slumped against the cabinets. I sat up in shock. *Was that a dream?* The mess across the kitchen floor answered my question. I saw the same setting as in my "dream," leaning against the cabinets with my legs sprawled out in a sea of crushed Cheerio's.

I jumped to attention. My thoughts tried to organize themselves in my head. I rolled my neck and stretched my back, sore from sleeping in such an uncomfortable position. I moaned as I felt my muscles cringe in my neck. Straining my body, I reached for the dustpan and broom. I swept the Cheerio's into a pile. *Is my life about to crumble along with them?*

Bryan snuck up behind me and wrapped his arms around my waist. "Good morning, beautiful."

"Good morning to you, my love."

"I'm sorry about last night." He rocked me back and forth.

"What…ah. Is that…um…true?" I was finally able to force the words out of my mouth.

He lowered his head and grunted, "Uh-huh."

I absently stared at him. "I'm so sorry that happened to you."

"You didn't do it to me. No reason for you to apologize. I'm going to pick up Phil; he's at his new girl's house."

"That didn't take him long."

"I shouldn't say 'new girl.' They used to date before Kelly came along. They're good for each other."

I couldn't help but wonder how to ask the questions still swarming in my brain without being too intrusive. "Do we need to…um…talk about that?"

He shook his head. "I don't want to get into details. You know it happened. I feel better, Hunter and all. I'd never hurt him, just so you know."

"I know. Are you okay?"

"I'm fine. It…um…got the best of me last night. I'm sorry."

"Don't apologize. I'm glad I was here for you."

He smiled. "Thank you." He kissed my lips and cupped his hand around my jaw. "I love you. I'll be back later."

"Love you," I mumbled as I watched him leave.

He shut the door behind him and called out, "Everything's going to be okay, Babe."

I stood in the hallway pondering what he had just said. *Are those words true?* I couldn't help but question the reality of the situation. I know anytime a child gets abused it haunts them for the rest of their lives. My stomach turned and my thoughts ricocheted as I pushed through the motions of my morning. I couldn't help but acknowledge the incredibly bad feeling lurking inside me.

As the days passed, I pushed my concerns about Bryan's past and probable future onto the back burner. We continued our happy life together.

My job continued to wear on me. The sales representatives blamed me for their own mistakes; more and more I began dreading going to work. My patience was wearing thin again, only this time for a different reason.

Chapter 18

I've never seen anything like it...

I called Bryan.

"Hello?" he answered.

"Hey, where are you?" I asked.

"I'm at the shop. You?"

"I'm driving through town. Can I stop by?"

"Yeah, we're just sitting here; slow day today. Aren't you supposed to be at work?"

"Yeah, but I left early. I'll be there in a few." I hung up the phone.

I walked into the office of the shop; no one was at the reception desk. I waited for a minute, admiring the artwork hanging in the lobby. The phone was ringing constantly. I peered around the corner down the vacant hallway.

"Hello?" I called out. "Anyone there?"

No one answered. I heard someone talking on the phone in the background. I called Bryan. "Hey Babe, I'm here but no one's up front."

"I'll be right there," he said.

I waited, continuing to look at the artwork.

Bryan appeared from around the corner and led me down the hallway into a board room. "Guys, this is Laurel. Laurel, this is Joe and Mike." We sat down at the enormous conference table.

"What brings you here?" Bryan asked me.

"Work sucked today. I told them I had a doctor's appointment so I could leave."

He pursed his eyebrows. "That's completely out of character for you. What's going on?"

I nodded and huffed, "I know it is. I'm just so fed up with how badly they treat me. When a salesman screws up it somehow gets put on my back. I didn't forward a call right or I didn't get the proper mail to them. It's all bullshit. They just can't admit that they screwed up their own shit."

"Sounds ridiculous," Mike said.

"It is. I like to refer to the office as 'sporadically ridiculum.'" I made air quotes.

They all burst into laughter.

"That's hysterical," one said. "Bryan, she's great."

He smiled. "I know," he said, pretending to fix his collar. "She's the best."

A man came into the room. "What's going on in here? What's all the laughter about? I heard you all the way in my office."

"Bryan's girl said that her office is 'sporadically ridiculum,'" Mike said, imitating my air quotes.

"That's one I've never heard before. I like it though. It's funny." He looked at me. "I'm Paul."

"I'm Laurel. Nice to meet you."

"Where do you work?" Paul asked.

"I'm an office manager for a restaurant supply company on the other side of town. The people I work with are idiots." I added, "I have too much common sense to make the dumb mistakes that they do, yet they blame me for them."

"Sounds like they don't have their shit together," Mike chimed in.

"You have no idea. When I started working there, there was no organization, period. I went through and organized their entire filing system. Now they can find things but somehow they still screw it up."

I caught a glimpse of Paul giving Bryan an inquisitive look. "She left work today," Bryan explained to him. "Very out of character."

I looked at Bryan, wondering why he told Paul that. "I just wanted to come say hello. I needed a pick-me-up, but I won't hold you up any longer." I got up from my chair.

"We've got nothing to do this afternoon. Relax with us," Joe said. "It's nice to have a new face around."

Bryan grinned at me. "We finished our job three days early. We're waiting to see if there's a small job we can do before next week, but it's not looking so good."

"So, you'll get paid for sitting here? Must be nice." I shot him a wink and a smile.

Paul said, "Should we order lunch for everyone? Laurel, would you like to join us?"

In unison, Bryan and Joe said, "Carlini's." They high-fived and nodded their heads.

"Absolutely. I can't pass up Carlini's. It's the best," I said, rubbing my stomach and licking my lips.

Paul said, "Carlini's it is. I'll ask Stephanie to ord... Oh wait. She quit. I'll call." He disappeared through the door.

Bryan looked at me with a shit-eating grin. "What're your plans for the day, slacker?"

I chuckled and tossed my hair over my shoulder and spun side to side in my chair. "Don't know. I have class tonight."

The door opened and Paul sat down at the table with us. "Carlini's is on its way."

Joe asked, "What're you in school for?"

"Huh?" I said. "Oh, no. I coach gymnastics."

They all stared at me.

"Where?" Mike asked.

"At Broomall's Gymnastics. I used to train there, so it only seems fitting that I give back." A smile tipped my lips.

"So can you do those flippy things?" Mike asked.

I laughed as I nodded. "Yes. I can do back handsprings. Otherwise known as 'flippy things.'"

They all gasped. "Really? That's cool," Paul said.

"Bryan, your girl's the bomb," Mike added.

I huffed and lowered my head into my hands. "Yeah Bryan," I mocked in a silly voice. "You're girl's the *bomb*."

He jumped up. "Come on, I'll give you a tour of the warehouse. Show you what we do."

I got up from my chair and followed him out the other door in the room. We walked down a hallway which opened into a huge warehouse lined with ceiling-high shelves.

"What's all this?" I asked, astounded.

"Projection screens, LCD players, flatscreens, DVD players, video equipment. You name it, we got it."

"Wow."

"We rented our equipment for the premiere from here, obviously. I've got an 'in.'"

"Convenient."

I turned to look as one of the rear garage doors rolled up making a loud rumbling noise that shook the ground. James came walking into the warehouse. "Hey, Laurel. Good to see you."

"You too. How's everything?"

"Well, good. Except that our receptionist quit and no one knows what's going on any more."

"Ah, yes. I heard."

Bryan said, "We just ordered Carlini's. Should be here soon."

James grinned and cocked his head. "I love me some Carlini's."

We walked back into the boardroom.

I said, "James, come have dinner with us soon, I have a friend that wants to meet you."

"Oh, really? What's she like?"

Bryan said, "She's awesome. Actually, she set Laurel and I up and we both agree you'd be a good match."

James said, "I'm not guaranteeing anything, but set it up. I'd like to meet her."

I smiled, "I'll make it happen." I turned to Bryan, "Someone should watch for the delivery guy, if no one's up there, he'll be waiting for a while."

He nodded. "Good call." He grabbed my hand and we walked up to the lobby. Just as we entered, the delivery guy walked in.

Bryan picked up the phone, pushed a button, and in a goofy voice said, "Paaauuuuul to da lobby. Paul, to da laaaaabby. We needs yer maaah-ney." He dropped the phone in its cradle as he laughed at himself.

I rolled my eyes and shook my head, giggling under my breath.

Paul showed up right behind me, handed the guy a ten, and said, "You can add this to my account right, Ron?"

Ron nodded, "Yes sir, as usual."

I grabbed one of the two bags of food while Bryan grabbed the other and we went back to the lunchroom. As we walked in, the entire staff had gathered. Bryan's announcement had informed everyone that lunch had arrived and they flocked to the lunchroom. We set the bags down and starting pulling out hoagies, chips, and containers of peppers and condiments. It was a feast.

I leaned towards Bryan. "Do you guys do this often?"

He shrugged, "At least once a week, usually on Fridays. But today's special cause we're here," he said, motioning to the other installers.

"This is really nice that they do this for you."

"Paul's a great boss."

"He's the boss or the owner?"

"Both."

"Well, that's something that you don't see too often."

"What?" he asked.

"Most owners wouldn't sit down and chit-chat in the middle of the day. My boss would be flipping out if he were paying us to sit around."

"I guess Paul sees it like this: we make him a ton of money every day. He'd still make the same amount of money and would still be paying us if the job wasn't done yet. So why cause an issue when it's a win-win situation?"

"Yeah. Makes sense. My boss would find something to freak out about. But he's ridiculum." I laughed at myself.

"Really?" a voice behind me asked.

I turned to see Paul standing behind me. "Oh yeah. He's constantly got something to complain about. Even on good days, it's never good enough."

"Sorry to hear that, Laurel. You don't deserve to be treated like that."

"Yeah, well, I gotta work. I have benefits and my son is taken care of."

"How old's your son?" he asked.

"Hunter just turned four."

"Do you mind if I ask how old you are?"

"I'm twenty four. Had him young. It's been rough but it's definitely been worth it."

Bryan said, "He's a really good kid."

My smile broadened. "My heart and soul."

284

Bryan shot me a wink.

"Thank you for lunch. I appreciate it," I said to Paul. "It's delish."

"No problem," Paul said.

As we finished up our lunch I said to Bryan, "I'm gonna stop by the grocery store on my way home. Anything you want?"

"Not for me, but Hunter's almost out of Cheerio's." He shot me a crooked smile.

"Okay. Do you want me to make anything for dinner for you before I go to class?"

"Nah, I'll pick something up on my way home."

"Thanks again for lunch. I'm going grocery shopping, my favorite," I said sarcastically as I rolled my eyes. Bryan stood up and followed me as I said, "Bye everyone, nice to meet you all."

The crowd called after me, "Bye! Nice to meet you. Come again soon."

I waved as I disappeared down the hall. Bryan walked me out to the car, kissed me good-bye, and disappeared back into the shop.

I picked up a few things at the store and went home. Normally, I would've picked Hunter up early, but that afternoon I needed time to myself to unwind.

I dozed off on the couch for almost two hours. The alarm on my phone woke me up. I rolled off the couch and went into our bedroom to change for class. I walked Nimbus and then went to pick Hunter up. As I walked into his Pre-school, Hunter saw me. He jumped up and ran over to his cubby and put on his jacket. Papers in his hand, he came running over to me. "I'm ready for class, Mommy."

"Let's get moving so we aren't late," I said.

We walked out and got settled in the car. As we pulled away, he sang, *"The wheels on the bus go round and round, round and round."* He abruptly stopped singing. "Hey Mommy, guess what?"

"What?"

"A boy named Hunter started at my school today! He's four too, but he's really tall."

"Wow. That's pretty cool, don't you think?"

"Yeah. Now everyone calls me 'Little Hunter.'"

My skin crawled. "'Little Hunter'?"

"Yep. They call me that now. 'Little Hunter.'"

I chose my words carefully. "Sweets, your name is Hunter. That's it. I don't want them calling you 'Little Hunter.'"

"Yeah. I don't like it but everyone just started calling me that."

"Your teachers, too?"

"Yep, everyone."

"Did you tell them not to call you that?"

"Yeah, but they did anyway."

"When they call you that, you say, 'My name is Hunter, not 'Little Hunter,'" I clenched my teeth as the words crossed my mouth. "And I'm going to tell them that I don't want you being called that, okay?"

"Okay, Mommy."

We pulled into the gymnasium parking lot as I fumed about educated professionals in the school system creating a demeaning nickname for my son. *'Little Hunter.' The nerve.*

As I began teaching, I was able to focus on my students. Class went smoothly as usual. As I wrapped up the night, I started thinking about my full time job. It was slowly starting to hinder my life. I really didn't want to stay there with how miserable everyone was being. But I knew I unfortunately didn't have too many options for a new job. Many places weren't hiring at the time; I'd done enough research along the way to know that.

I weighed my options in my head as Hunter and I closed the gym and drove home.

After bathing Hunter and getting him to bed, I sat down on the couch with Bryan. "How was the rest of your day?" I asked. "Any jobs come along?"

"Nope. Seems as if you made quite an impression; everyone raved about you."

"They seemed great, too." I recoiled into the couch. "I'm really not looking forward to work tomorrow," I sighed. "It's becoming a chore to go to work."

"Did you start looking for a new job?"

"Yeah, but nothing fits right now."

"As you always say, when God closes a door, he always opens a window. Maybe you need to leave in order to be able to find what you're looking for."

"Yeah, but I don't feel right not having a job lined up. I'm late enough on my bills to begin with."

"Well, now you have me to help. So don't stress over it."

"I know, but I'm also not going to make a rash decision immediately. I'd rather stick in there and see if things will change."

"Whatever you want, Babe. I just want you to be happy."

"I'm happy with my life, just not my job right now. We'll see what happens." I paused. "Oh, and listen to this shit."

His curious eyes met mine.

"There's a boy who just started in Hunter's class who's also named Hunter. They have now started referring to my Hunter as 'Little Hunter.'"

He stared at me with disgust. "'*Little* Hunter?'" He saw the look on my face. "You're going to take this up with them, right?"

"Oh, hells yes, I am. He's not little and calling a child little is demeaning to them. I'm not having it."

"Good. Give 'em hell."

"Oh, believe me, I will. I'm going to go to bed. I'm really tired," I said, getting up. I kissed him on the forehead. "Good night, Babe."

"Good night. I'll be up soon."

The next morning my alarm went off. I sat up in bed. Bryan had already left for work and Hunter was sitting at the bottom of my bed watching SpongeBob. I went into the kitchen and poured him a bowl of Cheerio's and some chocolate milk.

"I'm going to hop in the shower and get ready for work. Do you want me to dress you today, or do you want to do it yourself?" I asked.

"I'll do it myself," he answered.

"Okay, I'll be back in a few minutes." I couldn't wait to see the outfit he picked out for the day; they were always entertaining.

I quickly got ready as I called out to Hunter, "Did you brush your teeth?"

"No, Mommy. I'm getting dressed," he yelled from his room.

"Meet me in the bathroom as soon as you're done," I said.

A few minutes later, he skipped into the bathroom. "I'm ready." He jumped to a halt and stretched his arms wide, showing off his outfit.

I looked at him and smiled. He had on blue and tan plaid pants, a green and white striped shirt, and a black bow tie.

"Look at you! I love it," I giggled. "You're all sorts of mismatched colors and styles. Are you sure that's what you want to wear?"

He nodded, shoving his toothbrush in his mouth.

"If that's what you want to wear, then that's what you shall wear."

We finished getting ready for the day and headed out.

When we got to his school, I whispered to his teacher, "Miss Amy, can you let me know how the outfit works out? He dressed himself this morning."

She giggled. "I will. How cute is that?"

"He's a piece of work, that's for sure."

Miss Amy said to Hunter, "I love the bow-tie; it makes your outfit, Hunter."

He smiled as he adjusted it. "Thank you."

I kissed him good-bye. "Have a great day! See you later."

"Bye, Mommy. I love you," Hunter said as he joined the other kids.

I turned to his teacher and said, "Miss Amy?"

"Yes?"

"Hunter informed me that there's another Hunter who started here?"

"Yes, there is. He just started yesterday. As a matter of fact here he comes."

I looked as this really tall kid entered the pre-school. He was definitely tall for a four year old, but it still made no difference to my concerns. "He also told me that everyone has started to refer to him as 'Little Hunter.' I'd appreciate it if that could stop. He's not little."

She looked at me as if I had some nerve. "No problem. Have a great day."

"Thank you." I walked out of the school, wondering if she cared at all about my request. I sang along with the radio as I headed to work. I pulled into the parking lot and ran right over a newly formed pothole. My driver's side front tire deflated almost instantly. *What a way to begin my day.* I parked my Jeep and stared at my deflated tire. *At least I have my spare. Looks like I'll be changing my tire on my lunch break.*

I walked into the office and got organized for the day. I checked my messages and found that there was a complaint about an oven that was delivered to Milltown SteakHouse. I jotted down the information and pulled the file. I knew this was going to fall on my back. I called the manufacturer and confirmed the product numbers and information.

"Well, as far as I can tell, the invoices match up." I continued, "Let me call Christian and find out what's going on."

I called Christian, the owner of the steakhouse. "Hey, I hear we have a problem?" I said.

"The oven doesn't fit. It's too big!" he screamed, deafening my ear.

"What's the product number that you gave me?" I calmly asked him.

"Seven. Five. Four. Six," he spit back.

"Christian, that's the correct oven that's sitting in front of you. Are you sure the measurements are correct? Or maybe something isn't set in its place yet?"

"It's wrong, as usual." He paused. "I can't believe this. Why can't you guys get anything right? I'm always having issues with your company; I don't know why I bother."

"Again, I'm sure it's because the fryers aren't in place yet. Let me call the installer, Tom, and see what he says. In the meantime, please steer clear of the kitchen until I call you back." I hung up before he could say anything else.

I knew I was in no mood to get into a back and forth disagreement with him; I was liable to say the wrong thing today. I got our installer on the phone. "Tom? What's going on at Milltown Steakhouse?"

"I'm pulling in right now. I just have to finish installing the fryers and the oven."

"Well, I just got off the phone with Christian and he's saying the oven doesn't fit."

292

"It doesn't right now. I'm not done putting the fryers in place."

"That's what I told him, but he's having a cow. So be prepared when you see him. I asked him to steer clear of the kitchen."

Tom chuckled, "Good. That guy has no idea what's going on, but he thinks he knows it all."

"Typical. Do you want me to call him back, or do you wanna handle this one?"

"I got it. Don't worry about it."

"Well, call me if you need me," I said.

I hung up. *Problem deflected.*

I sent Bryan a text: *I handled the issue at the preschool, and then got a flat tire. A know-it-all owner first thing in the morning. Great day so far.*

I took an early lunch; I just wanted to get "the changing of the tire" over with. I struggled loosening the lug nuts, so I bounced up and down on the tire iron to loosen the tire. I jacked up my Jeep, pulled the spare off the back, and set the new tire on the bolts. Then I screwed on the lug nuts on as tight as I could with the tire iron and removed the jack. After realigning the tire iron so it was flat, I stood on the tire iron and bounced on it, hoping my weight was enough to tighten it.

Just as I finished tightening the bolts, Bryan and Mike pulled up it their work van. Bryan looked at me and shook his head, saying, "I was right."

"Did you come to rescue me?" I asked.

"Yep. But as usual, I'm too late."

"You're so sweet." I kissed him. "Thanks for coming. Next time I'll wait."

Mike called from inside the van. "You were right, Bryan. She did it herself. You feel like a man, now?"

Bryan rolled his eyes. "I told him I knew I'd be too late to help cause you do everything yourself."

I thought for a minute. "Isn't that a good thing?"

"Sometimes it just feels nice to be needed. That's all." He kissed my forehead. "Have a good day, Babe." He climbed back in his work van and I stood there feeling guilty for being able to change a tire.

I watched him drive away. He didn't even look as he passed by me. I couldn't believe it.

I wasn't used to having someone's help. It was still weird for me to have someone around to do things for me. I'd become so dependent on myself, I didn't realize I made him feel unneeded sometimes.

I called him.

"Hey, Babe," he answered.

I was relieved by the tone of his voice. "Thanks for coming to help me. I'm not used to having someone to rely on, so it's nice to know that you're here for me. I'm not used to it, but I'm grateful for it."

"We've been together for almost a year. When are you going to get used to it?"

I didn't answer.

"I'm sorry," he said. "I just want you to know that I'm here when you need me."

"Okay. Thanks for coming to my rescue and I love you for it."

"Love you, too. Bye," he said before hanging up.

I cleaned up the tools and noticed my hand prints in the dust on my Jeep. "You need a bath," I mumbled, swiping my hand in the dirt.

I cleaned myself up in the bathroom and then inhaled an apple as I sat down at my desk. I filed the orders I took, made a few phone calls confirming purchase orders, and ended my day. I locked up the office and began my evening.

I wanted to get a car wash before picking up Hunter. I also realized that my tires needed air as I kicked them. I got in and drove over to the Auto-Wash. I filled up the tires and sent my Jeep through the automatic wash. I watched from inside the building as it got pulled through the giant spinning sponges and pushed out the other end. I hopped into my glistening Jeep and headed towards Hunter's pre-school.

I sat at the traffic light noticing all of the hawks flying around in the sky. They swarmed as if they were hunting. The light turned green and the birds started diving towards the ground. I put the engine in neutral and revved it, trying to scare them away. I watched in the rear view mirror as the birds scattered behind me. I shifted the transmission back into second gear and watched the road in front of me. A hawk dove right towards me, clutching a squirrel in its claws. "Bam!" I jumped as it smashed the squirrel into the windshield and splattered blood all over the glass. I slammed on my brakes as my heart jumped in my chest. I slowly pulled off the road, barely able to see where I was going while the squirrel's blood and guts oozed down my windshield. I turned on my hazard lights and sat there stunned and gagging. I sprayed the washer fluid as the wipers smeared the blood across the windshield.

A hawk just smashed its prey across my windshield. I gagged again from the sight of it. *Thank God that's something you don't see too often.*

After rinsing most of the blood off the windshield, I drove back to the Auto-Wash. I sent it through the automatic car wash again.

I watched from inside the building again as the squirrel blood washed away from the Jeep. *Thank god I didn't have the top down or I would've been covered in blood.* I gagged as the thought spun in my mind.

The attendant walked over to me. "Thanks for coming back so soon. What'd you hit?"

"A hawk dove down and smashed his dinner into my windshield." I dry heaved as the words rolled off my tongue. "So gross," I shuttered.

"That's one you don't see every day," he huffed.

"I hear that," I mumbled.

"She's clean again. Come on." He waved for me to follow him.

I followed him out of the door and watched as the guys dry it again. I folded a five and dropped it in their tip bucket. "Thanks again, guys. Much appreciated."

"No more surprises, please," I said to myself. "Let's just get Hunter and go home."

I drove on the back roads to Hunter's school, avoiding the massacre scene.

I quickly walked into the daycare and got his things in order. I really didn't want to talk to anyone; I just wanted to get home. I almost felt cursed to be on the road. A flat tire and a murdered squirrel in one day.

"Home sweet home, and no more problems," I thought as I pulled into my driveway, collected my things, and shut the door. I heard an argument behind me towards the end of the cul-de-sac. I tried to see what was going on as I peered down the row of cars. I helped Hunter out of the Jeep and locked it up. When we stepped up on the sidewalk, the arguing got louder and louder. I saw two ice cream trucks parked at the other end of the parking lot. It appeared the drivers were having a standoff in between their trucks. By this point they were screaming at the top of their lungs.

I watched as the Ice Cream Man screamed, "This is my territory. Follow your own route."

The Mr. Softee guy giggled and shook his head as he climbed back inside his truck. "I'll go where I want."

I stared in astonishment; they were fighting about their territories. *There's something else, that you don't see every day.*

Nimbus was barking profusely, so we hurried inside. Hunter ran right upstairs to play in his room. I put down everything that was in my hands and opened the back door for Nimbus. I checked my phone and saw I had three missed calls from my boss.

I kicked off my shoes, changed into my favorite velour pants and went outback and sat in my lounge chair as I called my boss back.

"Hi, Mr. Nelson. What can I do for you?"

"I had another complaint about you today, Laurel, from Christian Miller."

My jaw tightened. "Really? What's his complaint this time?"

"He said that you completely disrespected him and told him to stay the fuck out of the kitchen.

And that *you* didn't help him solve his problem today, but *Tom* did."

I took a deep breath. "He left a message this morning. After I called the manufacturer and confirmed that the proper oven was delivered, I called Christian and he explained to me the problem. I told him that I was going to call Tom, the installer, to find out how far along he was in the kitchen. When I talked to Tom, he told me the kitchen wasn't set in place yet and he would talk to Christian because he was just getting there." I paused. "All I said was for him to please steer clear of the kitchen. I did my job and didn't curse, nor was I disrespectful."

"Well, I've been getting a lot of complaints about you. From what I understand, you're getting very short with the customers and it's affecting your job situation."

"It's affecting my job situation? What does that mean?"

"I'm afraid I'm going to have to let you go, Laurel. I tried to make it back to the office before you left, but I got stuck in traffic. I can't have you on staff if you're being ignorant to the customers."

My jaw hit the ground. "You're firing me?"

"I am. I've had too many complaints. I'm sorry. You can come clear out your desk on Monday." He hung up the phone.

I sat there stunned. I shifted in my seat and tried to understand what just happened.

I sat there, in silence, until there was a knock on the door. I jumped up, calling, "Hunter, your dad's here." Almost grateful that Hunter was going to his dads, I pulled open the door. "Come in. I didn't pack him a bag yet; I'll be right back." I skipped up the steps.

Hunter helped me put clothes in his bag for the weekend. "Have a good weekend, honey," I said.

"Bye, Mommy." He kissed my cheek.

I shut the door behind me, spun on my heels, and froze in thought. *What am I going to do? I just lost my job.* I looked around my house.

I stared at the pictures of Hunter that hung on the walls and the pictures of the three of us decorating the fireplace mantle. I felt absent.

Where am I supposed to go with my life now?

I flopped on my couch, listening to the silence. Tears trickled down my cheeks; I felt robbed and cheated. I couldn't believe he fired me.

I thought of my Grandmother and I heard her voice say, "This, too, shall pass.'

"I know," I said out loud and nodded. "I know." I drew a long, deep breath and exhaled. I laid back and closed my eyes, trying to distance myself from the absurdity of my day.

I heard the door shut and jumped out of the daydream in which I was saying, right to his face, "Fuck you, Mr. Nelson."

Bryan stood there and looked at me. "So, how was your day?"

I sat up and remembered my present life. "Ridiculum," I mumbled. "And horrible."

"Want to tell me about it?"

I went into the kitchen and cracked open a beer. Bryan stood in the doorway of the kitchen, staring at me. "That bad?"

I nodded as I swallowed a sip. I gained my composure so I could tell the story of my day. "Well, I talked to Amy at the pre-school; I think she understood but we'll see. Then I got the flat tire. Then dealt with the know-it-all restaurant owner." I sipped more beer and set it on the counter next to me.

He nodded.

"After I left work, I decided to put air in my tires and wash my Jeep, so I did that. As I left the car wash and drove down the road there were hawks swooping everywhere. One was carrying a squirrel and smacked it onto my windshield, squirting squirrel blood all over my freshly washed car."

He started cracking up.

I shifted my weight into my right hip, flopped my hands to my sides and joined in with the giggling. "Right? But wait. It gets better."

301

Bent over grabbing his stomach, he stuttered, "There's more?"

I aggressively nodded. "Oh, there's more. So I turned around and went back to the car wash and sent it through the car wash, again."

He started giggling in anticipation of the next occurrence.

"Then, I took the long way to pick up Hunter and then came home. I get out of the car and the Ice Cream Man and the Mr. Softee guy were screaming at each other at the other end of the parking lot, fighting about territories."

He burst into laughter again. "You're getting it from all sides today aren't you?"

"Right? But wait; it gets even better." I put my hands on my hips and breathed a deep breath.

He had to force himself to stop laughing. "Okay, I'm ready."

"So, I realize in the chaos of all this 'ridiculum' I missed a few calls from my boss. Soooo, I called him back." I stopped the story there and looked at him and started giggling.

"Well?"

"He fired me."

We both stood there staring at each other. Slowly his jaw dropped to the floor as he absorbed the information. "He fired you?"

I nodded as I smiled and shrugged my shoulders. I took a sip of my beer, never removing my eyes from his.

"Well, I was expecting a funny ending. But that's not funny."

"Right?" I squinted as I nodded.

"I can't believe that."

"Neither can I."

Chapter 19

New Job

On Tuesday, Bryan called me from the job site. "Hey Babe. What're you doing?" he asked.

"Putting the box of stuff from my office desk in the hall closet so I don't have to be reminded that I have no job."

"Out of sight, out of mind."

"Something like that. I guess I'm still in denial."

"I'm headed back to the shop. Do you want to stop by and say hello to me?"

"Sure, I've got nothing else to do before class. How far away are you?"

"Give me about a half an hour so I can get my paperwork done."

"Okay, see you then." I hung up the phone.

Trying to accept the fact that I had no job, I paced around the living room. I knew the one person that would make me feel better was my mom. I hadn't told anyone yet.

I called her up. "Hey, Mom."

"How are you?"

"I'm okay, but not really."

"What's going on?" she asked.

"I lost my job. They said I was getting too ignorant with the customers, which is bullshit."

"I'm sorry to hear that. What are you going to do?"

"I have no idea. But I know I need to accept it and move past it."

"Yeah, well. God doesn't close a door without opening a window," she assured.

"I know. Well, I'm going to meet Bryan at his work. I'll call you later."

"No worries, Laurel."

"Alright, bye."

I pulled my shoes on and grabbed my keys. Nimbus danced at the door, hoping to go for a ride.

"Ah, why not?" I opened the closet door to grab his harness and leash and there sat the box of stuff from my desk. It sat there, laughing at me in my face. I slammed the door shut and huffed. Nimbus stood still as I put on his harness. I shut the door behind me, buckled Nimbus into his seat, and hopped in the Jeep.

As we drove, Nimbus rode with his head out of the window and drooled. Singing along to the radio, I drove into town. Nimbus barked at the dogs that were being walked through town. When I got to the office, I parked right in front of the office door. I fed Nimbus a treat and said, "Wait here."

I called Bryan. "Hey Babe, I'm out front."

"We're in the boardroom. C'mon in."

I went inside the building, knocked on the door to the boardroom, and cracked it open. Bryan was sitting at the board table with the same group of guys from the other day. "Hi everybody."

I received a chorus of: "Hi, Laurel."

I sat down next to Bryan. "How's everybody doing?" I asked.

Mike said, "Ridiculum."

We burst into laughter. "Did Bryan fill you in on my recent ridiculum?" I asked, giggling.

Joe said, "Oh, we heard. That's some bad luck."

"I often say if it weren't for bad luck, I'd have no luck at all," I said.

Mike asked, "Did your car really get covered in squirrel blood?"

"Sadly, yes it did." I dry heaved recalling the massacre. "Right after I pulled out of the car wash, too. Go figure, right?"

"Murphy's Law," one of them said.

"That's crazy. I've never heard of such a thing," Mike said.

"Me either." I paused. "Did he tell you about the ice cream truckers fighting? That was ridiculum too. And then I got fired over the phone."

"Wow, that's just bad luck," Mike said. "I've never seen or heard of anything like it."

I stared at Mike, realizing that a few versions of that statement had been said to me about six times now: *I've never seen anything like it.*

I was starting to believe that the more people said that to me, the worse things were going to get. Maybe I should stop telling people about these things, and that'll make this series of events stop.

"Let's not talk about it anymore; it gives me the willies," I said, shaking my body. *Get rid of the bad karma. Shake it off.*

My eyes watered as I resisted another dry heave. The thought of the squirrel incident grossed me out.

I lounged in my chair, making small talk with Bryan and trying to avoid thinking about it.

"I have to go get Hunter. I'll see you after class?"

"Sounds good to me. Have fun."

"I always do," I said.

I quickly dropped Nimbus off at the house, then drove to pick Hunter up and went to the gym. My Tuesday night classes were more advanced, so Hunter just watched from the playroom instead of joining in. My mind twisted and turned over why I got fired. *What am I going to do now? Where do I go from here? School? Another job? What do I do?'*

As I did a total review of my life and my future, the head coach sensed that I was upset. "What's going on? Are you okay?" he asked.

"I'm fine. Why?"

"You've been sulking more than ever."

Nodding, I agreed, "Yeah, I guess I have been. I got fired from my job. My boss said I was being ignorant to the customers."

"Pfft, I doubt that. You're great with the kids here and that shows a lot of character. If you can handle dealing with kids, well, you can handle adults. Something else will come along. I'll ask around to see if I know anyone looking for someone."

"Thanks, I'd appreciate that. I've been trying to figure out why this is happening to me, but I can't seem to put my finger on it."

"Don't try to figure it out." He put his hands on my shoulders. "You'll end up driving yourself crazy. Just except it for what it is and move forward."

"Ok, I will. Thanks for the chat."

"See you Thursday, with a smile on that face."

"Have a good night." I walked out of the gym, put my shoes on, and headed home.

I knew Coach was right, but it didn't stop me from worrying; I had a child to feed.

I drove home in silence. I listened to Hunter singing in the background. I felt like my life was in shambles and I just kept shaking my head in denial. I finally decided that Coach was right: *Accept it and move on.*

That night, I tucked Hunter in, and we said our prayers:

Now I lay me down to sleep,
I pray the Lord, my soul to keep,
If I die, before I wake,
I pray the Lord, my soul to take.
God bless Hunter and Mommy, Grandmom, Danpop,
Aunt Sarah, Uncle Lance, Aunt Hillary.
God Bless Daddy, Gina, and Gianna, and Angel.
God Bless Bryan, and all of our family and friends.
Amen.

I kissed him on his forehead. "I love you."

I began feeling a bit more relaxed and accepting of the fact that I was fired. I began looking forward to the next chapter of my life. I couldn't change it, so I moved on.

I lay in bed, staring at the ceiling tiles. My head had re-wrapped itself around the thought of having no job. The situation was totally out of my control, but I really hoped for more of an explanation. I reviewed the years that I had worked there and my "incidents" were very few. I figured he had some underlying reason to fire me and just used this issue as an excuse. I closed my eyes and stopped my brain from spinning.

The next morning I decided to keep Hunter home from school and spent the day with him. We stayed in our pajamas all morning and watched movies.

My phone rang, but I didn't recognize the number. "Hello?"

"Hi, Laurel. This is Paul, Bryan's boss."

"Hello, Paul. How are you?"

"I'm great. Thanks for asking."

"What can I do for you? Is everything okay?"

"I was hoping that you would come in to interview for our office position."

"Really?"

"I think you would be a great addition to our office. So does my staff."

"I'd love to." I hesitated, "Does Bryan know that you're asking me to interview?"

"Yes, he does. We've been discussing it over the last few days."

"Well, that's great then. When would you like me to come in?"

"Any chance you could come in today?" he asked.

"I'd love to but I kept my son home from school and I can't drop him off now."

"Why don't you bring him? I'd love to meet him."

"Are you sure? I wouldn't want to be distracted during the interview."

"That's not a problem at all. The ladies will be thrilled to entertain him, I'm sure."

"Well, as long as you say its fine, I'll bring him. What time would you like me to be there?"

"Let's say 1:00. I have a tee time at 2:30."

"1:00 it is. I'll see you then," I said.

"Alright, bye."

"Bye." I hung up the phone and immediately called Bryan.

"Hellooooo?" he answered.

"Hi. How's your day?"

"Excellent. Yours?"

"I just got a call from Paul."

"Good. I was wondering when he was going to call you."

"Would you really be okay with me working there, too?"

"Well, we figured I'm mostly on the road and you'll be in the office, so it's not like we'll be around each other all day. And as long as we don't bring our personal life into work it'll be a good situation for all of us," he explained.

"Well, we pretty much don't fight. So that's not an issue."

"That's what I said, too. I know you're good at what you do and honestly, we need someone reliable in the office. Our orders and services are a mess right now. We need the help and you need a job, so why not solve all the problems at once?"

"Okay, I was just checking. I'll talk to you later."

"Love you, and good luck."

"Thanks, Babe. Love you, too." I hung up and jumped for joy. "Hunter, we need to get ready. I have a job interview."

"Yeah, Mommy!"

We quickly got ready and rode to the office.

"Please be on your best behavior, Spark," I said, pulling into the parking lot. "This is very important for me."

"I will, Mommy." He pointed his pinky finger at me. "I pinky swear." I wrapped my pinky around his as he jumped out of his car seat into my arms. "Good luck!" He kissed my cheek.

"Thank you."

We walked into the office. Paul and Mike stood there waiting for me. "Hello," I said with a huge smile.

In unison they said, "Hi, Laurel."

Hunter bellowed from below. "Hi, I'm Hunter."

"Hello, Hunter. I'm Paul and this is Mike."

"Hi! You're the boss?" Hunter asked Paul.

"Yes, I am."

"You want to hire my mommy?"

"Yes, I do."

"She got fired and she's been sad," Hunter said.

"I'm sorry to hear that, but I'm also glad to hear it. We need an office manager and I hear your mommy's pretty good at it."

"My mom's the best." He grabbed my hand and swung it back and forth. "She taught me how to do a forward roll. Do you want to see it?"

Mike said, "I know I wanna see it."

"Me too," Paul said.

Without hesitation, Hunter did a forward roll and stood to his feet. "Tada!"

They clapped and cheered. "Way to go."

"What else can you do?" Paul asked.

"I can do a handstand, too. Wanna see?"

"Absolutely."

Hunter braced his hands on the ground and kicked his feet up above his head, leaning to the left. He dropped his feet down to the ground, and kicked them up into the air again and again.

Bryan came around the corner and watched as Hunter performed.

"Wow! What a great job. I'm so impressed," Paul said.

"Me too," Mike said as he clapped. "I can't even do that."

Hunter said, "That's 'cause you're old."

We all burst into laughter. Hunter turned and saw Bryan standing there. "Bryan!" He jumped up into his arms. Bryan tossed him over his head and said, "I saw your handstands. Good job, Spark."

"Thanks, are you gonna do one, too?" Hunter asked, and then looked at Paul and Mike. "Bryan can do one, too. We have contests."

Paul said, "I definitely need to see that."

Bryan shrugged his shoulders, set Hunter down and did a handstand. The change in his pocket came tumbling down to the floor. Hunter crawled around and collected the change, saying, "Money, money, money."

We all laughed as Hunter shoved the change in his pocket and jumped around in circles.

"Why don't you come with me while Paul talks to Mommy? I'll show ya the machines in the warehouse," said Bryan.

Hunter's eyes lit up. "Cool." They disappeared down the hallway as Hunter called over Bryan's shoulder, "Good luck, Mommy."

"Thank you."

Paul said, "C'mon we'll talk in my office."

As I followed him down the hallway, he said, "What a great kid you have. How old is he?"

I smiled. "Thank you. He's four."

"He's so full of life and speaks so clearly."

"He's a great kid. I'm blessed."

Paul sat in his large executive leather chair behind his incredibly immaculate desk. "Well, I'm happy to say that the job is yours if you want it. As far as I'm concerned, all we need to discuss is your salary."

My eyes lit up. "That's fantastic. I've been so worried."

"No need to worry anymore. What were you making at your last job?"

"Eleven fifty an hour," I said.

"Really? How many people worked in the office?"

"There were about eight employees, but we out sourced a lot of our jobs. I handled scheduling the installations for them too."

"Well, we've got almost forty employees that you'll be handling. Most calls are for the sales reps and the rental division."

"Alright, that's easy enough."

"I'm going to start you at sixteen an hour plus benefits."

I tried to speak without showing too much of my excitement. "That's great! Thank you."

"I believe in taking care of my employees. I always say, 'a happy employee makes a happy client and a happy client keeps this ship sailing.' I work closely with my staff and clients, so I know if things aren't sailing smoothly on my ship."

"I'm very happy to hear that. It's a rare find in an owner."

"I know. I've worked for many assholes in my days, also."

I chuckled, "Me too."

"When can you start?"

"Well, there's no need for me to give any two weeks' notice, so as soon as I can."

"Do you want to start Monday or would you like to start tomorrow? We could really use your help as soon as possible."

"I'd love to start tomorrow. I feel useless being at home."

"Perfect. Welcome to Audio Visual Communications. I'm looking forward to having you on board."

"I'm very thankful to be on board."

"I think this will work out wonderfully," he said.

"So do I."

"I'll have Jane prepare the paperwork and she'll show you the ropes tomorrow. She'll be ecstatic to have the help. She runs our accounting division but has been carrying a lot of the weight since Stephanie left."

"Why'd she leave, if I may ask?"

He shrugged his shoulders. "We have no idea. She just simply stopped showing up for work and won't return any of our calls. I can't wait any longer to fill the position and everyone I interviewed didn't seem to fit the role that we needed. Then Bryan came to me about hiring you. I was thrilled at the idea."

"Bryan came to you about this?"

"Yes, he did. I couldn't believe that I didn't think of it myself. You're a perfect fit here."

"That's good to know. Our relationship isn't an issue for you?" I asked.

"Not in the least, actually. I think it'll be fine. I have a married couple that works here and they work side by side. The fact that Bryan's mainly on the road also adds stability to the situation. You two seem to get along incredibly well and he adores your son."

I smiled, "Those two are a hoot together."

"Well, I'm looking forward to having you around here. I think it'll be great."

"Thank you. I do, too."

"Let me show you around a bit and we'll find Bryan and Hunter."

I followed Paul back down the hallway and he introduced me to a few of the sales reps along the

318

way. "This is Laurel, Bryan's girlfriend. She's our new office manager. She's starting tomorrow."

"Nice to meet you, Laurel. Welcome aboard. We need the help," they said.

"Thank you. I'll do my best."

We walked into the board room and through the door into the warehouse. I heard Hunter in the distance. "Vroom! Vroom! honk, honk!" We followed the noises around the ceiling-high shelves. Bryan was standing next to a forklift and Hunter was turning the steering wheel and bouncing around on the seat like he was driving down a rocky road.

"There's Mommy," Bryan said looking over his shoulder. "How was your interview?"

"Very good. I start tomorrow."

"Good. I'm glad to have you here." He shot me a wink.

"Thank you for the recommendation." I winked back.

"Yeah, Mommy! Are you happy again?"

"Yes I am, Spark."

"Do you want to drive the fork lift, Mommy?" he asked, standing up on the seat.

"No, I don't want to get all dirty."

"Yeah, you don't want to get your pretty clothes dirty like mine." He stretched his shirt out and frowned. "Look at my mess."

I lifted him down from the forklift. "It's okay. Your clothes are washable."

Hunter skipped around as we walked back into the board room. "Do you want to go get some ice cream?" I asked.

"*Ice cream,*" he sang. "*It's a treat for you today.*"

I giggled as Bryan squatted next to Hunter and handed him a ten dollar bill. "Today, you treat Mommy to ice cream, okay?"

His eyes lit up as he grabbed the money from Bryan and shoved it in his pocket. "It's Mommy's special day."

"It sure is." Bryan peered up at me. "She's got a new job and her beautiful smile is back."

Hunter said, "Mommy loves to smile."

Bryan nodded. "We love to see Mommy smile."

I listened to the conversation they were having about me and I felt as radiant as the sun. I loved watching them interact. I could do it all day, every day, for the rest of my life.

Under his breath, I heard Paul say, "That's so cute."

I felt like the luckiest person on the face of the planet. I knew, at this moment in time, I had it all. My heart overflowed with love. There was no better feeling in the world that existed. I felt my blood flowing gracefully through my veins as my heart danced with pride. My lungs filled up with a quiver, my eyes locked on my son and the love of my life.

The next day, I started my new job. It felt like home from the moment I stepped into the office. The entire staff was welcoming and appreciative. While Jane was training me, she said, "We're all so glad you came aboard. We've been looking for the right person even before Stephanie was hired. None of us thought she would last long. We all have our sights set on you doing well here."

"Wow, thank you. That means a lot. Especially since I came from a place where every little mistake was blamed on me."

"Well, you won't have that problem here. Before we even move on a job, we make sure everything's in place."

"Preparation. I love it," I joked.

"Bryan's also excited that you're here. He knows you're good at your job. Not to mention, he's our top installer here and his opinion's respected," said Jane.

"He's great at what he does, that's for sure," I agreed.

As the days passed, I settled into my new position rather quickly. I'd been an office manager for years, so all I really needed to do was get used to the way they ran the office here. That was easy.

Chapter 20

Unit

Over the next few months, Bryan's and my work relationship proved to be flawless. Bryan was out on the road consistently and I ran the front office. Our coworkers were impressed with our relationship and often commented on our solidity as a couple. We somehow became closer to each other as a professional couple at work, and as a family unit at home. The three of us were inseparable. The mutual admiration between Hunter and Bryan was undeniable. They'd build forts in his bedroom for hours upon hours. They'd read books, play cars, and act like superheroes.

"Are you gonna marry my mommy and have babies?" Hunter asked him one day.

"Well, we've talked about getting married. I just want to make sure I make a lot of money first so I can take care of you and your mommy." He paused. "Do you want a little brother or sister?"

Hunter nodded. "I want a brother. I already have two sisters."

"I know you do. I bet having a little brother would be nice."

"I wanna teach him lots of cool stuff, like what you taught me," Hunter said.

Bryan smiled. "What cool stuff did I teach you?"

"Like how to tie my cape better so it doesn't fall off and how to build bigger buildings with my legos and taller ramps for my cars."

Bryan smiled.

"And you help me make the best forts."

"We do make some cool forts. Your bunk beds make it easy." He paused. "Do you think your mommy wants more babies?"

Hunter nodded intently. "She does. She told me."

"When did she tell you that?"

"When I asked her if she wanted to marry you."

Bryan's eyes widened. "Well, what'd she say?"

"She said she does."

"Well, that's a relief."

"Are you gonna buy her a ring soon?"

Bryan nodded as he put his finger up to his lips. "Shhhhh. Don't tell her but I've already started looking for rings."

"Yeah! You're gonna be my other Daddy?"

Bryan hugged him and kissed his cheek. "That's right! I can't wait."

"Me either." Hunter crawled around the fort, pushing his cars around.

"Time for bed, Buddy. We need to clean up."

"Can we leave the fort up tonight?"

"I don't see why not, but let's double check with Mommy."

Hunter came downstairs. "Mommy, can I leave the fort up tonight?"

I lay my book down next to me on the couch, "No problem. You ready for bed?"

"Yeah, I'm tired."

"Me too. I'm gonna have an early night tonight."

Bryan appeared halfway down the steps. "He can leave the fort up?"

"Yep, as long as you go right to sleep and don't play in it," I said to Hunter as we walked up to his room.

"Okay, Mommy." He jumped into his bottom

bunk and Nimbus curled up at the bottom of his bed.

We said our prayers and then Bryan and I kissed him good night.

"Sweet dreams," I said.

We quietly went back downstairs. Bryan said, "He asked me if we're going to get married and have babies."

"Really? What'd you say?"

"I told him yes."

"I'm so glad we found each other; I thought I was going to be single forever," I said.

"No way. I'm going to make you mine." He hugged me. "You've made my life perfect. Now all I need is for this show to happen and then we'll have it all. Two weeks until the final meeting. Then we'll know."

Chapter 21

The beginning of the end...

My cell phone began to ring, "Hello?"

"Hi, Babe. Guess what!" Bryan said.

"I miss you. How are you?"

"I'm unbelievably great. Guess what just happened!"

"What? What?"

"Spam just signed the papers for the show. Isn't that awesome?"

"I don't know what to say. That's amazing!"

He said, "I know. I can't believe it. It's like, overnight we're gonna be rich and famous. We're on our way."

"Tell everyone I said 'congratulations.'"

"Well, they're keeping it quiet for now. I'm not even supposed to tell you, but fuck that, Babe. I'm going to be on *TV*."

"I'm so proud of you. I love you," I said.

"I love you, my soon-to-be bride."

"Ahh, I love when you say that."

"I love saying that. Bye, Babe."

"Bye, Sweets."

Happy and bewildered, I hung up the phone. I stood in the middle of the living room. *This is happening.* A surreal sensation over took me. My chest began to quiver with joy as the reality set in. I sat down on the couch. "Holy shit! He's going to be famous!" I said aloud.

I jumped up and spread my arms out like an eagle soaring and spun around the living room. I jumped up on the couch, bounced on the cushions, and plopped face first laughing loudly in to the throw pillow.

The phone rang. I froze and contained my excitement before I answered. "Hello?"

It was Bryan again. "I love you, Mrs. Cease."

"I love you, Mr. Cease."

"I gotta go. Bye." Click.

I inhaled a deep breath. *In through your nose, and out through your mouth.* The excitement burst from inside me as I did a crazy dance across the room. I couldn't wait to see him. I missed him so much because he'd been in New York for the past few days for work. But he was coming home the next day and my excitement was jumping through my skin.

I could barely contain myself at work on Friday. As my day zipped by, I called him in the late afternoon to confirm our evening plans.

"Hello?" he answered.

"Hi, Baby."

"Hey, beautiful. We're almost finished loading up the truck and then we'll be on our way."

"Yeah!" I clenched my fist with excitement. "We goin' out to celebrate tonight? I was thinking we'd go to Giovanni's."

"My favorite place."

"We're celebrating your success, so we should go to your favorite restaurant."

"That's why I love you. You're so sweet," he said. "I'll call you after I get back to the shop to unload so be ready. I'll need to take a quick shower and then we'll go."

"Alright. Talk to you then. Drive carefully and tell Kevin I said hi."

"Will do." Click.

After work, I picked Hunter up from daycare and went straight home. I straightened up the kitchen and living room and I found anything I could do to keep myself busy until Greg arrived to pick Hunter up for the weekend.

As soon as Hunter left, I jumped in the shower. I did my hair and makeup quickly and dressed in Bryan's favorite outfit of mine: my tight black top that hung off one shoulder and a pair of tight blue jeans with my knee high boots. I couldn't wait to see him. I skipped through the house, singing as I went.

I checked the time: 5:45. He'd be there in about fifteen minutes or so. I sat down to watch TV.

Around 7:30 I started to worry. I hadn't heard from him, so I gave him a call.

"Hey Laurel, what's up?"

"What time do you think you'll be home? I'm ready and waiting."

"Me and Kevin met up with a couple of the guys from work for a drink. I'll be on my way soon."

"Okay. I'm getting hungry, so hurry."

"I'll be on my way in a few minutes."

"Okay."

I cracked open a beer and relaxed.

Six beers and three hours later, I went upstairs and changed. I ordered a pizza and called Karen. She immediately knew something was wrong from my voice.

"What's going on? What happened?"

I filled her in.

"That's very out of character for him," she said. "You two are glued at the hip. It's like you're conjoined twins."

"I know. He disappeared on me. He's never done anything like this before." I thought for a second. "Maybe I'm reading too much into it. He deserves a night out, but why didn't he just call me and tell me? He's never left me hanging like this."

"I'd be a hell of a lot more pissed off than you are, that's for damn sure. I think if anything, you're *under*reacting."

"Well, I'm not his keeper. I'm just his girlfriend."

"My ass, just his girlfriend. You two are the couple of the century. When I find a man, I want our relationship to be like what you two have."

"Well, thanks. But right now I don't feel like we're a couple at all. I mean, he's at happy hour with people from work. Um, *we* work together. Why didn't he invite me to come and meet up with everyone?"

"I don't know. Is it just the guys?"

"I don't know. I didn't ask for details when I talked to him. It was short and sweet."

Ding dong.

"I gotta go. My pizza's here. I'm so fucking upset right now. I'll call you later."

After I ate, I cried. Midnight came and went and I still hadn't heard from him.

I called him again...and again. No answer.

I got in the shower hoping to freshen up but all I did was cry some more. 12:30 rolled around and left without a trace of him. As I got out of the shower I was finally able to contain my emotions. He still wasn't home. I went upstairs, curled up in bed, and fell asleep.

At 3:36 in the morning he came stumbling into our bedroom, drunk as shit. I jumped awake as he tripped over everything and nothing. He fell onto the bed, passed out, and started snoring.

I lay there staring at the ceiling tiles. I don't think he realized he woke me up. If he did, he didn't care. I tried to fall back asleep but his snoring got louder and more frequent.

Annoyed, I got up and went down stairs. I curled up on the couch with Nimbus and cried myself back to sleep.

The next morning he woke me. "Good morning, my love. I'm so sorry about last night. I got so caught up in the atmosphere. I ran into so many people who, by the way, were very shocked that you weren't with me. I told them I was supposed to be out for dinner with you and that I was going to be in so much trouble."

"Why didn't you call me? I was so upset and so worried."

"Babe, I'm so sorry. I'm going to make it up to you."

"Please don't do that again. I felt like I didn't mean anything to you. One phone call, that's all it takes. I want you to spend time with your friends, but please don't leave me in the dark. I don't like being in the dark when it comes to us."

"I know. I'm sorry"

"Well, did you have fun?"

"We had a blast. Time flew and I got really drunk really quick. And that was the beginning of my fuck-up with you. I didn't eat dinner, so it hit fast."

"And then...you drove home," I added.

"I know. I was so terrified on the way home; I was all over the road. I won't ever do that again."

"Please don't. I don't want to lose you."

"You are never going to lose me," he promised.

"Let's go out to breakfast and then we'll come home and have a 'Naked Saturday.' How's that sound?"

"That sounds perfect."

He helped me to my feet. "You look beautiful when you wake up. I love that about you." He grazed his hand across my face and into my hair, leaned in, and kissed me.

I wondered if my face showed that I'd been crying all night. The concern quickly left my mind as we kissed.

"Your dragon breath is sexy too," he teased. We burst into laughter as he pulled me towards the bathroom.

"We both need a little help in that department," I replied.

We brushed our teeth and snuck a couple of toothpaste-flavored kisses. "Much better," we agreed.

I needed a shower in the worst way. He followed me in and we started soaping our bodies. I noticed that he was standing very still. "You alright over there?"

He giggled, "I'm marking my territory."

I turned towards him. "Are you peeing on me?"

He started cracking up. "I figure if I start peeing on you, I won't have to worry about you leaving me for some other guy because my scent will keep them away."

"Well, in that case," I turned and started peeing on him. "I need to keep those bitches away from you, Mr. I'm-going-to-be-Rich-and-Famous."

We both grabbed our stomachs as we laughed. I rested my head against the shower wall. "S-stop. My abs h-hurt."

"Mine t-too," he forced out between howls.

I handed him my loofa puff sponge. "Clean up your mess."

Giggling under his breath, he scrubbed the back of my thigh. He obnoxiously imitated my singing in a girly, high-pitched voice:

"Ev-reybody, ye-aah,
Wash yer body, yeeaaa-aaaah."

I grabbed the loofa back, vigorously cleaning my calf. "Pee runs downhill. Gotta get rid of your scent."

He grabbed the soap and started re-washing his legs, still singing:

"Ev-reybody, ye-aah,
Wash yer body right."

We fed off of each other's giggling; the more he chuckled, the more I did. We would break for a second and then I'd burst into laughter and he joined right in. I did a final rinse, kissed him, and hopped out. We dried off and quickly got dressed.

"Wanna take the Jeep?" I asked.

"Hells yeah. It's gorgeous outside."

I tossed him the keys as we walked out the door and headed to The Station Diner.

He grabbed my hand as we crossed the parking lot and opened the door for me.

When we got there, he asked the hostess, "Can we have a booth in the corner, please?"

She nodded and led us to a booth in the corner near the front glass window.

"Perfect," he said.

"Andie will be right with you," said the hostess.

"Thanks," he said as we sat down.

The server approached our table. "Hi, I'm Andie." She paused, her eyes fixated on Bryan. "What can I, uh, get you?"

In unison we both said, "Coffee."

"Sure, I'll be right back."

The waitress returned with our coffee and set them in front of us. She paused for a second, fumbling for her words. "Are you, ah…"

As I added sugar to my coffee, I realized she was staring at him again. Bryan chimed in, "I think my future wife's ready to order."

She snapped out of her stare. "Of course. I'm sorry." She fumbled with her pad of paper. "What can I get you?"

A smirk peered through my lips. "I'll have two pancakes, scrambled eggs, and a side of sausage, please."

"And for you?" she said, turning to Bryan.

"I'll have the same except with a side of bacon, well done."

"No problem." She turned to walk away but lost her balance and fell into the table next to ours. She hopped around grabbing her knee and cursed under her breath.

I said, "Are you okay?"

Without much of a response she turned and limped into the kitchen.

"She seems a little odd," he said.

I giggled, "Well, I think you flustered her."

"I did? How could that be? She doesn't know me."

"It's your dashingly handsome good looks, my love. It's a good thing I marked my territory this morning, or I might have competition." We burst into laughter, startling the people around us.

He leaned forward and grabbed my hand. "You don't have any competition, Laurel. I love you; you have my heart."

"And you have mine," I assured him. "I have so many questions to ask about the show. How'd they approach Spam with the deal?" Before he could answer, I jumped right into the next question. "Do you know what the name of the show's going to be?"

He giggled to himself and nodded his head. He looked at me and with an obnoxious tone said, "DumbAss."

I stared at him for a second.

"What do you think about that?"

337

"Surprisingly, it's very fitting." We burst into laughter.

"They want to have a premiere in New York next month. While we're there, Spam wants to film some skits, ya know, to get some New Yorker fans. The sooner we do it, the sooner we're huge."

I sat there as a single thought suddenly crossed my mind: "Is this show going to end up breaking us up?" I wondered.

"Spam already designed the website with video clips and pictures. He wants us all to put together a biography of ourselves. I don't really see the point, though. Do you?"

"Yeah, I see the benefits. People are nosy and they like to know everyone's business. You're bound to have a larger fan base quicker if they have more access to your personal information. Makes them feel like they know you."

"I can't believe it; you just said the exact statement that our agent said, word for word. That's why I love you so much; you're right on the same level."

"On the other hand, you'll have no privacy. And if I'm still dating you, I'll..."

He cut me off. "What do you mean if you're still dating me? You'll be married to me."

I took a deep breath. "All I'm saying is, the deal was signed yesterday, and already you gave me a taste of what your new life is going to be like. And I didn't like it."

"I messed up. I didn't mean to. It won't happen again, I promise. I don't want to lose you. I know how you must've felt last night. I'll never let you down again."

"You have a once in a lifetime opportunity in the palm of your hands. You're talking TV, radio, videos, travel, touring; It's going to be one big constant party."

"It's not gonna be a constant party," he protested.

"I don't necessarily agree with you." I hesitated. "Not to mention, Spam hates me. He wants me nowhere around."

"We've been together for over a year and a half, and it's been great. And Hunter's like my son. I want to give you both everything in the world. I'm doing this for all of us, not just for me. And I don't care if Spam doesn't like you or doesn't want you around. *I* do. Enough said."

I continued to make my point. "The show's called 'DumbAss.' Doesn't that give you an idea of what you guys are going to be doing?" I hesitated. "I don't know if that's going to be wise for me to try to raise Hunter in a situation like that. I have to consider his life, too."

He stared across the table at me. "You and Hunter are my life and I'm not going to lose you over this."

"I don't want to lose you, either. I'm just trying to put everything in perspective, that's all. You're my world, and Hunter's world. This is going to be a dramatic lifestyle change for all of us, not just you."

"I know, I can't wait. Oh. I told my mom; she wants us to go visit her next week. She wants to celebrate with us."

"Sounds good to me. I have to work Friday night. Should we leave Saturday morning?"

"We should take off on Friday; we won't be worrying about money soon," he said.

"I'll see what I can do."

As we finished up our breakfast, Bryan was eager to go home. "Time for 'Naked Saturday!' My favorite."

Chapter 22

Naked Saturdays

We walked into the house and I opened the closet, pulling out our blankets and pillows. I spread the large comforter across the floor in front of the TV and pulled the cushions off of the couch, propping them along the front of the couch for us to lean on. I heard Bryan rustling around with a bags of chips in the kitchen. "What movies should we watch?" I asked him.

"Let's start with 'Spaceballs,'" he said in a goofy voice.

341

"Monty Python, my favorite." I tossed the pillows in front of the couch cushions and laid the other two blankets overtop of the comforter. As I put the movie in the DVD player, Bryan shuffled in with glasses of iced tea, chips, and popcorn. We got naked and curled up under the covers. As the movie began, we quoted the lines word for word, giggling.

About a half an hour later, there was a knock on the door and it flew open. Bryan and I both turned, looking over our shoulders as our friend Jake stood there, shocked by the scene. Jake covered his eyes, "Ah. You're both naked."

Neither Bryan nor I flinched. "That's why we call it 'Naked Saturdays,'" I said.

Jake said, "Well, sorry to burst in on you. I just wanted to say hello. Next time I'll know better than to just walk in."

Bryan said, "Well, at least on Saturdays, don't just burst in. Wait for a reply."

Still shielding his eyes, Jake said, "No, no. I think I learned my lesson. I'll wait for an answer no matter what day it is." He turned his back on us and looked out the front door. "Call me later; Jess and I wanted to know if you wanted to go see a movie later."

"Sounds good," I said. "Dinner first. then a movie?"

"Okay. Call me later." Fumbling for the door knob, he let himself out. "Enjoy your nakedness."

"Thanks," we said.

I said, "Do you think he felt awkward?"

He huffed and nodded. "Yep. I do."

We adjusted in our makeshift bed and curled back up together, intertwining our bodies.

"Why don't we see if James and Kelly are able to hang out tonight?" I said.

"Good idea. I'll call him right now. You call Kelly."

We both grabbed our cell phones and placed the calls. As I mentioned it to Kelly, she answered, "Hells yeah, I'm in."

I looked over my shoulder and nodded to Bryan as he talked to James. He nodded and gave me the thumbs up.

"Why doesn't everyone meet here at seven? We'll pre-game and barbecue instead," suggested Bryan.

I dialed Jake. After filling him in on our idea for the night, he agreed on dinner at our house and then to go out to a bar. "See you around seven?" he confirmed.

"Okay, see you then," I said, and hung up the phone.

We both looked at each other. Bryan said, "This'll be a good night."

"Hells, yeah." I snuggled back into his warm chest. "I'm probably going to crash; I didn't sleep well last night."

343

"Whatever you want, my love." He kissed the top of my head. "Whatever you want."

I nestled into him and let my eyes close.

Around 1:30 my eyes flew open. I heard Bryan on the phone in the kitchen. I stretched my naked body under the covers, releasing a childlike yawn.

Bryan stepped into the hallway at the kitchen door and waved his fingers at me. He was fully dressed.

I pulled the covers aside, flashing my body, and rolled over to my knees. I stood up and sauntered past him. As I danced past him he slapped my bare ass. I scurried away into the bathroom.

He appeared in the bathroom doorway. "That was Spam."

"Oh, yeah? What'd he say?"

"We're going to Nova Scotia instead of New York."

"Nova Scotia? What for?"

"He's always wanted to go. So now that he's got a corporate account, he's making it happen."

"Wow, that's freaking awesome."

"We leave in a few weeks, for two weeks."

I stared at him. "Two weeks? What about work?"

He shrugged his shoulders. "Paul will have to understand. I don't want to lose my job, but I can't pass up this opportunity, either. Spam said if I don't go to Nova Scotia, I'm out for good."

"Ouch. So you kinda have to."

"Yup."

"Do what you need to do. You'll never get anywhere if you pass on opportunities that present themselves."

"I knew you would understand." He disappeared from the doorway.

I got in the shower and let the hot water trickle down my body. *Nova Scotia? We're at the bridge now. Are we going to cross it together?*

I searched for an answer as the shower filled up with steam. My thoughts came to a halt. *It's going to be one of two ways: either it's going to work, or it isn't.* I decided to let it go. I couldn't force it to work, but I could help keep it going.

I finished my shower and dressed for the evening. "Bryan?"

The empty house answered back with silence. I looked at Nimbus. "Where'd he go?"

Nimbus barked and pawed at the back door. I slid open the door and he chased a squirrel. Nimbus jumped at the base of a tree barking as I had a flashback to the squirrel massacre. I shook the vision from my head. "Gross."

I put a pot of water on and I took the meat and rolls out of the freezer. *I'm sure he'll be right back.* I cracked open a beer and poured it into a frosty glass.

I pulled a bag of potatoes out of the closet, rinsed them off, and put them in the pot to boil. Everyone loved my famous potato salad.

I went into the living room and started straightening up. I folded the blankets and put the cushions and pillows back on the couch and ran the vacuum.

When the potatoes were done, I went outside on the back porch to peel and cut them into little pieces. Time snuck by as I prepared for our guests.

I began to wonder where he was. I called him, but he didn't answer.

I set the phone down and looked at the clock. "6:30." I hoped he'd be back before our friends got there. I set the table on the back porch and brought out all the condiments.

Nimbus barked as there was a knock on the door. "Come in," I called from the kitchen.

Jake cracked the door open, "Is everyone dressed?"

"Yes I am. 'Naked Saturday' is over."

He pushed open the door. Jessica stood behind him giggling and shaking her head. "Hey girl. I heard about your naked asses today. That's so funny."

"Can't help it; they're the best days."

Jake asked, "Where's Bryan?"

I shrugged. "When I got in the shower he was here, and when I got out, he was gone. That's all I can tell you."

Jake called Bryan. "No answer."

I nodded. "Yup, that's what I got too."

Jessica started shucking the corn on the cob.

Kelly burst into the front door. "What up, bitch-ass."

"Hey. C'mon out back," I yelled.

Kelly carried her bags of goodies into the kitchen and pulled out the chips and salsa. She poured each into bowls and brought them to the table. "How's everyone?"

"Fantastic," I answered. "You?"

"Good. Excited to meet James," she said flipping her chin length mousy brown hair.

"He's excited too," I told her. "He's gonna be here any minute."

"Where's Bryan?" she asked.

"I have no idea. He took off earlier and I haven't heard from him since."

She huffed, "That's odd. What's going on with the show? Any news?"

I nodded my head. "I should let him tell you."

Knock, knock, knock.

I grinned, "That must be James. Kelly, can you grab the door?"

She smirked at me. "No problem."

James stepped inside. "You must be Kelly. I'm James. Nice to finally meet you."

"You too," she said as he kissed her cheek.

James walked towards the back porch. Behind him, Kelly peered over his shoulder, mouthing the words, "He's so cute" as she fanned herself.

I nodded and giggled as they walked out back. "Hi, James. How are you?"

"Good, good. Can't complain. And you?"

"Fantastic. How was your trip last week?"

"Chaotic. I don't want to talk about it."

"That bad?" I asked.

"Yup. My ex showed up at my shore house. Needless to say, there was drama."

"How long have you been broken up with her?" I pried, searching for some answers for Kelly.

"Long enough that I shouldn't have to deal with that crap; it's been over five months." He stiffened. "She should've moved on by now. I have."

"Why do people drag it out?" I asked. "I just don't get it. If it ain't gonna work, it ain't gonna work. Why bother draggin' it out? Let it go." I shook my head in disgust and shot a wink at Kelly. "Right, Kelly? Let it go." I flicked my hands.

James dug into the chips and salsa. "Where's Bryan?"

"He took off while I was in the shower. Why don't you try to call him and see if he answers you?"

He dialed Bryan's number. "Hey man, I just got to your house. We're all sitting here waiting for you. Hurry up." He hung up. "Isn't it odd that he'd up and disappear? And not answer any of our calls?"

I took a deep breath. "Yup. Very odd."

I stared at the porch in silence. In my head, questions were starting to swarm. I assumed he was with Spam; I'd already gotten the feeling that Spam was becoming very controlling and taking advantage of the power from his newly acquired status.

Kelly said, "I have no worries. Things'll be fine. Maybe some rough spots along the way, but just fine in the long run."

I started making hamburger patties as I shook off the thoughts of how wrong I thought she was going to be. "Jake, will you text him and tell him we're eating soon? I've got meat all over my hands."

After I finished making the burger patties, I called Bryan again. "Hey Babe, it's me. Everyone's here and we're all hungry. Hope you're on your way. Love you."

I looked at the clock: 7:46. "At eight, I'll start the burgers. That gives Bryan a few minutes to get here." I told everyone. "If he's not here, we'll eat without him."

Around eight Jake's cell rang. "Yo. Where you at?...Oh, okay," he said. "I'll tell her. Bye." He hung up the phone and his eyes met mine over the rim of his sunglasses. "He's not coming. He's filming with Spam. In Philly."

I stood there. I didn't know how to respond. *Do I brush it off, or burst into tears?* I said, "Philly? He's in Philly?"

Everyone stared at me.

Jake nodded, "That's what he said. And he's sorry he's not gonna be here."

I snorted, "Don't you think he could've told me this hours ago? He just up and left while I was in the shower. Poof! Gone. No good-bye. No nothin.' And now he's in Philly?"

Kelly, James, and Jake shot glances back and forth. I flipped the burgers in silence as my gut turned with disgust.

"And why didn't he call *me* to tell me? Why'd he call *you*?"

They all sat in silence as I continued to rant. "They signed the papers for the show yesterday. He blew me off last night, and now tonight, too. That's two for two."

Jessica said, "He blew you off last night? Wait, they signed the papers? For the Show?"

"They aren't telling anyone just yet, but yeah. They did. We were supposed to go out to dinner to celebrate last night but instead he ditched me and went to the bar and got trashed. He stumbled in around 3:30 in the morning."

James said, "He told me and everyone about the show when I saw him last night; he practically announced it in the middle of the bar." He glanced at me. "I couldn't believe you weren't with him. I just assumed you had other plans or didn't want to come out."

"He's been away all week, why wouldn't I want to be with him? Why wouldn't he want to be with me?" I shook my head in disgust. "No phone call. No nothing. I sat here all night and bawled my eyes out."

Jessica said, "He left you hanging? I don't know Bryan too well, but he's always put you at the top of the list, no matter what."

James said, "I agree. This is all so out of character for him."

Frustrated, I flipped the burgers and slapped cheese on them. "He told me that Spam wants them to go to Nova Scotia next week, for two weeks. Spam said if Bryan doesn't go, he's off of the show for good."

"Ouch," James said. "What about work?"

I threw my hands up in the air. "What about it? He's going to Nova Scotia." I could feel the bitterness creeping around in my brain. "I can say this: if my life is going to become a constant battle between me and Spam, we aren't going to work. Obviously, Spam's his first choice already," I said shoving the burger patties into the rolls.

James said, "I wouldn't go there just yet, Laurel. It's new for him. I'm sure they have a ton of filming to do before they air the show."

I nodded, "I'm sure."

"I don't like Spam. He's an asshole," Jessica said.

"Yeah he is." I paused. "And man, does he hate me."

Jessica asked, "Why's he hate you?"

"No idea," I said, shaking my head. "I guess I'm a threat when it comes to Bryan."

Jessica nodded, "I could see that."

James said, "It's pretty cool if you think about it. They're going to be famous."

Through my clenched jaw, I spit, "Yup, cool." I placed the plateful of burgers on the table.

While we ate, everyone tried not to discuss Bryan.

James asked, "Where should we go tonight?"

"I don't care, but I think I want to get drunk," I said under my breath.

Kelly said, "I'll drive you to make sure you're safe."

"Thanks," I said.

Jessica said, "Let's go to Johnny's. I haven't been there for a while."

Everyone agreed.

"Johnny's it is," said Jake.

As we walked into Johnny's, the owner, Matt, said, "Where's your husband?"

I smiled and said, "Filming with Spam."

He said, "Yeah I know; they were just here."

My heart plummeted into the tips of my toes. "Oh, yeah? I wasn't sure where they were filming." I cracked my knuckles and rolled my neck.

"Don't worry, they'll be back," he assured me.

I pushed past him and went to the bar.

Kelly said, "I heard what Matt said." She handed me a beer. "I'm sorry."

"I've got a very bad feeling, Kelly," I mumbled. "I'm already feeling the backlash of this situation and I don't like it."

Kelly nodded. "I understand; I wish I didn't, but I do."

Jake joined the conversation. "That's so fucked up. Bryan told me he was in Philly."

I shrugged, "Maybe he was." Changing the subject, I said, "Let's go up front."

We all walked towards the stage as the band was finishing their first set. During the break, we chatted with people we knew and everyone kept asking me, "Where's Bryan?"

My only response was, "Filming."

"Can I have your attention please?" Matt said into the microphone from stage. "I'm Matt Johnson, the owner of this lovely establishment. I'd like to personally introduce you to a few friends of mine. Milltown's own Spam and his Crew, just signed with MusicVision for a reality TV show, 'DumbAss.' We've worked all day to bring you the celebration of the year."

The crowd roared with applause as, one by one, the crew stepped up on stage. My spirit took a nosedive.

Matt continued, "Ladies and gentleman, Spam, and his girlfriend, Ali." Ali was wearing a black bikini with a white see through cover up and black stiletto heels. My pulse began throbbing in anger as I clenched my jaw.

"Ace and his girlfriend, Barb." Barb was wearing a red bikini with a black off the shoulder sweater and black stilettos. My anger funneled into my brain.

"Bryan, escorted by Heather." Heather was wearing a sunset colored bikini with white stilettos. I felt a surge of fury jolt down my spine. The hair on my entire body stood on end. My jaw hit the ground and I gasped for breath, but I couldn't breathe. I began to twitch and everything started to glow white, reliving the moment at the cabin. I just got struck by lightning; an emotional strike of lightning. Everything went silent. Everything went numb.

Kelly tugged my arm, "Come on."

I stood still. I couldn't move. I was frozen at the sight of it all.

Jake and Kelly each grabbed one of my arms and pulled me back towards the bar. Jake was saying, "Relax. Don't overreact until you find out the details. His cell signal was in and out. I may've misunderstood him."

The gut wrenching gurgle in my stomach told me otherwise. "I'm sure you didn't. He lied."

Jessica said, "I'm sorry, Laurel. That's so fucked up."

I wiped the sweat from my brow and I suddenly became dehydrated; I chugged the rest of my beer.

Jake had another one in my hands before I was finished. "Shot?" He handed me a fresh beer.

"Yep." I stood there, digesting the situation: Spam's girlfriend was on his arm and so was Ace's. *Why wasn't I up there?* I felt stripped of my position. Scathed, I glared across the crowd, watching Bryan being escorted around by some bimbo. "What the fuck?" I spit. I looked at Kelly. "Well, I guess this answers my questions."

Kelly tried to rationalize, "There must be some reason why you aren't up there with him. Maybe because of the barbecue."

My jaw clenched. "No. I'm not welcome. That's why."

Jake said, "I don't believe that. Why wouldn't Bryan want you there?"

I shifted, "It's not Bryan. It's Spam."

Kelly rolled her eyes. "Why wouldn't he want you up there? You're hotter than any of those girls, and you definitely have a better body."

I pursed my lips. "Cause Spam can't stand me. I guess I take the focus off of him and his girlfriend."

Jake asked, "Since when?"

"Always," I admitted. "From day one, he's had a problem with me."

Kelly shook her head. "I don't believe that."

"Oh, believe me. Wait till you see the way he glares at me."

She shrugged it off.

The band joined the crew on the stage. As the crew slowly rejoined the crowd, the band began to play. Jake whispered something to Jessica and they disappeared into the crowd.

I felt frustrated, angry, embarrassed.

Jake reappeared with Bryan.

He kissed my cheek. "Hey, Babe. You made it."

I looked at him absently. "I made it? As if you invited me?"

"I told Jake what was going on."

"Jake didn't know anything about this either."
I stared at him. "Is there a reason that you didn't
invite me or have me escort you on stage?"

"Well, everyone was having dinner at the
house, so we improvised."

"You improvised?" I nodded in disbelief.
"You disappeared earlier without saying goodbye,
didn't answer my calls, then I show up here and
you're being pranced around on stage by some
fuckin' girl in a bikini?"

He shrugged. "It was no big deal."

"You left me completely in the dark all day
about where you were, and lied to us about being in
Philly. And you say it's no big deal?"

"I didn't lie; I was in Philly, now I'm here," he
snipped at me. "Stop being a bitch."

I glared at him. "Am I being a bitch, guys?" I
asked everyone. "I don't think I'm being
unreasonable."

Everyone shook their heads.

"See?" I said. "You're two for two."

"Don't drag this out. I'm going to celebrate.
You comin' with me?"

I looked at Kelly and back at Bryan. "We're all
comin' with you," I answered.

We followed Bryan upstairs into the mob of
people. There were cameramen following Spam
around. He jumped from person to person, acting as
if he owned them while the film crew ate up his

every word. He grabbed Bryan and Slash and started moshing between them then shoving random people around the bar. The crowd laughed and joined in. I watched as they all desperately wanted to be included in the videos.

"Incoming!" Spam grabbed a stool and tossed it into the crowd. Most of them dodged the stool as it descended into the crowd, but the leg of the stool nailed some dude in the face and the crowd roared with laughter. Spam high-fived the guy.

Spam chugged his beer and smashed the empty beer bottle onto the floor. "Give me more." Ali promptly handed him a beer and he quickly chugged it. Spam pointed at Bryan. "Dude, he snorkeled in raw sewage today. It was fuckin' hysterical."

Bryan chuckled and nodded his head.

I stood still and hollow. *No way. No way he'd do that.*

"Give me a shot of Jager!" Spam screamed and Ali darted off to the bar to retrieve his shot.

I noticed as his demands were quickly met by anyone around him. No one stopped him; they only laughed and fueled his stupidity. Any other person on earth at this point would have been kicked out of this bar by now. Not Spam. The whole town was immediately obsessed with his fame.

"Great, this is what I'm in for," I thought as I walked over to the bar and ordered another shot. I swallowed it down and sipped my beer.

I glanced over my shoulder. Spam was glaring at me. My blood started furiously pumping in my veins and I got hot. My eyes squinted as I met his glare. I clenched my jaw as he stomped towards me.

"What're you doing here?" he demanded.

I calmly said, "Why wouldn't I be here?"

He snorted, "I told him I didn't want you here."

Kelly gasped behind me.

I continued. "Yeah? Why is that?"

"'Cause you're a controlling cunt."

I laughed in his face, "That's funny. Isn't that the pot calling the kettle black?"

He snapped, "I'm not controlling. Go fuck yourself." He spun and vanished in the crowd.

"Yeah, you are and *you're* a cunt," I called behind him, hoping he heard me.

Kelly said, "I don't believe that."

"I told you."

"What the fuck?" she gasped.

Unable to form a sentence, I spun towards the bar. I grabbed the ledge of the bar and stretched my back out. As I did, Kelly whispered, "Spam's burning a hole in your back. He's bitching at Bryan."

I shook my head. "I don't understand what I did to make him hate me so much."

359

Kelly said, "He's a dick. Don't worry about him."

I huffed.

"Here comes Bryan," she said.

He wrapped his arms around me. "Hi, Babe."

"Hi."

"Spam told me what he said to you. I'm sorry about that. He's just stressed out, ya know?"

I nodded. "Stressed or controlling?" I looked at him absently, "Did he tell you not to invite me tonight?"

"Yes. But I did, anyway."

"Oh, you did, did you?" I countered.

"It was a misunderstanding, Laurel. Don't start with me. Do you want to go home soon?"

"Well, I wouldn't want to interrupt your party, I mean, any more than I already have," I said obnoxiously. "Did you really snorkel in raw sewage?"

He nodded, "It was so gross. I had to get decontaminated afterwards."

"That's foul, Bryan."

He shrugged his shoulders. "That's the point. Give me about another hour, and we'll leave."

I nodded.

"You look beautiful." He kissed me on my lips.

"Thank you."

As the next hour crept by, Bryan mingled with the crew. They were signing autographs and taking pictures.

Knowing that we were nowhere near ready to leave, I wandered downstairs and had a cigarette with Kelly.

"You okay?" she asked as we walked back inside.

I inhaled a deep breath. "Uh-huh," I lied.

"Good, 'cause here comes more trouble."

"What?" I asked.

"Here comes Diablo."

My heart jumped into my throat. Suddenly, my feet were off the ground and I was being spun in circles.

"Hello, my beauty," he whispered in my ear. "I was hoping you'd be here."

"Hello, Vince."

"You look incredible." He rubbed the back of his hand down the side of my face. "I've missed you."

"How are you?" I pulled away from his hand.

"Good. Home for the week, then back to the tour. I was going to call you, but I heard you were still with this guy." He cocked his head towards the front door.

I followed his eyes; Bryan was shoving his way through the crowd, toward us.

"How're you two doing?" Vince asked.

361

I stared at him. I couldn't answer. I swore, he had a radar go off at the most inopportune moments of my life. When I first met Bryan, bloop! He popped up. When it was unraveling, bloop! He appeared. It drove me crazy.

Bryan pushed himself right in between Vince and I, wrapped his arm around my shoulder, and kissed the top of my head. "Hey babe, I want you to meet our producer."

Vince rolled his eyes. "I heard you finally got signed. That took a while didn't it?"

"Yeah, but it was worth the wait. Now I've got everything I want: fame, fortune, and the love of my life." He kissed my cheek.

I felt like he was dangling me in front of Vince.

Vince chuckled, "You smart enough to keep it all?"

I'm a trophy on a mantle.

Bryan grabbed my hand. "Come on, my love. Darrin's over here." He pulled me through the crowd and upstairs.

I asked, "Where's Darrin?"

"I don't know and I don't really care. I just wanted you away from that guy. I didn't want his hands all over you. He's a creep."

A vision of the bikini bimbos hanging all over Bryan flashed in my brain. I had every desire to counteract his comment, but I didn't want to start a fight right now. For once, I was smart enough to keep my mouth shut. After all, Diablo was the reason we broke up to begin with. I wasn't willing to have this fight tonight. It was Bryan's night to shine.

Bryan stayed at my side the rest of the night. As we passed Spam, I saw his jaw tighten. I smirked and rolled my eyes. "Ridiculum," I thought.

Jake and Jessica left around midnight but the rest of us ended up staying for the remainder of the evening. James and Kelly were hitting it off famously; they couldn't get enough of each other. I was thrilled to see Kelly smiling. Phil was in the past, thank God.

After the bar closed, Bryan and I stayed to hang out with the crew.

Perched at the bar, Ali struck up conversation with me. Within a short second, Spam was in between us, pulling her away from me. "Come here, come heeere. I gotta tell you something," he said. In the blink of an eye, they disappeared.

I chuckled. He made numerous attempts to try to make me feel like shit but I didn't let it bother me. He didn't need to like me, though I wondered if he was going to drive Bryan and me apart.

I nudged my head under Bryan's arm. "Can we go home soon? I'm tired."

"Yes, we can. Thank you for being here tonight."

"I wouldn't want to be anywhere else."

"I'm not letting you fall asleep tonight, not until I have my way with you." He pulled me against his chest.

"Then let's get moving; I can't wait to have you." I nuzzled his blonde curls and kissed his neck.

Spam huffed. He stood right against our shoulders, glaring at us.

I looked at him. "Can we help you?"

He rolled his eyes and spoke to Bryan, "I'm gettin outta here."

I said, "Have a good night."

He glared at me.

Bryan said, "Call me tomorrow and let me know the details."

"Yup." He took a step away, turned around and his eyes met mine. "Bye, you fuckin slut-whore."

Bryan spun towards Spam. "Dude, what the fuck? Don't you dare disrespect my girl like that. You don't have to like her, but you have to respect her."

Spam's eyes sliced through me. His glare chilled my body and his silent threats tingled my spine. My fists clenched. Everything around Spam began to fade to black as a dark cloud formed around his head. Despite my tunnel vision, I glared right back into his eyes.

He spun back around and pushed through the crowd.

I looked at Bryan. "What the hell did I do to make that guy hate me so much?"

Bryan shook his head, "I don't know."

"I don't get it," I said. "I just don't get it. You don't know why he hates me?"

He shrugged his shoulders. "He just found out, ya know, about you and Vince."

I nodded. "Ah, so that's why he called me a slut. But for the record, he hated me long before he found out about that. And he thinks that gives him the right to treat me like shit?"

"Pretty much. I told you before, his girl cheated on him, and now he thinks all girls are whores; not just you."

I stood in silence as a numbing chill swept down the length of my back and into my legs.

"Isn't he dating Ali? Shouldn't he be over it by now?"

Bryan shrugged. "He's just bitter at the world, I guess."

"It's just him, right? No one else has a problem with me, do they?"

"Not at all. Everyone thinks you're great. Everyone except Spam. Let's go home so I can feel you."

"Yes, please. Oh, wait. You swam in raw sewage. I ain't touching you."

He chuckled, "I got decontaminated, no worries. The guys at the plant assured me."

"That's just gross. Period."

"Yes it is. But it's still funny."

We said our goodbyes to everyone and walked towards his car.

I turned to Bryan. "Do you think Spam's trying to break us up?"

"Are you serious?"

I nodded. "I feel like he's trying to force obstacles between us. He already told you not to invite me tonight. I just think…"

"I won't let him," he assured me. "Things are weird; a lot's changing right now. Once we get into the swing of things, then it'll be better."

"Did you see Spam tonight? He was acting like a nut case: throwing stools into the crowd, smashing beer bottles. He's already out of control. And no one's even attempting to stop him. He's famous now and he knows it. If you ask me, it's just going to get worse." I paused as he stared at me. "He's going to take his fame to the extreme and everyone around him's free game, including you."

"It's just cause it's new, ya know? He was celebrating, that's all."

"I disagree." I slowly turned and stared out the window as we drove home in silence. *I know Spam's going to destroy us; He's already begun.*

As we pulled up to the house, he broke the silence. "I'm sorry again, about the misunderstanding

366

tonight. I guess my signal was bad when I called Jake."

I nodded. "I just felt left out again. I don't want to feel that way."

"Never again, my love, never again."

I stared at him. *I've already heard that before.* A fake smile tipped the corner of my mouth. "I love you. Very much."

"I love you with all my heart. I'm gonna beat you to bed," he whispered.

We both fumbled as we raced to get out of the car; I got caught in the seat belt. He slammed the car door as I tripped over the curb and stumbled across the grass.

We raced inside. I kicked my shoes off, practically tripping over them. I opened the back door for Nimbus to go outside as I pulled my top off. Bryan ran upstairs into the bedroom. I quickly followed as I removed my bra, unbuttoned my pants, and pulled them off, turning them inside out and hopping as I tried to get them over my feet.

I jumped under the covers, wrapping my chilled skin around his chest. As we kissed so passionately, my head spun; I realized that I felt some resistance to kiss him. I felt a wave of disgust and nervousness as my brain reminded me of his actions. *You've screwed me over twice. Your friend has deliberately shunned me and you swam in raw sewage.*

He paused, "You okay?"

I shook the disgust from my brain and for the first time ever, I forced myself to have sex with Bryan.

Chapter 23

My New Life

As the weeks passed, I quickly became acquainted with my "new life." Every moment that slipped by, Bryan became more unreliable. Almost every night he disappeared for hours on end.

I tried to justify his actions. I tried to understand. I knew they were filming. But, then again, he was trashed every time he came home. I couldn't help but wonder if he was cheating on me.

Often I sat staring out the living room window, trying to sort out my fears. I knew he couldn't be here all the time; he was working all day and filming all night. I also knew he had become different. He wasn't the guy I fell in love with. He had morphed into a totally different person. "We" were not "us" anymore. There was "him" and there was "me."

I felt the absence. I felt the fear.

He became a party animal over a short period of time. Everyone and everything else became more important. He made excuse after excuse and came home trashed every night, waking both Hunter and me up. Then he'd wake up late for work, hung over, and blame me for it.

Our hearts seemed to become more distant and our lives began to separate. Every time we'd bicker, he'd make promises to me and we'd talk things out.

"You're not the guy I fell in love with," I'd say. "If you don't want to be with me, it's fine. Just tell me and we'll stop dragging it out. This *drunken asshole* isn't who I want to be with."

"I know, I know. I fucked up, Laurel. I'm sorry."

"I know you're sorry, but how many more times are you going to do this? I can't take much more of it. It's not fair to me or Hunter either. You come in stumbling and banging into shit, waking both of us up. It's *ridiculum*."

He dropped his head in his hands. "I'm so sorry. I'll make it up to you both."

"I won't live like this. I can't."

"Please don't leave me, Laurel. It won't happen again."

"It's almost inevitable at this point. I don't believe what you're telling me, not anymore."

"Please, Laurel, I love you. It won't happen *ever* again."

I reluctantly believed him.

Within a day or two, he was back at it.

Every time I thought we'd worked through our problems, he started all over again. He'd call me in the middle of the day to plan our evening, and then he'd cancel on me again to "film." He'd ask me to make a certain dinner and then wouldn't show up until the middle of the night, trashed again. I didn't believe anything he said, not anymore.

He barely wanted to see me anymore, let alone talk to me or have sex. My patience was close to non-existent at this point.

I thought after a month or so it would calm down. I was dead wrong; it amplified. He started sleeping at his friends' houses and would show up late for work. We'd make plans to go snowboarding and then he'd sneak in during the middle of the night to get his gear and then sneak back out.

I finally got frustrated with the situation. He came in late on a snowy Sunday night when I approached him on the subject. "What's going on? You're not happy anymore?"

He rolled his eyes. "Yes, I'm happy. I'm just living a different life now."

"Oh, I know. You don't want to be around me at all. I can't do this."

"Everything's fine. Stop trying to control me."

"Everything's *not* fine. All you do is get drunk and party with your friends. You haven't spent any time at all at home with Hunter and me. How's that controlling you? Why don't you start dating one of them?"

"Ya see? This is what I can't take anymore," he said.

"Anymore? You haven't been here to see my face, let alone fight with me."

"I hate you!" he screamed at me.

"What? What've I done to make you hate me? You're the one who can't tell me what's really going on. You're running from the issue. If you don't want to be with me anymore, just *say so*."

"I didn't do anything wrong. Stop making me feel like it's all my fault," he said.

"This *is* your fault. You're the one causing this bullshit. Bryan, stop lying to both of us. If you don't want to be with me, just tell me."

"I don't have time for this shit right now; I'm going snowboarding with my friends and we leave in two hours. You're *not* my friend. I. Hate. You."

He showered me with spit as he spoke. I stood there with my jaw on the ground. My mouth dried instantly with disgust. I got faint as my heart hammered in my throat. I reached for the stair rail and slowly lowered myself to sit down. He slammed me into the wall as he barreled up the stairs. I heard him searching for something in the bedroom.

I sat there, shocked.

He slammed the bedroom door and blew back past me. His bag nailed the back of my head. "Ouch. What the hell, Bryan?"

I reached out and put my hand on his shoulder. As I touched him, he jerked away from me, catching my ring in his sweater. He jerked harder, twisting my finger and I fell into him.

He started screaming like a little girl as if I were attacking him. "Ahhh! Get off me. You're an abusive girlfriend. What're you going to do, hit me? I just want to get the fuck away from you right now."

Stunned. I was stunned. I had never, in all my life, felt so much pain all at once. My head emptied. My blood went cold. I lowered myself back down onto the steps.

He shoved his arms into his jacket and grabbed his gear. He snatched his snowboard and kicked the door closed behind him.

I crept over to the window. He ran to his car as if I were chasing him. He slammed the door and peeled away.

I stood at the window, tears streaming down my face.

"Mommy?" Hunter said sleepily.

I jumped when I heard his voice.

"Why're you and Bryan fighting again?"

"I'm sorry we woke you. Um, Bryan and I got into a little fight, and, uh, it'll all be okay." I wiped my tears away quickly.

"You guys woke me up. I thought I was having a bad dream. I thought a bad man was coming to take you away."

"No, Sweets. There's no bad man. We just had a misunderstanding." I slowly turned and climbed the steps. "Let's get you back to bed." My entire body was shaking; I had no strength. I braced myself with my hands on each step. I felt like I was scaling a mountain.

I followed Hunter into his bedroom and tucked him back into bed. "Is Bryan coming back?" he asked with fear in his eyes.

I forced a smile on my face. "Of course he is. But he won't be around for a few days, so don't worry."

"Where's he going?" he asked with confusion.

"He's going snowboarding with his friends for a few days," I whispered. "We're going to visit Grandmom and DanPop's for a few days anyway." I hesitated. "Sweet dreams, my baby."

I went into our room and packed a bag. I grabbed everything I needed for Hunter and me so we could go to my parents' house after work the next day. I passed back out, hoping and praying that all of this was just a bad dream.

I jumped awake in the morning, searching the room for answers. I hardly remembered anything. *Was that a dream?* I stared across the room. *Did he leave for work?*

"Mommy?"

"Yeah, what's up?" I asked, as I grasped for reality.

"Did Bryan come back?"

A cascade of reality set in. *It wasn't a dream.* I shook my head and swallowed the knot in my throat, which got wedged in the lumps in my chest. "No, Honey. He left. He, ah, went snowboarding."

"When'll he be back? I miss him."

"I'm not sure." I stood up, my legs felt weak under me. "Let's get ready."

Hunter turned and ran into his bedroom.

I went through the motions of getting ready. I didn't know what I put on. I didn't care if it matched. I don't know if I even brushed my teeth. None of it would have made a difference anyway; I was a Nothing, walking through my day.

It was one of the longest and most solemn days of my life. He never showed up for work. I knew why, but they didn't.

I went through the motions, with no effort or care. I gathered my belongings and left for the day. As I walked into Hunter's daycare, I heard someone say, "Little Hunter, your mom's here. Get your things together."

I looked over my shoulder at the Director. "Crystal, I *do not* want my son being referred to as 'Little Hunter.' It's demeaning. I've already spoken to Amy about this. Please don't let it happen again."

"I'll handle it. I'm sorry about that."

Hunter grabbed my hand as we walked outside. We got in the car and drove to my parents. I zoned out as I followed the tail lights of the car in front of me. I was even more annoyed after realizing that my first request was ignored by the school.

When I got there, I cried to my mom. I let it all out. I told her everything as she just listened.

I stayed at my parent's house for a week.

We avoided each other at work. Everyone knew something was wrong. He was late every day. He was hung over every day. I was not.

During the week, I began to realize I wasn't part of the big picture anymore. He was no longer in love with me. I was an obstacle to avoid. He didn't love me back.

I cried. I cried on the inside all day and all night on the outside. He saw none of it. He had no idea how I felt because he didn't pause long enough to care. He didn't care about us anymore.

I went back home that Friday night, hoping that the week away would have put enough distance between us so we could have a decent conversation.

Greg came to pick Hunter up. To him, it appeared to be a normal Friday.

After Hunter left, I sat there in silence. I felt empty and numb.

I walked through the house, feeling like I was in a strange place. I looked in the fridge and saw that it was filled with beer. I looked in the trash can: nothing but empty bottles. He'd been partying here. *With who?*

I sat down on the couch and turned off the lights and sat in the silence of the house. I zoned. Alone. I was alone. It actually felt nice.

As I enjoyed the silence, I heard his car pull into the parking space right in front of our door. *Here goes nothing.* I walked out the front door and towards his truck. I traced my fingertips in the snow on the driver's side window. He cracked the window about four inches.

"Hey, what's up?" he asked from behind the snowy glass.

"Um, I need to talk to you. Without fighting."

"I'm headed out."

"I see that. Can you roll the window down, please?"

"I don't want snow in my truck."

"Bryan, roll down the damn window and talk to me."

The window didn't move.

I took my hand and swiped the snow off the window. There, in the passenger seat, sat a girl.

"What the fuck?" I screamed.

Bryan quickly rolled his window down, "It's not what it looks like, Laurel."

"How fuckin' stupid do I look?"

One... I began to count to 10.

"It's not, I swear."

"Really? Then why wouldn't you roll the window down if there's nothing to hide? You brought another girl to our house? To *my* house?"

"You moved out, remember?"

"*I* didn't move out. *This is my house. You* moved in with *me.* I gave us some much needed distance."

Two...

The girl gasped. Her face was so familiar to me. "You have a girlfriend?" she asked Bryan.

Three...

I dug my nails into my palms. "Yes, he does," I spit at her. "*Who the hell* are you?"

Bryan said, "This is Heather. Don't over react, she's just a friend."

I watched the look of disgust cross Heather's face as she said, "Oh, really?"

Four...

Heather...Heather, how do I know her? I clenched my jaw. My ears and neck started burning. "I don't believe that for a second, you ignorant fucking pig. How dare you bring her into our house? Into my son's house?"

Heather was surprised again. "First you have a girlfriend. Now you've got a kid, too?"

Five...

A vision flashed in my head: I jumped through the window and smashed her face into the dashboard, multiple times.

"We've been together for almost *two years*," I said as I envisioned drilling her head into the window until I deemed her dead.

I chose to take a breath deep. My inner demon was aroused, and she was *pissed.*

"You've got a girlfriend and a fuckin' kid? What the fuck?" Heather continued.

My jaw clenched harder as the trigger went off in my brain: *Heather is the bimbo that escorted Bryan on stage at Johnny's that night.*

Six...

"He ain't my kid," Bryan said.

I cringed as I restrained myself from breaking his nose on the steering wheel. *Don't do it, Laurel. Keep it together.*

Seven...

My fists were balled and my nails were digging into my palms. "Get the fuck outta here right now before I beat the shit out of you and her."

Eight…

There was a rush through my veins as I maintained my composure.

He opened his door. "We'll leave after I get my…"

I slammed the door shut, knocking him back into his seat. "You'll get *nothing*. You're *not* coming inside." My jaw locked and my shoulders clenched as I spit and realized that I didn't recognize my own voice. *Nine… My inner demon has emerged.*

He recoiled, realizing the extent of my fury.

Spit began spewing out of my mouth with each exhale. My brain felt like an inferno as my muscles sparked. My eyes beamed like lasers. I was so furious, I felt like I was going to ignite.

I locked eyes with Bryan. *"Get off my property now. Do not ever come back."* I sounded like a demon.

"He obviously doesn't want to be with you, or he wouldn't be cheating on you. Wake up, *bitch*," she said. Bryan's eyes grew in fear as she spoke. Then she turned to him, saying, "Since I'm obviously nothing to you, Bryan, I guess she should know I fucked you in her house."

I shifted my stare to her. I felt my blood run cold. I gripped the inside of the door, ready to pounce as I balled my right hand and punched Bryan in the face, not once removing my eyes from her. His head bounced off the head rest as he screamed in pain. I grabbed him by the back of his hair and slammed his face into the steering wheel. I lurched through the window and grabbed for her. Bryan pulled me away from her and opened the door. I was, once again, face to face with him. I punched him in his eye again and dismounted from the window. I kicked the door and it slammed shut on his ankle.

My inner demon won. At this point, I was perfectly fine with that.

Fear overtook her face as I glared at her. *"Get the fuck out of here, before I..."*

He put the truck in reverse and frantically backed out. His wheels spun as he tore out of the parking lot.

My head spun. I looked up at the moon as snowflakes fluttered down from the sky. My stomach churned as I breathed in the crisp air.

Tears began to crystallize on my cheeks and the noises around me began to fade behind the buzz in my head. Flickers of white flashed in front of me. *Did I just get struck by lightning again? Yep, an emotional strike of lightning.* My knees buckled under me and I collapsed forward onto the ground. My eyes rolled back in my head as I leaned forward, my hands freezing in the fresh snowfall. I inhaled, gasping for air as my stomach churned and I puked. I felt my insides relieve as I heaved again. I braced myself on my Jeep's bumper, slowly turned, and stood up. My head spun with confusion. I stumbled backwards, reaching for the hood of my Jeep and tried to pull myself forwards. I stepped and slipped in the snow, hitting my head on the bumper. As I collapsed face first into the snow, I faded into the light once again.

Chapter 24

This too, Shall Pass

I groaned in pain as my eyes fluttered open. Unfamiliar voices surrounded me.

A paramedic leaned over the gurney I was strapped to. "Can you hear me?"

"Uh-huh."

"Your neighbor called 911. He found you lying in the snow. What's your name?"

"Laurel F-Forte." I quivered from the cold. "Let me up."

"Can you tell me what happened?" she asked.

"Hit my head. Passed out."

"What caused you to pass out? Do you remember?"

My eyes shot open in disgust. "Yep, I remember."

A male paramedic chimed in, "Could you tell us what happened?"

My vision twisted as I tried to focus. "Let me up. I'll tell you. I don't like being restrained."

"I can't let you up until I know if you're okay. What happened?"

I forced the words out. "My boyfriend's cheating on me."

"Were you drinking or doing drugs?" she asked.

"No, I don't do drugs and I rarely drink." I paused. "I guess I was in shock. Please let me up now."

Hesitantly, she unstrapped me.

I could hear Nimbus barking inside.

I sat up and swung my feet over the side of the gurney. The knot on my head was the size of a golf ball. "Ow, I hit my head pretty hard."

I noticed my neighbor ending his conversation with another paramedic.

"What'd you hit your head on?"

"The bumper of my Jeep. I tried to stand up after I puked. I slipped and fell into it."

She proceeded to check my eyes. "It doesn't look like you have a concussion; your eyes are

384

dilating fine. However, you should go to the hospital and get a thorough exam done."

"I'm not going to the hospital. I'm fine. I coach gymnastics three days a week and you wouldn't believe how many times I get nailed in the head, and not to mention land on it. If you knew me you'd know that a bump on my head isn't going to stop me."

"Well, then we'll need you to call someone to be here with you. Can you do that?" she asked.

I grabbed my phone from my pocket and called my mom. "Mom, I'm fine, but the paramedics are requesting someone be here with me."

"What happened, Laurel? Are you okay?"

"Yes, just please come over here."

"I'm on my way."

"My mom's on her way," I said, turning to the paramedic.

She continued writing on her clipboard.

After a few moments of silence, I heard my Grandmother's voice in my head: *This, too, shall pass.*

I said aloud, "I know it will."

She looked at me. "I'm sorry. You know what will?"

"I was thinking out loud. Sorry."

She studied me carefully. "You going to be okay? About your boyfriend, I mean?"

"I have someone more important to focus on. I'll be fine."

385

"You have a child?" she asked.

"I do. He's almost five."

"Is your boyfriend the father?" she asked.

"No, thank God."

She nodded, agreeing with me. "I've got a four year old daughter. They're amazing, aren't they?"

"Yes, they are."

She continued, "They make you realize a whole different side of you that you didn't even know existed until they came around."

"That's very true."

She went up to the driver's side of the ambulance, filling out more paperwork. I sat there wondering what I was going to tell Hunter.

My mom pulled up and spoke with the paramedics. I lowered myself down from the gurney and walked towards them. "I'm going to go take a shower if we're all done here."

"We filled her in on everything. She's going to keep an eye on you. I hope you feel better," she said.

"Thank you." I stretched my hand out. She looked down at my hand, pausing to shake it. I realized my hand and my jacket were covered in frozen puke.

Embarrassed, I nodded and lowered my hand, turned and trudged inside. I tossed my cell phone on the couch and walked upstairs towards the laundry room. I removed every article of clothing and shoved them directly into the washer, doubling the laundry detergent and softener.

I stood naked in my hallway and glanced towards our room and then towards the spare room. *Where, in my house, did he fuck that bitch?* I stared at myself in the bathroom mirror and it hit me: *He cheated on you in your own house. That means that he doesn't want to be with you, Laurel. Time to move on.*

I stepped into the shower and absorbed the steam. I felt empty and hollow.

I soaped my body. My skin was a shell; it existed only on the surface. My insides were hollow.

I washed my hair twice; it felt like rope.

I zoned into another world until the water ran cold.

I put on my favorite pajamas. Then I stared at my bed. *Did he fuck her in my bed?* I stripped my bed of the sheets.

I went downstairs and tossed the dirty sheets next to the washer and then grabbed a bag of frozen peas for my head. *Did he fuck her on my couch?* I grabbed the blanket and threw it in the pile of dirty laundry and then sprayed Lysol all over my house. I grabbed a fresh blanket from the closet and curled up in it on the couch and lay back with the peas on my head.

My mom watched me from the kitchen as I tried to get comfortable. I flipped through the channels, unable to find something to watch.

She handed me a cup of tea. "Do you want to talk about it?"

"What's there to talk about? I got my answer."

She nodded her head. "Well, I'm all ears if you want to talk."

"Talking about it's not going to change the fact that he fucked that ugly whore in my house."

"Well, I don't want you to do something crazy."

"I did what I needed to do. I punched him in his face." I nestled deeper into the couch. "I got it out. I'm fine. I still have Hunter."

"Did you really?"

"Fuck yeah. He earned it."

She smirked. "That's my girl."

"I'm going to go to bed. You staying here or going home?"

"How do you feel?"

"I feel great. Life is perfect."

"Laurel, don't."

"Yeah, Mom, I'm fine. I just wanna sleep."

"The paramedics said you shouldn't sleep; you should stay awake."

"I don't care what they said. I'm tired because my emotions went berserk, not 'cause I bumped my head. We both know I've had worse. I'm going to bed."

"Well, then, I'll go home. Dad's worried."

"Tell him I'm fine. No need to worry."

"I will. Remember, Laurel, *this, too, shall pass.*"

I stared at her as a chill shot through my spine. The hair on my arms and neck stood on end. "I know."

After a few minutes of collecting her thoughts, she said, "I'm going home."

"Okay, be safe," I said.

"I love you."

"Love you too, Mom."

There was an eerie feeling that spread itself through my house after my mom left. I felt like a stranger in my own home. My exhaustion was overtaking me. I shut off the lights and the TV and sat in silence. I was alone, but it no longer felt nice.

Chapter 25

Lease

Saturday morning I called off my class and then shut my cell phone off. I was in no mood to deal with coaching children right now.

My brain felt frozen. I had no desire to leave my house or talk to anyone. I sat on my couch and drank myself into oblivion. Saturday came and Saturday went.

Sunday morning I awoke on the couch. I heard a noise upstairs and instantly I knew Bryan was in the spare bedroom. I darted upstairs. "What the fuck are you doing here?" I demanded. "Get the hell out."

He rolled over and looked at me. His left eye was a deep purple and blue swollen bulge. "I'm fuckin' sleeping, bitch. Leave me the fuck alone."

I thoroughly enjoyed seeing his black eye. "I want you out. Now. It's moving day."

"Fuck you. I'm sleeping. I'm not moving anywhere, so shut the fuck up."

"Get the fuck up *right now*."

"Try to make me get up, bitch. Fuck off!"

I ran downstairs and put on a sweat shirt and a pair of boots.

I grabbed his car keys and twisted his house key off the key ring and put it in my pocket. I stomped through the house and pushed the panic button to set the alarm off on his Lexus. I let it go off until I heard him screaming.

"Don't touch my fucking car, you fuckin' crazy bitch!"

"Look who's up." I ran to his car, acting like I was going to take it.

He burst through the door, dressed only in his boxers and boots. "Get the fuck out of my car."

"Oh good, you're awake!" I got out of the car and kicked the door closed. "You're moving out today."

"Fuck you. I'm on the lease. I'm not going anywhere."

"Oh yes, you are."

"No, I'm not, you psycho whore!"

I turned and threw his keys down the street.

He ran through the snowy parking lot searching for his keys, cursing me the entire time.

I walked into the house and locked the door behind me. I watched through the window as he found the keys buried in the snow behind someone's tire. Shivering, he turned the door knob, which didn't budge.

He fumbled through his keychain, looking for his house key. "Fuckin' bitch stole my key."

He looked in the window and saw me as I stood there smiling, holding the key.

He ran to his car as I peered through the blinds. I could see him fumbling with the heating controls while he was yelling on the phone.

I grabbed my cell and called our landlord. "Hi Adam, it's Laurel."

"Hey Laurel, what's up?"

"I'm sorry to do this to you, but Bryan's moving out today. I know it's very sudden, but I caught him cheating on me. Can I get a new lease in my name only?"

"How soon do you need it?"

At this moment, I was thankful for the fact that my landlord was my dad's best friend. "Um, right now?"

"Oh, um, can you give me a few minutes?"

393

"Yes. Thank you. And again, I'm sorry it's so sudden."

"No worries. I'll call you back."

I went upstairs into my bedroom and threw his clothes onto the front yard. He jumped out of his car and started collecting his clothes. He tried to remove a boot as he put on his jeans and toppled over into the snow. He jumped up and hobbled to his car dusting the snow from his hip.

I chuckled.

He angrily sat in his car and pulled his pants on. Then he got out and ran over to his sweatshirt and quickly put it on. He gathered the articles of clothing spread across the yard and threw them in his car.

I stood there, rather enjoying watching him scramble.

My cell phone rang. "Hey, it's Adam. Where can I fax it to?"

"My parents' house. You know the number?"

"Yep. It's on its way."

Next, I called my mom and informed her what was going on. "Can you make a copy of the fax and bring both copies here as soon as it comes through?"

"Yep, I can."

"Thanks, Mom." I hung up and looked out the window as two cop cars were pulling up. I spun on one heel and darted upstairs into the attic.

I wasted as much time as I could rooting through boxes before I went back downstairs.

There was a pounding on the door.

I grabbed the pen sitting on the coffee table in the living room and shoved it in my back pocket before opening the door. "Can I help you?"

The officer said, "Miss Forte?"

I nodded. I recognized him from high school.

"Bryan needs to come inside and collect his personal belongings."

"His personal belongings are scattered across the front yard."

"Is his name is on the lease?"

I shook my head. "He's not welcome in my house."

The officer continued, "Is his name on the lease?"

"For the moment, but he doesn't get mail here. I have a new lease on the way."

"Until it shows up, he has every right to come in and get his things."

I peered over the officer's head and watched my mom pull in.

"Without the new lease, you cannot prevent him from entering the property," he added.

Bryan (and his black eye) stood behind the other officer, leaning on his car. When he saw my mom get out of the car, he started yelling, "I want my shit, Laurel. Stop being a fucking bitch and give me my shit!"

My mom walked around the police cars and hustled to my front door.

She handed me the new lease and I quickly signed it, smirking at the cop. "Perfect timing, done deal. Tell him to get off my property, before I have him arrested."

Bryan was flabbergasted.

The officer turned and looked at Bryan, shrugging his shoulders. "You got outsmarted there, my friend. There's nothing I can do."

"Tell him to check the curb Monday night; it'll all be in the trash."

Bryan got back in his car and slammed the door, cursing me as he called someone.

My mom snuck past the cop and came in and locked the front door. I turned around and looked at my mom as I burst into tears.

She grabbed ahold of me. "It's all going to be okay, Laurel."

I sobbed in her shoulder, "I know, b-but it h-hurts so b-bad r-right n-now."

"I know, hun, I know," she whispered. "No worries. It'll all work itself out in the end."

"I can't believe that he had the *audacity* to come back here after I caught him cheating on me in my *own home*."

"He just ruined the best thing that ever happened to him, you know that. *He* knows that. And he's got a black eye to remind him of it."

I tried to laugh. The truth was, as much as he deserved everything he just got, I didn't want any of this to end this way.

I sat down on the couch and stared at the wall. I couldn't cry anymore because my emotions were drained. I fell sideways onto the couch, pulled a throw pillow under my head, and stared at the wall some more.

My mom said, "How about I call Greg and have him drop Hunter off at my house? I'll take him to school in the morning."

"Yeah, I could use another night alone. I'm gonna be a mess. I probably won't be worth much tonight."

She called Greg and confirmed the new plans with him. "He's going to drop him off around five. If you'd like to come over for dinner, please do."

I inhaled a deep breath. "I doubt it. I probably can't focus enough to drive the three miles over to your house."

She nodded, "I have a lot to help Dad with, so I'm going to head home. You gonna to be okay?"

I nodded.

"Do you need anything else?"

"Nope. Thank you."

"You're welcome, Laurel. *This, too, shall pass.*"

I nodded.

"By the way, Laurel, I'm glad you gave him a black eye. He asked for it." She let herself out the front door.

I closed my eyes.

At 6:30 Monday morning, I jolted awake. I looked around the living room, taking a moment to focus. I peeled myself off the couch, walked Nimbus, and went upstairs to shower, trying not to think about what was going to happen at work today.

I drug myself through the motions of the morning. As I stepped into the closet, the sadness overwhelmed me. Half of the closet was emptied. I recalled throwing his clothes out of the window onto the snowy ground. I spaced my hanged clothing out across the rod. *Put a smile on that face, Laurel. You'll get through this.*

Chapter 26

Apathy

I pulled into the driveway at the office. I walked into the office that morning pretending like nothing was wrong and hoping Bryan was already out on the road. "Morning, Jane."

"Good morning, Laurel. How was your weekend?"

"Fantastic. Yours?"

"It was good. We have lots going on this morning, so I hope you want to be busy."

"As a matter of fact, I do." *Whatever keeps my mind off Bryan will be perfect.*

I listened to my messages and made a fresh pot of coffee. Slowly, I returned the calls. I caught myself staring at my computer screen, pondering the future. I jumped when I heard Paul call me on the speaker phone. "Laurel?"

"Yes, Paul?"

"Can you to my office please?"

"On my way." I grabbed my cup of coffee and walked towards his office. *Please don't ask me about Bryan.*

"C'mon in, Laurel."

I opened the door and stood at the corner of his spotless desk. "Do you ever actually *do* work at your desk? It's always in perfect order."

"Yep. Most of it's phone calls, so I don't make too much of a mess."

"What's up?" I asked.

"Is Bryan sick?"

A chill swept through me. "I, ah…I don't, um…know." *He probably doesn't want anyone to see his black eye.*

He looked at me in disbelief. *"You don't know?"*

I shook my head trying not to make eye contact with him.

"Did you break up?"

Solemnly, I nodded.

"When?"

"Well, I guess it was official yesterday. But we've been having a lot of problems over the past few weeks."

"Interesting."

"Do I dare ask why?" I pressed.

"Well, Bryan called me over the weekend to tell me that he was leaving for Nova Scotia for two weeks to film some show," he explained.

Trying not to react, I nodded and tapped my finger nails on the cup as every muscle in my body cringed.

"Obviously, I wasn't happy to hear that my best installer was going away. Not to mention that he gave me *pretty much* a week's notice about a two week vacation."

"I didn't think that was fair, either. But, um…either he goes or he loses his place on the show."

"That's what he said. I agreed to his time off, but, um, I guess my major concern starts here: why didn't he show up for work today? And why can't anyone get a hold of him?"

"I can't help you, unfortunately. But welcome to my world." I stared out the window, making sure I kept my composure. "I've been dealing with that for over a month now. This show has taken over his life."

"His life or his work?"

"His life. He's done a complete one eighty. Our relationship has become a total landslide of bullshit since they signed the deal. He's just not the same person anymore." If I was going to cry, it would have been right then. But nothing. I was numb.

"How're you handling this?" He studied my face.

"I don't really have a choice in the matter. If you love someone, set them free." Still no emotion.

"What's the name of this show and what's it about?"

"They just signed with MusicVision for a reality show. They do stupid skits and ridiculous stunts."

"What's it called?"

I lowered my eyes. I adjusted my shoulders as I cleared my throat. "DumbAss."

He laughed, "I thought he was joking when he said that. Is that really what it's called?"

"Yep. And surprisingly it's very fitting."

"Well, I guess that's good for him, right?"

Emotionless, I lied. "I'm excited for him." I felt the weight of this conversation pressing down on my shoulders.

"If you don't mind me asking, why did you two break up?"

"Long story short, it's because of the show." I sipped my coffee and stared at him absently.

"Well, that didn't take long, did it?"

I shook my head. "If you love someone, set them free."

"I think you two will work things out. Just give it some time. You two are so good together."

I stared at him, aware that apathy, at this point, had completely taken over. My emotions were non-existent and I was numb.

I knew Paul's intentions were good, but I also knew better than to believe him. He knew Bryan had started partying all the time and was always late for work. What Paul was completely unaware of was that Bryan was cheating on me, that I kicked him out, and that I gave him a black eye. Though there was a part of me that wished everyone would find out about the black eye.

"Is there anything else?" I asked, trying to end the conversation.

"No. Thanks for the insight, Laurel."

I quickly recoiled out of his office, pulled the door shut behind me, and walked directly to the bathroom. I didn't have any tears left to cry, but I needed to regroup. It was only day one and the burden of all of this had started to reflect on me.

The rest of the day drug by as I forced myself to keep my thoughts busy with issues at work. Unfortunately, everyone directed their questions and concerns regarding Bryan to me. I was still Bryan's girlfriend in the eyes of our coworkers.

After work, I picked Hunter up from daycare. Amy saw me coming through the door and called for him. "Little Hunter, your mom's here."

I glared at her and then turned towards the director of the pre-school. "I *do not* want Hunter being referred to as 'Little Hunter.' If I have to address this subject again, I *assure* you it *will not* be done politely."

"I apologize, Miss Forte. It won't happen again."

I glared at her in disbelief. "It *better* not." I picked Hunter up and burst through the front door of the school. After I got Hunter situated in his seat, I drove home.

I pushed through the motions of my evening with Hunter, pretending everything was just fine. My heart was empty and my brain was fried. Hell, I was still in shock over the whole situation. I couldn't find the words to tell Hunter what happened even if I had wanted to. I decided that it'd be best to give myself a few days before I tried to explain it to Hunter. I knew he'd be heartbroken and I couldn't deal with that at the moment. I'd tell him soon, but not just then.

I laid Hunter down for bed, and we said our prayers:

Now I lay me down to sleep,
I pray the Lord, my soul to keep,
If I die, before I wake,

I pray the Lord, my soul to take.
God bless Hunter and Mommy, Grand mom, Danpop,
Aunt Sarah, Uncle Lance, Aunt Hillary.
God Bless Daddy, Gina, and Gianna and Angel.
God Bless Bryan, and all of our family and friends.
Amen.

I kissed his forehead. "I love you, Hunter."

"I love you, Mommy." He touched my cheek, "When Bryan gets home, tell him I said goodnight and that I love him."

If I could cry, this would have been the moment.

"I will."

"Good night, Mommy."

"Good night, Sweets."

As I turned, it was like a wave of nothingness washed down my body. I shut down. My soul went numb and completely detached itself from my body. My brain silenced; it was vacant. Every emotion in my body went white.

I stood there for some time before I slowly made my way into my bedroom. I stared into the room, feeling its void. There was a huge presence missing: *Bryan.*

I *forced* myself to move.

I slumped down the stairs and let Nimbus outside, supporting myself with the door as my face smashed into the glass. I was vacant from life. When

405

he ran back inside, I climbed the mountain of steps and went to bed.

I tried to cry, but I couldn't. I was emotionally dead.

Tuesday and Wednesday drug by as if I were in a trance. Predictably, Bryan called off of work both days. My interactions with coworkers were shallow and habitual. I participated in the day, but I was indifferent. The world around me continued to move at its fast pace as I stood still. I was where I needed to be when I needed to be there, but it wasn't *me*. I was merely my shell, my skin and bones. The blood in my body pumped at its own pace, independent of me. I was seen among society, only I didn't engage with life. Nothing fazed me. I shunned interacting in conversation. I avoided everyone I could. I only spoke with the people I *had* to speak with.

I awoke the next morning as Hunter jumped on my bed. "Wake up, Mommy. It's time for breakfast." He darted downstairs and opened the door for Nimbus.

I followed him into the kitchen and poured him a bowl of Cheerio's. We got ready for our day and out the door we went. I drove absently, staring at the tail lights of the cars in front of me. I dropped him off at school and drove to work.

I brewed coffee and listened to the messages. Then I walked down the hallway towards the warehouse. I heard James and Paul talking in one of the offices.

"What'd you think I should do?" Paul asked.

I heard James say, "I really don't know. Neither Kelly nor I can get a hold of him, either. He went from being your number one installer, to completely unreliable in a matter of days. Did you talk to Laurel?"

I clenched my jaw.

"Yeah, I did. She said he did a complete one eighty with her too," said Paul.

"Yeah, he did. I saw it with my own eyes," confirmed James.

"I feel bad for her."

"So do I. He left her and Hunter high and dry. He was cheating on her, too."

"He was? She didn't tell me that."

"Well, why would she? She's not going to tell *you* that; you're his boss too. I don't think she expected him to bail on her or work."

"Should I talk to her about this, or just fire him?"

I stepped in the doorway and answered, "As I said the other day, set him free. It's what he wants."

They both stared at me.

I continued, "He doesn't want to be here anymore. Not for work and not with me. Let him go."

Paul said, "I'm sorry about all of this, Laurel."

"Well, Paul, it's certainly not your fault. But thank you. I understand he didn't show up again today?"

James shook his head.

Paul said, "I had a voicemail on my phone; he called at four in the morning and left a message that he wasn't going to be in today. He was slurring his words."

"Yeah, that's what his new life's like." I felt a little spark of resentment, the first sign of any type of emotion in days.

I handed James a folder. "Here's the file on the job today." I barely made eye contact.

"Thanks, Laurel."

I walked out of the room feeling the pity lurking behind me. I drug myself back to my desk and plopped into the chair. I stared at the computer screen as I sipped my coffee. I stretched my jaw and rolled my shoulders. My entire body hurt.

I called Coach. "Hey Coach, its Laurel."

"Hey Laurel, you okay?"

"I'm not really feeling well today. Is there any chance you can do the class without me tonight?"

"I'll ask Shane if he can do it. He's on his way here now. Either way, it shouldn't be an issue. Is everything alright?"

"Yeah. I guess I'm just exhausted."

"Well, rest up. I'll see you Saturday?"

"Definitely."

I pushed through the rest of my day, picked Hunter up, and drove home. The absence of Bryan was beginning to wear on me. I felt like I'd lost a limb.

Over dinner, I began to ease into the conversation with Hunter. "Bryan and I haven't been getting along very well."

"I know, Mommy."

"You do?"

He nodded. "Yeah."

"I, um, don't think he's going to live with us anymore."

Hunter's eyes glassed over. "What? He's not coming home?"

"I think it's best, Spark. He doesn't want to be here anymore."

"He doesn't love us anymore?" His eyes filled with pain.

I shook my head slowly. "He's got a new life now; one that doesn't include us."

"So he's not coming back?" Tears streamed down his rosy cheeks. "He said he wanted to be my other daddy. He's gotta come back." He threw his fork across the table, slammed his fist beside his plate, and began to cry hysterically. "He said he wanted to be my other daddy!"

I hugged him tightly. "I know what he said. Things change. People change." I hesitated as he kept crying. "Bryan changed. He doesn't want us in his life anymore. I know it hurts, but it'll all be okay."

He tried to push out of my arms. "No, Mommy. He can't leave. He loves us, he told me."

"I know what he told you, Babe, but he's moving on with his life. And we have to let him."

"No, Mommy. I don't want to let him. Call him right now. I wanna to talk to him." He stomped his foot and slammed his fist on the table.

"Hunter, I know it hurts but it's best for all of us right now."

"Call him, Mommy. I want to talk to him."

"Hunter, I'm not going to call him. We need to leave him alone."

"I wanna talk to him, please. He told me he wanted to be my other daddy." He slid off my lap, kicking his feet.

"Not right now, Hunter. This is hard enough for me as it is."

He glared at me through his tears. He spun on his heel and stomped upstairs. His bedroom door slammed. I could hear him crying and slamming his toys in his bedroom.

I sat at the table, my stomach churning. I stared at my half-eaten chicken breast. My head spun and my eyes fluttered. I jumped to my feet and ran to the bathroom, barely making it to the toilet as I puked my guts up. My stomach cramped as I continued to hurl. My body was sweating though I was shivering cold. I looked at myself in the mirror. My eyes were glowing with fire. I stared at the person in the mirror. *Who is she?* I turned and puked again.

"Mommy? Are you okay?"

I looked at Hunter; his eyes filled with sadness. "Yes, Sweetie, I'm okay. Just a little upset, that's all."

"I'm sorry, Mommy. I just want him to come back."

"I know, Sweets, but I need you to know that it's not going to happen. He's gone."

"Did I do something wrong?" he quietly asked.

"No, hun, not at all. Bryan changed, not us."

He nodded as he played with my hair. "You need a bath."

I smiled, "Yes, I do. And a toothbrush."

"You have puke breath. It's okay, Mommy. You'll be alright."

I nodded. "I know. After all, I still have you."

"I'll take care of you."

"I'm going to take a bath, you go watch TV. I'll be out soon."

I closed my eyes as I soaked in the water. I became hypnotized by the reddish black haze behind my eyelids. I twitched in the water as my sadness began to spark with flashes of anger. *How could you walk out on us?* I closed my eyes as blackness engulfed my mind. I twinged again. *Who the hell do you think you are?* My mind sparked with anger and resentment. *Cheating on me in my own house. Fucking Asshole.*

My eyes rolled closed in my head as I slipped into the darkness. I spasmed as I envisioned his face. "Asshole," I spit through my clenched jaw. I reached forward and turned on the hot water. I felt the hot water wrapping around my calves and I slumped down under the water with my eyes open. The water stung my eyes for a few seconds until they adjusted. I gazed through the ripples of the water.

I squeezed my eyes shut as I surfaced my nose to breath in air and lowered myself back into the icy hot water.

A vision of us getting married jolted in my brain. I cringed. A vision of having a baby together plowed across my mind. My hands balled into fists of rage.

I sat up as I felt a rush of disgust and a surge of anger. My stomach churned. Every time I closed my eyes, I saw a vision of what our future was supposed to be. It made me sick. It made me angry. It made me stop closing my eyes.

Friday morning, I heard Hunter crying. "Mommy, Mommy, look!"

My eyes quickly adjusted.

Hunter stretched his arms out. "Look, Mommy! My skin's itchy and red."

I turned his arms; his skin was red and scaled. "Oh my God, what happened?"

"I don't know, Mommy, but it itches bad."

I removed his clothes. Everything from his neck down to his feet were scaled and red. I quickly called his pediatrician. "Dr. Morgan, Hunter has had an allergic reaction to something. His entire body looks like lizard scales."

"Give him children's Benadryl and use a hydrocortisone cream. Call me in two hours and let me know how it looks."

I quickly followed the doctor's directions and then called off of work. All morning, Hunter wined and complained about his skin burning. I gave him a cool bath and reapplied the hydrocortisone cream.

The pain continued, so we decided to go to the doctor's office. "Come on back, Laurel." The nurse motioned us into one of the exam rooms. As we got situated, Dr. Morgan appeared right behind us. "Good Morning."

"Sorry to just show up, but he's in agony." I stepped aside, exposing Hunter to his view.

Dr. Morgan took looked at his skin. "Laurel, that's not an allergic reaction."

"What is it?"

"Psoriasis."

"Psoriasis? How does a four year old get psoriasis?" I was baffled. "It's all over his entire body."

"I've never seen someone break out so badly, all at once." He looked over Hunter's chest and back. "He's never had any sign of this before?"

"No, nothing even close. What brings an outbreak like this on?"

"Stress."

I froze in my skin. "Stress?" I huffed as I stared at his scaled body. *Is this because I just told him that Bryan's not coming back? Or did the fights between Bryan and I stress him out this much? Could it be a combination of everything?*

"Mommy, it itches." Hunter broke my thoughts.

Dr. Morgan said, "I've got an Ultraviolet light we can use on him; it'll clear up the scales faster than anything else. I'll give you scripts for corticosteroids and for an antibiotic to prevent an infection."

Under the lights, again. My head went silent as I flashed back to the hospital when Hunter was born. I slowly sat down in the chair in the exam room. I couldn't help but feel responsible, again. *My poor baby.* A tear kissed the corner of my eye as Dr. Morgan said, "Laurel, its okay. These things happen. He's not in any danger. It's just a skin irritation. It's not contagious, just itchy."

"Okay. How many times does he need to go under this light?"

"Just once. It'll stop the cells from reproducing. Then use the topical cream for the next few days."

Slightly relieved, I said, "Okay. Let's do it. He's really uncomfortable."

"Hunter, we're going to take this stick and shine it everywhere on your body. It'll stop you from being itchy."

Dr. Morgan turned it on and passed it over Hunter's arms, chest, and back. He had Hunter sit down so he could pass it over his legs. "Is it feeling any better?" he asked.

Hunter said, "It still burns, but different now."

"That's a good sign, Buddy." Dr. Morgan turned off the light and turned to me, saying, "Get this cream immediately and apply it. The other's an antibiotic; it's just a precaution so he doesn't get a streptococcal infection."

.   I checked out of the office as I leaned into the counter wondering, "Why did this happen? How did this happen? Is this my fault again?"

Chapter 27

Interview with a Dumbass

Hunter's skin cleared up almost immediately. I had barely eaten or slept for days. After a few days, my exhaustion began to wear on me. My energy level plummeted to the floor. I felt weighed down more and more as the reality of my life continued to set in.

I sat at my desk one day in a daze, wondering if Bryan was ever coming back to work.

I thought to myself, "Laurel, stop dwelling on this. You're strong, beautiful and positive. Move forward with your life and stop worrying about him. He's gone." I dropped my head into my hands. "Be strong. Focus on Laurel," I repeated constantly in my head.

I was organizing my work for the day when Paul called on the speaker phone. "Good Morning, Laurel."

"Happy Monday, Paul."

"How're you today?"

"Every day's better than the last."

"How's Hunter feeling?"

"Much better, thanks for asking. What can I do for you?"

"I need the files for the Town Builders account. Could you grab them for me?"

"I'll be right in with them. I'm going to grab a cup of coffee on my way. Did you have your morning coffee?" I asked.

"I picked one up on my way in, but thank you."

"See you in a few."

"Alright, Captain."

I started down the hall towards the file room with a forced smile on my face. As I walked past one of the offices, I heard Bryan's voice. Like a ton of bricks, my heart dropped. I continued past the next office and I heard him again. *He's on the radio. Shit. Shit, shit, shit.*

I stopped to listen. I just *had* to know. I could tell they were talking about the TV show as landslide of fear cascaded through me.

In the office, a group of my coworkers were listening. *They all know him, they all know me. They all know we were together and why we're not anymore.*

"How cool is it that he's famous now," I heard one of them say.

Just as I had myself convinced that Bryan wouldn't say anything about me, the female radio DJ asked, "How's life changed for you since you signed with MusicVision?"

Spam's voice came on. "A lot's changed so far, but the show doesn't premiere for another few days, so no one really knows who we are or what we do. I'm sure after that happens, it'll be a landslide of fame and chaotic bullsh-*bleep!*"

She asked, "So, is anyone from your past trying to jump back on the bandwagon?"

Bryan's voice came on. "My ex-girlfriend Laurel's trying so hard to get back together with me since she found out that we signed. She's such a *bleep!* She called me the other night crying about one thing or the other. So I told her to f-*bleep!* off and hung up on her. She cheated on me and punched me in the face and wonders why I can't stand the sight of her or the sound of her voice."

Suddenly I couldn't breathe. Tears formed in my eyes. The hallway started getting very tight and very long. Sweat started beading on my brow and my legs weakened as I slithered down the wall. I set my coffee on the floor and put my head between my knees. "Slow, deep breaths," I thought to myself. "Laurel, you deserve better. He's bitter and angry and a liar. You're his target.' I continued to breathe. I wiped away my tears and forced myself to listen to the interview.

He wasn't done yet. "I'd never take her back. She's an abusive, dirty, cheating whore."

A rush of embarrassment heated my body as all the crew laughed hysterically.

"Good for you," the DJ said. "She doesn't deserve you. Look at you now: you're famous and she's a nobody."

"She's so *foul.* I'm glad her and her son are out of my life," he continued.

I felt like an industrial sized vice grip tightened around my chest as they all laughed, *at me.*

"She's a mother? Poor kid. Is it yours?" asked the DJ.

"Hell. No. Thank God I didn't knock her up. I don't have to put up with her sh-*bleep!* for the rest of my life. I'm *soooo* much better off without her."

My breath escaped me. *You bastard. You self-righteous, disgusting, ignorant bastard.* The room spun in my head.

Jane turned the corner and saw me on the floor. "Laurel. Are you okay? What's wrong?"

I slowly lifted my head. "I don't feel good. Can you get me water?" I fell to the side.

Jane said, "Jason. Can you get me water? Hurry."

He and the other coworkers who were listening in the room came rushing over to me. "Laurel, we're so sorry. We shouldn't have listened to it."

"One of our own became famous. Pretty cool, huh? Something to be proud of," I said.

Jane led me into the office and sat me down in the chair. I heard the DJ announce: "We'll be right back with more from…" I hit the radio switch off; I couldn't stand to hear anymore.

I leaned back in the chair, took a sip of my water, and wiped away my tears.

Kara said, "Don't let it upset you, Laurel. He's just bitter."

"Don't let this upset me? He just said that on the radio. Do you know how many people just heard that? Everyone in this town knows exactly who he's talking about," I huffed. "Except for the part about the black eye, he twisted everything to make him look better."

Kara sarcastically said, "Well, of course he did. He's a guy. They can never get anything right."

Jason asked, "You gave him a black eye?"

I nodded with what little pride I had inside me.

"Well, did you cheat on him too?" he asked.

Kara slapped his arm. "Don't be an asshole. That still wouldn't give him any reason to say that on the air."

"Bryan and I had known each other for 2 days when I ran into my ex, Vince, on the way to one of Bryan's premiers. And very long story short: Vince decided to show up at the premiere and all hell broke loose between Bryan and I. Vince ended up driving me home and shit happened."

"Well, that's not cheating. You barely knew each other," Jane responded.

"We weren't a couple but apparently that didn't matter to him. He flipped out and we didn't talk for about two weeks." I quivered through my tears. "Then, we saw each other at the Dairy Queen in town and we both apologized and from that day forward we were together. Up until a month ago, when he and his buddies got offered this show, then suddenly Hunter and I became a burden."

Jane asked, "Why would he say those things about you? Does it make him feel like more of a man?"

I shrugged my shoulders. "I guess so. He's bitter." My eyes filled with tears. "I found him at our house with some chick about a week ago; that's why I punched him in the face."

Everyone gasped.

Kara said, "Good for you, Laurel."

"Yeah. Look where we are now," I said.

My cell began to ring: it was Jake. I slumped my head in my hands and took a deep breath. "Hello?"

Frantically, Jake said, "Yo, did you just hear him on the radio talking about you?"

"Yep. I heard it. So did my coworkers. We're talking about it as we speak. Where are you?"

"I'm at work too. We're all sitting here listening as well. We thought it was cool that he was going to be on the radio, and then he goes and pulls this shit. I really can't believe that he'd stoop so low. By the way, didn't you break up with him?"

"Yes. And I didn't cheat on him; we weren't together. Last Friday, I caught him cheating on me with that bitch in the bikini. That's why I punched him. Funny how that information got twisted, too."

"You punched him? You go, girl. Fuck him, Laurel. You don't deserve this."

"Yeah, well I'm gettin' it. I'll call you later."

"Okay, bye."

I shut my phone and set it on the desk. I looked at everyone around me as my eyes welled up. "And so it begins."

Jane said, "Maybe you should take the rest of the day off. Go home and relax."

"That's the *last* thing I need right now: time to think about this bullshit. I'd prefer to keep my mind busy. Thank you anyway."

I got up and forced myself back to work.

On my lunch break, for the first time ever, I left the office. I went to the park down the street and sat at the picnic table with my head in my hands and I cried.

My phone began to ring. I realized that this call was going to be much worse when I saw that it was my brother.

I collected my emotions. "Hello?"

"Laurel? Are you okay?"

"No. No, I'm not," I admitted.

"Did you hear it on the radio or through someone else?"

I huffed as I started to cry, "I h-heard it on the r-radio."

"Fuck, Lala. I'm sorry he said those things about you. Don't believe a word of it. I almost fell off the roof when I heard it."

"Did Dad hear it?"

"Yeah, he's pissed."

"Oh, Fu-u-uck. What'd he say?"

"Nothing. That's how you know he's pissed."

"Great. That's just what I need on top of everything else. Should I call him?"

"Ah, I'd leave it alone right now. Just wait and see what happens."

I nodded my head as I rubbed my hands through my hair. "Okay."

"I'll call you after work. Maybe I'll stop by."

"Yeah. I need to get back to the shop. I'll talk to you later."

"You left work?"

"Yep. First time ever. I needed to get away."

"Where are you?"

"Sitting at the park freezing and crying."

"Okay. You'll be fine, Laurel."

I wiped away the tears racing down my face. "I know."

"Bye, Sis."

"Bye, Lance." I snapped my phone closed and dropped it on the picnic table.

There it was. My dad knew. My brother knew. It was all downhill from there. Fuck.

I got up from the bench, trudged back to the Jeep, and went back to work.

Back at the office, no one brought it up, not in front of me at least. I was sure much was said behind my back. But today, that was just fine with me.

I felt shame piling up on my shoulders; I didn't deserve this.

My work day ended and I drove to pick up Hunter. When I walked into the pre-school, Hunter was putting his coat on. I helped gather his paperwork for the day and tried to rush him out of the door because I had no desire to talk to anyone. We were walking towards the front as I heard Miss

Amy call out, "We'll see you tomorrow, Little Hunter."

I froze in place. I glared over my shoulder at her and then spun on my heel and stomped towards her. "I've asked you *multiple times* to stop calling him that. His name is *Hunter.* Not *'Little Hunter.'*" Everyone was staring at us. "Do you have any idea the trauma that a nickname like that can cause for a child?"

She shook her head with the fear of God in her eyes. "Yes, I'm sorry."

"*Sorry* doesn't cut it anymore, Amy."

The director of the pre-school quickly appeared, "What's the problem ladies?"

"Amy continues to call Hunter, 'Little Hunter' after I've asked her multiple times to stop."

"I'm sorry, Miss Forte. We got another Hunter in our class and that's the way she distinguished the two of them. I assure you, it won't happen again."

"I've been *assured* before. I don't believe you now."

Amy said, "I'm sorry. I thought it was cute 'cause the other Hunter's so tall."

"Then why don't you refer to him as *abnormally tall Hunter*?" My glare met her eyes as she stumbled over my question.

I looked at the director. "Isn't your first name Amy, also?"

She nodded.

"So should I refer to you as *Fat Amy*?" I heard a gasp across the school. I stared at her, waiting for her to answer. "Would you like that?"

"No, I wouldn't."

"Then I suggest you address this problem before I contact my lawyer. Do you *finally* understand me?"

They stood there, afraid to answer. "Yes."

I picked Hunter up and burst through the front door, pissed off to the high heavens. As I drove home, I calmed myself down, replaying the look on their faces when I embarrassed both of them in one shot. *Two birds, one stone.* I smirked. *You picked the wrong day to fuck with me.*

I felt as if my entire life had exploded into oblivion. I was trying so hard to keep it together and to keep my wits about me, but the entire world rocked my boat today. I was in distress. *Who do I call? What do I say?* I had no idea how to explain the happenings in my life then, nor did I know how to deal with them. I drifted. Mentally, I drifted far off course and turned off my radar.

Chapter 28

'Fargle'

A few days passed as I had very little interaction with people. Thankfully, Hunter's skin had cleared up perfectly. I know the stress of the situation brought on the psoriasis. But Hunter kept asking to call Bryan. I'd battled the decision in my head: *If I keep telling Hunter that he can't call Bryan, I'm the bad guy. If I let him call Bryan, and Bryan doesn't call back, Bryan's the bad guy.* I had to tell Hunter that, despite his hopes, Bryan was never coming back.

I sat him down one day. "I've got to talk to you about Bryan."

His beautiful eyes looked into mine with a great sadness. "Is he coming back?"

"Um, no, hun."

"Did you talk to him?" His eyes lit up.

"No, I didn't. However, he was on the radio a few days ago and said some very hurtful things about me."

"What'd he say?"

"That doesn't matter. I'm more concerned that you'll understand that I can't be around someone that'd treat us like that. He's out of our life for good."

His eyes welled up with tears and his bottom lip quivered.

"I'm sorry. I didn't want it to turn out this way. I loved him just as much as you did. But he's out of our reach now and we have to accept that."

He looked at me; his big green eyes glistened with tears. "What'd he say?"

I sat there in silence as I chose my words wisely. "He said that I mistreated him and that I was mean. He's glad to never have to see my face again." A tear rolled down my face. Hunter wrapped his arms around my neck as I continued. "I'm sorry it didn't turn out the way we'd hoped, but everything'll be okay. We'll get through this."

"Don't cry. I love you, Mommy. I know you're not mean. We've got each other. That's all we need."

"I know, Babe. I love you."

"I love you too, Mommy."

"Can I read you a book?" I asked.

"Um, my favorite show's on. Wanna watch it with me?" he asked.

"Absolutely." I curled up with him. Nimbus joined us as he flopped across the bottom of the bed.

This was always my favorite part of the day, spending time with the main man in my life. After Hunter fell asleep, I snuck out of his room with Nimbus.

We went into the living room, I checked my phone. I had multiple texts telling me that 'DumbAss' aired that night at ten. I checked the clock and realized that it would start in twelve minutes. I grabbed a beer, sat on the couch, and tuned in to the channel. I watched intently as a fearful realization ate away at my brain. *This is it. They did it. It's officially official. They're famous. I was thrown aside, just as I had feared.*

As the first episode aired, I began to relax. It appeared to be a compilation of parts from the movie that I had already seen, edited down to a half hour version. I watched as I recalled each of the clips shown. The show ended and a huge wave of relief passed through me. I felt as though I'd escaped torture. I grabbed myself another beer as I heard a second 'DumbAss' begin. I stared at the TV screen: four guys chicken-fighting each other, dressed in medieval attire. The two guys perched on the shoulders (one of whom was Bryan) were carrying lances as they pretended to be jousting. I chuckled a little: the humor behind it was obvious. I recoiled back onto the couch, wishing I could be proud of them but instead I felt very little.

As I watched the second show I realized I had never seen these clips before. Some guy named Jack-O was teasing Spam and Bryan, saying, "Dude, no way. There's no way that just happened."

Spam pointed and laughed at Bryan's black eye and said, "Yeah she did, that *Bitch*."

Bryan nodded.

"She beat you up?" asked Jack-O.

Bryan nodded as he pointed to his blackened eye. "Punched me in the face, she did."

Spam laughed, "She's such a bitch and a fucking whore. I hate her."

Jack-O shook his head in amazement as Bryan played the part of the abused boyfriend.

"Fargle," Spam said. "That's what I call her. Short for 'Fu-*bleep!* Laur-*bleep!*'"

Jack-O chuckled, "Why'd she punch you again?"

432

Bryan said, "Cause I caught her cheating on me in my house with her piece of shit asshole ex-boyfriend that she calls Diablo."

I gasped, "No fuckin' way."

My phone rang: it was Diablo. "Yeah," I answered.

"So, we're a hit. Literally. D'you really punch him?"

"Yep."

"Is he crazy? Does he think that I'm going to let him talk shit and make up lies about either one of us without beating the shit out of him?"

"Apparently. But for the record, I vote you pulverize him. I gotta go." I snapped my phone shut and kept watching.

"Bryan Cease's ex-girlfriend's a dirty slut that runs trains on anybody that'll give it to her. She's gotta have Hep C or some disease in that nasty pus-*bleep!* of hers," Spam went on.

My phone rang again: it was Diablo, again. "Uh-huh," I answered.

"I just have to say: *I told you so.*" Click.

I turned my phone off. I sat there, staring at the TV as his words rang through my head: *I told you so.* Once again, Diablo popped right up, and this time, we both knew he was right. I couldn't believe it. *I can't believe that Bryan is saying the shit he is saying. I can't believe Diablo was right, and I can't believe the position I'm currently in. Fuck Me.*

"She's a dyke bitch manly lezbo." Spam almost fell off his chair he was cackling so hard.

Jack-O asked Spam, "Is she really that bad?" He nodded profusely. Jack-O turned to Bryan, "Why'd you date her if she's that much of a whore?"

"My dick got wet every night. Why else?"

"Thank God you ditched that nasty cow," Spam said. "You made the right choice."

I turned off the TV and sat in silence. I felt violated. *Raped.*

I *knew* everything they were saying wasn't true; it didn't change the defilement stomping on my soul. It was a compilation of many stories churned into one extra-large lie. My problem was that they had said that on *national television.* Everyone that knew Bryan and Spam knew exactly who they were talking about. Unfortunately for me, I lived in the same town as they did.

Fuck me. I'm going to get pummeled.

Chapter 29

Blur

The next few weeks were a blur.

Everyday, I got phone calls about 'DumbAss' from people telling me what they said and did on the show. I couldn't turn on the television or radio without hearing something about them, or another ignorant crack about me.

I just kept to myself. I didn't discuss the situation with anyone.

I had no power or control; they had both. They used every chance they could to demolish me. Their lies spread like wildfire. I remained focused on my priorities as I felt myself go into defensive and protective mode. I'd made a commitment as a mother. For the life of me, I was going to remain devoted to it.

I was a lioness who needed to protect her cub.

I took time to try and sort out the chaos. I needed to make sense of what had just taken place and to understand what I was in for in the very near future.

I still had so many things that I wanted Bryan to know: *If you tried to break my heart, you've succeeded. If you tried to make me cry, you've succeeded. If you tried to keep me from loving again, you've succeeded. All I wanted was for you to be happy and you've succeeded. You got everything you wanted. I got everything I didn't want.*

I weighed it all out and came to terms with each and every aspect of my life. I organized it.

I understood where his life was.

I understood where my life was.

Chapter 30

Little 'Ol Me

'DumbAss' had another radio interview. Mounds of worry engulfed me as I forced myself to relax. *The more his fame grows, the quicker he'll forget about me, right? That only makes sense. I mean, seriously. At this point he can already have anyone he wants, so why bother worrying about me?*

The DJ said, "I understand you're making a movie about Bryan and his ex-girlfriend?"

My brain spasmed. *No. He wouldn't, would he? He couldn't have turned this into a movie, right? No. No. No.*

Spam said, "Absolutely, we are. She's such a dirty whore; we just can't pass up the opportunity to mock that bi-*bleep!*"

I turned the radio off.

Little 'ol me? They're making a movie about little 'ol me? What did I do to deserve this?'

My mind went blank.

A couple of the installers walked into the office. Apathetically, they shot quick glances in my direction as they rounded the corner. I knew they heard the interview.

I walked into Paul's office.

"What's up, Laurel?"

"Can I go home? I'm not feeling well."

"Sure, no problem," he said without looking at me.

I knew he'd heard it too.

I found Jane. "I'm going home."

"No problem, Laurel."

She didn't look at me either.

I grabbed my purse and left. I had six missed calls: James, Kelly, Lance, Hillary, Karen and my dad.

They all heard it. I didn't call any of them back. I didn't have it in me at the time, and their questions would still be around later.

I sped out of the parking lot at work, headed straight to the beer distributer, and bought a case of beer and a pack of cigarettes.

I called my mom.

"Hello?"

"Can you take Hunter for a couple of days?"

"Yes, I can. Lance told me what happened. Are you okay?"

"Will you pick him up from daycare after work?"

"Yes, I will, Laurel. Are you alright?"

"Nope." I hung up.

She called me right back. I didn't answer.

I went home and started drinking. I laid in my lounge chair on the back porch and cried. My head spun and my heart bled.

At 5:30, there was a knock on my door and Nimbus darted inside.

I didn't get up.

I heard the front door open as I drunkenly gazed at the tree in the back yard swaying in the breeze.

"Laurel?" Lance asked. "You here?"

I rolled my head towards him. When he saw my face, his eyes widened. "Uh-uh," I said.

He grabbed a few napkins from the kitchen. "Here, you've got mascara all down your face."

"Don't care."

"I can't believe that he's gonna do this to you."

"Neither can I. What did I *do* to deserve this?"

He shook his head and shrugged his shoulders. "Lala, you did nothing. He's bitter and angry at the world right now."

"Why? He wanted fame and he got it. What's he mad at?"

"He doesn't have you and Hunter anymore. Maybe he's regretting his actions and taking it out on you."

"Why? *Why?* What did I do *to him? He* did this, not *me.*" I stared at him, hoping he had the answer.

"You did nothing. He figured it out the hard way. Maybe that's what's wrong. Maybe he's looking for some type of reaction from you."

"Like what? *Running back to him?* Begging him to be with me? I don't want him."

"If you think about it, Laurel, it makes sense. He's telling the world that you're begging him to come back already. Maybe that's what he wants you to do."

"Well, if he wants me back, this is the *wrong way* to go about it. Right now, I'd like to find him in a dark alley and beat the shit out of him."

He chuckled, "You'd absolutely destroy him, She-Ra. He's such a pussy."

"I know I would; that's the funny part. I'd destroy Spam, too."

He giggled from his gut, "One punch from you, She-Ra, and you'd break both of their jaws. Not to mention destroy their egos, too. They'd have to explain to all their fans how *one girl* kicked both of their asses at the same time. That'd be priceless."

"I thought a black eye would've been enough of a warning, but now I'd like to rip Bryan's head off and place it on my mantle."

"So why don't you go confront him? Teach that dickhead a lesson and *kick his ass.*"

"Cause I'm better than that. And I'm obviously a better person than he is; I'd never treat someone like this, no matter what the circumstances were. Never. Who *he* is now, I want nothing to do with. And I certainly don't want Hunter around him."

"I know, but maybe he already figured out that he fucked up with you and wishes you'd forgive him. Maybe the fans have gotten to him already and he can't find anyone better than you."

"Yeah, so he goes on the radio and slaughters me and *my son* and then announces that they're making a *movie* about me? That makes perfect sense." I threw my hands in the air as tears raced down my cheeks. "What a fucking *Dumb-ass.* Literally."

Lance chuckled, "Can I have a beer?"

"Absolutely. Grab me one too?"

He walked into the kitchen and returned with two beers. "When'd you buy that case?"

441

"After I left work."

"You know you've drank like eight so far."

"Yes I do. Today, I'm just fine with it. I deserve to get drunk."

"Yeah. You gonna make it to work tomorrow?"

"Probably not. But that's just fine with me, too."

"Don't lose your job because of this shit."

"I won't; I've accrued plenty of sick days. Right now, I deserve to use them. I've never been this *sick* in my life. Where'd I go wrong?"

"Laurel, just make sure you keep your *life* going without Bryan or his bullshit. Hunter's worth it. You're a great mother and he's a great kid. You *need* to keep your head on straight for you and for him. Take a few days to deal with this, but don't give up. You can't."

As I thought of Hunter my eyes overflowed with tears.

"Stay gold, Ponyboy," he quoted from *The Outsiders.* "Stay Gold."

I giggled through my tears and dabbed my raw face. "How'd I do? Did I get all the mascara?"

He looked at me and giggled. "No, no, you didn't. You look like a gothic witch. You'd be better off washing your face."

"I gotta pee anyway." I got up and stumbled to the bathroom and washed my face three times to get rid of it all.

I checked my phone: nine missed calls. Two from Lance before he got to my house, two from Hillary, one from my parents' house, three from Kelly, and one from Jake.

Then there was a knock on my door.

I pulled open the door. It was my mom, Hunter, and Hillary.

"Hi, Mommy." Hunter lurched into my arms. "You don't feel good?"

"No, I don't. How was your day?"

"It was good. I made a new friend. His name's Brian; but it's spelled different the Bryan's name. Pretty cool, huh?"

"Yep, that's cool. I missed you. I'm so happy to see you."

"Me too, Mommy. I need clothes for Grandmom and DanPop's house." He slid down my legs and ran upstairs.

Hillary quietly asked me, "Are you okay?"

"As best I can be."

"What a jerk off."

"Tell me about it."

"You don't deserve this."

"I know, but for some reason I'm getting it. And from what I understand, it's only going to get worse."

443

My mom said, "I'd like to punch him in his face."

"Feel free."

"What…the…hell is he *thinking*?" she asked angrily.

I shrugged. "Beats me."

We all walked back to the porch.

Hillary said, "Dad's on his way. He's pissed."

My stomach churned with a spurt of anxiety. "Great."

I sat down on the lounge chair. "What do I do? What *can* I do?"

"There *has* to be some way to stop this," Hillary rationalized.

"How? Sue them for *saying* that they're gonna do it? Until they release it, you can't do shit."

We all shook our heads, lacking direction.

My dad burst through the door and stomped out back. "Hi, Laurel." He kissed the top of my head. "You okay?"

"No, not really," I admitted as the tears welled up in my eyes again. Facing my dad was the worst part of this whole situation. I felt like I let him down most of all.

He said, "What the *hell's* he thinking?"

I looked down at the deck in shame. "I don't know, Dad. I just don't know."

"Does he think this is going to drive you back into his arms?"

I shrugged. "If he does, he's sorely mistaken."

My dad said, "Well, that's good to know. Neither you nor Hunter deserves this after everything you've done for him. After what *we've all* done for him. *We* don't deserve this. I'm embarrassed to admit that I know him."

I glared at him. "You? Think about me. I lived with the guy; I was planning a *life* with him."

He huffed, "All the guys on the job site know exactly who he's talking about. And they all know that you're my daughter."

"I'm sorry, Dad. I didn't see this coming."

Mom said, "None of us saw this coming, Laurel. He was like family to us."

"And for the record, Dad, I feel the same way at work. Everyone knows everything."

He rolled his eyes, "Oh God, I didn't even think about that."

Hillary said, "Are they treating you different there?"

"At first they felt bad for me. After today's radio interview, the few that *did* talk to me wouldn't make eye contact with me. Some glared at me and some of them didn't even look in my direction."

Lance said, "That'll change. Give it some time."

Hillary said, "If you let it control your life, it's going to take over. If your ignore it and continue living your life, you'll conquer it."

"I know," I huffed. "I'm not going to let this control me. It's not worth it."

My mom sat down next to me. "This, too, shall pass."

"I know. But right now I'm dealing with all of the emotions at once. Sadness, anger, embarrassment, and a multitude more that I haven't addressed yet. I've got to push through all of these feelings in order to get to the other side."

My mom said, "I know and there *is* another side. You're such a strong woman and I admire that in you. You were on your own before and you can do it again."

I wiped away a single tear. "This will only make me stronger 'cause it ain't gonna kill me."

Obnoxiously, Lance said, "Great, *that's* just what you need: to be *more* independent."

"After this, I may never need another man in my life, *ever.*"

My dad said, "You didn't *need* him. You were doing great on your own *before* he came around. You're too strong and independent to let someone control your life, so don't start by letting this control you, Laurel. You deserve a great man. Bryan's a scared little girl."

"I'm so sorry, everyone. I feel like I've embarrassed this whole family."

Lance and my dad said, in unison: "You didn't do this."

My dad continued, "*He* did this. No, scratch that. *They* did this."

"I know, but I brought him around. I feel like this is *all my fault.* I certainly didn't do it on purpose. But he did, obviously."

We all sat in silence for a few minutes.

Then my dad said, "Well, Lance and I have to go back to a job site real quick. Are you going to be okay?"

I huffed. "Yeah, I'll be fine."

"See you later. Love you, Laurel," my dad said.

"Bye, sis," Lance said.

"Bye. Thanks for stopping by."

My mom asked, "Do you want us to stay for a bit?"

I shook my head. "No, I really just want to be alone right now. To think about things."

"Well, don't think for too long. You've got responsibilities to attend to." She pointed towards Hunter.

"I know, Mom. I just need a few days, that's all. Hacunna Mattata."

Hillary started singing the *Lion King* song, "*It means no worries, for the rest of your days. It's our problem free philosophy, Hacunna Mattata.*"

I giggled, "Yep." I walked inside and made sure Hunter packed enough clothes that matched.

"Bye, Sweets. Be good for Grandmom and Danpop. I love you."

"I will, Mommy. I love you, too." He kissed me and darted out the front door. I hugged Hillary and my mom goodbye. "I'll talk to you tomorrow. Thanks again."

"Bye," my mom said.

Hillary said, "He's a dick. Don't worry about him."

I nodded and watched them all get into their cars. After they pulled away I wrapped a blanket around my twitching body and went back outside.

As the sun set, the early spring evening welcomed a chill in the air. I curled up in the blanket and drank the beer. I stared into the evening sky gazing at the stars. As much as I tried not to focus on what I was in store for, I couldn't help but imagine the worst.

I got very scared. I was about to feel a landslide of hate and ignorance. *What am I supposed to do? I have no power to change what's going to happen to me. I have to turn my back to their bullshit and move forward with my life and pretend that it doesn't bother me.*

I inhaled a deep breath. My head felt clustered and my heart was empty. I felt my muscles tighten as my head swarmed around my options.

What happens if you love someone, you set them free, and they never really go away? Is there a happy ending there? Is there a way for me to salvage what's left of my life? Is there

448

something there that God intended to remain? If so, what is it? Is this torture just meant to break my soul? Dear God, I don't understand.

I had to remind myself to unlock my jaw and release my fists. I was festering in heartbreak, anger, and embarrassment. As a tornado of memories ransacked my thoughts, I allowed myself to cry.

I thought about all of the dramatic changes he had made since this show began. He cheated on me, he stopped showing up for work, radio interviews, comments on the show. And *now* they announced there was a movie being made about me.

He was no longer the person that I loved. His actions quickly turned him into my nemesis.

He went from loving Hunter and me, to slaughtering us on national television and radio. Bryan had declared war. It was unacceptable that he had put my son in jeopardy. I knew that the next few years were going to be treacherous.

I've got to prepare for this battle. I will not let them destroy the life that I've built for my son. I will not let them take it away. I will not let them have the power over me that they are searching for. I will move forward. I will watch. I will learn. And in the end, I will win this war.

I had no idea how I was going to conquer my future. As each event arose, I'd have to rise to the occasion. I had no other choice.

I'd keep my mouth shut for the time being. I allowed my emotions to fester and stir inside as I prepared to be attacked verbally, mentally, emotionally, or physically.

When the time came, I *would* stand my ground.

I *would* put on my armor.

I am now a warrior.

Chapter 31

Stalked by Fame

As the weeks passed, the fans of the show started ganging up on me. I received threatening phone calls at all hours of the night. Sometimes they'd hang up. Others would breathe heavily into the phone. Most frequently, they'd threaten me: "I hope I *never* run into you in Milltown, *Bitch*. You'll never see me comin'." Click.

You're a mass that has consumed me. I've tried to fight it. I've stood my ground. I'm doing my best to move forward. You seem to always be there. Even though you're not in my life, you're here. You haunt me. Your fame stalks my

451

life and so does your hatred. My life has shifted. I cannot rid myself of you. The masses will not allow it.

I began to fear for my safety. More importantly, I began to fear for Hunter's safety. If they were able to get ahold of my unlisted home phone number, then they were able to find my address. *They know where I live.* I began to document every call I received: male or female, date and time.

My days were filled with fake smiles as I became more alert of my surroundings. I looked over my shoulder more and more. *Are they lurking in the shadows watching me?* I began to watch my back. *Are they really coming after me? Were they just threats?*

The crew's fame spread like wildfire. Every time "DumbAss" had an interview, they made remarks about me. Spam had interviews with skateboard magazines and television shows and in each one he spread rumors about me.

My friends told me about rumors they heard around town and in the bars. I decided check their web sites. As I opened the first one, there was the face of *little 'ol me.* They posted pictures of me on the internet. My skin froze and my heart pumped with anger. My hands shook as my adrenaline sky rocketed. There was *my* face and *my* name followed by threatening and ignorant comments from fans:

"She's fuckin' ugly."

"She looks like a cunt."

"She's got a kid? I pity it."

452

"Laurel, the cunt-bitch-whore stalking Bryan Cease...Get her."

"Is that really her? Does she even bathe? I can smell her pussy from here."

"When I see her in town, I'll beat her to a pulp. She ain't got nothing against me."

"Bryan, really? She looks like a nasty cunt. I think you should give me a chance...I'm ready when you are."

And the comments just kept on going. My fears were coming to life. I knew I was in for it and there was absolutely *nothing* I could do about it. *Should I call a lawyer?* Maybe if I continued to keep my cool, it'd go away. I didn't want to engage in their stupidity. I had much more important things to worry about.

The rumors about this movie were everywhere I turned and every person I knew knew about it. I was swarmed.

I felt like I was six years old again when I was taunted and teased by some of the boys in my neighborhood. They had built a tree fort in the middle of the woods. I remember riding my bike down the dirt path when I heard giggling and came to a skidding halt. I listened to the whispers coming from the fort as I slowly snuck over to the rope ladder. I quietly gripped onto the ladder and began to climb ever so stealthily. The three boys' whispers silenced as they stuck their heads out of the fort. Then, like a war cry, one of them screamed, "Fire!!!"

Suddenly, each boy launched large water balloons at me as I dangled a good six feet off the ground.

"No girls allowed," the dark haired one said.

I dodged each oncoming barrage of water balloons as best I could. Then, a direct hit, smack on my forehead. The blow dislodged my grip and I fell from the rope and landed on my back side.

All the boys popped their heads out. They were quiet as they try to see if they actually hurt me. Soaked, I simply sat there for a moment and gathered my thoughts. I stood to my feet, brushed myself off, and rode home in tears.

I, once again, gathered my thoughts as tears streamed down my face, much like I did when I was six. *What can I do? I feel like I just got hit with a tractor trailer that pinned me against a wall.* I wiped my tears away, closed my eyes, and inhaled a long deep breath.

Hunter. Stay focused on Hunter.

I *chose* to preserve and maintain my life. I would *not allow* this control my world. But damn, it made it extremely hard to venture out into town: *their world.* Going into to town became a nightmare. I had no idea who these people were, but they knew *exactly* who I was. They felt like it was their duty to attack me: "There's that fucking ugly whore that

454

used to date Bryan. You fuckin' whore. Get out of the car, bitch. I'll give you what you deserve!"

I stared at the group of punks who were tormenting me standing on the corner. I was half tempted to get out, just to see what they'd do. *Hunter. Stay focused on Hunter.* I took deep breaths and gripped the steering wheel as I shifted in my seat, anxious for the light to turn.

"I didn't think you'd have the balls, whore! You scared?"

I turned my head and met her glare. I smirked and shook my head. "Quite the opposite, dumb bitch. I'd kick your ass," I thought, turning my smirk into a smile. "Come and get it, bitch." The light turned and I began to drive.

She yelled, "I knew you didn't have it in you!"

I won't engage in this stupidity. My life is better without him. Hunter's worth it.

On episodes of the show they referred to me as "Bryan Cease's ex-girlfriend." Every time they mentioned me, I received threatening phone calls. My ledger of phone calls and episodes grew quickly.

I randomly checked their web sites and kept tabs on the status of the movie. Fans wrote more and more threatening comments and ignorant accusations. I printed them out and filed them in the bottom drawer of my desk, which quickly overflowed. Each one pissed me off even more than the last, which made my spirit stronger and my soul more driven.

I collected the "verbal stones" as they were thrown in my direction. I gathered my ammunition show by show and month by month as they tarred and feathered me in front of the whole village. It was my name and my face, but their made up version of me. *Maybe it's time to talk to a lawyer. This is ridiculum.*

I had no desire to be in their world and that pissed them off even more. Things got worse. I hated where my life was. I needed something to change because I was scared to death.

Chapter 32

Twenty Five

On my birthday weekend, I went out for drinks with my friends. I tried not to think about anything before I left the house, hoping that because so much time had passed, no one would care anymore about little 'ol me.

But as soon as I walked towards the bar, the taunting started. Two of his friends were talking outside the front door. I acknowledged their presence as I shot a quick glance over my shoulder and a crooked smile.

They saw me, I saw them.

Shortly thereafter, a random girl came up to me and said, "You did him wrong. You're just pissed because he's famous and left you high and dry. Now he can get someone so much better than you."

I simply responded, "Famous? You're the one shocked by his fame, not me. I knew *months* before they signed. I hope you enjoy your talks with him now because they'll end. He *will* forget about you; he'll never forget about me."

She said, "You're a jealous whore, you ugly bitch."

I refrained from punching her square between the eyes. "Jealousy's not what I feel right now; it's more like disgust."

She rolled her eyes and huffed at me.

I laughed at her and found my friends gathered by the dance floor.

Chelsea said, "Hey, Sweetie. Happy Birthday. How you been? I haven't seen you for so long."

"Thanks, I'm good. It's so good to see a friendly face. What's new with you?"

"Same old shit, bigger pile," she huffed.

"I hear that. At least you're not dealing with somebody else's pile of shit too."

"You hangin' in, girl?"

"Yes. Barely, but yes," I admitted.

"Don't worry about anybody but you and your son. He's worth it. You both deserve to be happy."

"Thank you, I needed to hear that. He's the only reason I'm doing as well as I am. Gotta protect yer young."

"Keep it that way. You look great."

I continued watching the band, singing and dancing along with the songs. I needed to stop worrying about everything and simply be *me*.

An old friend approached me. "Ya know, Laurel. Every time I see you, I think of Bryan."

I resisted karate chopping him square in the throat. "Really? Most guys think about how hot I am and try to get in my pants. Guess that makes you gay, huh?"

"You're bitter. Should've expected that," he remarked.

"Not bitter. I'm over it. If you ask me, Bryan's the bitter one," I said.

Chelsea, overhearing the conversation snapped, at him. "Really dude? Don't be a dick."

"I didn't mean to bring it up. I'm…"

I added, "I see you *once* in a blue moon and *that's* the first thing you say to me? Try again."

"It was good to see you. You look great. Gotta run." He left us.

"Fuck him," Chelsea said.

"He's an asshole. I need another beer. Do you need a drink?" I asked.

"I'm good, Hun. Thanks for asking."

"I'll be right back."

I perched on the bar waiting for Teddy, the bartender, to see me. "Oh my God, I've wondered where you've been. How're you? You look stunning." He handed me a beer and leaned over for a kiss.

"I've been working a lot, being a mom. You know, living life."

"Life is doing you well. You're gorgeous, my dear. That beer's on me; have fun tonight. I love to see you smile."

"I will. I'll see you later." I headed back over to the dance floor where Jessica was dancing with Jake.

Jake came over and gave me a hug. "I miss you darling. How's that little man of yours?"

"He's wonderful. Thanks for asking."

I stood there, people-watching and minding my own business when, unexpectedly, I was soaked. My hair was drenched and my shirt was saturated. A cup rolled off my shoulder and landed on the ground.

Kelly, Jessica and Jake turned when it splashed them.

"Someone just dumped a beer on me from the balcony upstairs." I cringed.

Kelly gasped, "What the fuck?"

I looked up to the balcony; some chick was smirking at me. "That fucking bitch," I said through my teeth as I envisioned myself gripping her by her hair and using her face as a punching bag.

I took a deep breath, brushed myself off, and went upstairs into the bathroom to clean myself up. I dried my hair and shirt under the hand dryer.

Kelly came storming into the bathroom. "What the fuck's wrong with them? That's so ignorant."

My brain was boiling. *Happy Birthday, Laurel. You shoulda stayed the fuck at home.*

"Do you want to leave? We can go somewhere else," she asked.

"Why? To let them win? Let them think they can get over on me this way, too? I don't think so."

Stacy said, "Fuck them. They can't ruin your night out with us. You don't get very many nights out, ya' know?"

"It's so fucking childish," I said. "How'd I get myself into this position? He left me. He cheated on me. This is what I get?"

"They're losers, Laurel."

"Let's go sit down, I feel like I need to watch my back right now. I'd rather just chill," I said.

I walked out of the bathroom and downstairs and there she was; the girl who dumped the beer on me was right at the bottom of the stairs. At that second, I *knew* that Bryan and all of his friends were standing right around the corner.

461

I stared her right in her eyes as I descended and gave her an evil smile. "Nice shot, I was soaked. But I still look better than you." I batted my eyes as I walked past and slammed her with my shoulder.

She slammed into the wall and everyone around froze as they quickly realized I was standing there.

My eyes met Bryan's.

He started stuttering in mid-sentence and got very nervous.

My jaw locked, fists clenched, and my shoulders pulsated with adrenaline. It took every ounce of self-control I had not to split his face open with one Hail Mary of a punch and drop his ass. I felt the evil hatred pumping through my veins and out of my eyes. Visions of his face bursting through his pug-shaped nose flashed in my head.

Take the high road. Don't count to ten. Walk away now; he's not worth it.

I smiled a powerful, ignorant, and controlled, evil smile as I locked into his fearful eyes. His nervousness showed all across his body as he rocked back and forth, stuttering over his words.

I walked past him and didn't look back. I sat down at the table, ordered a drink from the waitress, and lit up a cigarette. It was one of the most pure and empowering moments I remember.

My friends quickly followed me to the table. They had been close behind me and watched the whole thing. But they also saw what I didn't see: the reactions.

Kelly said, "I'm so glad you shouldered her into the wall. Whatever you said to her pissed her off and she started ranting after you walked away. What'd you say?"

"I said, 'Nice shot; I was soaked. I still look better than you.'"

They laughed hysterically.

Jake said, "You want me to kick his ass?"

I didn't respond but I thought, "Yes."

Kelly said, "Bryan tried to follow you through the crowd. Jessica grabbed him and said, 'Don't you dare. You did this you fuckin' idiot. You don't deserve her.'"

Jessica continued, "He tried to say something but I didn't give him the opportunity to. I pushed him, turned, and walked away."

I tried to get comfortable as I adjusted myself in my seat. My back was on fire. My brain was overcooked. I stared at the stool in front of me. *Why's this happening right now? Is this a dream? I mean, a nightmare? What, in God's name, is going on? Please make it stop.*

Suddenly I wanted to leave but I didn't want to make a scene, so I finished my beer and slid out of my seat, saying, "I'm going to the bathroom, I'll be right back." I disappeared into the crowd towards the back door, which would set off an alarm. I knew the bouncers would flock to the door. I quickly jabbed the door open, walked out, and took off around the corner. I slowed to a quick walk as I approached the street and crossed towards my Jeep.

I set my phone to silent.

I got in my car and just sat there as tears started welling up. I said to myself, "Laurel, no. Don't let him do this to you. He's already proven that he doesn't deserve you; why give him the tears too?" I prayed, "Dear God, give me strength. Please make him leave me alone. Please make this stop. Please God, I'll do anything. Please make this go away."

I started the car, threw it in reverse, and left the parking lot. As I rounded the corner I had to pass the bar. As my luck would have it, he was standing outside.

I saw him look at my Jeep, and notice me in it. My mind started racing: *Why's he using me to make himself feel better? I did so much for you, asshole. I made sense to you when nothing else did. I would've done anything for you. And this is what I get? Bullied. I get bullied because you became famous. I'm glad I'm not with you anymore.*

My brain became absorbed with questions and my chest became tight with anxiety. After a drive that seemed to last forever, I finally arrived home and cried myself to sleep.

I awoke the next morning with tears in my eyes. I was thinking of him and wondering why I went out at all.

I stared at the ceiling as I tried to organize my thoughts. Hunter was at his dad's all weekend. I was alone. And damn, did I feel it.

I got up and sluggishly walked downstairs with my blanket wrapped around my body. I flopped down on the couch and watched romantic movies; I needed to cry.

I cried so much, I cried myself dry.

Somewhere in the middle of the first movie, my doorbell rang. *Go away. I don't want to be bothered. No more drama. Please. No more drama.*

It rang again. And again. And again, again and again. Whoever it was knew I was here and they weren't going away.

I heard keys in the lock. Kelly: she's the only one with a key to my house.

The door opened slowly. "Laurel? Are you here?"

I didn't answer. I couldn't find the word, "yep." I just laid there.

She pushed the door open and stepped into the living room.

"Hey, Laurel, are you okay?"

I weakly rolled my head towards her and answered with an empty stare.

She sat at the end of the couch. "Do you want to talk about it?"

I lowered my head and shook it slowly.

"Can I get you anything? Some soup, a drink, a nail file?"

I wished I could laugh. I just couldn't find it. A very weak and lifeless, "No" came out somehow.

"You left us last night. We've all been so worried. We've been calling your cell but you haven't answered; we thought something happened."

I rolled over and looked her dead square in the eyes. "Like what?"

"None of us knew. You disappeared on us and then we realized that he left, too. We thought maybe you were together."

I rolled back. "Hell no. I came home. It's where I needed to be. Home and alone."

"Do you want me to stay for a while?"

Pressing my palms into my eye sockets, trying to release some of the pressure in my mind, I mumbled, "No. I just want to be alone. I need that right now."

"You're sure?"

"Yeah."

She waited a few minutes, sitting with me in silence. After realizing that I was in no mood to talk she said, "Call me when you want to talk."

I grunted.

She kissed my forehead and left.

After the third love story, I forced myself to get up. I shuffled into the kitchen and stared into the cabinets and the refrigerator. I finally decided on a box of crackers and a beer.

I switched the DVDs and zoned into the next movie. I felt every bit of the character's pain.

I watched the love stories and compared each story to mine. Every single one of them had a happy ending. *Will my love story have a happy ending? No way. What good could come of this? Nothing good will stem from this. Nothing, at all.*

As I weighed my options of my life that day, I chose myself. I chose to focus on what I wanted and what I needed. I took a step back and looked at my life from a different perspective and saw things very differently. I began, for the first time in years, to focus on what truly mattered to me. I cut the world off and beautiful things began to happen. Whether my feelings or actions made sense to anyone else, they made sense to me and that was what mattered.

Chapter 33

There's No Place Like Home

I knew I couldn't remain on the path that my life was going down. Pregnant at the age of nineteen, never been to college, and I had no other avenues in my life. Every morning I woke up I was like a machine; I did the same thing over and over again. And at the end of my day, I despised the lack of opportunities I had in my life.

At twenty five, my life had become everything I told myself I didn't want it to be: normal and monotonous. I needed to get my life in order and buy a house. The only way for me to accomplish that goal was to move back in with my parents so I could save money. I presented the idea to them shortly after I'd thought of it, and after some convincing on my part, I was able to weasel my way into living there for free.

We moved in almost immediately. This was the safest place for me to be: home where I was needed, loved, happy, and understood. After all, there's no place like home. I focused on my son and myself.

I decided that I wanted to go to school for Cosmetology. I had always cut my friends' hair as well as my own; I had a natural talent for it.

The next day, I called off of work and applied to schools. I had to get out of the work atmosphere where I was; there were too many reminders haunting me. As much as I tried to ignore them, Bryan's continuing slandering made my interactions with my worse. My paranoia heightened and my ego bruised.

I had to get out of there; it was mental torture. I need to regain control over the things that I had the power to control. The day I received notification that I was accepted into Cosmetology school, I put in my two weeks' notice at the Audio Visual Communications.

I continued coaching gymnastics and started waitressing on the weekends. I could truly be focused on what was important to me. My life instantly began to change. As I worked my way through Cosmetology school, I quickly made leaps and bounds in life.

My smile began to surface again. I felt great about my future and my life. About halfway through school, I was at the top of my class. I started looking for assistant jobs in a salon. I knew if I was going get approved for a mortgage to buy a house, I'd need to be in a long term position. I began working part time as an assistant at Shear's Salon. I cut back on my coaching hours and began to strive for a career. As my days passed by rapidly, my pride and ego grew.

I passed the Cosmetology Practical Exam with flying colors: step one of my goals. I was thrilled with myself, and excited to start my future as a stylist. I began working full time as a stylist at Shear's Salon, quickly building my clientele book. I had to stop coaching gymnastics due to my new schedule, but continued waitressing on the weekends. My bank account quickly grew as I saved every dime to use as a down payment on a house for Hunter and me.

As winter began to set in, my waitressing hours were cut down. Hunter's birthday was right around the corner. "What do you want to do for your birthday, Sweets? Where should we have your party?" I asked, dreading the array of possible answers.

"I want to have a gymnastics party!" he exclaimed.

A feeling of relief overcame me. The only thing I was going to need to pay for was a birthday cake. I called the gym and scheduled a day for Hunter's party. Coach agreed to let me run the party, even though I no longer worked there.

I sat down at the computer and made birthday invitations. The next morning, he excitedly took them to school to hand out to his friends.

Chapter 34

Five Years Old

It was the day of Hunter's 5th birthday party. I had thirteen kids coming to the gym. As they gathered in the lobby, parents were excited to see how their kids would enjoy the party.

We bounced on the trampolines, jumped into the foam pit, and flipped on the bars. I high-fived each child as they finished their turns and their smiling faces overwhelmed me with pleasure. Nothing made me feel better than teaching a child something new. They all were so excited about what they could physically accomplish when someone showed them how.

Outside of Hunter, none of them had ever taken gymnastics classes. At the end of the party, I got to make them all "fly." They sat along the wall, waiting for their turn. Hunter, the birthday boy, went first. I hooked him into the belt, as he demonstrated what each of them was going to do. He showed them seat drops, back flips and, finally, how to fly. I held onto the ropes that extended up to the ceiling and jumped off the side of the trampoline, shooting Hunter up into the air and flying back and forth. All of his friends cooed in excitement. Back and forth he swung in the air, kicking his feet around and doing back flips. As I slowly lowered him back down onto the trampoline, the kids gasped and excitedly shuffled to be next. They each took turns flying as their screams of joy echoed through the gym.

As we finished flying, we lined up and went upstairs in the party room for birthday cake. They all found a seat at the long table, covered in a "Batman" tablecloth. Hunter sat at the head of the table. I set the "Batman" birthday cake in front of him, lit the candles, and we all began to sing. After the first line of the song, he burst into tears.

I jumped to his side, "What's wrong, Hunter? What's wrong?"

Sputtering through his tears, he said, "Y-you didn't turn o-o-ff the l-lights, Mommy."

Trying not to giggle in his face, I realized he was right. I stopped everyone from singing and said,

474

"Oops. I forgot to turn off the lights. We are going to need to start over." I flicked the light switch off, and said, "Okay, everybody, one more time."

"Happy Birthday to you, Cha-cha-cha
Happy Birthday to you, Cha-cha-cha
Happy Birthday dear Hunter, Cha-cha-cha
Happy Birthday to you. Cha-cha-cha"

With a huge smile on his face, he blew out the candles on his cake. I quickly removed the candles and cut the cake in pieces. I passed out the plates, and all the kids started inhaling their pieces. I walked back behind Hunter with a large piece on my plate. I set it next to him as he shoveled his cake into his mouth. He glanced over to my plate and smiled.

I sat down next to him, pushed the back of his head, and smashed his face into my piece of cake.

He giggled hysterically, "Mommy smashed cake in my face!" His friends giggled as he stood up on his chair and danced with icing and cake smeared across his face and up his nose.

Giggling, he said, "Mommy, I have something for you."

I said, "You do? What is it?"

He picked up a piece of cake and smashed it into my face.

The entire roomful of parents and kids burst into laughter. I leaned over and kissed him, smearing the cake and icing across our faces even more.

"Yummy, I love it." We chuckled so hard, my abs started hurting.

I wiped the icing and cake crumbles off of my face as best I could and grabbed a fresh napkin for Hunter's face. I cleaned him up and excused myself to the bathroom.

I washed my face making sure to get all of it off. As I double checked my face in the mirror, an overwhelming feeling of love overtook my body. Tears welled in my eyes, as I whimpered with happiness. At the same moment, I was overwhelmed with sadness and loneliness. Bryan infected my brain, and I started balling my eyes out.

I contained myself. In my head I started repeating, "Laurel, he doesn't deserve you, he doesn't deserve Hunter, he doesn't deserve to be here. Let him go. You have too much good in your life and that is what you need to focus on."

I stared at myself in the mirror, dried my face from tears and water, and went back to the party room. The second my mom saw my face, she knew something was wrong. Nonchalantly, she walked over. "Are you okay?"

"Yep," I said and walked away from her.

Hunter started ripping open his presents as I watched. I kept forcing thoughts of Bryan out of my head. I froze a smile on my face, pretending everything was fine. The emptiness crept into the back of my mind and I forced it out again. I released the tension in my jaw. I was overwhelmed. I always assumed Bryan was going to be here for Hunter's birthday. I forced myself to have a conversation with one of the moms. I needed to redirect my mind.

As Hunter finished opening his presents, parents started collecting their kids to head home. My mom and I cleaned up the mess around the room. As I worked in silence, she talked. "What a great group of kids. They had so much fun."

I nodded my head. "There ain't no party like a gymnastics party."

She continued, "Do you think they'll get any new students from this?"

I nodded. "Yeah, one or two."

"Well, that's good right?"

"Of course, Mom. The more kids that join, the more money they make," I continued, "The more money one makes, the happier they are, right? Isn't that the way it's supposed to be?"

She sarcastically agreed. "That's what they tell me."

I walked out of the party room, bags of presents in my hands, and went downstairs to the gym. I locked the garage doors and set up the floor for the classes tomorrow. We loaded the car and I locked the front door of the gym and headed home.

Chapter 35

Waiting to Piss

The rest of the world was speeding past me in the blink of an eye. So much time has passed, I wondered what would happen if I showed my face in town. I'd rebuilt the foundation of my life and I felt good. I was happy.

I decided it was time for me to have a night out. Unfortunately, I knew that where I liked to go was where he'd be. "Good," I thought as I planned a night with Kelly and Chelsea.

We decided to go to Johnny's. I hadn't shown my face there in about six months. That's a long time for someone who was so well known here and then simply vanished out of sight.

I prepared myself to see him. I knew I could handle this. Suddenly, I looked forward to my night out.

As we walked through the door, the owner, Matt, was standing there. When he saw me, his head dropped and he put his hand on his heart and smiled. He gave me one of his well-known bear hugs. "You've crossed my mind so many times. How are you?"

"Very good, and you?"

He smiled, "Life is good. I can't complain. Your ex-husband's upstairs."

My heart plummeted.

"I figured he would be. Thank you for being the first asshole to shove it down my throat."

He said, "I just wanted you to know."

I flicked him off as I walked through the crowd. He was the best known ball-buster on the face of the earth. His first love was ruining someone's day. I guessed I should've prepared myself for him, too. That was my first reminder of why I didn't come out any more.

I made my way through the crowd and ran into some old friends. In two years I hadn't heard

480

from any of them. They'd continued to go out and get drunk and that's just not how my life was.

The band was taking their first break, so I excused myself and went to the upstairs bathroom. *There's a long line. Of course.*

I inhaled a long, deep breath as Matt's voice rang in my head. *Your ex-husband is upstairs.* I held my breath. *Don't let this control you. Control it.* I repeated it in my head as I exhaled and removed all negative thoughts from my brain. I leaned against the wall, patiently waiting for my turn in the bathroom. I closed my eyes and rolled my neck and shoulders, releasing the tension that had built up since I arrived.

In the line I stood in, waiting to piss, I let my guard down and relaxed a little bit. Just as I opened my eyes and came out of my thoughts, there he was. He was coming out of the bathroom with a big smile on his face, until he saw me.

I felt a strike of heat spear through my spine. I felt myself get hot, pissed off hot. My body sparked with anger and danced at the edge of the fiery cliff, ready to ignite like wildfire jumping, from one muscle to the next.

This wasn't supposed to happen. My fingernails dug into my palms. He quickly dropped his eyes from my glare and cornered the wall.

I snuffed. *Pussy.* I thought I was prepared for this, but you can never really know until you experience it. I should've known. This had been the longest five seconds of my life. Nothing was said.

After recouping in the bathroom, I grabbed two beers from the bar and went back downstairs to hang out.

Kelly was standing next to the sound guy, whom she had known for years. I handed her a fresh beer as I joined her.

"Thank you." She winked at me.

I nodded as I took a sip of my beer. "Uh-huh."

She studied my face. "What just happened?"

"I'll give you one guess."

"Is he here? Is Bryan here?"

As my eyes rolled, I gave one solid nod.

"Did he see you?"

"Waiting in line for the bathroom."

"Did he say anything to you?"

"Not a word. But when he saw my face, it wiped the smile right off his. I think he shit himself a bit, too."

She burst into laughter, "Good. Maybe he can roll around in his *own* shit for the show."

"Swimming in raw sewage isn't funny enough anymore. He can one-up himself and walk around with shit in his pants for a week," I said.

We laughed at his expense, which felt really good. I'd found it rather hard to laugh at any part of this situation since he had drug my reputation through the mud and destroyed my ego.

The band continued to play their second set of the night. We bobbed along to the songs, occasionally breaking out in a funny dance. They began to play "Sweet Home Alabama" when Kelly grabbed Chelsea and I and pulled us towards the front of the stage. We sang and danced along with the band.

I noticed a girl, who I had never seen before, glaring at me from the other end of the stage. She whispered to one of her friends, who quickly glanced over her shoulder at me before disappearing into the crowd.

As I watched out of my peripheral vision, I felt her eyes glaring at me while she worked her way towards me through the crowd. She shoved through the group of girls standing slightly behind me. I glared over my shoulder and the second my eyes met hers, she pulled her right arm back, hand in a fist, ready to punch me.

I spun on my right heel and caught her fist with my right hand, clenched it and twisted her arm down. I pulled her by the back of her neck and whispered in her ear, "You don't want to do this."

The bouncer closest to me jumped off the ledge and forced his way in between us.

I released my grip from her as he braced her and guided her back to her spot at the other side of the stage.

He returned to his spot on the wall and he tapped me on the shoulder. "I saw that coming, Laurel. Do you know what that's about?"

I shook my head frivolously, "No, I don't, Joe. I've never seen her before in my life."

He nodded, "Keep your eyes open."

I nodded. I turned as Kelly and Chelsea were staring at me. Chelsea said, "What was all that about?"

"No idea." I looked up at the lead singer, Chris. He shook his head and winked at me. I smirked back at him and shrugged my shoulders.

We continued to dance along as they led into "Jack and Diane" by John Cougar Mellencamp. Jokingly, we imitated our 80's dance moves. As we danced in a circle, I saw a girl with jet black hair shoving her way through the crowd directly towards me.

I stopped in my tracks, as she lurched over the group of people standing behind me. One of the guys caught her around the waist as she threw punches at me. I reached out, grabbed her by the back of her hair, and slammed her face into my knee. I was quickly lifted from where I stood, still holding onto her hair. A huge hand reached around me and grabbed my wrist, forcing me to release my hold on her hair. The band immediately stopped playing.

The bouncer spun me around and set me in the corner behind Kelly and Chelsea. He looked at them and pointed his finger at me as he demanded to them, "She doesn't move."

They simultaneously nodded as he turned and helped carry out the girl while she was kicking and screaming, "I'm gonna kick your ass, Laurel!"

Kelly looked at me, "What the fuck's going on?"

"I wish I knew," I lied as my eyes began scanning the crowd; I knew this had something to do with Bryan. The crowd was watching the girl get dragged out and then glanced back towards me, trying to figure out what was going on.

My eyes ventured upstairs to the balcony. As I scanned for a familiar face, friend or foe, I caught a quick glance of Bryan. He tried to hide from my line of sight. As it all seemed to make sense suddenly as I took a sip of my beer.

I leaned in between Kelly and Chelsea. "Bryan's up on the balcony dodging my line of sight as we speak."

They both looked up towards the balcony. "You don't think Bryan put them up to this, do you?" Kelly asked.

"I don't know. Obviously it has something to do with them targeting me on the world wide web. Just sayin."

Chelsea shook her head. "What a Dumbass."

The band began fiddling on their instruments and Chris spoke to the crowd. "Let's get back to business, people."

The crowd roared.

Chris spoke into the microphone to me. "What was all that about?"

I shrugged my shoulders. "Never seen either one of them before."

Chris looked up at the balcony, his eyes searching for Bryan. "Can't we all just get along?"

The crowd roared with laughter and applause as he started singing again.

I leaned against the ledge and waited for the bouncer to return. I looked at him. "Can I move away from here now?"

He nodded. "What the hell's all this about?"

"I have no idea. I don't know either one of those girls, but I have many reasons to believe it involves Bryan."

He nodded. "That's what I thought. Sorry you had to deal with that."

"I'm sorry, but it just goes to show you the stupidity amongst them."

He smiled. "Believe me; I know how stupid they are. I deal with them every weekend. Watch your back."

I smiled. "I will and thank you."

He nodded and stepped back up to the ledge. People stepped out of my way as I walked through the crowd. I felt Joe watching me from his post.

I stepped up off the dance floor near the bar

and stood close to the wall. I ordered a beer from Teddy.

He quickly set it in front of me. "Was that about you?"

Slightly embarrassed, I nodded.

"Why? What'd you do to them?"

"I've never seen either one of them before in my life."

He nodded. "So it's probably about Bryan then, huh?"

"Yep." I clenched my jaw and forced a smile on my face. "Should I be offended?"

He raised his eyebrows, "That's a tough call. You'd think by now he'd have moved on. But then again, maybe he did and one of them is his new girlfriend and she's jealous of you." He paused. "You do realize how beautiful you are, right?"

I slightly nodded. "Jealousy is a bitch."

"Yes it is. You'd make any woman jealous."

"Well, thank you. Now get back to work." I shot him a smile and a wink.

"Always good to see you, Laurel."

"You too, Teddy." I watched as the band continued to perform.

I gazed over the crowd and settled my brain around the events of the evening. I shook my head in disgust. Inhaling a deep breath, I closed my eyes and ran my fingers through my hair.

As I opened my eyes, I saw a slight

commotion near the opening of the stairwell onto the dance floor. I paid no attention to it. *Thank God, I'm not involved.* I flipped my hair over my shoulder and leaned my back against the wall.

I looked around, avoiding the commotion as something quickly caught my eye. Bryan and Spam walked out onto the dance floor from the balcony stairwell just behind the ruckus.

Just as they stepped into my view, Spam glared at me with a smirk on his face. He turned to the slightly chubby girl behind him, nodded his head in my direction, and her eyes met mine.

She looked somewhat familiar to me. I rolled my eyes and smirked. She stomped towards me as the sea of people parted like the Red Sea for Moses. She had her right hand in a fist by her side and her gaze locked on me. As I watched her in my peripheral vision, she had no idea that I knew she was coming after me.

Time to end this, Laurel. Enough is enough. I thought to myself. My own thoughts were followed by my dad's voice echoing through my head. *Laurel, never start a fight, but make sure you finish them.*

She pulled her fist back, ready to swing. I clenched my fist and punched her with a quick jab in her nose. Blood splattered across her face and down her shirt. She toppled backwards, tripped over her own feet, and fell across the wet dance floor. She tried to get up, but her balance was altered and she fell forward onto the floor, blood gushing from her nose.

I stood firm as my eyes met Spam's shocked eyes which were outlined by dark circles and sunken into his face.

I smirked at him and then met Bryan's sunken eyes. His horrified face told me everything I needed to know. *That one's his new girlfriend. Where do I know her from?* He stepped towards her, his body language was tense. He cowered behind her as she tried to stand up. I knew he was scared to come anywhere near me for fear of me hitting him. *Well, you'd deserve it, too.*

As he bent over to help her, I envisioned punting his face like a football and hopefully splitting his face wide open, too. I twitched and constrained myself as I had a flashback to my childhood football days. My team always made me punt the ball; none of the guys could kick it as far as I could.

I chose to smile at him, as I spun around and went to wash my hands in the bathroom. My adrenaline was pumping through my veins. I took long, deep breaths as I dried my hands.

I looked at myself in the mirror, "Time to go home, Laurel."

I opened the bathroom door to find Joe, the bouncer. He said, "It's time to go home, Laurel."

"Yes, it is. Sorry about that. Again, I don't know who the fuck she is, but I believe she's Bryan's new girlfriend."

He nodded. "She is. The other two were her friends."

I took a deep breath, "Figures."

As he escorted me to the front door, another bouncer motioned for us to stop. I looked at him, "What's going on?"

The bouncer at the front door, Tim, said, "The first two girls are out front waiting for you to leave so they can jump you."

I rolled my eyes, "I'm not worried."

He laughed, "I'm sure you aren't. But I can't let you leave, knowing what's going on. Mandy, Bryan's girlfriend, has already been rushed to the hospital."

My eyes met his. I said nothing. *Mandy? Mandy? Do I know a Mandy? That's short for Amanda, right? Amanda, Amanda…* Then it hit me like a ton of bricks: Amanda was the waitress at the Italian Restaurant we used to go to. *Son of a fucking bitch.*

"You broke her nose and her cheek bone."

I smiled and said nothing.

Two police cars pulled up front. The officers quickly gained control of the two girls screaming out front.

I couldn't hear anything going on, but Tim started narrating for me. "The cop just said, 'So this girl attacked all three of you out of nowhere?'" He chuckled and looked over his shoulder. "They're

490

trying to pin all of this on you."

"Of course they are."

Joe called out, "Officer, can I talk to you?"

The second officer stepped into the front door and asked, "What can you tell me about this situation?"

Joe filled the officer in on the events of the evening: "I was bouncing on the dance floor. Laurel and her friends were minding their own business at the front of the stage. The blonde in the red shirt first went after Laurel on the dance floor. Then the one with the black hair went after her, too."

The officer looked at me, confused.

I smiled and said nothing.

Joe continued, "Laurel removed herself from the dance floor, and then Mandy, the girl that's on the way to the hospital, went after Laurel. And in one punch, Laurel split her face open and broke her nose and cheek bone."

Tim jumped in, "After all of that, the two girls that are out front are planning to jump Laurel when she leaves."

The officer looked at me. "Do you know these girls?"

I shook my head. "I've never seen any of them before. Though I did just find out that the one that I punched is my ex-boyfriend's new girlfriend."

"Ah. So there it is," the officer said. "He must still have a thing for you."

You have no idea. I forced a sweet smile, as I thought, "Maybe now it's time to contact a lawyer."

"Sounds like a case of 'don't know what you got 'til it's gone,'" the officer said.

Joe joked, "She sure as hell isn't as good looking as you are."

I smiled, "Thank you."

The officer said, "Did you drive?"

I nodded.

"I can tell you're not drunk. Can I escort you to your car? We have the other two in cuffed in the car."

I stared at him, "Why are you arresting them?"

"Public drunkenness. Are you going to be pressing charges?"

"For what? Kickin' their asses?"

Everyone burst into laughter.

I confirmed, "No, I won't be pressing charges. Is there a possibility that any of them will try to come after me?"

The officer shook his head, "We've got too many witnesses that are on your side. It would go nowhere in court."

I nodded. "Well, that's good to know."

He flipped his notepad closed, tucked it in his jacket pocket, and motioned for me to lead him to the car.

I looked at the bouncers. "Thanks again, and

sorry for the commotion."

"You're welcome. And none of this was your fault," Joe assured me.

"No worries," Tim said. "Have a good night."

"You too." I stepped onto the street. I looked in the back seat of the cop car and saw that the two girls were mouthing off at me. I smiled, waved my fingers at them, and allowed the officer to escort me to my car.

As we walked, I broke the uncomfortable silence. "The stars are beautiful tonight, despite the chaos."

He shot me a confused stare. "You just got attacked by three girls, beat *them* up, and you're more moved by the stars than worried about your safety."

I slowed my pace and stood still, looking up at the evening sky. "Look at the moon. It's huge," I whispered.

He stared at me. "Laurel? Aren't you concerned for your safety?"

I lowered my eyes to meet his. "No. I'm not worried about my safety. If you haven't noticed, I'm a very confident person. I don't get intimidated too often and I'm very physically capable of handling myself."

"Okay. Do you have a husband or boyfriend at home to protect you in case someone were to follow you?"

"Neither. However, I do have a five year old

son at home and a very well trained Pit bull. I wouldn't want to be the person who thinks they're going to threaten me at my home."

He slowly nodded his head.

"I was a competitive gymnast for thirteen years. I still coach and my father is a second degree black belt in karate; he taught me well. Strength oozes from my pores, as does discipline and confidence."

"So I don't have to worry about you, then?"

"Nope. Thanks for making sure I got to my car safe. Have a good night." I unlocked the door to my Jeep and hopped in. The engine roared to life as the officer crossed back over towards the bar.

As I drove home, I knew that what I said to the cop was true. I was a very confident person and I didn't get intimidated very easily. However, when I allowed myself to be overwhelmed by hard situations, I became scathed. And all of my strength, pride, and desire became tarred and feathered by the *ridiculum*. I became insecure, bitter, and angry. I took those negative feelings and fertilized the garden of my life.

This *was* my life. I had walked right back into what I wanted so desperately to be away from. The damage was done. *Enjoy your wake-up call into reality; he's gloating in it. You let him see you squirm. But in a week you'll be a much stronger version of who you are today.'*

The next morning awoke and the reality hit me; they had three girls try to jump me. Thank God I had the day off. It could be a Laurel day.

I knocked on Lance's bedroom door. "Hey, do you think I should call a lawyer?"

"Yes, without a doubt."

"Really? What can they do?"

"They've got to be able to do something, Laurel. They've put your name and face all over their websites and they're making a movie about you. There has to be something you can do."

"Okay, I'm gonna think about it."

"Don't think too hard. Just make the call, Laurel."

I backed out of his room as I felt the noose tighten around my neck. I felt slaughtered. *I can't believe it has come to this. I have to call a fucking lawyer.*

I cleaned my parents' house from top to bottom. I released my frustration by scrubbing everything I could find. I started in the downstairs bathroom, and then went to the kitchen. After cleaning all of the appliances, I dropped to my hands and knees and scrubbed the tile floor. I moved to the upstairs bathroom, and then vacuumed the entire house.

By the time I had finished, I was simply exhausted. I sat down and flipped through the channels. Nothing was on, so I popped in a movie and fell asleep on the couch.

Sunday morning I went to the grocery store. I was browsing the produce aisle when I heard an unfamiliar voice. "Hey, Laurel."

I turned around to see one of Bryan's friends. "Um, Robert?"

"Hey, you *do* remember me. How're you?"

"Good. You?"

"I'm good. You look great. How's your son? Hunter, right?"

"He's good."

"Are you still working at the audio visual place?" He wandered towards me.

Hesitantly, I said, "No. I'm not. It got too stressful." My eyes met his as my chest tightened.

"You know, he's sorry, Laurel."

I stared at him and cocked my head. "Huh?"

"He doesn't hate you and he doesn't want you to hate him."

"Why would he hate me? I never did anything to him. And for the record, I don't hate him."

"Bullshit. You haven't even acknowledged his presence in months."

"That's because he doesn't exist to me. I don't hate *him*; I hate what he's *doing* to me."

He stared at me, blinked slowly and said, "Yeah, well, he's sorry 'bout that."

"Well, if he's sorry, don't you think *he* should be apologizing to me in person instead of giving an empty apology through a guy that I don't know?"

496

He nodded his head in silence. "I know what he did to you. And for the record, we all laid into his ass about how fucked up it was."

"Really? Huh. Well, for *your* record, it doesn't change a thing that you laid into his ass. It didn't stop him or change anything. What's done is done. And what he did was completely *fucked* up. I didn't deserve that and neither did Hunter."

"Are you ever going to forgive him?"

As I widened my eyes, I cocked my head and spit at him, "Forgive him? If he wants forgiveness, he needs to come askin' for it. I'll never forget it. I'm over it and I'm over him but I'll never be cordial with him again."

"You'll never be friends with him?"

"Nope. I have as many friends as I want and need. I know what he brings to the table and I don't want it in my life. Been there, done that."

"Oh, but you don't hate him?" he asked, dumbfounded.

"I don't hate him, I hate what he's *doing* to me. I look at it this way: if he didn't do this to me, where would I be? I would've been right by his side, strung out on coke and pills, like the entire crew is. No, thank you. That's not who I want to be as a person, let alone as a mother." I realized I was almost yelling when I broke from my rant. *Calm down, Laurel.* "Not to mention, Ali, Spam's girlfriend. She lost custody of her daughter a long time ago and has been in and out of rehab multiple times. Did you know that?"

He shook his head.

"Oh you didn't? Then I also doubt that you know Bryan had his new girlfriend, Mandy and two of her friends try to jump me at the bar?"

He shook his head in disbelief. "No. I, um, didn't."

"Great friend you have there. I don't want a friend like that; I deserve better and my son deserves better. As far as I'm concerned, he does not exist. Not in my world. He's dead to me."

"I see."

"Let's look at it this way: *I owe him.*"

He cocked his head in disbelief.

"He's made me go through shit I wouldn't have wished on my worst enemy. I'm a much stronger and wiser person for it."

"Understood."

I continued, "And because I've gone through so much shit in my life experiences, I know he's not worth a second of my time or consideration as a friend, let alone a person."

"I guess I can agree with that."

"It doesn't matter if you agree or disagree with my choice. It makes sense to me; that's all that matters." I took a deep breath and ran my fingers through my hair. "If he wanted to come out of this with me as a friend, then he should've *left me the fuck alone*. That's all I wanted, but look what I got instead."

"Like you said: 'been there, done that,'" he confirmed.

"Good. I'm glad you see it my way." I spun on one heal and shuffled away.

As I stood in line, I kept my eyes completely forward, watching the checker ring up the lady in front of me. My chest began to loosen as I rolled my neck and shoulders. The weight of this absurd situation overtook me at the most random times.

I hated it. I hated everything they had done to me. But it only made me strive to be *better*. *Better* as a person and *better* as a mother.

Chapter 36

Better

Over the next few months, I put every ounce of my energy into making a better life for Hunter. I worked every single day. I refused to go out and barely spoke to my friends.

I focused on my goals and watched my bank account grow as I became more driven than ever. As I began looking for houses to buy, I started feeling the weight of the world lift as a result of all of my hard work and drive. But then I felt weighed down with more responsibility.

Either way, the search for a house was on. I

felt as if I had looked at hundreds of houses, but nothing even slightly moved me. As my frustration grew, I worked harder every day and night. I rarely had a day off.

I didn't mind, though. Being active kept my mind focused. I didn't have time to think about all of the bullshit and drama in my pseudo- life. Staying busy kept me focused on the great things I had in *my* life: my son, my family, and my health. The more I focused on the things that were important to me, the better my life became.

Every night before I went to bed, I prayed:
God grant me the serenity to accept
the things I cannot change;
courage to change the things I can;
and wisdom to know the difference.

Amen.

Sunday evening, after I had put Hunter to bed, my brother walked into the house. "Hey, Sis."

"Hey, how was your day?"

"Good, good. I think I found the perfect townhouse for you."

With little enthusiasm, "Oh, yeah? Where is it?"

"It's in Milltown Chase, an end unit."

I shifted in my chair as my interest was

piqued. "Really? That's the neighborhood Chelsea lives in. When can I go look?"

He nodded. "We have an appointment on Wednesday at 5:30."

"Wednesday? Perfect. I work 'til five."

"I know. That's why I made it for then."

"Tell me about it. How many bedrooms?" I inquired.

"It's a three bedroom, one and a half bath, end unit. Right next to the pool and tennis courts."

"No way. That sounds good so far. What's the price range?"

"Right where you want to be."

"That's a great neighborhood with lots of kids."

"Perfect for your little man. I drove past it earlier, just to look, but it's got a lot of yard for him to run and play."

"Awesome. Let's cross our fingers," I said.

Wednesday afternoon approached as I drove to the townhouse. It was about four minutes from my work and ten minutes from my parents' house; already, it was perfect.

I met Lance in the pool parking lot behind the townhouse. Immediately, I liked the location; there was a half an acre of yard behind the row of town houses. I was very interested. We walked across the backyard, along the side of the house, and looked at the front yard. "So far, so good," I said to Lance.

"I agree. Let's go inside."

We back-tracked to the side of the house and then to the front door. "It's gonna need a little makeover, but that's easy," Lance said as he unlocked the door and went inside.

"Yes, it is." I stepped in and took a first look around: the stairs were right in front of me, the living room to my left, and dining room to the right. Immediately, I knew it was the one. "It's perfect." I walked through the living room. "There's a good amount of light." I looked out each of the three windows. "The bushes need to be trimmed back, but that's an easy fix."

I followed Lance towards the kitchen.

"The half bath's right here." He opened the door to the left, "And the water heater's in this closet."

As I stepped into the bathroom, I saw the look on my face in the mirror. I wanted this townhouse to be mine.

We walked into the kitchen. "It's all brand new; the stove, microwave, refrigerator, and dishwasher," Lance said.

"Do all of the appliances stay?"

"Yes, they do. So do the washer and dryer. The windows and the roof are new also, and they stay too," he joked. "This is a good find, Laurel."

"I love it." I walked into the dining room towards the back door. I unlocked and opened it and stepped out onto the back porch. "Hunter will love this," I said as I looked out at the trees and yard. I stepped back inside and completed the circle from the dining room back to the front door. I darted upstairs and my brother followed.

At the top of the steps were the washer and dryer tucked into a closet. To the left was one of the bedrooms. I followed the iron rail around to the right. "The master bath connects to the hallway and the master bedroom." Lance stepped into the master bedroom. "It has a walk-in closet. The shelving isn't great, but once again it's an easy fix."

I followed the hallway to the end and on the right was the third bedroom. I stepped inside and knew instantly this was going to be Hunter's bedroom. I spun in a circle, looked at the ceiling fan and looked out the windows. I already knew how to decorate it. "This is it. This is the house. It's absolutely perfect."

He nodded. "Go look at the attic. The door is right here." I ran up the attic steps. It was cluttered with boxes and rather chilly.

"Make an offer," I said.

He smiled. "I knew you were going to say that. I've already prepared the paperwork. I'll put the offer in tonight."

I stepped back into the master bedroom. The walk-in closet was huge. I stood looking out of the back window across the pool and tennis court area, watching the neighborhood children playing in the grass. I fell in love and I knew Hunter would love it too.

With little restraint, my offer was accepted. My pride soared: I finally did it. *I bought my own house.*

When I came home from work, I ran inside to tell Hunter the good news. "Guess what?" I said, smiling from ear to ear.

Hunter looked at me with excitement. "Umm, we bought the house?"

"Yes, we did. We're going to have a place of our own."

Hunter started jumping in circles and sang, "*Mommy bought a house. Mommy bought a house.*" He stopped in place. "Am I gonna have my own room?"

"Yes you are," I said. "And I already know which one you're going to pick."

"I get to choose? How many bedrooms are there?"

"Three. But the one's automatically mine."

"I get to pick! That's cool." He ran over to me and hugged my leg. "When do we move in, Mommy?"

"In about two months. But it's gonna go fast."

I worked even harder as my excitement grew.

Hunter was so excited to move into our new home; he talked about it every day.

I began purchasing things for our new home: curtains, a new bedspread, accessories for Hunter's bedroom, and towels for the bathroom. As the settlement date approached, I found myself glowing with happiness. I finally did it. I finally accomplished my goal.

My stomach danced with nervous butterflies as I walked into the realtor's office to sign the settlement papers. My hand shook with excitement as I handed over my down payment check with pride, knowing every second of my hard working days had finally paid off. My pride gleamed across my face as I was handed the keys to our new home.

I did it.

I swallowed the lump in my throat and a single tear streamed down my face as I walked out of the office. I jumped into my Jeep, which was packed with cleaning supplies and cans of paint, and sped over to my new house.

I pulled into my new parking spot with pride. I stared at the front of my new house, feeling unstoppable. I walked across the front lawn towards the door. I inserted the key into the lock and pushed the door open into an empty and dirty house.

My house. Home sweet home. I smiled as I inhaled a long deep breath. *Damn, this feels good.*

My parents showed up a few minutes later

with tools, a vacuum, and a steam cleaner. "Congratulations, Sweetheart. We're so proud of you," my mom said.

"Good job, Laurel. I'm happy for you," my dad said.

We vacuumed and mopped the hardwood floors, steam cleaned the rugs, and painted the walls. We refreshed the entire house in one day. It smelled fresh and looked brand new.

My dad and brother moved in my couches and all of the heavy furniture while my mom, Hillary, and I hung the curtains in all of the rooms.

My hard work had finally paid off. A massive feeling of accomplishment and pride overwhelmed me. Success was mine.

Sunday morning, I focused on getting Hunter's bedroom put together. I wanted him to be comfortable from the second he arrived. I set up his bunk beds and hung his television in the corner of his bedroom.

Greg dropped Hunter off early Sunday afternoon. He ran up to the front door, flying like Superman. I jumped out of the front door, pretending I was Superwoman. "Welcome home, Buddy. Go in and check it out."

When he ran in through the front door, his jaw dropped to the ground. "Look, Mommy. It's our new couches." His face lit up with excitement.

I beamed with pride. My heart melted when I

saw him this happy. He ran around the living room, into the kitchen, into the dining room, and then jumped into my arms at the front door. "I love you, Mommy. I'm so proud of you."

"I love you, too. Now let's go look at your bedroom." He squiggled down to the floor and ran upstairs.

I chased him up the stairs, waiting to see his reaction. I heard him gasp as he rounded the corner into his bedroom. "Wow. I have my own TV! Look at my Superhero pictures! You hung them for me? I have bunk beds again. I love it, Mommy. I love it. All of my books and drawing stuff on my new desk. Way cool!"

Nimbus jumped on his bed, barreled off across Hunter's lap back out into the hallway, and back on the bed multiple times. We laughed hysterically.

I said, "Looks like Nimbus loves your room, too. Why don't you take him out back and check out the back yard?"

"Yeah." Hunter ran downstairs and darted out the back door. "Look, Mom, there's the pool. Look at our yard." He darted across the yard, Nimbus right at his heels. "Mommy, look at all of the trees I can climb."

My dad appeared along the side of the house. "Hunter, come here. I want to show you something."

Hunter circled around and ran back towards us. "What's up?"

My dad said, "Grandmom and I got something for you." He wheeled a bicycle out in front of him. "A new house with a new yard deserves a new bike."

His jaw dropped as he ran over to the bike. "Thank you, Grandmom and DanPop! I love it."

He jumped on it and rode across the grass with Nimbus running right beside him. He slammed his brakes, slid his back tire, and came to a skidding halt. He looked back over his shoulder as he waved to us, "I love my new bike. It's so fast."

We all smiled and chuckled. I said, "Thanks, Mom and Dad. It's so perfect. I love you."

"We love you too, Laurel," my mom said. "You should be very proud."

My dad added, "We know how hard you've worked to get here, Laurel. We're proud of you. You've raised a great son and he deserves all of this. So do you."

Hunter pulled up next to me on his new bike, hopped off, and put the kick stand down. He jumped into my arms and said, "I'm so proud of you. Thank you, Mommy. This is the best day of my life."

From that moment, I felt different. I felt like my world immediately started making sense again. *It feels so good, to be where I am right now.* I took a deep breath in my new back yard.

My new life is just beginning. .

Or so I thought...

\

Sketch Artist
A. Thomas

Cover Art
AMPN Design
www.ampndesign.com

Editor
R. Rafetto

Published by
Indifference Publishing, LLC.

Laurel Forte Series®
Little 'Ol Me®

Made in the USA
Charleston, SC
12 November 2013